THE TALE OF JACKSON

A NEVERLAND LEGACY STORY

NEVERLAND LEGACY SERIES
BOOK ONE

TERRI D. ROSS

Hardcover. ISBN 978-1-7389577-2-9

Paperback. ISBN 978-1-7389577-0-5

EBook. ISBN 978-1-7389577-1-2

This collection of words is for the lady who gave me the sentence which began it all.

'He looked both directions down the hall, then decided which way to go.'

He most certainly did decide, Karrie R.; irrevocably.

PAN MELODY

Lost Boy, Lost Boy,
Won't you come and play?
Stay here forever,
Never age a day.

Never go hungry,
Never read a book.
Battle the Pirates,
Defeat Captain Hook.

Lost Boy, Lost Boy,
Won't you take my hand.
Never be alone,
Here in Neverland.

PROLOGUE

She fluttered her wings in agitation at the sound of his laughter, the deep pitch a stark difference to the higher tones she once looked forward to hearing come from his lips. Needing a distraction, she bit down on her own lip; the reminders of their time together before always brought the now familiar ache to her chest. From her vantage point on the flat surface in front of the illuminated numbers of the speedometer, she took in his changed features; the interior lights high-lighting his more defined jawline and cheekbones in the night. If she looked hard enough, she could still see the boy he used to be.

His mocking laugh echoed around her again. The joy it contained felt like tiny pin pricks along her skin, and she hugged her knees tighter through the agony. Her eyes stung as her newfound tears began to collect along her lower lashes. He did this to her every time she sat in this spot, a torment she willingly endured to be close to her old friend.

When he looked down at her with those beautiful, pale-green eyes she adored, she held her breath in anticipation of his reaction: a glimmer of shock, a slight squint, or the crinkling at the corner of his eyes in happiness at seeing her.

Nothing.

Her shoulders slumped in defeat, and she dropped her forehead to her knees, heartbroken anew. It was a torturous habit for her now, this game she played. She suspected she would forever sit in front of the lights and gauges during these motor vehicle adventures to pretend —if only for a moment—those eyes were seeking her.

It had become a useless endeavor to try to make him see her again over these past years, but hope was impossible to let go of when the melancholy struck deep.

With age comes the responsibilities of the Real-World, leaving no room for memories of her to co-exist. Even his eldest son, who recently entered the age of adolescence, no longer noticed her presence when she ventured into their home. The youngest boy still smiled and sang with her at night like his father used to when the others were slumbering. The nostalgia during those times was her salve to the raw wound her friend's absence from her caused. When she was seen, she could seamlessly imagine belonging to his family—to him —again.

The other occupant in the car spoke words she didn't care to acknowledge, and his rich voice enveloped her once more causing another flutter of her wings.

He used to laugh with me *like that. That* laugh *used to be mine,* he *used to be mine.*

He had been her favorite; her companion in the dreary task of guiding and supervising the Lost Soul's guides. He made her responsibilities to the damnable island not feel as suffocating or desolate. With his absence though, she was drowning in loneliness.

Believing she was graced with her responsibilities on the island because of her gift with tinkering and creating new purposes with old things, she embraced her role with a level of enthusiasm many struggled to match. Surely, there was use for her skills on an island hosting a continuous flow of occupants from the forever changing Real-World. She had yet to discover the purpose for her talents there, and her role was beginning to hold the ambiance of imprisonment instead of opportunity.

A displaced ticking sound jarred her out of her thoughts of the island. She watched her shadow, haloed by an orange hue appear in front of her, disappear and reappear once more.

The direction arrow, she realized, it was blinking on and off.

The tick-tock sound that accompanied her shadow's game of peek-a-boo reminded her of a precious watch. A watch she helped him design which failed them both in the end; for surely, he was as miserable as her at times in his Real-World life.

The cold hard surface under her palm sent a chill down her arm as she caught herself before falling over when the motor vehicle shifted to one side, as it did when he altered the direction he travelled. She was thankful this time hadn't been as abrupt as some of the previous turns.

His companion's feminine laughter grated like razor-blades along her spine.

Is that blonde woman, his wife, *laughing at me? Is my almost falling* amusing *to her?* She stood and glared at the creature who bewitched her friend and stole him away from where he belonged.

Everything had been perfect until that creature igno-rantly trapped her in a jar and her friend gallantly saved her from that clear prison. Little did she know the scheme of bewitchment was only beginning back then. If her friend had known where it would lead, she was certain he would have flown to the island posthaste away from this enchantress. The life he was living now was one he adamantly rebuked when he was younger.

He'd loved the island and all its occupants until that crea-ture *introduced herself.*

He clasped the woman's hand and brought it to his lips, bestowing a kiss to the back of it and eliciting a giggle from its owner. The smile on his face and in his eyes while he looked at the blonde was irksome.

As he turned the large wheel with his free hand, her wings carried her above to sit on the highest point on the leather wheel. She crossed her legs, placed her elbow on her thigh and rested her chin in her hand, her foot twitching in irritation.

He said he wouldn't be happy without me in his life, so he's not as happy as he appears, she reminded herself. She tried to remember his words during times like these and it helped soothe her most days.

To her right, the lake's calm surface reflected the moon and stars in the night sky, beckoning to her from beyond the vehicle's window.

How simple it would be to bring him back. Yet, rules were rules and even she had to abide by the ones set out for her.

Although ...

She perked up from her position, her hands resting on the taut leather beside her. *There is nothing in the rules about a Guide reclaiming their role and returning from the Real-World after they decide to live out their life. No rules prohibiting me from bringing a guide back ...*

Her gaze darted from his pale-green eyes to the woman's conniving smile to the lake outside the window still calling to her. *I can save him from her and this life. I can bring him home and it will be like it was before. With that creature and her spells gone, he will be free and happy to be back with me.*

Giddy with the possibilities to come, she hopped to

her feet and clapped her hands excitedly in front of her, envisioning his reaction to her solution. *Surely, he will smile in pure delight for being returned once his memories of Neverland are restored. He will thank me profusely for helping him escape the Real-World.*

She glared at the woman as another sickening giggle escaped the temptresses lips. More of her lost friend's false laughter surrounded her but she smiled, knowing she would make his laugh real once more.

Sliding down the wheel to the contraption she once thought of as her greatest creation, her feet landed on the clear glass surface; her eyes following the movement of the copper hands as time continued predictably. Time passed differently in the Real-World: steady and predictable, unlike the island.

Tick. Tick. Tick.

Raising her leaf-covered foot, she brought it down hard on the face of her failure, smiling in satisfaction at the splinters in the surface spreading out. Then there was silence. Beautiful silence. The long copper hand twitched to continue its journey to mark the passing of another second but stopped shy of meeting its mark.

A squeak escaped her lips as she lost her footing and landed hard on the marred surface as her friend turned his wrist; brows knitted, and the corners of his mouth turned down. That was a look she knew well—one she used to receive from him whenever her emotions got the better of her but she knew his focus wasn't on the damage her temper caused.

A quick look out the window revealed they were fast approaching the end of her opportunity and she knew what she needed to do.

"Don't worry, Pan. I'm bringing you home."

THE TALE OF JACKSON

CHAPTER 1

CHANGE IS IN THE AIR

MERILEE

Emerging from the water, Merilee welcomed the heat of the sun's rays which had quickly become her addiction. Creatures such as she lacked the luxury of feeling temperature differences in the water because they matched their internal temperature to the waters— a convenient trait to possess when existing in a place with drastically differing regions such as the Ocean of Souls. Well, if the creatures were aware of their limits and exercised caution, that is.

She lost a few fledglings over the decades to the boiling waters of Lava Loch. The foolish youth believing themselves impervious to matters as simple as temperature variations. A well-placed challenge by the more seasoned mermaids resulted in the arrogant youth forfeiting their newly formed existence before being fully enjoyed.

There were the frozen remains of the poor souls

banished to Glacier Bay. A particularly morbid site she herself utilized often for introductions with the fledglings, in hopes of relieving them of the ignorance always present in the early ages. If the Fates willed it, a semblance of common sense would be blessed upon the youth to replace the ignorance after such a scene. The Fates were cruel with their apathy on most occasions.

Leaning back, she closed her eyes, allowing her senses to shift to each water droplet heating, shrinking and eventually evaporating from her skin.

The elements truly were miraculous in her opinion, but *water* was most extraordinary. A single droplet could evaporate and become a different entity or solidify and float above the collective—heat and cold permitting—eventually returning to its original liquid state, unaltered by the process. As a collective, it could shape ocean floors, carve landmasses into astonishing valleys or level ancient forests in a fit of temper. It ebbed and flowed in a beautiful dance with the other elements, at the mercy of its counterparts but trusting the process. All the while a formidable force on its own capable of irreparable damage.

Beautiful and dangerous. She smiled at the thought. *Admirable, indeed.*

With her arms gliding through the water at her side, her waist-long, cobalt-blue hair streaked with hues of turquoise danced and caressed her upper body, increasing her enjoyment of this moment. The lengthy tendrils were an extension of her being. The hypnotic way each strand moved, whether in still or rippling waters, consistently fascinated and soothed her. The sun's heat kissed her as her tailfins leisurely propelled her towards the object of her interest.

She opened her eyes to the crystal blue of the sky. A fluffy white cloud in the shape of a clam shell appeared so soft she envied those who slept in them.

This is a genuinely captivating place.

Echoing ripples through the water made her sigh as the source skipped along the surface beside her. "Joyful moment concluded," she said under her breath. Straightening, her hair blanketed her shoulders as she turned towards the impatient boy. "Your aim requires improvement, young one," she said, heading toward Peak Point Rock and the figure standing upon it.

"Ha!"—the older teen scoffed—"I assure you, there is nothing wrong with my aim," he said, his English accent carrying over the distance to her.

She smiled inwardly at the irritated tone from this Lost Boy she adored and assumed she always would while he remained there.

His right arm lifted back and swung forward; another stone to skip along the surface next to her—this time a little closer. She shook her head as she played with the water while making her way to their usual meeting spot.

Peak Point Rock had formed at the front of the narrowing passage to Mermaid Lagoon. The waterway was ten-feet wide, with cliffs on the left covered in vining leaves and the three gentle waterfalls from the

Hot Springs above. Peak Point Rock stood sentry on the right, often a place those like Simon waited for her, or other mermaids, to arrive for their leisure. The vegetation surrounding the lagoon was lush, and enchanting. Rich colors of green adorned the oversized leaves of the tropical plants and trees, complementing the deep blue-hues of the water. The sand making up the beach side, nestled deep in the back, was the lightest of beige. It was no wonder the mermaids claimed this as their oasis.

"You mermaids take your sweet time doing *anything*. As if others don't have anything else better to do than wait on you."

"And yet, you waited," she pointed out, trying to withhold her laughter and failing.

His blonde brows pinched down over clear blue eyes. "I'll have you know; I've been waiting here for hours."

"Patience is a virtuous trait. Imagine utilizing your time waiting more wisely by perfecting it." She pulled herself atop the sister rock to Peak Point Rock, which lay just below the surface. The fact she had yet to form an imprint in the stone with how frequently she visited this spot continued to baffle her.

Simon's toned figure lowered onto to the moss-covered rock with the predictability she'd come to expect from the Lost Boy. He, like Vincent, tended to be a creature of habit when he visited here. He was often seen sitting with one elbow resting on a bent knee, leg dangling over the edge, dagger tucked in his belt; a position he took now. The ragged, tan T-shirt he wore had been relieved of its sleeves long ago, the slash in the middle of the neckline splayed opened to show a leather strap holding his Coin of Passage beneath. His usual olive-green cargo shorts replaced with a washed-out denim pair.

Those shorts must be uncomfortable to wear, the material looks so abrasive. His feet are bare this visit though, she mused.

He placed his hand to his chest. "I have the patience of a saint." His blue eyes narrowed on her. "You're peevish today. Need a kiss from a handsome man to brighten your mood?" he asked, eyebrows waggling at her.

She rolled her eyes. "No." What she needed was to change the subject before he attempted to practice more of his newfound skill of flirtation on her. It was simultaneously adorable and painful to witness. Merilee had been observing his changes in interests, from sword play and pirates, to the maturing interest in the opposite sex recently as a late teenager would.

He smiled, then winked.

His more defined cheekbones and jawline were notable this visit; she recognized other signs of maturity emerging in his features, signifying this Lost Boy would be departing soon if he continued this path. "You've been gallivanting to the Real-World again. Is there appeal in joining the Hooks' ranks then? You're approaching the line of the maturity to do so."

Simon dropped his hand and recoiled, his face the

picture of horror. "I'll not be joining that bastard, and you damn well know it, Mer."

He looked so offended by her question, she almost laughed. "You, my dear Simon, are young," she said, wringing her hair of excess moisture to begin combing her fingers through the cobalt tresses, "and youth tend to believe they are clairvoyant, knowing which direction they will choose in future situations. They often surprise themselves when the reality comes to fruition."

He slid his dagger from his belt and began cleaning under his fingernails, lip curled. "I won't be surprising myself and becoming a pirate"—he cringed—"I'd rather not grow old in the Real-World either."

"What's drawing you there so frequently?" She knew for many of the Pans it was the magnetic pull of their Wendys—if they were fortunate enough to find them. No other who occupied Neverland felt a pull to the Real-World. Lost Boys either stayed in Neverland or utilized their Coin of Passage to the afterlife. They rarely ventured to the Real-World for enjoyment; therefore, Simons actions were unusual, piquing her curiosity.

"It started with visiting Vincent." He shrugged, focused on his task. "When he started to forget, I guess I missed him and wanted to stay with him in a way."

Merilee sympathized with the longing in his voice. It was a difficult transition for many, and she understood him wanting to hold onto his connection with his previous Pan. Those two had been inseparable for years.

"After, I needed to understand what is so great about

the present Real-World that he would give up this"—he held his arms in the air and then spread them wide—"because surely his Wendy wasn't the sole reason."

"Is he not happy with her?"

He huffed and continued his mission on the other hand. "Sure, he is. Even has children. Which, by the way"—he pointed the dagger towards her—"he said he did not want to have." He sat up straighter. "How many times did he say, 'Too many things go wrong all the time. With how many children I bring over, it's a wonder anyone wants to risk having one,'" he said in an American accent identical to Vincent and returned to his nails, scowling again.

"You imitate him well," she said, leaning back on her arms to allow more of the sun's rays to warm her. *And he called me peevish? Seems he is in a foul mood himself.* She flicked the clear surface of the water with her royal-blue tailfin, splashing him with droplets of water.

"He probably drank too much gin and *forgot that too*," he grumbled, wiping his T-shirt free of the droplets.

She barked out a startled laugh. "I imagine pregnancies have resulted from ingesting large quantities of alcohol." *Ah, that was the source of his ill mood, he missed Vincent.*

He smiled with a dimple, but his merriment refused to reach his light-blue eyes. She knew this one rarely spoke of matters that were closest to him and if he wanted to delve into this topic, he would. No sense in pushing the boy. She closed her eyes to the sky and remained silent, waiting for him to speak.

"I've just missed him, and Neverland's not the same

without him. The pirates killing Lost Boys, mermaids killing pirates, pirates killing mermaids, and Lost Boys killing pirates." He sighed. "It wasn't like this before."

Not like this before? He couldn't be serious. She cracked an eyelid open and peered at him, Simon's sun-kissed skin turning a rosier shade on his cheeks under her gaze.

"Well, we all weren't so *aggressive* about it. And"—he pointed the dagger tip in her direction again—"how many new Pans can Tink *possibly* go through?"

He began swinging the dagger through the air as he vented. She kept track of its movements in case he accidentally let it go in his enthusiasm.

"I swear the glow-bug goes through one every month. It's ridiculous. How can a new Pan possibly get to know all he is to know in that much time? The boy doesn't even have a chance!"

"Perhaps she's attempting to fill a void refusing to be filled." She gave him a pointed look.

"Tu shay," he said, deflating and inclining his head. "Maybe I'm doing the same by traveling back to the Real-World."

"Maybe." She was confident in her assessment. Simon was, in a way, more lost than any other Lost Boy without Vincent. He left the Lost Boys cohort shortly after Vincent departed to the Real-World; and, as far as she had been able to decipher, he followed neither the Lost Boy code of ethics, nor the pirates. He acted outside the parameters set for either group, and Tink was either unaware or apathetic to his actions because she had yet to correct him. Pointing out that he abandoned the other Lost Boys like he felt Vincent had abandoned him would bring about no revelations or peace; so, she kept that thought to herself.

Movement on the horizon caught her attention. In the distance she could see the Hook's ship: its black flag, with the white skull and two crossed swords, waving in the breeze; white sails arced by the wind and Hook's silhouette at the helm. She stopped herself from peering at the body she knew was pinned to the bow by swords.

"Have you seen Dorathea recently?" she asked distractedly, then tore her gaze away from the ship and toward Simon.

He appeared to have followed her gaze because he was looking in the same direction and a mischievous grin crept onto his face. "Yeah, she was delivering a message to Hook a day ago."

"Oh?" *What message did* that one *personally deliver to Hook?*

He chuckled. "Yeah. Brought the corpse of one of his crew to the beach, gutted, with his intestines wrapped round his neck like a bow. Left a bloody mess in the sand too."

Her eyebrows rose. *Quite the message.* "Do you know the reason?"

"Overheard the pirates saying *that* fellow felt the need to kill one of the Never-Beasts for the pleasure of it, and left it gutted on the forest floor." Simons eyes twinkled with amusement. "She returned the favor. Seems she wanted to remind them to not waste a life of her beasties."

Merilee smirked. "Effective."

"Very. She is one that even *I* would never want to cross. She's as terrifying as she is beautiful."

"As are all the Ancients," she said, barely refraining from rolling her eyes at the wistful look on his face. "To her, you're a mere zygote."

"You keep reminding me how young I am compared to all of you, but I'll remind you, according to Real-World calculations, I'm fifty-one years old."

"An embryo then. Too young to play with those knives you carry around."

He rolled his eyes. "That reminds me"—he began flipping his dagger in the air, catching it by the tip of the blade each time. The sapphire embedded in the ivory handle glinted in the sun's rays with each toss—"you need to return something."

"Such as?"

"Vincent's dagger. You stole it from me when you tossed me in the lagoon a few days ago."

His tone was light, but she knew by the dagger flipping he was agitated.

"I want it back, Mer."

"Your inability to remain on two feet is the reason for your dunk in the water. I do not toss humans into the lagoon." She flicked her tailfins again and splashed him with more than a few droplets.

"Bloody hell! Will you stop it? If I wanted to be wet, I

would be in the damn water," he said, a hint of laughter in his voice. "I would have been able to remain on both feet if you hadn't pulled on my boot."

"When was the last time you went to check on Vincent and his family?"

"Can't stay on topic today?"

Ignoring the question, she watched the water roll, bend, and slide over her tailfins as she moved them along the surface. *Another tug on his boot may be necessary.* The idea amused her. *He would squeal like one of those coil-tailed creatures Dorathea adored.*

"A couple weeks ago Never-Time, give or take a day." He stopped flipping the dagger. "His dagger isn't there. I never forgot it there if that is what you're implying. I may be young but I'm not an idiot."

"No such implication of your character was implied. Cease with the bristly attitude."

"Cease changing the subject," he countered, irritation leaking into his tone. "I want the dagger back."

"You notice Tink acting stranger than usual?"

"Really?" His dagger fluttered in his hand by the blade tip.

She guessed he was contemplating throwing it in her direction; it wouldn't be the first time he had done so, nor would it be the last.

"Truly." She lengthened the word, opening her eyes wide.

He sighed loudly and rubbed his middle finger along his temple, making her lips twitch. "The glow-bug isn't around enough for me to notice her behavior, or if it's strange." He moved to rubbing his forehead with his palm. "What does that have to do with you being a thief?"

She shrugged and submerged her lower half into the water. "Absolutely nothing." Pushing off the rock, she extended her arms forward and smiled at the small orange fish that brushed against her right forearm. Gliding her arms through the crystal-clear liquid, she took pleasure in the ripples spreading through the water while Simon got to his feet in her periphery.

"Hey! Merilee!"

She continued to increase the distance.

"I want it back!"

"It's where it needs to be," she said.

"It's not in my boot so I beg to differ!"

She smiled. If he knew where Vincent's dagger currently was, he surely would retract that statement. Time would tell if it would prove useful though.

Diving under the surface, she swam amongst the yellows, pinks, and purples of the coral reefs, and could hear Simon yelling at her above the surface. If there was time to spare, their conversation could have continued longer. She accomplished what she set out for and planted the seeds that she needed for him to grow; he would be venturing to see his old friend sooner, rather than later.

An important game was presenting itself on the Ocean of Souls, and learning the players was a necessity. She suspected Neverland depended on it.

CHAPTER 2
NOT THE SAME

JACKSON

CARSTON LAKE, MARCH 1998

The air hurt his face. Each inhale stung his nostrils, and he swore he could feel each individual nose hair freezing—not his favorite experience. If it wasn't for his little brother needing to find a silly stone for his collection, he wouldn't be outside in the cold and his nose wouldn't be suffering at all.

Why couldn't he live in a tropical place? Bright warm sun, hot sandy beach, and clear water. Now, *that* would be a wonderful place to live. He could almost feel the warmth on his toes if he thought hard enough; or was that the burn of frost bite?

Jackson peered down at his worn-down sneakers and found a small hole where the tip of his big toes rubbed. At least he couldn't see his socks this time, the last pair's

"

soles practically fell off before he got a new pair. Snow boots over sneakers on these walks down Carston Road during winter months was a better idea; he probably wouldn't be as cold—or bitter—about it then. Maybe he would convince Natalie to come with him to get a new pair afterward, throw in a stop for ice cream and call it a date.

His brother's laughter made him look up just in time to see the black and red winter coat spin around and fall into a snow pile on the side of the road. The kid's messy blonde hair covered his eyes, but the wide grin on his face was unmistakable.

"Hey, Jacks!" Patrick called out. "Wanna make a snow angel with me?"

"That's not gonna happen, buddy." No way was he willingly going into a pile of frozen water droplets. He shivered at the idea. *The kid could have all the fun in that department.*

"One day"—Patrick got to his feet and began wiping the snow off his blue jeans and winter coat, all the while laughing—"I will get you to do it."

"Not gonna happen."

"You're such a wuss!" Patrick said, shaking his head.

"And you're annoying me," he said with no heat. "Now, go find your stone so we can go where I can be warm."

Patrick rolled his eyes and continued towards the opposite side of the road where the snow piles were melting, allowing more stones from the road to appear.

For a kid who was twelve, he acted half that age sometimes.

He guessed it was a good thing that his little brother was still able to goof around, he just wished that the kid could find a different way to feel close to their mom other than coming to this place—especially in winter. At least his nose hairs wouldn't be frozen then. Even better if Patrick would stop acting weird so he wouldn't be so torn about wanting to leave for college. He didn't feel right leaving now that Patrick was regressing.

Breathing slowly into his gloved hands to warm them up, he put the less-than-adequate material to his nose to try and thaw his abused nose hairs. He knew he was a wimp when it came to the cold, but he didn't care. A guy had to draw the line at going outside when he could see his breath visibly leave his body.

A tiny snort from his walking companion made him smile behind his hands. She *would* find his discomfort funny. Glancing over at the fuzzy cotton fluff ball on the top of her toque, which happened to be eye level with him, he had the sudden urge to tug on it and make her as cold as he was for her little snort; but he refrained from doing it. He wasn't *that* mean of a guy. Besides, she probably wouldn't even feel the cold.

Her ugly moss-colored winter coat covered most of her body. He made the mistake of teasing her about the coat the first time he had seen her wear it. In retaliation, she'd given him a toque and gloves in the same ugly color saying, 'Now, we make a complete set!' with an impish grin on her face. Her smile and giddiness when she gave him the pink gift bag would always be a fond memory for him. She had been so excited; he didn't want to disappoint her. He realized then that he would do a lot of things he thought were silly for her.

She kept him curious, always did things with meaning, didn't expect much in return, and let him just be him. The more time he spent with her, the more he found he wanted to spend. Most importantly though, she gave him peace; she was his calm. Right now, her light-brown nose with its spattering of freckles was turning a cute shade of rose, matching her cheeks. The coloring was making him think of other ways he wanted to make her blush but that wasn't going to happen with his little brother down the road.

"You're staring again."

She lifted her face up to him with a smile he wanted to kiss; so, he did just that. Her giggle on his lips made him smile in return.

"Of course, I am." He tucked errant strands of copper-brown hair that escaped from her white toque behind her ear. "You're nice to look at."

"There are nicer things to look at out here, Jackson." She gestured in front of them with a wide sweep of her arm.

A fog had rolled in yesterday, blanketing every surface with hoarfrost and he knew it was her favorite climate event. He could appreciate *her* appreciation of it and the way her caramel eyes with golden flecks filled with happiness as she took in the sight.

"There are nice things to look at, but I want to look at you. You're prettier and you have a nice pink nose right now." He kissed said nose and threw his arm around her shoulder with a sigh. "One day you will learn to take a compliment, Nat."

She laughed. "I know how to take a compliment. You need to pay attention to what your brother is doing and not my nose," she said, nodding towards Patrick's direction.

Looking down the road to where he knew Patrick would be, Jackson rolled his eyes at the sight of Patrick crouched down twenty feet ahead, pushing around fresh snow on the side of the road. The kid's jacket was hanging open with obvious weight in the pockets, probably filled with random stones. He must not have found the one he felt was for their mom because he sure looked focused from over here.

"Do you think he has found one for her yet?" Natalie asked, her compassion towards the situation evident in her voice.

"Nope. He's still searching." He tilted his head and narrowed his eyes when the kid seemed to be arguing with himself, or with the friend only Patrick seemed to see. "He should be done soon though," he murmured, as Patrick's head jerked up towards him. His younger brother then gave him a wave with a too-big smile.

He raised his arm and waved back; Natalie doing the same in his periphery. *That's a don't-pay-attention-to-me smile if I ever saw one. What's the kid up to?*

"How many stones does your mom have in the garden now?"

"Thirty-five. One for every month anniversary since she passed. She has quite the collection of white stones in her garden now," he said, eyes following Patrick as he moved closer to the guardrail bordering between the road and Carston Lake, making his heart beat a little quicker.

That guardrail had been placed there to prevent another car going into the lake shortly after his parents' vehicle was found submerged. He could always visualize the top of the white Chevrolet Impala visible inches below the surface if he looked at the lake, so he avoided looking whenever he was down here.

He dreamt of that night, what it could have been like for his parents more often than he ever admitted. A conversation he wished he'd never overheard with details of the accident only a couple weeks after it happened was the cause of the dream's vividness. The dream was always the same: their mom alone, underwater, seatbelt caging her in the seat, lifeless; and their dad nowhere to be found.

Constantly visualizing his mom in the submerged car was the reason he hated coming down here, but Patrick needed him to bring him. Their uncles tried to bring Patrick a few times but that ended badly every time, resulting in the kid hiding away in his room for days, saying Jackson didn't care about him, or their parents, anymore. He didn't understand why Patrick jumped to the conclusion he didn't care if he didn't bring him down. Heck, he'd come down here every month for almost three years—what was one month? Not to mention he'd been pushing off the things he wanted to do for those three years to be there for Patrick because he cared about how his brother would feel about it, but his brother never seemed to notice *that*. So, he sucked it up and brought his little brother to collect the stones; he never wanted Patrick to think he didn't care about him or their parents. If his little brother needed it, he would do it no matter how much he didn't like it.

The collection was all part of Patrick's grieving and healing process. It was the way his brother was dealing with the deaths of their parents; well, assuming his dad was dead too.

"How is he doing?"

"Who?" *My dad? How would I know?*

"Patrick ..." Natalie looked at him with a frown between her brows.

Yeah, okay, that was a stupid thing to say. "Oh. Patrick's fine." He shrugged, feeling kind of stupid for his question and slightly irritated at his inner thoughts. His dad was dead, so why would Natalie be asking how he was doing? Unless his dad wasn't dead, and then that would leave room for a whole lot of questions. He felt his heart beat in his chest a little harder like it always did as he thought of his dad. Jackson hated not knowing and the possible scenarios that often ran through his mind about what his dad could be doing if he was alive somewhere.

"Uh huh …" She stopped walking, making him stop since his arm was still resting on her shoulders.

"Patrick, is being Patrick," he blurted out, flustered and feeling the anxiety starting to creep in. Hoping she would drop it and start walking again, he faked a smile and shrugged. "Want to go get ice cream after you come with me to get new sneakers?" By the way she folded her arms he guessed that was a no.

"Really, Jackson? Ice cream?" She shook her head a little. "I know Patrick has been—"

"Has been doing better than he was, and that is as much as we are going to talk about it right now." He only wanted to enjoy being around her and wait for Patrick to be done so they could leave.

Taking a deep breath, he blew it out slowly, attempting to relieve some tension.

She pursed her lips and tilted her head. "It's just that—"

"Patrick's fine," he snapped, feeling the familiar weight of his reality creeping into his chest. He clenched his fists until he could feel the blood flow leave his knuckles.

She asked because she cared, he knew that, loved that about her, she genuinely cared about him, but he didn't want to talk about it. If he talked about it, it made everything more real. Yes, some days for Patrick were good and it felt great, like he had his little brother back; but then Patrick had days like the past week and Jackson struggled to handle the situation.

"Hey, Jacks," she said, her voice soft. She uncrossed her arms and placed her hand gently against his stomach, stepping in front of him. "I'm sorry for pushing. It's just that you look tired and that usually means Patrick has had some bad nights ..."

At her pause, he raised an eyebrow. *Is she really trying to lie to me?* He knew she couldn't lie, well not in a way someone would believe her.

She bit her lip. "Your uncles may have mentioned it and asked me how you were doing with it. If you don't want to talk about it, I won't make you," she said, her voice smoothing over some of his tension. "Just know that I'm here. You need to talk, I'm here. You need me to be your sounding board, I'm your girl. You need me to just be here with you, I got you covered."

His freaking uncles needed to not use his girlfriend to get information about him—that's what he needed. If they wanted to know something, why didn't they just ask him? They didn't need to get Natalie involved. Sure, he had lost his temper a time—or two—but he was in the middle of losing it during a difficult day. It wasn't like he was hot headed; was he? Natalie's deep brown eyes, which looked mahogany in the sun and were bouncing back and forth between his, looking like *she* needed a hug, told him otherwise.

Well shit. He opened his mouth to tell her it was alright, but she continued.

"I told them you were alright, but I don't really know. So, I don't really know if I lied to them by saying that or if it's true. I hate lying and feel terrible if I do it, but if you want me to lie and say you talked to me, I can." She frowned. "Well, as long as you tell me sometime in the near, near future, then it wouldn't really be a lie per se, more like an early truth. Well, it would be a lie right then, but the sooner you tell me, then the sooner I will know whether it was a lie. And really your uncles just care about you and since you are quiet and don't say much about things, they think you might not want to say anything about your problems, worried it takes away from Patrick since he is struggling a lot. Which is dumb because you are just as important as your brother and I thi—"

He reached up and cupped both her cheeks, which she puffed out to hold her breath to stop her rambling. *My beautiful blowfish.* "Breathe, Nat." He kissed her puckered lips and applied slight pressure to her cheeks to get her to exhale. "You don't have to lie to my uncles for me. I know you hate lying and wouldn't make you do that."

She nodded; her gloved hand gave his wrist a gentle squeeze. "Thank you."

"You're welcome," he said, and bent down to be eye level with her and to stroke her cheeks with his gloved thumbs. "He is talking nonsense again. To his imaginary friend or about fairies being real."

"He hasn't done that for a few months," she said with a sad smile.

"No, he hasn't which sucks because I thought he was

getting past this and I could start thinking about those applications seriously—"

"You can go to college, Jacks. I keep telling you that."

"—and, he's sleepwalking again. I found him trying to jump out his window a few nights ago and then he was down the street by the Miller's last night around 2 am." It'd been one of the scariest moments for him, realizing Patrick was missing, and the thought of not finding him before something bad happened.

He shook his head and exhaled a long breath.

"How did you know he went out, or where he even went that late?"

"I woke up and was getting a drink of water when the motion light in the backyard went out. When I looked through the kitchen window, the backyard gate was open. I always latch it, so I went upstairs to check on him. He wasn't in bed, so I ran out and took a guess he was heading in this direction. We're all just lucky I was right. Who knows where he could have ended up this time."

He wasn't even sure the kid *was* sleepwalking anymore. When he reached him that night, he asked him what he was doing. When Patrick's eyes met his, they were clear and he said he was just getting some fresh air, then smiled like nothing was wrong with going out for a stroll at 2 am at the end of winter. His brother wasn't dazed, groggy or anything like he usually was when on his previous nocturnal missions. He was *fully* present, which made Jackson more concerned. It meant that he had knowingly left the house in the middle of the night. Or worse, consciously tried to jump out the window. Another reason Jackson couldn't leave Carston now.

Also, there was the way Patrick's eyes focused behind him repeatedly in the street when they were talking, which made the hairs on Jackson's neck stand on end. He looked of course, but nothing was there, only an empty street and dark houses. The entire walk back to the house he had felt watched. It was probably his imagination, but he still couldn't shake the feeling.

"So, no he isn't as fine as he could be, but he isn't crying all the time or screaming for mom, or saying dad is coming back soon. He's made some progress and he is better than he was. It doesn't help Hugh isn't doing well and the kiddo knows he's about to lose a close friend that's been around since he can remember. I think that is the reason he is having issues again."

Natalie reached up and held his wrists. "And *you*? How are *you*?"

"I'm okay. A little freaked out by the way he's behaving, but who wouldn't be? The more Patrick goes through, or regresses, the angrier I am at all of this but I'm dealing." He pulled her head close and gave her a kiss. "If I am not okay, I will tell you."

"Promise?"

"Promise." He wrapped his arms around her shoulders, resting his head on hers, and he smiled because she fit him exactly right.

She breathed in deep and sighed against his chest. "I

know you're not telling me something, but your hug feels amazing, so I'll let it slide."

He chuckled. "Your kindness knows no limits."

He felt her shrug.

"You give good hugs and smell nummy."

Movement on the lake caught his attention, and he lifted his head to see better. "What the hell is he doing?"

Natalie let go of him and turned in the same direction. She gasped, "Jackson, the ice is thick but it's thinning. He can't be out there."

Yeah, no kidding. Patrick knew the rule about the lake. *Stay the hell away from it, frozen or not.* He was only a few feet from the bank but that was too far where he was concerned.

"Patrick!" he yelled as he started jogging towards his brother. "What the hell are you doing?"

The kid didn't respond, only kept hitting the ice he was crouched on.

"Patrick! Get off the damn ice!"

"Patrick? Come on kiddo, stop playing out there!" Natalie yelled from behind him, a hint of panic in her voice.

He reached the guardrail and watched Patrick's small hand reach into his jacket pocket and bring out a fist-sized stone, which he raised in the air and brought down on the ice with a loud crack.

My brother has a death wish. That was the only explanation he could think of. Another crack sounded through the air making him flinch. He sure as hell didn't trust the ice, but he needed to get his brother's attention.

"Fuuuuck," he growled as he hopped over the railing onto the bank. He was going to beat his ass for this.

Crack!

"Dude, stop hitting the ice!" He sure as shit didn't want to have the ice break while he was on it too, because the farther onto the surface he got, the more his stomach churned.

"I found the perfect stone for mom," Patrick yelled excitedly, and poked the ice. "I can get it!"

His stomach dropped as he watched the raised arm come down to connect with the surface again. Images of Patrick's lifeless form trapped under ice and floating in the water flashed through his mind. *The kid's insane, he has to be.*

When Patrick's hand raised once more, Jackson was thankfully close enough to grab his wrist and pull him up causing a squeak from his brother.

"What are you doing?! Let me go!" he cried, his free hand trying to push him away.

Let him go? Not like that *was going to happen.* He wasn't about to bury another family member because of this freaking lake. "Stop it," he snapped, and Patrick started squirming from his grip. "You need to stop and get off the damn ice before you fall through!"

The kid stopped and frowned, then looked towards where he'd been crouching.

Jackson gave him a little shake until he had his attention again. "You *especially* can't try and break any part of the ice while you're on it. That is just stupid. It's deeper than it looks, and you can't swim well. Do you understand?"

No response.

"Okay then"—turning his brother in the direction where Natalie stood, he gave his shoulders a little shove for encouragement—"get moving."

Patrick looked back down at the spot for a second time, Jacksons eyes followed, and he noticed a white stone in the middle of the area. *That was what he was going to break the ice for? Un. Freaking. Believable.* His temper flared as Patrick's pace slowed.

"Now!" His shout louder and harsher than he intended.

The kid huffed and started walking towards Natalie, who was waiting by the railing, arms crossed and pacing.

What is wrong with that kid? He wanted to strangle him for being so stupid and lock him in a room to keep him safe. The kid either had no fear or didn't care enough about his own safety; he had a feeling it was the latter.

Muffled bells chiming behind him had him searching for the source, stunned to see a woman's face haloed by sparkling specks glaring at him from under the surface of the cleared-off area. He lurched towards the woman to help her but she was gone with his next blink.

Rubbing his eyes, he exhaled slowly. *There was no woman under the ice. Hadn't she been transparent? What is she then, a ghost?* He snorted. He was stressed, and coupled with thinking of his mom a few minutes ago, it made sense his mind would be playing tricks with him. *Yeah, let's go with that.* Or he was losing it. Lately, that seemed truer than he was comfortable admitting.

When he was safely on the right side of the guardrail, Patrick looked up at him like someone kicked his puppy. *Well, well, look who* finally *might have clued in to how stupid he had been.*

He was going to make sure he and his uncles sat him down to have a talk about what happened, although Natalie was doing a fine job telling him all about the dangers of doing reckless things on the lake. *Maybe coming from her it would sink in.*

"Stone finding is done for today. Time to head to the car," he said, not even remotely sorry for ending this stone search before Patrick was done.

His brother didn't argue; simply looked back at the lake, nodded, and headed up the road to the car.

"Well"—Natalie exhaled—"that was intense."

"Yeah, you could say that."

She wrapped her arm around his waist as they started walking. "You okay?"

"Nope." He put his arm around her shoulders and kissed the side of her head. "But I will be. Once I find out what is going on in his head, I'll be okay."

The trek back to the car was as silent as the drive to the house. He hated silence. Normally he would put on the radio or tap out a beat on the steering wheel to fill the silence in the car; but right now, he needed the quiet.

The same disturbing image of Patrick kept popping into his head; his brother's brown eyes staring sightlessly as his body floated in the water—it was making him sick to his stomach. It felt too real, especially when Patrick morphed into his mother. He shook his head to get rid of the image.

He had to figure out how to get Patrick to talk before he lost him too. The kid was becoming increasingly distant, acting in ways that went beyond grieving as far as he was concerned. He hadn't wanted to voice his suspicions to his uncles or Natalie, because then it would be so much more real and could set things in motion he couldn't stop. Would he lose him? Would Patrick be medicated like in those shows, and become an unfeeling living zombie? Would that be the outcome if he was open about Patrick seeing things that weren't there or his reckless behavior?

Grip tightening on the steering wheel, he peeked in the rear-view mirror. Patrick was resting his head on the back of the seat, staring out the side window, seemingly lost in thought. Worse yet, could he live with himself if something happened to his little brother if he didn't say anything?

CHAPTER 3
TRAPPED IN THE PAST
MERILEE

"That older boy is becoming more of a nuisance!" the five-foot-tall, translucent fairy yelled; her wings fluttering in agitation much like the tiny fairy it represented.

Merilee barely refrained from laughing at the fairy's disgruntled behavior as she observed the projection pacing the musky cave, stomping its imperial feet with each step. Biting her lower lip to distract herself from her amusement, she gazed towards the beautiful creature gliding through the clear, still water, the man the fairy was yelling at. She would have sighed if her lips weren't otherwise occupied, leaving her grateful for her previous decision. If she allowed her presence to be known, it would cease her entertainment and she wasn't about to let *that* happen.

The winged creature didn't know she had discovered Vincent in the cenote weeks ago and preferred it remain that way. Hal only knew she had enough drama to contend with on the island presently because of these two, she held no desire to manage more. Besides, it was *that* selfish fairy who trapped Vincent in her hideaway—not her. Hardly her fault. And oh, what a delightfully grown surprise he had been.

Her eyes followed Vincent as he pulled himself out of the water and onto the limestone floor—well, the eight-foot ledge. The muscles in his back and shoulders were highlighted with the movement, thanks to the combination of his clinging wet shirt and the sunlight shining in from the opening at the top of the cenote. It was as though the sun knew how spectacular that creature was and needed to touch him. She thought the feeling was mutual because he rarely ventured out of its warm rays when she was present.

He ran his hands through his dark, wet hair and rung out his olive-green T-shirt, exposing a sliver of a defined lower abdomen. She appreciated the elements in that moment, with a healthy dose of envy of their proximity. *Delightfully grown, indeed.*

"You know I almost had Patrick break the ice today." Smugness dripped off its words. "If only he hit it a few more times, he would be here right now."

Vincent's hollow laugh echoed off the tall walls. "Jackson won't let anything happen to his little brother," he said, pride in every word as he rung out his shirt.

It scowled at him and continued to pace, growing brighter. "He can't be there all the time."

"Seems to me he has been doing a damn good job of keeping his brother safe." He glared at it, leaning against the damp wall, crossing his arms and one ankle over the other. "He's always been a protective kid, and I can only imagine how losing his mother and me would have made that a thousand times stronger." His grin was all teeth. "Well done."

"You grew into an insufferable adult." It sniffed haughtily, putting its nose in the air. "Always so hostile now. After all I did for you." The translucent wings fluttered again.

"Sort of happens when your once-best-friend *kills* your wife," he gritted, "in front of you no less."

Merilee winced at the thought of how the experience would have felt for him. Well, she knew how that felt for him, he confided as much to her during one of their many visits. She also knew any friendship or tender feelings between those two was long lost and if she had to wager, Vincent would kill the fairy he used to call his best friend, and enjoy it—immensely.

The ethereal projection waved its hand dismissively. "You'll get over that soon enough. She took you away and I needed you back here. Therefore, she had to go. You'd see I'm right if you would stop being so stubborn."

"Leave my sons alone, Tink. You have me here, you got what you wanted. I'm back here, with you, and Annelise is dead." He opened his arms wide. "You've won. I'm all yours. Stop playing with Patrick."

"She took you away from me first, and you said you

wouldn't forget me or Neverland, and you did. So, *you* don't get to tell me what to do because *you* did this! This is *your* fault!" it yelled.

"Tink!"

Merilee looked up at the sound of the boy's voice yelling for the insane fairy beyond the cenote's opening, half expecting the new Pan to fall straight through the hole with how clumsy this one seemed. When a body didn't fall through the opening and a fainter "Tink!" reached her, she was disappointed.

Pity. Pan falling onto the cave floor, preferably atop of Tink would have been an amusing interruption. Well, for me anyway, she amended glancing at Vincent, *doubt he would find it amusing at all.*

The opening above was one of two entrances to her hideaway. To fly or fall through the opening high above, she guessed twenty-five feet at least; or to swim twenty meters down and thirty meters out to Neverland Cove. The latter was no problem for a mermaid like her but an impossible task for a human like Vincent.

The golden transparent form scrunched up its face and let out a shriek, fluttering its wings while glaring at Vincent. Its shape disappeared, becoming the small six-inch ball of light that was Tink herself and flew up out of the cave.

"She was pleasant," Merilee drawled, swimming out from behind the boulder. "You seem to have a knack for infuriating her."

Vincent started at her voice, then sighed and dropped his chin. "It's not hard, my existence pisses her off."

"No, the selfish fairy is pissed off you forgot *hers*." Resting her arms on the stone ledge of the floor, she stretched out her fins to lazily play peek-a-boo with the surface behind her. "Appears to me she hasn't forgotten about your sons though."

"How long do you think she will be gone?"

She met his pale-green eyes, the pain pulled at her heart.

Tink's involvement with his sons was a topic unavailable for discussion today; she allowed the topic change.

"All depends on which misfortune this latest Pan requires her for. Accident prone and awkward for a creature of his purpose. Who knows what has him calling for Tink this time."

She rested the side of her head on her arms, feeling the warmth from the sunlight absorb into her skin and the water droplets slowly evaporate. At the sight of his bare feet, she wondered if he longed to feel the heated sand of Lost Boys Beach in-between his toes instead of the hard stone. Either way, she was envious of his ability to experience such a sensation.

His feet moved, and she followed the movements as he sat down in the sunlight, leaning against the wall with his demin-clad legs stretched out. He sighed before crossing his ankles; the position recreating memories for her of more enjoyable times with him.

She remembered him as the boy he had been during

his first acquaintance with Neverland. Holding the purpose of Pan, he would sit like so at Peak Point Rock, play his pan flute for her and the others, or use bamboo sticks to drum a rhythm she and her kin would swim to. Discussions for hours about the ridiculous adventures he and Simon embarked upon, genuinely surprising her with their survival rate. When the reality of needing to be the Pan to guide young children, who lost their lives so young in the Real-World, to Neverland sat heavy with Vincent; she would find him sitting, leaning against a Peak Point Rock, legs straight and crossed at the ankles. A Pan's role was not for the faint of heart, and Vincent handled the Lost Boys with a grace she admired.

He cocked his head to the side, "Why do *you* think Tink came back for me? There were Pans before me, some went to the Ferryman when they were finished, and others went to the real world and grew up." His brows drew down and lips thinned. "She didn't care if they forgot her."

"Tink is a simple creature. You know that as well as anyone. Her motives aren't hidden." When he nodded, she continued. "I believe it's solely selfish reasons for her. I doubt she believed the rules of forgetting would apply to you."

"I really hope there is more to it than that," he scoffed, resting his head against the wall and closing his eyes to the sunlight.

She shrugged even though he wasn't looking at her. "I doubt it. You were her favorite Pan and everyone on the island knew it. Why do you think your Hook went after you often but never actually hurt you."

"That Hook didn't like hurting anyone."

"That Hook killed half your Lost Boys and many of my fledglings," she snapped. *That Hook didn't like to hurt anyone?! An absolutely naive statement.*

He looked at her. "What?"

"Pinned Dreilia to the front of his ship for all to see." She slapped her fin on the surface, angered by the thought. "Nothing like seeing the corpse of your charge regularly to reinforce a statement." She held no forgiveness for those men and their actions of late. Some transgressions were unforgivable.

"I'm sorry, Mer. I didn't know."

Vincent's words eased some of the pain his statement caused but the sincerity in his voice soothed her nerves. Afterall, she knew he wasn't to blame for what had been happening; that blame rested on Tink's shoulders.

"Don't delude yourself with the notion that your Hook lacked the enjoyment of inflicting pain on anyone." *The idea of a kind-hearted pirate is as absurd as a mermaid with legs.* "Your Hook never actually hurt you because he fears Dorathea," she explained, wanting to get on topic.

"Thea stays in the Neverland Forest. She doesn't intervene with the Pan and Hook cycle. That's Tink's area of expertise."

"Precisely, but the Pan and Hook cycle is Tink's *to observe,* not intervene. Tink is to remain neutral but became passionately protective of you. Dorathea keeps and guards balance with single-minded focus over *all things* in Neverland. If anyone upsets that balance, she wouldn't hesitate to remove them. Permanently."

"So, if Tink got upset at me being hurt …"

"She'd be reckless and anger Dorathea by responding in retaliation to Hook."

"Messing with the balance."

"Exactly. Tink was different with you, actively involved with your everyday plans. She was never like that with the others. Pans, Hooks, Lost Boys, and pirates are hers to observe. *That* is her task. Help the Pans and Hooks assimilate to the roles and be a guiding presence. She isn't meant to have an active role in Neverland, never did."

"Ah. But she interfered with me, proving that theory inaccurate."

"Not in Neverland."

"That the loophole?"

"Possibly. If she meddles in the Real-World, nothing gets affected on a grand enough scale for Dorathea to take notice and intervene. Tink ventures there regularly to find a suitable Pan, Hook, and Lost Boys."

"But she brought me back here *to Neverland* so that still makes your theory inaccurate."

She wanted to ask him how he had grown to be so handsome but remain so dimwitted, but then his brows drew together as he looked at her.

"Is that why Neverland has felt different these past few weeks? Is that the tension in the air?"

Not just a handsome face after all. "Things were fine until she brought you here. You aren't meant to be here again."

"… and by bringing me here Tink upset the balance of Neverland, but not enough for Dorathea to notice."

"I'm sure she has felt the effects of it but it may be sometime before she figures out the cause. No one's aware of your presence here to my knowledge. For now, she probably views us collectively behaving more aggressively as comparable to sibling rivalry." The temptation to inform the biped herself about the fairy's tinkerings clung to her, but due to the uncertainty pertaining to Vincent, she kept his presence silent. "But," she continued gently, "she killed Annelise."

His jaw ticked. "In the Real-World," he gritted.

"True, but Tink killed a human. Big no-no. Playing tricks and scouting for a new Pan or Hook is one feat. Making any decisions affecting human lives outside of the Pan/Hook parameters, is another interference in its entirety. She produced a massive ripple effect that will be colliding with us shortly."

She would pay in pearls to see a fight between those two beings though. Tink showed her temper often but only recently began crossing boundaries. Dorathea on the other hand, firmly acted within the black and white, coldly apathetic to anything outside the lines. Fire versus ice.

"And now she is amusing herself with my son."

Ah, a topic now to be ventured. "Another violation but I believe she has other motives with that move."

He sat up straighter. "What other motives could she have?"

She was hesitant in voicing her speculation about this Patrick situation. What if she was incorrect? She could cause unnecessary worry for Vincent and have him behave irrationally—possibly get himself discovered. Then again, what if she *was* correct?

She raised her head and pushed off the ledge, she needed to evade that calculated risk for the moment and raised her hand. "I'll return shortly."

Diving under the water, she swam to the pouch she concealed on the floor upon entering the cave. Opening the top, she reached in and grabbed the dagger she had stolen from Simon a few nights ago.

A vibration rippling through the water redirected her focus to the surface. Vincent was swimming towards her. His display of impatience being worse than Simon's would have made her smile but seeing him in the water made her anxious. She needed to keep him where he was safe.

Pushing up, she propelled herself towards him. Grabbing his shirt with her free hand, she pulled him to the surface, anger replacing the anxiety when the air touched her face, heating her skin and bristling down her scales. She brought the blade under his chin and growled. "You will not dive in this water! Do you understand me?"

He raised one eyebrow. At this proximity, his pale-green eyes had a rim of dark blue on the outside creating a stunning contrast. *Genetics blessed him.* She could feel the heat of his body spreading through the water between them, reminding her of the reason she needed said body to stay warm.

"Do you understand me?" she persisted, slower this time, needing him to acknowledge the importance of this. There were multiple reasons—some selfish, others not—why he needed to remain alive. Most pressing—Neverland needed him breathing.

His expression didn't change.

Very well, another approach. "Do you have your Coin of Passage?"

"Why does tha ..." he trailed off, his other brow joined the first. "Oh shit."

"Yes, oh shit," she parroted. "You die without that, and there will be no seeing Annelise. No pleading with the Ferryman to pass, no waiting for your sons to reacquaint with you two later." She removed the blade. "No diving in these waters."

He nodded, looking a bit pale. "No more diving." He brought his hand up under his chin and smoothed it over his dark stubble. Reaching for the ledge, he lifted himself up and sat with his legs dangling in the water. "Where do you keep that thing?"—he paused—"Wait. Why do you even have a dagger? You prefer to drown your prey."

She laughed. "I do. We all do. It's more satisfying to watch them struggle to breathe under water while we can do it effortlessly."

His knuckles turned white as he clutched the ledge and peered into the clear water. "Yeah, can't say I share the satisfaction of watching someone drown."

For a second time in an hour, she inwardly winced. "No, I imagine it isn't a sentiment you share. I apologize for my thoughtlessness." She wanted to dispose of the fairy for Vincent and aid in ridding him of that haunted look. Until then …

"This is for you." She placed the dagger beside him on the ledge. "Stabbing me isn't a wise choice though." She doubted he desired to do so but felt compelled to make the statement in case her carelessness had created a change of heart.

His eyes widened as he picked it up, touching the garnet surrounded by rubies. "My old dagger?" His fingers caressed the ivory handle and embedded gems reverently. He reached up, flicking his thumb over the blade and grinned. "Sharp as ever." Flipping it into the air, he caught it by the blade. "Hello, old friend."

"Collected it from Simon while he was swimming in Mermaid Lagoon."

His lips twitched. "Simon abhors the water, Mer."

She shrugged. "Doesn't mean he wasn't swimming. I never claimed he was doing it *willingly*."

He laughed. "You knocked him into the water again, didn't you?"

"He was being an arrogant pest and particularly annoying the other day," she said, smiling. "Growing up quicker than usual too."

Vincent cocked his head to the side, but before words traveled from his lips she continued. "More importantly, there is purpose for that dagger here and Simon has the one you made him, so he isn't left defenseless."

"Simon wouldn't allow himself to be defenseless. He could make a weapon out of a fallen twig if need be," Vincent said.

She would wager he was recalling a time, or several, where his friend had done just that by the way he smirked as he flicked the blade's edge with his thumb once more.

"I can't be here to keep you safe all the time." She nudged his leg in an attempt to tease and bring him back to the present.

"Thank you." He nudged her hip with his foot in return.

"You're welcome," she said as she pushed away from the ledge and sunshine. "If I'm right, it's only a matter of time before you'll need it."

CHAPTER 4

TORN DECISIONS

JACKSON

ap. Tap. Tap.

The pen connected against the cracked watch face of his father's watch as he read the text on the page, an unconscious habit Jackson picked up whenever he was studying or needed to concentrate.

There was something about the sound he found comforting, almost like a connection to his dad wherever he may be. Once the investigation was completed on his parent's Chevrolet Impala after the accident, their belongings were returned in a brown envelope; the old-style watch on his left wrist being one of the items. His father had always worn the watch, so it felt right for him to wear it, broken or not. Sure, he could have taken it to get fixed, but it didn't feel right to have it done—not yet.

Patrick's laughter from the backyard caused him to pause in his study. He'd not a clue what Patrick was doing but the laughs coming sporadically through the crack in the window were worth the chilly nighttime breeze entering his room. His lips turned up at the corners at another heartfelt chuckle and he would willingly put on two pairs of socks and a sweater if it meant he could hear it.

Besides, he didn't have much of a choice concerning the window being cracked open since he wasn't comfortable with him being alone—especially outside—and there was no way he was going to sit outside studying. The weather may be warming up fast, but snow was still on the ground with a chill in the air. So, he would deal with a slight breeze for his own peace of mind.

A knock at his bedroom door had him looking up from his biology text to see his Uncle Alex walking through the doorway.

"Come on in," Jackson muttered, more to himself than to be welcoming. He still wasn't impressed with how his uncles had tried to use Natalie last weekend. She still insisted on apologizing to him for intervening and being weird about it, but what he kept hearing in his mind was her nervous ramblings that day. He didn't like it when she was uncomfortable, and she should *never* be uncomfortable around him. So, whenever the source of her discomfort came to chat with him this week, he left the room.

Unfortunately, that source entered his space and took a seat at the end of his bed wearing a weathered gray thermal shirt stained with some sort of oil or grease, and blue jeans in no better shape. The standard get-up for his

Uncle Alex when working on the old car in the garage. If he had to take a guess, his uncle was as concerned for Patrick as he was and was dealing with it his favorite way.

Jackson went back to studying. He may not work on cars like his uncle, but he could lose himself in a textbook. The outcome was the same.

"We need to have a little chat."

"Why talk to me when you can ask Natalie to do it for you?" he said dismissively. Sure, it was childish, but damnit he was still irritated. The past week had been stressful for so many reasons and he was about at his limit with drama.

"Seriously, you need to get over that. You were acting off and weren't talking much, so we asked Natalie." Uncle Alex's annoyance showed in his tone.

Good, and he can continue to be annoyed. I will get over it when I am good and ready.

Continuing writing his notes on the human genome, he ignored his uncle's statement. Maybe if he ignored the man long enough, he would get so annoyed he would go away.

A throat cleared behind him instead: loudly.

He dropped his pencil on his notepad and swiveled his desk chair around, doubting he was going to like whatever he was about to hear. *Might as well get this over with.* "Alright, what's up?"

Uncle Alex reached into his back jeans pocket and when his arm came forward, a folded letter was in his hand. "This"—he waved the bent envelope in the air—"want to tell me about this?"

Yeah, he wasn't going to like this chat. He knew exactly what that was. "Looks like a bent piece of paper with none of your business on it."

His uncle let out a huff of air. "None of my business, hey? You got accepted into a college, the college you had been talking to your parents about going to and—"

Jackson raised his eyebrow at *that* bit of news. He didn't remember telling his uncles about those conversations. "Huh?"

"Your mother called and told me when you mentioned it back then. She was all excited, and twins tell each other everything." He waved his hand dismissively but grimaced.

Ah! That made sense. Although he wondered what his mother had overshared that Uncle Alex wouldn't have wanted to know. An image of his dad popped into his head, and he grinned. She would have overshared about her love life and she had been the *honest-in-an-awkward-kind-of-way* person.

"Anyway, I find this letter in the bottom of the junk drawer, and you say it's none of my business?"

Jackson shrugged. The look of incredulity on his uncle's face was priceless. *What? Is he offended?* There was some satisfaction in that, maybe he *would* enjoy parts of this conversation.

"It's my business because we need to figure out housing, whether on campus or off, and you'll need furniture most likely. Then there is tuition and fees, funding, grant applications, I think." His uncle ran his hand back and forth in his short blonde hair clearly agitated. "Hell, I don't know. I never went to college. I don't have a clue." He sighed. "But it's my business because your parents wanted us to make sure you were taken care of if something happened to them, and I intend to. We are financially responsible for you and the funds until you're twenty-one, if you choose to go to college. *And* not just that, I want to see you succeed. So, if I can help, I want to."

"I'm not going."

Silence.

He shrugged again when Uncle Alex just stared at him because there was nothing to say about it. "Can I get back to studying?"—he pointed behind him with his thumb—"Finals are coming up and I want to see if I can get honors."

"You're joking right?"

"Nope"—he popped the 'P' for emphasis—"Honors would be cool to get." His lips twitched as Uncle Alex's face screwed up like he tasted something sour and pinched the bridge of his nose.

He *loved* making him do that, it was a favorite pastime for him since Uncles Alex and Marcus moved into the house. Especially when this particular one pissed him off —which he had. Uncle Marcus would have just popped him on the back of the head for being irritating; not hard, but enough to let him know to smarten up.

Still holding his nose, Uncle Alex leaned forward and rested his elbows on his thighs. "So … you don't want to go to this college, but you want to study enough to get honors … for fun?" He spoke painfully slow.

Jackson waited for him to look up before he nodded. "Yep." Popping the 'P' again to be extra irritating. *Maybe I can get the man's eye to twitch too.*

And really, there wasn't anything difficult to understand about the school situation as far as he was concerned. It was 100% plausible he would want to get honors just for the hell of it, and not do it for an appealing transcript. He excelled in his classes, always had; so yeah, graduating with honors would be fantastic.

What wouldn't be fantastic is another family member leaving Patrick. The kid had big enough issues as it was with being separated from him. Jackson had to get a cell-phone for the sole purpose of being able to reassure him he was coming home when he left without him. Like clockwork, he would receive a phone call if he took a minute longer than when he said he was going to be home. What would Patrick do if Jackson left for college? He couldn't have his phone on him all the time and if he was honest, he didn't like the idea of being tethered to the thing. He felt restricted enough the way things were now, but he could deal with it here until Patrick got better. He promised he would never leave him and would keep him safe, and that was one promise he was determined to keep.

Uncle Alex let go of his nose. "Why did you apply if you didn't intend on going?"

He broke eye contact with his uncle's too-observant brown eyes and looked at the picture frame on his wall: a picture of him with Patrick on his shoulders when he was fourteen and Patrick was nine. His father had taken that picture a week before the accident. A pain shot through his chest at the memory.

His uncle sighed. "I understand you don't want to leave him, but you need to have a life outside of Patrick. Marcus and I have been taking care of you both for three years, you need to understand this isn't your burden to carry. You can't make choices like these"—he gave the letter a shake—"based on what your brother is going through, Jackson."

Sure I can, and I will. He wasn't leaving his brother, he wouldn't, not after the last couple weeks.

"His appointment to get reassessed is in a couple days. Hopefully, we will have more of an idea on how to help him after that."

An appointment Uncle Alex made with Patrick's psychiatrist after Jackson had brought everything up to his uncles the day of the Carston Lake incident. That had been a nerve-wracking experience for Jackson.

After he dropped off Natalie, he had dragged Patrick into the living room where his uncles had been sitting, watching T.V. and told them what happened on Carston Lake. There may have been some pacing and some swearing on his part, he had gotten himself worked up by the 'what ifs' that had been running through his head while driving home. His uncles were rightfully pissed, and grounded Patrick from the lake for two weeks before sending him to his room for the night, which was when he decided to tell them the rest. How he thought Patrick was seeing and hearing things, and his total lack of fear for his own safety, him displaying subtle signs of being suicidal. The words felt thick on his tongue and his heart pounded in his chest, he felt like he was betraying his brother in some way; but worse than those words, was the fear he was right about all of it.

Thinking about it afterwards, he felt—well still did feel—stupid about being worried his uncles wouldn't believe him or tell him he was overreacting. Uncle Alex had always been more observant than he let on, he just wasn't usually intrusive about it. Until lately, that was.

Standing up from the edge of the bed, Uncle Alex held out the letter. "Give it some more thought, okay? No rush decisions. You aren't helping him if you set yourself up to resent him later for a decision you made based on him. That's not fair to either of you."

"I won't resent him," he said, scowling, and took the envelope.

His uncle's mahogany-brown eyes felt intense as he studied him, reminding him of his mom's stares when he was younger. Jackson couldn't hide anything from her either when she did that.

"You might not now, but why would you put yourself in a situation where you could?"

Patrick's laughter floated from outside his cracked-open window and they both turned to the sound. Moving to the window, he looked down into the backyard where Patrick appeared to be sword fighting an imaginary foe.

His brother's smile was huge as he dodged and swung one arm as the other was tucked behind his back, until his smile disappeared and he stopped. "That swing didn't count!" he yelled, "girls are supposed to lose, not cheat!"

Jackson frowned and looked over at his uncle, seeing him frowning as well.

"Girl?" he asked hesitantly. "Think he's playing with Mom?"

"I don't know, Jacks," his uncle placed a hand on his shoulder and squeezed, "but we are going to find out."

Patrick stomped his foot in the slushy snow and headed towards the back door. Once out of view, the telling squeaks of the porch bench swing began.

"Go talk to him. Bring up the idea of you going to college and see what he says? He could surprise all of us." With a clap on his back, Jackson listened to the receding footsteps while he stared out at the spot where Patrick had been playing.

The backyard light shone on the snowmen and ice castles Patrick and his uncles had built the other day, and a light behind one ice castle caught his attention. It was as if a little flashlight was moving inside, highlighting the yellows and blues of the dyed ice blocks. *Did Patrick put a candle inside one? Because that was a neat idea.*

"Go away!"

He started at his brother's tearful shout and the light from the ice castle came out of the front opening and shot through the backyard up to the night sky. *A firefly? Do we even have fireflies here in winter?*

He could hear sniffling and decided the firefly didn't matter; he needed to talk to Patrick about leaving for college. If his brother reacted badly—no college; but he dared to hope, if Patrick seemed okay with the idea, he would look more seriously into the programs. He didn't want to admit that Uncle Alex had been right, if he didn't get to go and had to miss out on this experience, he had a feeling he *would* come to resent Patrick; and that resentment was the last thing he wanted to feel.

* * *

The wall of cold air hit him as he opened the back door that led to the deck, a fleece blanket over his shoulder and Thermos in hand. His boots clunked against the wood of the deck as he walked towards a sniffling Patrick. *Maybe I should wait.*

Dark-brown eyes looked up at him as he sat on the bench swing. Pulling the blanket off his shoulder, he passed it to Patrick. "Can't let you freeze out here by yourself."

Patrick gave him a half smile and put the blanket over his lap. "It's above freezing, Jacks. I can't freeze if it's not cold enough to do that."

"Fair enough, but it's still cold out here." The Thermos lid twisted easily, releasing the sweet smell of fresh hot chocolate and he poured some of the liquid in the lid. He loved the smell of the stuff, it brought memories of their dad pestering their mom about never putting in enough marshmallows.

Patrick took the lid and frowned at the contents. "Where are the marshmallows?"

"Ask Uncle Marcus. Couldn't find any in the pantry. I think he ate them all watching a movie with Marium last time she was over."

"Is Marium the tall one or the strong perfume?"

Jackson grinned into the Thermos before taking a sip. "She's the high-pitched giggle."

"She owes us marshmallows," his brother grumbled, looking up from the drink and towards the night sky.

"I'll let him know." He doubted Uncle Marcus had realized there wasn't a backup bag because he was fairly good at keeping those stocked for Patrick. The learning curve the uncles had with adjusting to suddenly being responsible for a nine-year-old and a fourteen-year-old was steep, but they managed well. Jackson had even idolized his uncle Marcus at one point due to his way with women, but then he witnessed the morning after of awkwardness one to many times and realized that was not a situation he ever wanted to be caught in.

Patrick had made the mistake of calling one—of five ladies—by the wrong name in greeting when they came into the kitchen for a morning cup of coffee. Uncle Alex had choked on his coffee the first couple of times it happened which encouraged Patrick to say the wrong name to others for fun. The whole routine had been amusing for all of them, watching Uncle Marcus try to calm down his companion of the week; it was comparable to trying to sooth a feral cat.

He swung the bench gently as he pulled himself back to the present. *Is now a suitable time to bring up the acceptance letter? How do I mention this? Ease into it or just straight up and say it, like ripping off a Band-Aid?*

Letting out a long breath while he rubbed the back of his neck to relieve the tension, he decided to stop hesitating. "Hey, I want to ask you a qu—"

"Did you hear about Hugh?" his brother said, sadness in his tone.

"Yeah buddy, I did hear." He knew Uncle Alex had broken the news to Patrick about his classmate earlier that day. "How you doing with it?"

"I miss him … but he isn't hurting anymore."

"No, he isn't hurting anymore." No kid should have to go through what Hugh had.

Jackson could still remember Hugh being over for sleepovers with Patrick and the campouts in the living room they would have. Scaring them during a late-night show was his big-brother duty, and oh how he made them scream a time or two. He smiled at the memory. Then Hugh got sick and the sleepovers and visits with Patrick dwindled and eventually stopped all together once his chemotherapy treatments started. Patrick went to see him as much as he could when Hugh had good days, but even those eventually became rare.

He reached out and rubbed his brother's shoulder. "Remember mom saying that any grief we feel is all the love we have left for the person who died?" At his brother's nod, he continued. "It makes it easier to bear the sadness some days for me to think about that."

"Do you think mom is happy where she is?"

He followed his brother's gaze and looked to the sky. The stars were bright tonight, and the moon was full. It was the kind of night their mom used to love; she would come out here and watch the stars on the bench swing, often with one or both of them curled up to her side and listening to her sing or tell stories.

"Yeah buddy, I think she's happy."

"Sometimes I think of how great it would be if there was a place where we could go to visit them. Mom, Dad, Hugh. Not Carston Lake, but like really see and talk to them. To say I love them. To smell mom's perfume or feel one of dad's hugs." He smiled slightly. "I would give anything for that, you know."

His throat felt tight as his own emotions crept up. "Yeah, that place would be pretty amazing."

"Yeah, it would." Patrick took a sip of his hot chocolate. "One day I'll get to see them again."

He wasn't sure what to say; because yeah, family meets at the pearly gates and all that, but something was off. Patrick's tone maybe? Too much certainty?

"I look forward to it. It will be a great day." Patrick smiled. "I'm going to go to bed, I'm tired." He stood up and handed him the blanket. "I already know what you want to ask me. It's fine, Jacks. You do what you need to do. I'll be fine. I have Uncle Alex and Uncle Marcus here, and it's not like you won't come home to see Natalie and I'll never get to see you. Stop worrying about me. I'll be good soon."

Sitting back, he straightened his legs to stop the swing's momentum. That went better than he thought it would. He had expected anger, accusations of breaking promises and tears. "Hey Patrick," he called out, "how do you know what I was going to ask?"

His brother toed small, melted slush pile on the deck with his boot. "There's been a lot of mail lately, Oliver was talking at school about his sister getting accepted into a college overseas on a culinary scholarship, so I figured you would talk to me about college sometime because it's your last year in high school."

"Did you find the letter?" He thought he had hidden it well.

Patrick looked past him and sighed. He followed his brother's gaze; nothing out of the ordinary stood out in what was illuminated by the light. He half expected to find something or someone staring at him when he turned. He looked back at Patrick and raised an eyebrow.

The kid shrugged and took a sip of hot chocolate. "I thought I saw something"—another sip—"Can I go inside?"

"Yeah, go get ready for bed." He leaned forward, adopting a position similar to one Uncle Alex sat in earlier, Thermos tapping against his pant leg. "Thanks for talking to me about missing mom and dad. It's good. I miss them too, buddy."

Patrick smiled at him, and he smiled back.

His smile grew larger as he heard his brother whistling the lullaby their dad used to sing to them. This was a step in the right direction. Patrick had opened up a little and it was one of the most honest conversations he had had with him in months. Real felt good and now the lullaby, he hadn't heard the song in almost three years. It made his chest hurt realizing *he* had forgotten it.

Hearing the back door shut, he took a sip from the Thermos. *Well, what to do now?* He needed to make a list of things to do over the weekend now that college wasn't off the table. He thought he would be more excited, elated, but he felt nervous and a little uneasy after talking to Patrick; like he was saying goodbye to his brother in a different way.

He stood up and stretched, the off feeling lingering. Maybe he would convince Natalie to give him a massage tomorrow after he told her the news. Smiling at the thought of what else they could do after the massage, he threw the blanket over his shoulder and went to head inside.

A chill slithered down his spine. He looked over his shoulder and searched the yard one more time. *Nothing.* Maybe it was all the movies he and Uncle Marcus had been watching, but he could have sworn he felt someone behind him.

Jackson shook his head and reached for the cold door

handle. Turning it, he caught the reflection of a woman standing behind him, glaring. He spun around, dropping the blanket and spilling the remaining hot chocolate on the deck into the empty space where the woman should have been standing. *There is no way anyone could have moved that fast.* He picked up the blanket and squinted into the darkness. *Yeah, need to take a break from those thriller movies.* Shaking his head at his ridiculousness, he went inside. The image of the woman's angry face flashed in his mind as he crossed the threshold and he felt satisfaction in hearing the click of the deadbolt on the door.

Flicking off the outside light, he left the kitchen and headed up to his room to start with that list he was going to make, but he knew he was going to spend more time trying to figure out who that woman tonight looked like than planning his new future. The disturbing part though: he was almost certain the reflection was the same he had imagined at Carston Lake.

CHAPTER 5

HIDDEN DANGER

"Hey pretty girl, what's up?' Jackson put the cellphone between his ear and shoulder as he searched his pocket for his keys.

"Hey, just checking that we are still going to see *I Knew I Loved him* tonight."

He groaned inwardly. *Never should have agreed to bet against her.* Now he was stuck going to some ridiculous chick flick. He opened the door and threw the keys onto the side table in the entrance way. "You said 'horror' wrong."

"You wish I did," she said through a laugh. "I won the bet fair and square."

That she had.

"Yeah, yeah. What time is the movie again?"

"Four-thirty at the Monarch Theatre."

"Alright, I'll pick you up in an hour. But you have to tell me what your surprise is afterwards." He really didn't like surprises, but she was adamant about telling him after he fulfilled his part of losing the bet—her way of making sure he followed through.

"Sounds good. And yes, after you suffer through the movie, I'll tell you."

"Perfect, see you in an hour. Love ya."

"Love you too."

He pocketed his phone as he walked down the hallway towards the stairs, needing to check in on Patrick. Uncle Alex had called to tell him the appointment went well today and that he had dropped him off before heading to work. He wasn't sure what 'went well' meant to his uncle, but wanted to see how Patrick felt about it because his opinion was the one that mattered.

Taking the stairs two at a time, he ignored the family photos that lined the wall as always. He wished he could take photos down; some memories he still had a tough time visiting.

"Hey, Patrick!" he called out as he hooked onto the banister and swung himself to the right, past his room, linen closet, and headed towards his brother's room at the end of the hallway. His brother's shadow moved across the floor from the sunlight shining through from under the door.

"Hey Buddy, I wanna chat with you." Opening the door, he frowned as he took in the empty room. His brother kept his room habitually tidy, yet it looked as though a notebook had exploded from the desk. Papers, some crumpled, littered the floor.

"Patrick?"

The closet doors' hinges creaked as he opened them, half expecting his brother to jump out and scare him. Nothing. Hangers hit each other as his hand moved the clothing around to check behind to be sure.

Turning, he bent down to look under the bed. Books, candy wrappers and a few figurines. A chill down his spine made him straighten and turn towards the curtains moving with the breeze from the partially open window.

Papers crinkled on the floor as he walked over to the window. Sliding up the windowpane, he peered down into the side yard.

The snow had mostly melted—thanks to the nicer weather—but small clumps of snow lingered where the snowmen had been and dark puddles from ice castles made the side yard a soupy mess. The shed door creaked as it swayed in the breeze.

He really needed to oil those hinges.

Wait, why's the shed open? A paper from Patrick's desk floated to the floor by his black sneaker. Picking up the crumpled sheet he examined his brother's messy scribble.

"Lost boy, Lost boy, won't you take my hand. Never be alone, here in Neverland," he read aloud, curious about the multiple lines under the word 'Neverland.' He'd have to ask him about it later, after they had a chat about his appointment, once he found the kid. Placing the paper back on the desk, he headed out of the room.

Down the stairs, he turned to the left entering the kitchen, passed the dining room and out the patio door.

"Hey buddy, what are you doing in the shed?" He opened the shed door wide, intent on telling his brother that not responding was rude; but once again, it was empty. It was emptier than it should have been, Patrick's bike was gone.

Taking out his cell, he dialed his Uncle Alex and noted the gate was open. His phone rang in his ear as he jogged to the patio door, hoping to find a note in the kitchen he'd missed.

"Hey, Jackson. I can't talk long; I have a meeting in five minutes."

"Did Patrick tell you where he was going?" he asked as he scanned for a note.

"Going? He told me he was going to take a nap. Why? Isn't he there?"

"No, and his bike is gone."

His brother had been acting more like his old self these past few days and instead of it making Jackson feel better, it was having the opposite effect. The churning in his gut intensified.

"Maybe he just went for a bike ride because it's been so nice out."

Even his uncle didn't seem to have much faith in that answer. The last time Patrick touched that bike was two years ago, and that was only to put it in the shed because biking reminded him too much of their dad.

Patrick's messy scribble written in erasable marker on the fridge caught his eye.

"I don't think so," he said slowly. "He wrote, 'feeling lonely, going to find a stone for mom.'"

"He went to the lake then?" His uncle's voice was laced with worry and rustling paper could be heard through the phone.

"That would be my guess. I'll go check there and I'll stay with him if he is," he said, making his way to the front entrance and picking up his keys. "He feels lonely, so I'll cancel my date with Natalie and hang with him tonight."

"Sounds like a good plan. He said he had a good appointment, that the doctor helped him understand some things. He seemed fine. I know where your mind is going, but maybe this is a good sign he is going down there without needing you."

"Seems like you're trying to convince yourself, not me." The front door slammed behind him and he jogged to his car parked on the street.

"Maybe a bit of both." His sigh was loud over the speaker. "Just call me and let me know when you find him. I'll talk to Marcus about a trip to the cabin this weekend. Might be good for all of us."

"Sounds like a plan. Gotta go." He snapped the phone closed and yanked open the driver's door.

He put his seatbelt on and started the engine, urgency clawing at him as he did a U-turn and headed towards Carston Lake. His thoughts were going a mile a minute, running through conversations he'd had with Patrick lately and how he had been acting, trying to find a reason to not think the worst. Then the reoccurring images of Patrick floating lifeless in the lake flashed in his mind and he almost threw up.

Needing to hear the voice that could always settle him, he picked up his phone from the cup holder and dialed Natalie's number. Putting it on speaker, he listened to it ring twice before her voice filled the car.

"You better not be cancelling because you don't want to watch a chick flick," she teased.

"I am. Patrick wasn't at the house and then left a note saying he felt lonely and went to find a stone for mom—"

"Alone?"

"—Yeah, so I'm going to hang with him tonight. I hope you aren't too mad about postponing it. I'll make it up to you." He took the left turn to Carston Road, and wondered how Patrick could have gotten this far on his bike already, it wasn't that long after he was dropped off that Jackson got home. *The kid had to have biked fast.*

"I'm not mad, Jackson." Natalie sounded a little offended. "Your family comes first, and really, I think of Patrick like a little brother too. If he needs you, he needs you."

"Have I told you I love you lately?"

"Everyday." She laughed. "Don't worry about me, go check on Patrick. If he isn't there, come pick me up and we'll look for him, okay?"

"Two chick flicks. Double feature night. No complaining about any cheesy lines."

When the car crested the hill, he spotted a small

person on the surface of the lake. The blood drained from his face.

"Nat," he drew out wearily.

She was silent for a beat. "What is it?"

"He's on the lake." His voice monotone, not expressing any of the fear he felt at the sight. It was like his brain didn't want to register what he was seeing. The closer he got the more he couldn't deny the figure wearing the red and black jacket was indeed his brother. Like a tidal wave, the brain fog lifted and clarity of the situation crashed into him. "He's on the fucking lake, and he's jumping on the surface."

Jackson could even see water leaping into the air each time Patrick's boots connected with the surface as he jumped from one spot to another. "No, no, no, no, no," he repeated, stomach in his throat and pulse pounding in his ears.

"Jackson!" Natalie's sharp tone snapped his focus from Patrick just before the tires went off the road. "Jackson, is he still above the surface?" She spoke as if this wasn't the first time she had asked him.

He parked the car next to the guardrail. "Yeah, he's still above the ice." Shoving the gearshift into park, he unbuckled and got out of the car. "With how much water he's kicking up, I doubt he'll be for long."

Patrick's laughter met him as he rounded the car.

"Patrick!" he yelled. "What the hell are you doing out there?" His brother didn't respond, just kept looking down at the surface and then jumped to a new spot, like some Russian roulette whack-a-mole. That's when he heard it: the echo of cracking in the lake.

The ice splintered towards him from Patrick's direction. His brother was going under; he knew it.

"Patrick!" he yelled again, but still no response. What was he supposed to do? If he went out there, he could fall through because he was heavier than Patrick, or even take Patrick under with him. He could hear Natalie's voice coming from the phone in his hand, but the words were muffled by the sound of blood whooshing in his ears.

His decision was made for him when Patrick shrieked and his legs went through the surface. Jackson stopped thinking and dropped the phone, volleying over the guardrail. The inch of water covering the ice like a blanket splashed up, soaking his shoes and pant legs as he ran. He tried to run as lightly as he could, focused on Patrick's desperate struggles to pull himself up.

What had he learned about frozen waters? *Disperse the weight, widen the contact surface to lessen the pressure?* He bent down, sliding on his stomach as he neared his panicking brother. Freezing water soaked into the front of his clothes like he was on a frozen Slip-and-Slide.

"Jacks!" Patrick cried. "Help me up!"

"Working on it, buddy. Just try and stay calm for me." He felt like a hypocrite because he was anything but calm.

"It wasn't supposed to break! She said it wouldn't!" Patrick wailed, reaching for him as he got closer.

What the hell is he talking about? He grabbed his brother's hand and pulled him close. He felt Patrick's other hand clench the back of his jacket. He wrapped his arms around Patrick's trembling form under the arms to keep his upper body out of the water. Worried his brother would shake out of his hold, he increased his grip.

"I got you. I got you." Jackson kissed his brother on the side of the head, and breathed him in, needing the reassurance his brother was okay. He backed up enough to look into Patrick's tear-streaked face. "I'm going to get you out of here, okay. I got you. But I need you to listen to me and do what I say before we both go through." He gave the kid what he hoped was a reassuring smile and tried to keep his voice as calm as he could.

The sound of cracking let Jackson know they needed to move, and quickly. Patrick's lips quivered. "What do we do, Jacks?"

"I'm going to start backing up. You are going to kick your legs and help me lift you onto the ice. If we keep our weight dispersed enough, we should be good." At least he hoped that was true, seemed logical enough to him.

Patrick sniffed and nodded his head, tears still falling. "I'm sorry."

"Not the time for that, buddy. Say it all you want when we are in the car." Readjusting his grip, he grabbed as much material of the coat as he could. "Hey." He looked in his brother's eyes to make sure he was present;

nothing but his brother peered back at him. "On the count of three."

At Patrick's nod, he took a deep breath and started counting with him.

"One. Two. Three!"

He braced his elbows and pulled. Shifting back, he made room for Patrick to rest his upper body flat on the ice. Jackson's shirt rose to expose his abdomen to the frigid surface, stinging his skin. *Really, really, hate the cold.* He let go of Patrick with one hand and pulled his shirt down for the little relief it gave him before repositioning his hand back under Patrick's arm.

His brother looked at him and chuckled a little. "Snow angels wouldn't be so bad compared to this, hey?"

He couldn't help it, whether it was the relief of them staying topside or the adrenaline coursing through him, he chuckled too. "Still not gonna happen."

They both let out a nervous laugh. "Let's not do this again, okay."

Patrick nodded. "Yeah, no worries there."

"Let's get out of here. This lake freaks me out."

Tinkling bells had them both looking towards the hole Patrick was half submerged in.

"Jacks …" Patrick's weary tone raised the hairs on the back of his neck. "We need to get out of here. Like, now!"

He didn't need his brother to yell the last word to get him moving because the face of the blonde woman appeared and that was all the motivation he needed. It was the same woman he kept seeing, and every time he did, he felt uneasy—like prey being stalked. Jackson didn't know who or what she was, but malice radiated from her.

"What the fuck is that?" he asked, trying to pull Patrick up; except his brother didn't budge. He pulled again, but still nothing. It was like Patrick was caught on something.

The woman smiled a cruel smile.

"Jacks!" Patrick scrambled to get a grip on his arms when he was yanked backwards. "Don't let her take me, Jacks! I don't want to go anymore. I want to stay with you! Don't let her take me."

He had no idea who 'she' was but like hell anyone was taking his little brother from him. Tightening his grip, he pulled as hard as he could, Patrick's pleas and apologies fueling his efforts. Then, he was jolted forward, and Patrick's terrified scream filled his ears. There was no stopping their momentum and he knew it.

The splash of the inevitable wasn't as terrifying as the sound of his brother's scream being garbled by the lake water. Then there was nothing but silence and the biting, icy water surrounding him. Patrick's hands grabbing at his arms and holding onto the fabric with a pinching grip. He tried to kick up towards the surface, opening his eyes to make sure he was heading in the right direction, but his brother's grip pulled him down.

Panic surged through him as it became darker as he moved towards the bottom of the lake. His lungs burned with the need for oxygen, skin stinging from moving through the frigid water. *This is it. We're going to drown. Drown like our parents, in the same damn lake.* He didn't see a way out of this, didn't understand what was happening, and—man, his lungs burned. He needed to inhale.

The breath he was holding was knocked out of him as he collided with something hard. *The bottom? No, not the bottom.* He still had hold of Patrick's jacket in one hand, and that arm was being forced through something that felt like thick sludge. His side was next, then his face, making him realize being buried alive was one of his top ways to not want to die, and finally the rest of him went through. Then he was floating, suspended in the warmest water.

The hand that had a hold of Patrick was empty and he moved it around frantically trying to feel for something solid. There was nothing. He reflexively opened his mouth to call for Patrick and felt it fill with the warm water. *Well, that was dumb.* Jackson looked towards the shimmering surface and used the energy he had to reach for it.

After several useless movements of his arms, he realized it wasn't going to be enough and stopped trying to reach the impossible. Shimmering sunlight from the rippling surface touched his face and it was then it registered how far below he truly was. A calm washed over him as the burning in his lungs subsided; even the accompanying lightheadedness was welcome as he accepted the truth of the situation.

Yes, this is it. Why is it so bright though? Is this what if felt like for mom? What's swimming in the water? His eye lids felt heavy, so he let them close. He promised he would never leave Patrick and would keep him safe; but he failed him in that. Jackson hoped he would see Patrick again to tell him he was sorry. He only wished he had gotten to hold Natalie one more time.

The tick-tick-tick of his dad's broken watch was the only sound he heard as everything faded to black.

WELCOME TO NEVERLAND

MERILEE

The tiresome task of consoling the Lost Boys whenever that reckless fairy decided she found a more suitable choice for Pan was becoming daunting.

Merilee huffed as she swam towards the object floating at the Neverland Cove bottom.

Every time the Lost Boys began to build a relationship and stability with the Pan, Tink removed him, leaving his incompetent replacement to fumble in his place. It left Mermaid Lagoon riddled with melancholy Lost Boys needing mothering and consoling. Of course, the children would come to her home; her kin resembled women of a maternal age.

Unfortunately, the majority of her kin would rather drown the Lost Boys to stop the whining drivel instead of consoling them. Take the easier route and continue on their merry way. Which left her demanding the mermaids to leave Mermaid Lagoon to deal with the Lost Boys herself. A truly distasteful task she would rather not have bothered herself with; but to save the lives of the children, she acquiesced. If she wished any semblance of peace for her and her fledglings, this Pan matter had to be dealt with.

Her last completed task was listening to the four remaining Lost Boys whining and crying about how they missed their Pan already; how they didn't want a new one and were set on not liking his replacement. The boys weren't even willing to give the new Pan a chance, which caused her patience to be worn dangerously thin. Funny though, she accused Simon of lacking the very thing she struggled with now—patience. Life had an irritating way of proving judgement was only a reflection of self.

She growled. The idea of turning around and drowning them all for occupying her afternoon was sorely tempting. Each Lost Boy really should be grateful she wasn't as cruel as she wanted to be. Perhaps she should drown just one, so the remaining would lose the delusion she was motherly. It would surely get her point across that they weren't welcome to invade Mermaid Lagoon to whine whenever Tink replaced their guide.

Now that incompetent fairy had carelessly brought something to Neverland Cove when she brought the newest addition through. She knew it was Tink because she almost collided with her—and who she presumed was the lifeless Pan—a moment ago. If she hadn't been paying attention to who could see her, she surely would be sporting an injury or two.

She had half a mind to find Dorathea and tell her to put a leash on Tink. Perhaps she still would, because there was more chaos now than ever, and wasn't that Dorathea's job? Why was she responsible for keeping a semblance of order instead of the Biped herself? Her task was fledglings, pleasure, and taking the broken souls to Hal. Simple. Nothing about Lost Boys, Tink, or responsibility for the island's ebb and flow.

She would discover the location of Vincent's coin of passage, then let him loose on the island. Surely, he had building rage towards Neverland and its occupants. Might be therapeutic for him; it surely would benefit her if he disposed of Tink, Hook and the whiny Lost Boys polluting her lagoon. *Entertainment at its finest.*

The blob floating motionless was a man, she realized as she neared it. Dark hair about five-inches long, was dancing about his face, and a black coat billowed like a cape of sorts behind him.

Being level now with the man, she waved her hand before his face to displace the water and encourage the hair back to allow her to see his features. Sharp brows and nose, high cheekbones, thin lips, and the start of a goatee growing in. The hoop in his ear caught the light and twinkled at her.

Where did you come from, young one? And he *was* young, hugging the line of adulthood but keeping the softness of youth in his face.

Tick. Tick. Tick.

The sharp sound in the water drew her to his wrist, which happened to be the source. She leaned in closer and examined what appeared to be a pocket watch fashioned into a wristwatch. The face of the watch was two-thirds gold with lines running diagonally across, while the remaining third had a tarnished metal peeking through: small birds in a 'v' formation, wings extended, pointing towards the center of the watch. She touched the metal and felt a shiver course through her, similar to displaced energy that didn't belong. *Interesting.*

Who is he? She moved back slightly and became ensnared by pale-green eyes peeking through lids half open, watching her. Well, no, looking through her. She cupped his face with her right hand, and his lips curled slightly before his eyes closed and face went lax. Not only did he *look* familiar, but something also *felt* familiar.

She gripped his shirt and flexed her fin, pulling his motionless body up to the surface.

Birds chirped in surrounding hills that bordered the cove's water, which was a deep hollow pool from the hill's sharp incline under the surface. The spring falling from above, at the far end opposite the cove entrance, mimicked the incline under the water that had been eroded over time. It was behind that spring the entrance to her sanctuary, and recently Vincent, hid. The pitch-black entrance repelled any cautious mermaid away in fear of getting lost in the channels, but she slowly explored those channels over the years and memorized each one.

The sandy portion of the bank had a steeper section, allowing mermaids to accompany those lounging on the sands. She pulled herself from the water and onto the gloriously warm sand, before pulling the male out of the water, leaving his legs dangling in the deeper section and laid him beside her. She pushed on the male's chest to lay him flat on his back. The left arm gracelessly fell to the side with an accompanying sopping-wet noise. Hair covered most of the attractive features. His black jacket was halfway off his right arm, white shirt was partially raised revealing the reddened skin of his abdomen.

She reached out to touch the angry looking flesh. Frigid cold seeped into her fingertips and she hissed, jerking her hand back. This one had been freezing when he was brought over.

Plunging her newly frigid fingertips into the warm sand behind her, she took note that he was wearing denim cargo shorts, similar to those Simon had been wearing recently. *Must be the modern style, just proves common sense is lacking in both worlds.*

Taking care to avoid her bare arm touching the frigid man, she leaned over and wrapped her fingers around his left wrist, noting his incredibly thready pulse. As she suspected, the Coin of Passage was materializing into a corporeal state in his palm.

The coin had the usual intertwined vines on the

outside. *A little old for a Lost Boy, but perhaps he is going to take the role Simon held as Pan's second of sorts.*

As she continued to watch the design take form, her brows drew together and lips turned down. *Well, that's peculiar.* Where she suspected an oak tree would appear, instead a ship with skull and crossed swords overlapping it, materialized.

"A Hook," she breathed, delightfully surprised because she had yet to be in the presence of a Hook prior to him assuming the role. It was comparable to touching a unicorn. Her intrigue faded as realization of what his presence indicated took root. *New Hook, new enemy.*

"What chaos will you bring?" she asked aloud. She should rid Neverland of this Hook before he replaced the present one, take the coin and toss his body back into the water to be taken back to where he came from. It was this human's first time dying, in Neverland no less, so he had a long grace period to be resuscitated. If she tossed him back in, there was a chance he would be found by another in time.

Staring at the coin, she debated her options. She hadn't been expecting Tink to bring in a new Hook and Pan with one trip; it was a rather impressive feat. *Unless Tink isn't aware she had done so.* She recalled how oblivious Tink had been to her presence. It was a possibility the fairy wasn't aware because although she was careless, she wouldn't leave a guide to die.

"Better the devil you know at times." She went to remove the hair from his face but a splash from the cove lifted her eyes to see Simon emerging from the water—glaring at her.

The quiet spring flowing behind him made a beautiful view. Water droplets glided from his wet, dark-blonde hair and chased down his face to return home.

"Forget to mention something important, Mer?" Bitterness soaked his words as he swam towards her.

Once he met the shallow waters, he stood and began stalking in her direction. She studied how the water retreated from his hair, leaving his face and shoulders. It was akin to being soaked with water from the head down, except the water was returning to where it came, leaving Simon void of its moisture.

He grabbed the man's legs and moved them to the sand, taking him fully out of the waters.

Yes, indeed she had omitted facts, but it would be foolish to admit as much.

"What you deem important, may be insignificant to me. So do be more specific with your accusations," she retorted. "It's been a trying day."

He let out a humorless laugh as he ran his hand through his dry hair, removing it from his eyes. "I would think the fact that Vincent and Annelise are dead would be a significant fact for both of us."

True. But technically Vincent isn't dead, so Simon was only partially correct in his assessment. "You would have found out quicker if you visited him regularly."

He pointed an accusing finger at her. "How long have you known!? And are you saying it's my fault I didn't know sooner even though you could have told me? Wait, how did you even know?" His voice became louder with each word.

Another agitated Lost Boy to deal with. Wonderful.

"I didn't know Vincent died; I knew *Annelise* did." She would apologize but the words were a pointless gesture because she would not have done anything differently given another chance.

Merilee rested on her elbows and flicked the water with her fin. Why must humans be such emotional creatures when she wasn't willing to deal with them. Usually she enjoyed all emotions, they caressed her being in separate ways, mostly enjoyable, but she was having an extremely unpleasant day. All these emotions were purely agitating, like sand against an oyster's flesh.

"And you should have bloody told me!" he shouted. His eyes looked to be brimming with tears.

She should feel guilt over causing him distress, but he truly needed to focus on the grander outcome. Yes, she withheld information, but she did give him the inclination to seek the information himself. If she straightforwardly told him, she meddled with the balance of Neverland, but if his actions led him to the same conclusion by her guidance, the balance was maintained. It was in the nuances.

Simon inhaled deeply, seeming to be collecting his temper. "I went to his house and no Vincent or Annelise. I watched from the window as Tink messed with Vinnie's little boy." His fists were clenched but he was no longer shouting. "She was singing him the Pan melody."

Okay, he gritted that last part.

"Convinced him to go to Carston Lake while it's barely frozen and play hide-and-seek."

Simon's voice began rising in volume, increasing her agitation.

"Do you know how hard it was to watch and not intervene when the boy fell into the lake?! Then, this one"—he jabbed a thumb at the unmoving figure—"came and tried to save him like a protector out of a fairy-tale."

Her head snapped up from Simon's fists to his face. "Protector?" *Is that where this one came from? Trying to save Vincent's son from drowning? Right place, wrong time?*

Simon nodded. "Aye, ran onto the barely frozen lake and tried to pull him out of the water." He cocked his head. "You know who this is, don't you?"

She retook the man's left hand and raised the Coin of Passage for Simon to see. "A Hook, Simon. He's a Hook."

"Nooo." Simon's eyes went wide as he looked at the hand she held, then looked at her. "He can't be a Hook." He shook his head vigorously. "It's Jackson, Vincent's oldest boy. His boys can't be the Pan *and* the Hook."

"This"—she gently shook the hand she held to empha-size her point—"claims otherwise."

"Doesn't make sense," he said while looking heartbro-ken. "He doesn't fit a Hook's criteria. He cares for Patrick. Hooks don't *care* for Pan's. Doesn't work that way."

"While you two are disputing the probability of the present situation, this one *will die* and directly cross to the Ferryman without intervention. A reality I refuse to allow to manifest," a distant smoky voice said.

Merilee looked toward the bend of the cove as Dorothea came into view. The Ancient's white sheet-dress skimmed her knees and exposed her upper thighs as she approached. The golden rope tied around her waist held a dagger similar to the one Vincent had made Simon, except embedded green emeralds glistened in the sunlight from the handle of hers. Braids in her mahogany-colored hair adorned with leaves throughout fell to her waist. She looked like a goddess, which in a way, she was.

At the not so subtle 'wow' that came from beside her, she released the chilled wrist and hit Simon in the chest.

"Close your mouth. You look ridiculous," she snapped.

His teeth clacked as he snapped his mouth shut. A slow grin spread across his face. "Envious much?"

Certainly. She had always been envious of Dorathea for a multitude of reasons. Especially on days where she was exhausted by her tasks; so yes, she envied her counterpart's relaxed nature. Granted, she was ignorant of all the beautiful Ancient was responsible for but understood the spectrum was vast. The fact Dorathea seemingly managed those responsibilities with more grace than she was capable of at present, irritated her. *Theme of the day.*

"Wow," she drawled, "we are worthy of your presence?" She attempted to be pleasant but couldn't keep herself from making the sarcastic comment.

"Seriously?" Simon choked out, motioning to the approaching figure with his eyebrow shooting up to his hairline.

Merilee snorted. He was behaving as though she slapped a Larnack on the snout. "If that repulsive fairy had been dealt with, I wouldn't have been subjected to sniveling Lost Boys for several hours this afternoon." She sniffed haughtily, then cringed for how similar her behavior was to Tink's.

Dorathea's lips twitched and she nodded her head, seeming to agree with Merilee's thoughts. "In due time, Tadpole. Your nasal cavity may benefit from a clearing in the near future."

"Biped," she muttered.

"Irritable?"

"Yes," Merilee and Simon both said in unison.

I should throw him in the water for that.

Simon looked up at the beauty as she paused beside him. The wonder in his eyes made her want to drown him. "Oh, sorry." He got to his feet and took a few steps back, making room for her.

"My gratitude." Dorathea knelt where Simon had vacated. She smoothed Jackson's hair away from his face gently. "He is early." The back of her fingers caressed his cheek almost reverently before she brought her hand down to his Coin of Passage, removing it from his grasp.

Merilee narrowed her eyes. "What do you mean by early?"

"He is early."

The Ancient lifted the coin level with her amber eyes and smoothed her thumb over the face of it. "By almost a decade Real-World time"—Dorathea held out the coin towards Simon—"I trust you will keep this safe until it's required."

Simon's eyes bugged out comically and Merilee rolled her own at his behavior. His hand even had a slight tremor while he reached for it.

"What will happen if I lose it?" he asked as he white knuckled the metal.

"Best not find out."

She not only saw but heard Simon gulp at the subtle warning. His discomfort eased her irritation slightly. He was terrified of the person who tasked him with keeping this Hook's coin safe, and his coloring went to a lovely hue of green.

"W-when will it be required?" Simon stammered.

"When it's his time to return of course." She placed her hand on Jackson's chest. "I will make you aware when the time comes."

"How do you know when he is supposed to come to Neverland? What else do you know that you aren't sharing?" It was annoying she wasn't privy to all the knowledge Dorathea was.

"I could ask the same of you," Dorathea said.

Well, that's concerning. Just how much was Dorathea

aware of? And if she knew Vincent was in Neverland, why had she not intervened?

"Simon, I trust you will keep that safe," she reaffirmed; and at his nod, she continued. "Return him to the Real-World and when you do, rub *his* right thumb counter-clockwise on the coin to remove the water. Be prepared, for his lungs will expel our water and he will become conscious. Be out of sight shortly after the task is complete."

"Wait, won't he require the coin in the Real-World? What if he dies again without it since he's a guide?" she inquired.

"He won't," was all Dorathea said.

"It works with inhaled waters too! Not just clothing?" Simon sounded delighted with this news. She could envision Simon inhaling water and expelling it as a trick now.

"Correct. Now take him back to Carston Lake and when you return to Neverland, I require a word." Dorathea stood and began walking back to the cove's bend. "And Merilee," she called over her shoulder as she continued walking.

"Oh, Thea," she mocked, already tired of feeling inferior.

"You have already found the object you seek. You only need to recognize it."

She stared at the retreating figure, mulling over the knowledge she had gained within the brief encounter. It appeared she wasn't the only one keeping secrets and hers weren't tantamount to the plethora Dorathea was privy too. It didn't settle well.

Perhaps she didn't know all the players, or even the board anymore. What with the Biped's cryptic and vague parting words. She was searching for many things lately. A more concise clue would have been useful.

She turned to Simon to see him holding the Hook coin up with wonder on his face.

"Can you believe it?" he said in awe.

"Do get a move on before you forget your task. The longer he is here, the more time passes there." She looked down when she heard the ticking of his watch. *What a loud contraption.*

"Oh, relax Mer." He knelt to pull Jackson onto his shoulders. The two were of equal height and stature, causing Simon to stumble a little with the task. He held onto Jackson's left wrist and leg as he gained purchase. Simon blew his hair out of his face and grinned at her. "She said all I have to do is this"—he released Jackson's leg to move the coin in a counter-clockwise motion around the limp thumb—"and he will be fine."

She wasn't as confident all would go as smoothly.

Simon readjusted his grips, palming the Hook coin as he did. Jackson jolted straight, violently, and started projectile-vomiting clear water.

Simon released his grip and dropped him onto the sand before looking over at her with horror on his face. "I didn't even touch his thumb to the coin!"

She didn't respond, dumfounded as she watched

Vincent's son roll onto his hands and knees, vomiting water. *No, Simon did not, so why is the water retreating? And if he isn't meant to be here yet, what are the ramifications of him becoming aware of them or Neverland now?* She bit her lip. *How to resolve this?*

Well ... she could drown him again, then Simon would be able to take him to the Real-World like he was meant to. Yet, he would remember being drowned in Neverland, his awareness of the location wouldn't matter, he would remember the feel of this place. Or worse, he could remember her drowning him, which might cause a teensy ripple when he is the Hook. Not a first encounter that would gain favors anyway.

"Merilee, what do I do?!"

His boyish tone full of uncertainty brought her out of her thoughts and the metal of the coin caught her eye. "You have the coin, take him before he's fully lucid."

Jackson turned to her as she spoke, Vincent's pale-green eyes taking her in. She felt his gaze from the top of her head to her very-exposed mermaid scales, fins, and all.

"What the hell?" his voice raspy, eyes widening.

Simon needed to move quickly. "Now, Simon." Her tone brooked no argument.

CHAPTER 7

LAND OF CONFUSION

*N**ow, Simon? Who's Simon? Is that a mermaid? It looks like a mermaid. Bright teal-streaked blue hair, human arms, white fabric wrapped around its breasts, and a very, very scaly blue fish tail.*

He took in huge gasps of air. Wow, his lungs buuurned. It felt like he couldn't get enough air. Why was his head so fuzzy?

Hands grabbed him under his arms, and he was lifted to his feet.

"Hey there, I am going to take you for a trip," said the English guy's voice.

Head spinning, he was turned around away from the mermaid, and now faced a blonde guy about his age. Jackson felt his eyes go impossibly wider when his focus went past the guy's shoulders.

Straight ahead, two huge hills covered in the greenest trees gave way to smooth rocks at the bases, creating a

"V" for the bluest water to flow in between at the apex. Further still, he could see a ship sailing the horizon, backdropped by a setting sun with the most brilliantly colored sunset highlighting the clouds.

Jolting out of the hold on his shoulders, he turned in a circle, taking in the hill formations and vegetation. *It is spectacular.*

Tropical trees blanketed the hills, steaming water cascading down from the top of a sharp cliff opposite the entrance where the opposing hills met. It smelled like fresh water, leaves, and damp soil. The sound of fluttering wings made him look to his left in time to see a flock of enormous brightly colored birds of every hue, fly above him and into the sky.

"Hello?"

A hand vigorously waved in front of his face. He blinked. Then turned to face the guy who was talking and blinked again. There was something familiar about the look of him. Whether it was the guy's overgrown, wavy blonde hair, his slightly slanted eyes, or how everything came together, he wasn't sure, but he knew he had seen him before.

"Who are you?

The guy held up his hand with his pointer finger raised, opened his mouth, then snapped it shut. "I am the guy that needs to get you home," he said with a nod and seemed to puff his chest up a bit.

Okay, he was weird … "Where am I?" *Maybe this question wouldn't be hard for him to answer.* Jackson was starting to feel a pounding behind his eyes, probably from the freakishly bright colors everywhere.

"Somewhere you're not supposed to be. So"—he gestured towards the water beside them—"Let's get you home." The guy grabbed his arm and started leading him into the shallow water.

"Am I dead?" He honestly wasn't sure. It felt like it was a possibility, or a high probability, but he couldn't exactly remember why that was. What was the last thing he remembered?

"Let's just get you home."

There is the cove I'm standing in, because that's what it is, a cove. Not sure how I got here but here I am. The giant rainbow birds and the ship sailing in the distance.

"Now that you're awake …"

Then there was the stunning mermaid, with bright blue hair and aqua eyes, who had called to Simon. That must be who this is. Simon.

"… you get to do this part."

Something metal was shoved into his hand. It sent a shiver down his arm that wasn't unpleasant. "Are you Simon?" he asked.

"Hold onto this for dear life, you understand? For the love of Dorathea don't lose it," his escort muttered, "if she doesn't gut me and use my innards as a bow for this muck up, then she surely will if you lose the darn thing."

Gut him and use his innards as a bow? What's a Dorathea?
"What?"

The guy stopped them from walking farther when the

water level was knee high. Jackson looked at the water where the bottom dropped off into a deep blue void a few steps away.

"Alright, now the fun part." The blonde took a deep breath. "Think of home or where you want to go."

"Home." *Yeah, I can think about home.*

"Now, you're going to rub the coin clockwise while thinking of where you want to go."

He could see Natalie and tell her about the mermaid. Wanting another chance to see the creature, he looked for her and frowned at the now vacant spot. *Where did she go?*

"Focus, Jackson." The guy sounded impatient now.

"How do you know my name?" *I didn't tell him, did I?*

"You want to go home, right? So let's focus."

Home. Yeah, home would be good. Home made sense. The pounding in his head was getting worse, so he did what the guy said. He pictured the home he'd grown up in. He rubbed the coin clockwise with his thumb, feeling the raised surface of a design he didn't know.

The temperature of the water around his legs dropped and a chill went through him. *Why is the water getting cold?* He hated the cold.

Images of Patrick crying and pleading with him to not let go echoed in his mind. His eyes popped open. "Patrick," he whispered.

"Hold your breath," the blonde guy instructed before pushing him into the frigid water.

Pressure surrounded him as he was pulled farther

below the surface. His body hit what felt like sludge before he was engulfed by it. Panicked by the thought of being buried alive under the water, he increased his struggles, fighting against whatever was surrounding him. Patrick's pleas continuing to echo loudly in his ears.

Then it all stopped. No pressure, no thick mass, no pounding in his head. Nothing but dark, bone-chilling water and blessed silence surrounding him. A muffled tick-tick-tick was the only sound that penetrated the dark water. *Dad's watch? It had been dead since it was recovered from the car. What the hell just happened?* He didn't even know. What he did know was that he needed to breathe.

Kicking off the gravelly bottom, he swam towards the moonlight shining among the blocks floating along the surface. *Pieces of ice,* he realized.

He gasped big gulps of air, filling his lungs with the much-needed oxygen, puffs of breath following each exhale. Jackson turned in a full circle. He knew it was Carston Lake by the hill, guardrail, and boating dock on the opposite side of where he and Patrick often walked. Unfortunately, his car was no longer parked where he left it.

Teeth chattering, he swam the short distance to the empty boating dock trying to ignore the sting of the ice hitting his throat as he went.

His body felt heavy as he crawled up the cement pad. Cold and drenched, he collapsed with no energy left and rolled onto his back. *Why was I in the damn water anyway?*

Man, it's freezing. His eye lids felt like anvils were pressing down on them.

Clink.

He turned his head at the sound and saw a metal coin beside his palm. *Did I drop that?* He stretched out his fingers and picked it up to bring it closer. It didn't seem familiar. The vines on the outside were raised and poked his thumb. The skull and crossed swords in the center overlapping a ship was cool though. *Did I find a pirate coin like in the movies? Arrrr.* He chuckled.

"Bloody hell! You couldn't have lived in a tropical place, could you?"

A blonde guy was walking towards him up the launch pad dripping wet and looking pissy.

He let his head and arm fall back to the unforgiving ground, too tired to care why where he lived pissed off a stranger. The guy obviously had as much sense as a rock because he was swimming in a lake this time of year. "What an idiot."

The guy snorted and his boots made a squishing noise as he stopped beside Jackson and knelt. "I've been called worse for less, my friend."

He raised an eyebrow. "I'll bet."

The guy's face was illuminated by a vehicle he could hear coming down the road. *Where have I seen him before?* He wanted to figure it out, but he couldn't keep his eyes open anymore. His brain felt too foggy, and his body weighed down. He didn't even feel cold anymore, surprisingly, and wasn't sure if that was a good thing or a bad thing, but he'd take it.

"Help will be here soon, Jackson. See you when you're ready."

Ready for what? he wanted to ask the guy but his eyelids and mouth didn't want to work—his whole body refused to move. Cold fingers picked the pirate coin out of his hand and he wished he had the will to protest; he wanted to keep his treasure.

"Rest now."

Squishing sounds of water in the stranger's boots passed his head and went in the direction of the road. He listened to the sounds as the squishing was replaced with the sound of boots hitting pavement and an engine rumble of an old muscle car. It all faded to the background as the tick-tick-tick of his dad's watch lulled him into sweet oblivion.

CHAPTER 8

HOUSE OF MEMORIES

JACKSON

CARSTON, MARCH 2011

Jackson yawned and flicked on the signal light. "Yeah, I'm almost there. Turning onto Sterling now."

The streetlights illuminated the green leaves and shone patches of shadows onto the pavement from the familiar elm trees bordering each side of the road. His wife loved how it created a canopy of green above the street every spring and always marveled at how magical it appeared no matter which season. It had seemed magical to him once too, but that was before life took the magic away.

"I'd have told you to stay at a hotel instead of driving six hours after your shift, but I'd doubt you'd have listened." His uncle's annoyed tone came in crystal clear through the truck speakers, which was one of the reasons he kept in touch with Alex over the years. The guy was predictable and easily irritated; a perfect combination for his amusement.

He imagined Alex pinching the bridge of his nose collecting his patience, which made his lips twitch.

"Nope." He popped the 'P' for nostalgic reasons and laughed out loud when Alex sighed. "I'm fine," he said, laughing. "If I needed to pull over for a short power nap or stop at a hotel for the night I would've. I'm not an idiot."

"Debatable."

"Ouch. So, are you coming by tomorrow to help with the reno's or to make sure I don't cut off a limb?"

"Bit of both."

He rolled his eyes and raised his middle finger to the phone in its holder.

"Calla also told Janet that her and her mom were going to be baking because we are coming into town."

"You're coming for Natalie's baking, aren't you?" *The man never changed.*

"Guilty, and if I gotta sit through a make-over session to get some of that baking, I will."

"I'll be sure to tell Calla you hate chocolate and only eat their baking to be polite. You really just love the way the pink eye shadow brings out your eyes."

"Don't you dare! That'd just be bad form." Alex chuckled. "She wouldn't believe you anyway, your daughter is too smart for that."

"True enough. So, see you at eight? I'll have the morning coffee on so don't pick any up."

"You got it. See you at eight."

The triple beep of the disconnected call sounded as the house came into view. The two-level house with white siding and blue trim looked the same as it had when he was growing up. The only difference being the siding was yellowing and the trim had begun peeling with age. Natalie's silver SUV was parked in the driveway in front of the side yard, where he often remembered his parents' white Chevy Impala being parked.

He parked in front of the walkway leading to their blue front door, the tarnished brass number twenty-three highlighted by the outside porch light.

Home, sweet home. He snorted at the ridiculousness of that saying. Yes, there were great memories here but those were always overshadowed by the memories he drank to forget.

Removing the keys from the ignition, he pushed away the depressing thought and grabbed his cellphone from the holder. The driver's door creaked as it opened and he stepped out; the sound of the truck door closing echoed in the quiet street. His steel-toed boots on the pavement a percussion as he headed to the back of the truck. The street was eerily still, making his movements overly pronounced. Dropping the tailgate, he pulled the hockey bag filled with all his out-of-town necessities from the truck bed and threw it over his shoulder. His back ached from the long drive and the weight of the bag only exaggerated the pain, making him feel older than his twenty-nine years.

Maybe Alex was right, and I should have pulled over for a stretch or two. He'd be damned if he was going to tell his uncle that though.

The last object to grab was the grey cooler he used as a lunch box when he was working, and he closed the tailgate—the latch snicked into place.

He refused to acknowledge the guy standing across the street as he stepped to the sidewalk. The blonde was leaning against an Elm tree—watching him like he always did. A long time ago he learned if he didn't engage, the guy kept his distance. Natalie, or anyone else, never seemed to notice the guy and gave Jackson weird looks when he mentioned him; exactly the way the police had when he tried to report the guy when he first noticed him three years ago.

Nothing was done of course. There was never any video footage with him on it. No evidence of foul play, nor evidence of anything at all, for that matter. After receiving too many odd looks from law enforcement and the locals when he asked around if anyone spotted the guy—he dropped it.

Carston was a small, close-knit city and it only took a few inquiries before the rumors started circling about him and the speculations about his family began again. He wasn't about to be labeled insane; he remembered how people had looked at and talked about his brother. *No, thank you.*

Pressing the lock button on the key fob for the horn on his truck to sound once, he walked up the path towards the house. A white bike with pink tassels on the handles rested on its side in front of the metal 'For Sale' sign staked into the lawn. There were other miscellaneous items which didn't belong, like the skipping rope he stepped over, and the soccer ball in the flowerbed. *Someone needs to be putting things away when she is done with them.* He would be having a talk with the little lady tomorrow about keeping these things off the lawn.

The front door swung open, and a little body flew at him, barely giving him enough time to drop his cooler. He took as step back as he absorbed her slight weight and hugged her closely, blonde hair caught on his stubble and stuck to his mouth. He puffed the fine hair out of his face, making his daughter giggle; a sound he missed far more than any father should have to.

"Hey there, Petal"—he squeezed her tighter—"Why aren't you in bed?" The last time he had checked in the truck it was past 10 o'clock, and that had been when he drove into the city limits.

"Mom said I could stay up until you got home since there is no school tomorrow."

Wow ... That was almost *believable.*

"When in reality, I put you to bed but you refused to sleep until your dad came home."

Ah, there it is. He looked up to see his wife leaning

against the door frame with her arms crossed and grinning in his direction. *As beautiful as always.*

Her brown hair was up in a loose bun, hair sticking out everywhere, and she was wearing his worn blue sweater that went to just below her hips, and black leggings he was always fond of.

"Yeah. That's what I said, Mom." His daughter turned and smiled brightly at Natalie.

"Uh-huh. Dad's home, so time for bed, Calla." Natalie pointed over her shoulder into the house.

He kissed the side of Calla's head. "Better listen to your mom. She gets grumpy if you don't." Jackson set her on her feet and smiled as she ran past a scowling Natalie, which made him laugh.

"I do *not* get grumpy."

He raised an eyebrow. "No, not at all."

"Oh, shut up," she said through a laugh. "Fine, this grumpy mom is going to tuck our daughter into bed. *Again.*"

Picking up his cooler, he started walking to the door. "I'll be up shortly to say goodnight."

Natalie nodded and gave him a too-short kiss when he reached her in the doorway. "Welcome home."

His gaze fell to her tempting backside peeking out from under his sweater as she headed towards the stairs. She knew he appreciated seeing her in his clothes and she made fun of him for it, but he never complained about it. *Going to thank her thoroughly later.*

Walking into the foyer, he dropped the oversized bag

and heard it hit the floor before rotating his shoulder. He breathed in the smell of cleaner, baking, and Natalie. The smell of home. *Always bittersweet walking through that door,* he thought. He closed and locked the front door before throwing his keys in the old cow-print bowl on the side table and toeing off his boots before heading to the kitchen on the right to put his cooler beside the fridge just past the entry.

The plate of cookies on the counter made him grin. *Should hide those from Alex and watch sadness ensue.* He debated if his uncle's reaction to no baking would be worth the wrath of the women upstairs as he went to the sink. Turning on the tap and grabbing the soap, he watched the suds accumulating on his hands turning dark brown from the residue of work. Seeing the suds flow down the drain was satisfying; like watching the stress of the job leave him and go where it was no longer his problem. This set had been a long stretch away and he missed Natalie and Calla.

He felt the tension of work leave his neck and shoulders whenever he was home, but the constant deep ache in his gut became more noticeable without it. It was one of the reasons he had decided to sell the house; to help him move on with his life more completely. He doubted it would work some days, but Natalie seemed hopeful. Their daughter, on the other hand, was more resistant to the idea of moving these past couple months than she had been when they first sat her down to talk about it.

Past his reflection in the window, the water in the

birdbath fountain reflected the kitchen light shining out into the side yard. The water pooled off into the red lava-rock bed below, littered with the stones Patrick had collected for their mother.

When he was installing the fountain, he wanted to get rid of the reminders of his brother's habit, throw the stones into the cursed lake and start anew. Deep down, he was still torn about seeing them but didn't say anything. Natalie insisted he keep the stones because it was important to her to keep reminders of his family. *Keep their memories alive, for one reason or another.*

He picked up the dish towel from the side of the sink to dry his hands. *It's supposed to get easier to see reminders of them, isn't it?* Not the case though, it was only easier when not looking at them. He looked up and a woman looked back at him through the kitchen window. "Jesus!" He staggered back away from the sink.

With a blink she was gone.

"Jackson, you coming upstairs? Calla wants to say goodnight." Natalie's voice came from upstairs.

"Uh, yeah … I'll be two minutes. Finishing cleaning up." He raised his voice loud enough to be heard upstairs while keeping an eye on the window, preparing to see someone walk past it. The larger window to the left in the dining room showed nothing but the reflection of the dining table and picture on the opposite wall.

He walked to the door in the dining room leading to the deck. *Why did people peep into strangers' windows? It was creepy as hell.* Opening the patio and heading outside, he was greeted by the sounds of the fountain and not much else. Nothing seemed out of place. In the artificial light lent by the kitchen and dining room windows, he could see the backyard was empty; the shed latch closed.

"Don't have the patience to deal with another one of you," he muttered. *The blonde guy is disturbing enough, now there is a damn woman lurking about. Not gonna happen.*

A quick trip around the small deck to see if anyone was crouched down beside it, revealed nothing. No woman, no creaking fence gate left unlatched and swinging. Only the trickling of the water falling from the fountain, but he felt eyes on him. Maybe he needed to stop being so paranoid because it was probably fueling the feeling. *This is why we need to get rid of this house.* Maybe he would be able to finally relax and not feel like a lab rat being watched when he was home.

Going back into the house, he refused to see any reflections in the windows around him. He learned his lesson to not look for a source when he felt like this. People tended to find what they were looking for, and that was not what he wanted right now. The sounds of his brother's laughter echoed quietly in his head as he walked through the dining room, heart beating heavily in his chest. *Not tonight, man. Don't do this tonight. Take a deep breath.*

One glance at the newer stainless-steel fridge and it flashed to his parents old worn white one, his brother's scribble—which he refused to wipe off for months—present again in black erasable marker.

The whooshing of blood in his ears didn't drown out Patrick's laughter, nor the tinkling of bells which was almost deafening. He pinched his eyes shut, his breath coming in short, shallow bursts of air. Shaking his head to dispel the images of the past, he looked back at the once-again stainless-steel fridge. *Focus on the present, find something to ground to.*

A white paper kept in place by a sunflower-shaped magnet caught his attention. It was a drawing he assumed Calla had done, two figures holding hands. Jackson went over and removed the magnet, holding the paper higher to focus on the drawing. His fingers sat amongst the pencil crayon colors of the girl's yellow hair with brown lines mixed in, feeling the smooth lines of color, focusing on the contrast of it against the rougher texture of the paper. He inhaled, concentrating on the smell of the soap he used earlier, the plate of chocolate chip cookies on the counter, and the faint aroma of colored pencils mixed with paper.

His breathing began to slow as did the sound of his pulse in his ears. Even Patrick's laughter and those chiming bells began to dim. Next to the girl was a drawing of a boy, same yellow hair with brown lines mixed in, brown eyes and a large smile. The initials JP were written above the boy's head, along with a yellow circle with a lighter halo beside the 'P'.

"Hey." Natalie's soft tone relaxed him further. Her hand rubbed slow circles over his lower back as he put the paper back on the fridge with the sunflower magnet and let out a final deep breath—feeling almost normal.

Jackson turned, cupping Natalie's concerned face and captured her lips for a deep kiss. He needed to feel something real. She was his solid ground: always had been. He met her surprised squeak with a satisfied groan as he felt her body melt into him. She knew him and what he needed; knew how to mend him when he felt like he was unravelling. *Natalie is Home.*

Letting go of her face, he bent down to cup the backs of her thighs and lifted her for her to wrap her legs around his waist, which she did. He pinned her between him and the wall, one hand stayed on her backside supporting her weight and the other found the hem of his sweater and delved up to cup her breast. She moaned but broke the kiss.

"Calla's not asleep yet."

"So be quiet, and it won't be a problem."

She laughed softly and flicked his bottom lip with her tongue. "I went shopping when you were out of town this time."

"Oh yeah? Chiffon or silk?" He loved her shopping trips, probably more than she did. Her neck smelled heavenly, so he nuzzled in and kissed below her ear, he felt her thighs squeeze his hips in response and he smiled against her skin.

"Lace," she said breathlessly.

Now it was his turn to groan. She laughed, so he nipped her neck.

"Red and black, too."

The image of her dressed in strips of red and black lace had him groaning a second time as he rested his head against her shoulder and removed his hand from her breast. He placed his newly unoccupied hand above her head on the wall to keep it off her. He used the other to tap her outer thigh to get her to release her hold of his hips. "Go change."

She kissed him softly, but he stole one deeper kiss before slapping her on the ass as she scooted out from between him and the wall.

She chuckled. "Don't forget to lock up."

Natalie was going to keep him in the present, he knew it by the smile of promise she sent him before she ascended the stairs.

Blowing out a breath, he got on with the task of checking the doors were locked and turned off the lights before heading upstairs. He still felt that sliver of unease but ignored it the best he could with each step he took. He'd become accustomed to masking the uncomfortable feeling while functioning, especially around his family. What worried him was the episodes were becoming more frequent and he was sure Natalie was going to figure it out sooner rather than later. She didn't know how much he was struggling; he wouldn't let her. *Well, panic attacks not included. She'd known about those since my recovery from the lake.*

Jackson could hear Patrick's phantom laughter coming from Calla's room at the end of the hall—

Patrick's childhood room. The sound seemed to be getting louder every time he came home from work which was why he knew they had to get rid of this place.

The door was slightly ajar as he poked his head in, noticing Calla was asleep and snoring softly. Walking in as quietly as he could, he leaned over and kissed her on her forehead.

She smiled and opened her eyes slightly. "Love you, Dad."

"Love you too, Calla. Goodnight."

"Goodnight," she said through a yawn and snuggled deeper into her pillow; her face going lax once more and her quiet snores resuming.

He smiled at the adorable little person he and Natalie created. She was his heart, this little pint-sized human, and he was wrapped around her little finger. This little lady had his uncles wrapped around her finger too—and she knew it. He had caught her being the little opportunist a few times with his uncles and laughed at how gullible Alex and Marcus were at times. He understood, he would do anything for her.

The pale-pink floor-length curtains moved and caught his attention. Little feet poked out from the bottom. *What the hell?* He walked over, determined to find out who Calla had snuck in while he and Nat were occupied downstairs, but when he moved the curtain, he frowned. Nothing.

"Dad?"

"Nothing Calla, thought I saw something. Go back to sleep, Petal."

"Okay," she said through another yawn.

It had been a long shift and the drive home made it longer, he was probably overtired and feeling stressed about what transpired earlier. He peeked out the window, taking a final scan of the backyard and was satisfied when he didn't see the blond guy or a woman.

Jackson left his daughter's room and headed to his own at the opposite end of the hall. When he opened the door and saw Natalie leaning against the dark wood post of the four-poster, king-sized bed, he forgot how tired he was.

He was right, she looked like a wet dream in red and black lace. The black stockings were a brilliant touch. He reached down, grabbing the hem of his shirt and pulled it up and over his head. Seeing her eyes widen slightly, he grinned.

"You can buy as much red and black lace as you want when I'm working, as long as you dress like that when I come home."

CHAPTER 9
WHO IS JP?
JACKSON

Mentally listing off the materials he needed for the backyard project he was going to tackle today, Jackson descended the stairs and grinned when he spotted Natalie leaning against the counter by the coffee machine, sipping on the delicious-smelling brew, her hair up in a messy bun, in a white tank top and pale-yellow pajama pants. Seizing the opportunity to be close, he went up behind her to kiss her neck and rest his chin on her shoulder. Wrapping his arms around her waist, he smiled when her hand rested on his forearm. "Morning, Nat. How'd you sleep?"

"Quite well thank you, someone tired me out." She lifted one of his hands and kissed it. "How about you?"

Seeing the full pot of brewed coffee, he straightened and released one arm to grab a coffee mug from the counter and poured himself a cup of black coffee. He didn't like cream or sugar in his morning brew and

Natalie said only psychos drank coffee black. She on the other hand was a bougie coffee snob to him. Who wanted to have a coffee that took two minutes to order?

"It was a solid sleep. Real solid, in fact." It'd been a long time since his first night home was sans nightmares.

He let his other arm drop as she turned to face him. Her spattering of freckles stood out in the sunlight pouring in; that, paired with her deep-brown eyes reminded him of a fine brandy—he doubted he would ever get tired of looking at her.

"Want to talk about what I walked in on last night?" Her warm eyes were filled with concern.

"Nah, not much to talk about. The usual minor panic attack." He shrugged. He hadn't told her about the hallucinations, or how frequent they had become when he was home lately. Didn't see much point because he only got them when he was here, and since they were obviously connected to this house, once they sold it and moved, the hallucinations should stop.

At least I hope like hell I'm right and that's the case.

"You promised you would tell me if you weren't okay. That was the deal."

"And I will tell you when I'm not okay. Right now, I'm good. I can handle the attacks and they're getting easier to come back from. That therapist you suggested had some useful suggestions." Catching the picture on the fridge from last night, he nodded in its direction. "Who is JP?"

Natalie caught her bottom lip between her teeth. "Calla says he's her friend."

"From school?" *She hasn't mentioned anything to me about a JP.*

"I think so. I've asked her and she said she found him crying, sad that we are moving. That's all she said."

He gestured with his coffee mug to the drawing. "So, you haven't met the kid?"

"No, I haven't."

"He's not her boyfriend, is he?" He was not ready for his baby girl to start liking boys, or girls for that matter, in any capacity other than platonic. "She's not old enough to have a boyfriend or girlfriend, is she?" He really didn't know when that started for girls. He knew he started noticing girls in a different light when he was a preteen.

Natalie chuckled. "Don't look so horrified. No, it's not her boyfriend. She has a crush but wouldn't tell me his name."

"Oh, hell no." He shuddered.

Natalie laughed again. "So now that that's settled, what are your plans for today?"

"Probably head to the hardware store to pick up a few things. Some shingles need to be repaired and the yard needs some work"—he blew on the coffee before taking a sip—"Figured I would see how much I could get done while I'm home. Get the place to sell faster."

"Sounds good. Just remember to relax a little."

"I'll relax when the house sells, Nat."

It was the same argument every time he had days off, but she didn't seem to want to hash it out again, because she let it drop. "I'm taking Calla out for a girl's lunch today with Janet before I have a quick nap before work. Alex is coming by to help since they're in town, right? Calla is excited to give him a make-over."

"He'll be here …"—he glanced at the clock on the stove—"in about twenty minutes. And he can't wait for the eyeshadow." Jackson smiled into his cup.

"You mean cookies."

"Maybe."

"Oh, just a reminder, I work nightshift the next three nights; so, try not to do the shingles while I'm sleeping in the afternoons if you could." She set her empty cup in the sink and leaned in for a kiss.

"Wouldn't dream of it, Love."

* * *

The sun beat down on his back while he poured another bag of black lava rocks onto the landscaping fabric. The realtor suggested they do some landscaping in the side-yard to clean up the look of it, so he and Natalie decided to rip up the garden bordering the fence and replace it with the lava rock. The white landscaping stones for the trim around the rock beds gave it a sharp-looking touch.

Bending towards the wheelbarrow, he sliced open another bag of black lava rock with the utility knife. As he poured the rocks over the small patch of visible land-scaping fabric, he had to admit the realtor had been right, the side-yard did look cleaner without the graveyard for plants Natalie called a garden.

"It's looking cleaner without the garden cemetery. Good call," Alex commented as Jackson walked back from putting away the extra landscaping fabric in the shed. His uncle had been enthusiastic about helping him with the renos, even offering to stay while Jackson went back to work to get things completed faster—which he appreciated.

"Yeah, it's definitely an improvement." He wiped the sweat from his brow and tossed the empty bag back into the wheelbarrow. "All it needs now are a few planter boxes for whichever flowers Natalie wants and I can cross this one off the list."

"Janet loves flowers. I'm sure she will drag Natalie and Calla to the greenhouses tomorrow morning. Come" —Alex waved him over to the deck and the cooler he had brought over—"you could use a refreshment."

Ascending the three steps to the deck, he took the open beer Alex held out, nodding in thanks. His uncle had acquiesced regarding bringing beers instead of coffee.

Taking a drink, he looked over the condition of the exterior of the house and relished the feeling of the cool liquid. "The siding could use an update"—he pointed to the multiple dents from a recent hailstorm that passed through—"and the shutters around the windows need work."

"A quick coat of paint can take care of the shutters."

Alex put a hand in his pocket and took a drink of his own beverage. "I'll give Marcus a call and see when he has time to help replace the siding. I don't think it has been replaced since your parents bought the house."

Movement in Calla's bedroom window drew Jackson's attention. The curtains were settling as though someone had let them fall back into place. *Were the girls back already?* He checked his watch. *It isn't even 12:30 yet.*

"That work for you?"

The a/c unit isn't turned on, so it wasn't the air flow from the vents.

"Jackson?"

"Huh?" He looked over at Alex and rubbed his arm where he had smacked him.

"When is your next set of days off?"

He frowned. "Umm, in three weeks. The next job is a bigger project, so I'll be working until the last week of April. Did you hear the girls come home?"

"No, why?"

"Thought I saw something. I'll be right back."

He set his drink down on the patio table and went inside. "Natalie? Calla?" The sound of the fridge motor humming was all the response that met his ears. Maybe his eyes were playing tricks on him. *Wouldn't be the first time.*

"You alright?"

He turned at his uncle's voice. "Yeah, just checking if the girls were back."

The sound of something hitting the floor above him

had him looking up and Alex doing the same. "You heard that, right?" He glanced at Alex, who nodded.

"The girls finally convince you to finally get a cat?"

The echo of heavier footsteps sounded above them, heading towards the kitchen. *Into Calla's room.* "Did *that* sound like a cat?" He raised an eyebrow.

Alex shrugged, looking back up at the ceiling. "Maybe you were right about the place being haunted. Your mom thought it was."

Really? Did she see the blonde guy too? Maybe his mother passed down some nondisclosed mental ailment to him and his brother. Haunted sounded like a less permanent problem though. "I never thought I would hope that was the case."

The sound of multiple objects hitting the floor made him move towards the stairs. "Clumsy Casper," Jackson muttered, taking the stairs two at a time. *Maybe it was the mysterious JP.*

He looked through the wooden railings as he made his way up the stairs, catching a shadow cross Calla's room under the door.

Clasping the cold doorknob, he turned it and anticipated seeing a young boy, or maybe the blonde guy who stalked him. Yet, it was anticlimactic because the room was unoccupied, although there was the smell of something he couldn't place; perhaps Calla's plant had been knocked over? Maybe that was the sound he had heard. He scanned the floor for a potted plant or spilled soil. *Nope.* He checked behind the window curtain like he had the night before, and went to continue looking for the source of the noises when Alex cleared his throat.

"So … whatcha looking for?" Alex's hands were in his pockets as he rocked back on his heels. "Calla's pencil case spilled on the floor over there." He pointed to his right at the scattered colored pencils on the floor and open pencil case.

"Oh, didn't see that." Jackson bent down and picked up the colored pencils and placed the case back on the desk. Her cork board on the wall above the desk had more drawings of the little boy and the initials JP. One drawing he presumed was Calla and this JP fighting pirates; underneath she had written in her bubbly writing: Never go hungry, never read a book. Battle the pirates, defeat Captain Hook.

Captain Hook?

"Is Captain Hook a video game character or something?" he asked aloud, but more to himself.

"I have no idea. Probably, or a school yard game?" Alex guessed, coming to look over his shoulder at the drawings. "I can ask her while we have tea this afternoon." Alex patted him on the back. "Let's get the side yard finished up and pick up some paint for the shutters before the girls get home."

"Yeah. Sure, ask her about JP while you're at it." He pointed to the pictures. "She hasn't told Nat much about him."

"Calla's keeping something from Natalie?"

"Yeah, strange, huh?"

"You could say that. No worries, I'll play detective."

He took one last look around the room, because the hairs on the back of his neck were standing on end. *The slatted closet doors would be the only option for someone to hide unless they went the ol' under the bed route.* He reached for the door but paused when Alex cleared his throat again.

"You sure you're okay there, buddy?"

He knew that look; he had seen Alex give it to Patrick numerous times before calling the psychiatrist. *Better stop acting weird if I don't want history to repeat itself.*

He dropped his hand and shrugged. "Yeah, just feeling a bit off lately is all."

"Does it have anything to do with the missing kid in the area?"

He blew out a breath and rubbed the tension in his neck. *Did it?* When Natalie told him one of Calla's schoolmates was missing and search parties were about again, it had brought back memories of when Patrick's classmates and friends had gone missing a few months after Patrick drowned. Those were memories he tried to keep buried.

"Maybe. I've been thinking a lot about that time in my life lately and it isn't pleasant. But it's life." He dropped his hand and shrugged.

"You still haven't talked to anyone, have you?"

"Nah, I stopped. It's not going to change anything or bring them back. I'm good. Only a couple rough days is all." He smiled even though he knew Alex would see through the lie. "You said something about roping Marcus into helping with the siding?"

Alex pinched the bridge of his nose and took a few deep breaths, eventually he nodded and dropped his hand to look up at him. "Yeah, I'll give him a call tonight and see if he is available the end of April."

"Sounds good. Hopefully sell the place in May if that's the case."

"Which reminds me, while I was going through the storage unit I found a small box of your parents' things. Must have accidentally packed them when Marcus and I moved out of here. I have it in my truck."

He was having a hard enough time trying to numb himself with Natalie insisting on keeping their memories alive in everyday things. The fact he'd come to blame their deaths for Patrick's careless actions and death, having more objects of theirs might make his skin itch. He wasn't sure he wanted more of his parents' things.

* * *

After saying his goodbyes to Alex and Janet, tucking Calla in for the night and Natalie leaving for her night-shift in the palliative care unit at the hospital, it left him alone with the box filled with his parents' things in the downstairs living room. He refused to go through it in front of his family, not wanting to upset them or be made to keep things he would rather see the burn in the firepit.

Might as well get it over with. He set his spiced rum down on the end table and reached for the box, placing it on the floor between his legs. Opening it, he was pleasantly surprised that it was only about a third full—mostly what looked like journals and sketch pads. He guessed the journals were his father's because his father was always writing in leather books. His mother would be sketching on the bench swing while he and Patrick played in the sprinkler or entertained themselves with whatever game they found amusing at the time.

He picked up the sketch book on top of the rest, bypassing the journals he considered keeping for reading later. Flipping the cover page open, he was greeted by a younger version of his father. His features were drawn with clean, sharp lines. His hair was drawn shorter than Jackson recalled his father preferring before he died. The shading his mother did was impressive, even if she was younger as the date at the bottom indicated.

Calla must have gotten her talent for drawing from her, because even at the youthful age of nine, Calla was close to matching the skill on the page.

Flipping through sketch book, he was presented with page upon page of his father's face, other people he didn't know while they laughed, or smiled; then beautiful scenery of valleys, waterfalls, and the oddest-looking animals. He smiled at the beauty of his mother's sketches, how she captured the smallest details to make the image pop off the page. One portrait almost made him drop the pad of papers entirely.

There, staring back at him with a mischievous grin, was a younger version of the blonde guy that he kept seeing. Younger, but Jackson had seen that smile numerous times, most recently last night while he got out of the truck. Had he seen this drawing before? He didn't think so, but why else would he see the same guy whenever he was home. The name Simon was written in cursive at the bottom right corner. Uncomfortable, he turned the page and then couldn't breathe. The stone-faced woman he had sworn he'd seen in the lake with Patrick that day was drawn in lead on the page.

The sketch pad closed with an audible 'thwomp,' and he dropped it back into the brown box.

Nope, burning it all.

He grabbed his drink and downed it in two large gulps relishing the slight burn in his throat.

Nope, that woman doesn't exist.

Yet, that woman had been all he could recall when he woke up in the hospital the next day. When the police officers talked with him, he was told Natalie had called emergency services after she lost connection with him. They also said there was no evidence or witnesses of someone fitting her description at the lake when they were there earlier. Granted they were more concerned about where he had been for the nine hours he was missing, and he couldn't tell them that either—he had no clue.

After getting 'the look' whenever he brought the woman up in his therapy sessions, he stopped. He almost convinced himself that he conjured her to cope with the idea of someone else being responsible for Patrick's death than Patrick or him. But that page. That page made him doubt everything surrounding that moment with

Patrick, and he knew he had seen her in the window last night.

Definitely burning the box; journals included. The fleeting thought of diving down the rabbit hole of unanswered questions was too tempting for him to keep his father's musings. Jackson had lived this long without reading them, he would keep it that way.

Pushing the box to the wall farthest from him, he flicked off the light and went upstairs. Sleeping it off sounded like a great idea. Calla's voice made him slow and turn towards her room. He stopped outside her door to listen. It was the laugh accompanying Calla's that had him turning the doorknob and walking in. *JP snuck in? Not sure how the kid made it to the window, but right now anything seems possible.*

Calla gasped as she hopped into her bed, cheeks flushed and hair everywhere, looking as guilty as any kid could. His shoulder rested against the door and he waited as she tried to look calm and not out of breath, eyes shifting towards the open window.

"So … what were you doing?" He kept his tone calm, even though the thought of her sneaking a kid into her room at night made his temper rise. *What parent let their kid out this late anyway?* The thought made him angry and sad at the same time, feeling sympathy for a child who could parents who were that inattentive.

"Umm …" Her lip trembled as she looked to the window again. "We were … I … I was just umm …"

She looked like she wanted to cry. He took pity on

her and walked over to sit beside her on the bed and smoothed some bedraggled hair behind her ear. "What were you doing Petal? I'm not mad. I'm curious why you aren't in bed because your mom has mentioned you doing this more often lately. You having trouble sleeping?"

She peered down at her clasped hands. "I was playing hide-and-seek with a friend," she said in a rush. The wind chimes outside sounded obnoxiously loud rather than soothing at that moment to him. He guessed Calla had the same thought when she winced at a particularly high note.

"Who is this friend?" He peered around the empty room, relieved she was talking because Alex hadn't been able to get answers.

"Umm, he … says to call him JP." She plucked at her blanket as she spoke.

"And where is this JP?"

"I can't say." She peeked up between her lashes, her gaze shifting to the side toward the nightstand. "Well, I can but you won't believe me."

"Why not tell me and find out? Is he under the bed?" If the kid needed a place to sleep, then he was more than welcome to sleep on the couch. He held no issues with helping a child out who needed it; he wasn't about to allow the boy to sleep in the same room as his daughter though.

Calla rolled her wrist and pointed beside him where she had gazed earlier. "He's standing there …"

He slowly nodded, trying to formulate a plan to navigate this situation. "No one is there, Calla." Reaching over, he tucked more errant hairs behind her other ear.

She lowered her eyes and deflated, giving him a sad smile that made him feel like he had disappointed her.

"Yeah, I know, Dad. No one sees him but me. Adults don't believe, so they don't see."

"Don't believe what?"

"Never mind, it's okay. He's a friend I made up, so I didn't feel so alone." She shrugged her small shoulders. "It's hard sometimes being the quiet one at school."

"Why don't you invite a classmate or two over to hang out after school sometime? Is there anyone you want to be friends with outside of school? What about that girl Amber from your homeroom? You seemed to get along with her at the beginning of the year, why don't you try and build a friendship with her." That way she didn't have to pretend to have someone to play with. He had too many bad experiences involving imaginary friends with his brother for the idea to sit well.

She knitted her eyebrows. "Yeah, I can ask her."

"Okay, you do that on Monday. But now, it's time for bed little lady."

She scooted down under the covers, and he pulled the blankets to under her chin and leaned in to kiss her on the forehead. "Goodnight Calla, love you.

"Goodnight Dad, love you too."

He straightened and walked over to close the window because those wind chimes were annoying as hell.

"Can you leave it open?"

"It's getting chilly. You sure?"

"No, it's not"—she giggled—"Wow, you really are a wuss about the cold."

"Hey! That's not nice," he said through a chuckle. "A person isn't meant to be cold, we are warm blooded: emphasis on *warm.*"

He left the window open a few inches while scanning the side-yard for the eyes he could feel on him. *We need to move,* he thought.

"I am warm with the window open." She smiled.

"See you in the morning, Petal," he said, and smiled to himself as she snuggled back into bed. Closing her door, he listened to hear if Calla started talking but she remained quiet.

Natalie hadn't mentioned anything about Calla having problems with making friends at school to him; but then again, he never thought to ask. That he neglected to notice his little girl was struggling with feeling lonely—so lonely she found comfort in making up an imaginary friend—didn't sit right with him.

His mind swam with other possibilities that he could be missing about her as he made his way to his room. *Working out of town has its downside, and this is part of it.* He'd have to talk with Natalie about what Calla had told him, maybe she would elaborate on the subject too.

Closing his bedroom door, he promised himself to be more aware of what was going on with his little girl.

CHAPTER 10

JUST A DREAM

JACKSON

Bubbles were everywhere in the frigid water, obstructing his view. The burning in his lungs was becoming increasingly unbearable with each second that passed with him under the surface. Patrick's terrified scream came deafeningly from every direction. He had to find his brother, the sounds of those terror-filled screams felt like razor blades along his skin and ice inside his stomach. *Where is he?!*

A break in the bubbles cleared the way for him to see the translucent blonde woman laughing and smiling cruelly with her hand wrapped around the back of Patrick's neck as he struggled. He tried to swim towards his brother, panicked the woman was going to hurt him —then they were gone.

What the ...?

A hypnotic voice humming a melody increased in volume. "Won't you take my hand, never be alone, here in

Neverland." As quickly as the woman and Patrick vanished, a beautiful blue-haired woman appeared in front of him. She was so close, her blue tendrils surrounded them like a veil in his periphery; mesmerizing aqua eyes were all he could see. A thin hand cupped his cheek and he closed his eyes, and he leaned into the woman's delicate touch. Feeling a sense of peace come over him, he smiled; the burning in his chest disappeared.

"Jacks!" Patrick's scream reverberated through the liquid, and his eyes popped open. He was standing on the surface beside a beach and surrounded by the vibrant greens of tree-covered hills. He marveled at the clarity of the crystal blue waters beneath his feet. A reflection of a kaleidoscope of different-colored birds flying above him had him looking to the sky. Each vibrant color of the feathers shining bright in the sunlight against the backdrop of white clouds; the shapes of skulls and crossed swords gliding through the sky.

"Time to go for a little trip."

Jackson turned toward the source of the familiar English voice. The blonde stalker stood on the water two feet away from him, smirking, head tilted to the side. The guy came into his personal space, blue eyes filled with mischief, and pushed him backwards into the water.

More bubbles, pressure squeezing around him; then darkness. No water, no tropics, no Patrick; the sound of his heavy breathing all that accompanied the all-encompassing void of nothing.

"Hello?" he called out. Then he heard it. The tick-tick-tick of a clock.

He spun around, trying to find the cause, but he couldn't even see his own hands when held out in front of him making it impossible to locate anything.

"Hello?" he called out again, the ticking getting louder as did, along with the sounds of bells chiming.

"Jackson."

Patrick's whisper in his ear had him jolting upright. Breathing heavily, he rubbed his chest above his pounding heart. Movement to the right caught his attention. "Nope, not happening!" He scrambled to Natalie's side of the bed, away from Patrick standing beside his nightstand.

Not okay, not real. The warmth on his earlobe contradicted that statement so he shook his head trying to get rid of the feeling and make the image of Patrick in his room disappear. It didn't.

Patrick still stood there, looking like he had the last day Jackson had seen him—which was not much older than Calla was now. His black pant legs had been cut off unevenly to make shorts, his beige T-shirt was dirty, and he had a leather strap necklace of sorts. His messy hair framed a face Jackson wouldn't allow himself to admit he missed the point of pain most days. Except his brother was kindness and innocence, not like this. Dirt-smudged face with a cruel smile and chocolate brown eyes that had a faint outer glow of amber.

"You can see me," the hallucination said gleefully as it

hovered higher towards him, its black shoes dragging on the comforter.

"You're not real, you're *not* real," he repeated aloud, slicing his arm through the air, trying to get this to stop. His heart pounded even harder as the sound of Patrick's laughter filled the room. "You're not real."

I need to wake up. Wake up. Wake up. "Wake up!"

A chill spread over him as the thing lifted its small hand and reached to touch his shoulder. He damned near stopped breathing at the pressure he felt where the thing contacted his skin. "You're not real," he whispered.

"Now you see me." It smiled.

A tapping on his bedroom door diverted his attention from the thing touching him and his door began to open.

"Dad?" Calla's whispered word broke whatever was happening because the pressure on his shoulder disappeared along with the thing that looked like Patrick.

"See you soon." Patrick's voice was barely a whisper in his ear sending a chill down his spine as Calla came into the room.

"You okay, Dad? I heard you shouting." She looked around the room while wavering on her feet—obviously half asleep. "Having one of your nightmares again?" Calla asked through a yawn.

"Yeah, a nightmare," he breathed out, running a shaky hand over his face. *What kind of nightmare was that?* He usually dreamt of Patrick and the drowning, which his old counselor—Mrs. Webster—told him was normal for what he survived, but not the other nonsense. That was an unwelcome new addition to his nocturnal endeavors.

He scooted over to his side of the bed, straightening the comforter where the material had bunched from the shoes, or what he thought were the shoes.

"You don't seem okay."

"I'll be okay, just felt real. That's all." He turned on the end table lamp, flooding the room with a soft, warm glow. He gave her a reassuring smile. Reaching out, he rubbed her arm and gave it a gentle squeeze, taking comfort in her presence.

Her small hand came up and held onto his, giving him a little squeeze back.

"Thanks for checking on me, I appreciate it. But you should go back to bed. Sorry I woke you up."

"You're welcome." She gave him another little squeeze and then heading out the door, stopped in the doorway. "I love you."

"Love you forever, Petal. Goodnight."

Once the door shut, he rested his head in his clammy hands and let out a trembling breath. *What the hell was that? That was some freaking exorcist shit.* Jackson lifted his head and ran his hands through his damp hair; thankful for the little stabs of pain his fingers caused when they caught on the knots. The sight of his comforter had him reimagining how the tip of those small black shoes caught on the fabric and bunched it, like some ominous wave of cotton as their owner floated—*floated*—towards him.

He shivered. The worst part of that whole nightmare was how real it felt; from the sound of Patrick's voice in his ear, the pressure of its touch, to the smell of earth and sea water he swore still lingered in the air. This wasn't like the blonde guy, because that one never did anything, just stayed silent and uninvolved but observant. Whatever that thing was, it talked and touched him, and violated his personal space which crossed a line he didn't know he had.

Reaching up to the spot he felt the apparition, or whatever it was, touch he cringed. *Maybe this place* is *haunted.* Talking to Alex tomorrow about what he remembered of why his mother thought the place was haunted seemed like a great idea now. There might be some wisdom in whatever his mother had shared.

A soft tick-tick-tick came from the direction of his closet. He reached between the headboard and night-stand to grab the aluminum bat he kept there. Pushing the blankets back, he swung his legs off the bed and onto the plush carpet. Slowly, he walked towards the sound, preparing himself to see whatever that thing was, or an intruder. His hand shook a little as he grabbed the cold handle, pulling back the closet door to find an empty closet. He blew out a relieved breath and pushed aside the two shoe bins of Natalie's to expose the worn banker boxes.

The box labelled Keepsakes came into view and he knew what he was going to find. Removing the lid, he rummaged through the trinkets and bobbles. He felt the old newspaper clippings of his parents' and brother's obituaries, as well as the clippings of the missing children that Patrick had known. Then he felt it. The smooth, chilly metal.

His father's broken watch. It had worked when he had awoken in the hospital the day after Patrick had fallen into the lake. The steady tick-tick-tick was what lulled him awake. For two days after it had continued to work, then stopped: until now.

He held up the watch, studying how the hands were moving once again.

"Let's see how long you stay working this time around, shall we?" Jackson murmured, as he flipped the small watch over to see the engraving he knew was written on the back.

Stay here forever, never age a day. VP.

CHAPTER II

POOR DECISIONS

MERILEE

She believed when the time arrived of Pan's awareness of his father's survival and location in Neverland, the boy would promptly release him from the cenote and away from the safety of his prison. This concern was unfounded and lacked merit, because he indeed kept his father in his prison, but for alternative reasons.

Merilee sensed, more than witnessed, this Pan's descent towards the morally grey. She presumed it resulted from the trauma a particular, irresponsible fairy inflicted on the young child prior to being brought here. Eagerness with a hint of desperation surrounded the boy when presented with his role as guide for Lost Boys, similar to when a fledgling experienced her first capture of an immoral soul. The fledgling's enthusiasm she understood, expected; each one had a hurt in their being often from the usually brutal way they were brought to the Ocean of Souls.

"You wouldn't believe it, Dad! He has a daughter about my age! She is so fun to play with. She looooves hide-and-seek—and drawing!" Pan clapped his hands repeatedly, the sounds reverberating against the damp walls. "She draws like mom used to. She's already so good at it."

"Is that so?" Vincent asked.

"Time is sooo weird here." Pan ran his hands through his hair, then began pacing, an eerily familiar Tink mannerism. The boy's sporadic, almost manic energy began filling the cenote, making her edgy, her skin and muscles pricking uncomfortably with the need for movement. She felt tempted to submerge herself until the boy's departure to spare her excess discomfort.

"I thought it was only a few weeks since Tink brought me here, but she is nine!"

"Does Jackson know you are playing with his daughter?" Vincent's casual tone contrasted with the excitement emanating from his son, but she could see his hands fisted, white knuckled under his crossed arms.

"No, he doesn't even see me." Pan waved him off dismissively. "I was standing right in front of him when he moved the curtain in her room. Looked right at me! It was cool." He paused in movement and tapped his lips with his finger. "Well he didn't then, but I'm sure he can now." He turned to Vincent who was leaning against the damp wall. "He doesn't believe enough yet. I'm going to change that," he said, nodding repeatedly. "Move some things on him, wake him up from another dream! That one worked well! He looked so shocked! I can see if I can get Calla to help. OOOO! I can bring her here! Jackson would come then too!"

"You are responsible for *guiding* Lost Boys to Neverland, Patrick, not bringing kids here of your choosing."

If he only knew what his son had been up to, he wouldn't be pleased. She thought even Tink was becoming hesitant with the adventures of her new Pan. The foolish fairy may have underestimated the damage to his psyche when she began this quest of misdeeds.

"Why not? Why can't I bring her here? Everyone comes around here eventually." The child shrugged and lifted his hands to his sides.

"What's the girl's name?"

"Calla Annelise, like Mom," he answered through a smile that reached his eyes. "Jackson wanted to have a boy, but never had one."

"That's a pretty name. Does she talk to Jackson or her mom about your visits?" Vincent asked, and Merilee was impressed that it was so calm.

"No, I told her not to. That would make Tink super mad too. She doesn't like Jackson or Calla much."

"I imagine she doesn't."

Merilee rolled her eyes at the insecure fairy's tactics. Tink always needed to be the center of attention and loathed anyone who competed with her.

"Okay, I'm going to bring Calla over. She needs to see

Neverland"—Pan perked up—"I'll tell her she can meet you! Oh, she would be so excited!"

"Patrick, leave Calla alone," Vincent said, waving his hand as if dismissing a bug. "She needs to stay with her dad, and you need to take care of the Lost Boys you brought over."

The boy stood still with his head tilted slightly and seemed to study his father. "The ones I brought over are happy and are enjoying being here. Don't you want to meet Calla?"—His brows pinched together—"She isn't as boring as Jackson; she actually likes playing in the snow!"

"The Lost Boys are your priority. Focus on them or guiding others to the Ferryman."

"Wait, if I bring her over, then Jackson will come over too." He straightened and returned to smile widely. "That's a fantastic idea! You'll see Dad, then we will all be here!" Pan bent his knees, lifted an arm to the sky like those superheroes Merilee had watched earlier Pans and Lost Boys imitate, and flew out of the cenote with the telltale trail of Tink's pixie dust behind him.

"Patrick!" Vincent yelled, putting his hands in his hair and pulling on the strands. "Fuck!"

"What a terrible idea for him pursue," Merilee said as she leaned against the side of the boulder, making herself partially visible in the shadows.

"No shit, Mer. Where is Simon? He needs to get to Jackson."

"Probably with Dorathea or tracking your Jackson.

He very well could be right where you want him." She wouldn't be surprised if that was the case. Simon had an uncanny ability to be in the right place at the right time.

"We need to stop him from bringing Jackson's daughter here. I can't imagine what it will do to Jackson if he takes her." Vincent began pacing, much like his son had. "What the hell is Tink teaching him?"

She debated relaying the facts of events past but decided now was not the time to tell him of his son's actions. No remorse was the least of her concerns about the new Pan. How he actively encouraged children to harm themselves in the Real-World to become Lost Boys here in Neverland—that concerned her. She overheard the boys talking at Mermaid Lagoon about the many horrific actions Pan told them to do to cross and be with him in Neverland forever. Some encouragements seemed innocent enough, until the source of the words was considered.

"He's different, Mer."

"He's your son, it's natural to view him differently amidst this world in the role you held. Being a Pan is much to process and its purpose difficult to absorb. Include all facets of Neverland and it's bound to change an individual."

Vincent had started shaking his head halfway through her first sentence.

"No, that's not it." Shaking out his arms, he stopped pacing and leaned against the wall putting his hands in his pockets. "There's a carelessness, a … I don't know, lack of the softness that used to surround him."

"The boy has had Tink interfering with his life for years, which is bound to influence him. Give him some time to acclimate to the new life. He could surprise us and find the median of his parallels."

"Us? You have concerns regarding him?"

"I am aware of his enthusiasm for certain aspects of his purpose that are concerning, but it's premature to predict which way it will go for him."

He was quiet, she assumed processing. Then his lips curved in a slight smile.

"Calla Annelise. I'm a grandfather." The sound of him scratching his stubble echoed as he tilted his head. "That sounds strange."

"Truly."

"Patrick can't really believe he can bring her here. We need to get me out of here so I can fix this and deal with Tink."

"We are working on it, and if I know Simon, he is in the Real-World with dual purposes in mind. Keeping an eye on Jackson and making sure Pan doesn't hurt the girl if he is aware of Pan's interactions with her."

"I hope you're right. I have a feeling Patrick won't hesitate to bring Calla here, especially if he believes Jackson would follow; and that is the exact thing I don't want to happen. I don't want both of my boys in this place. They deserve so much better."

That was her fear as well, only she knew Jackson was meant to return one day. She only hoped that the other son wasn't as volatile as this younger one and Vincent would take the news well when he found out.

CHAPTER 12

REALITY CHECK

What types of cheese did Natalie say she needed *for supper tonight? Gouda? Parmesan? Ricotta?* He regretted not bringing the list she left on the fridge this morning, it would have been mighty handy now. Why were there so many types of damn cheeses anyway? He was good with cheddar and mozzarella, throw in some marble to keep it spicy once in a while and call it good.

"Dad."

A tugging on his shirt sleeve grabbed his attention away from the multitude of cheeses in the deli cooler, to his daughter who was more interested in getting to the bakery section of the store than the deli.

"Dad." Calla was balancing on her toes, neck stretched, and tugged on his shirt again without even checking if she had his attention. She raised her hand with her index finger pointing somewhere across the store. "Do you know that man?"

"Who?" Jackson followed her finger's direction to see the blonde guy waving at them, grinning.

He brought her arm down towards her side before she waved back, garnering a frown from her.

"I don't know who that is." He looked back to see the guy tip an imaginary hat to him and start walking in their direction.

"He's been following us around the stores today. You sure you don't know him? Seems like he knows you."

"He's been following us?" He kept his eyes on the guy's progress.

"Yeah, he was at the hardware store by the checkouts. Didn't you see him? He waved at you."

When he tried to recall if he had seen the guy, he came up blank. It was possible he overlooked the blonde; he'd been actively ignoring the guy for so long it was pretty much second nature.

Wait ... Calla can see him. Unease trickled down his spine. He wasn't sure what was more concerning: the fact Calla could see the guy he figured was part of his own delusion, or that a real human being had been following him for so long. *Is he real, or isn't he?*

It was a busy grocery store, so he watched people move out of the guy's way which meant they could see him. Right? But the cameras never recorded him ... *The guy wouldn't do anything drastic in front of so many people, would he?* The blonde had never been violent before; and if he was being honest with himself, his presence had never come across as threatening. Noting the tan T-shirt and cut-off baggy jean shorts, he didn't get *I'm-going-to-stab-you* vibes.

"Maybe he wants to be friends?"—Calla's sweet voice sounded hopeful—"You do need friends, Dad."

"Yes, he does," the English blonde agreed with laughter in his voice as he came to stand in front of Jackson. The blonde extended his arm and offered his hand to shake. "Name's Simon."

Peering down at the offered hand, he wasn't sure what to make of this. Simon was the name written under the drawing his mother had done with this blonde's likeness. He clasped the offered hand when Calla went to shake it and gave it a firm shake while guiding Calla slightly behind him with his other hand. "Jackson."

"I'm Calla," she volunteered happily.

Simon released Jackson's hand and smiled at his daughter. "Nice to meet you, Calla."

"Why are you following us? Did you need to get cheese too?"

"Actually, I need to talk to your dad."

"Why don't you call him? It's easier than following people, you know."

"That would be easier wouldn't it, but I don't have a phone."

"You should get one. How did you get that scar?"

Calla pointed to a thin scar about three-inches long.

Simon turned his arm slightly and grinned. "Fighting pirates. That battle was a fierce one."

Her eyes went wide. "You know pirates?"

"Lots of them." Simon nodded his head.

"Do you know …" She paused and peered up at Jackson. When he raised an eyebrow, she leaned closer to Simon and cupped her hand around her mouth. "Captain H?" she whispered.

Simon bent at the waist and cupped his mouth as well. "Who do you think gave me that scar?"

Her eyes went impossibly wider, and she gasped. "Can I come with you next time?" she said excitedly.

"And we're done here," Jackson said as he moved in front of his daughter. It's one thing to talk to a stranger, it was a whole other thing to ask to go with him. *What the hell is she thinking? The Stranger-Danger talk obviously didn't stick.*

Simon straightened and held both his hands up in a placating gesture. "I am not about to take your daughter anywhere, so relax."

He didn't care anymore what Simon wanted to talk about. Catching sight of the leather strap around the guy's neck with a medallion dangling from the center, he recognized it from Patrick's doppelganger the other night. *This is too much.* The urge to leave pulled at his senses. He could feel his skin prickling like it had while that, *thing,* had hovered over his bed. To top it off, Calla asks the guy to take her to battle pirates. *Who battles pirates nowadays? It's not the 1800s.*

"But Dad," Calla protested as he grabbed a hold of her upper arm and turned them from Simon. "Hey, you forgot the cart!"

A warm hand landed on his shoulder, bringing him to a halt.

Simon appeared beside him. "I only need five minutes of your time and then you can go."

He shrugged off the hand. "I can go whenever I want to, and you don't get five minutes. Don't talk to me or my daughter again. Leave me and my family alone."

Simon shook his head. "Wish I could. It's not that simple."

He poked his index finger into Simon's chest, saying, "It is, and you will. Leave. Us. Alone," emphasizing each word with a jab because had no qualms about defending himself and his family from anyone that meant to hurt them. He didn't think there was anything he wasn't capable of if pushed far enough. Natalie and Calla were his world.

Simon's eyes dilated, streaks of blue snaking through his irises. A current of electricity flowed through Jackson where they made contact, extending up his arm and through the rest of his body. He felt wired, energized; a feeling of contentment filled the hollow of grief the had been his constant companion, before it dissipated as quickly as the current appeared.

Simon tilted his head in acknowledgement but remained silent.

Turning, Jackson put his hand on his daughter's

upper back and guided the waving Calla towards the exit. The farther away from his stalker, the better. When they reached the automatic doors, he looked back to where he had left him. As he suspected, Simon was nowhere to be seen.

* * *

"She's all tucked in," Natalie said as she walked into the living room. She took a seat beside him and rested her head against his chest. He moved his arm from the back of the couch and around her, and began rubbing her side absently.

"Too bad she wasn't feeling well when you guys were at the store today, I was kind of looking forward to making lasagna tonight."

"We'll go tomorrow and this time I'll remember the list too. Do you know how many different types of cheese there are?"

Her body twitched with her chuckle and he smiled at the sound: soothing and melodic. He tucked errant strands behind her ears before placing a kiss on her head. "Glad you find my ignorance of cheese amusing."

"I do, I really do."

Delicate fingers began scrolling letters over his abdomen: something she'd been doing since the first movie they watched together. He lifted his drink of spiced rum and ginger to his lips, the tinkling of ice cubes in the glass breaking the silence.

"How many have you had tonight?"

"Has Calla told you about JP?" he asked and took

another drink, needing the liquid courage for this conversation—whichever way it went.

The finger tracing letters stopped, and he looked down at the chocolate strands of hair. When she didn't respond, he stopped rubbing her side and ran his hand through her hair.

She sighed. "Not really."

"She talked to me a bit about him last night."

Natalie moved her head, dark eyes looked up and bounced between both of his. "Really? What did she say?"

"That he's her imaginary friend and that she's lonely. I guess she's having trouble making friends at school. Did you know that?"

"No, she never said anything to me." She bent her head back down and resumed writing with her finger on his abdomen.

He couldn't make out what she was writing but he enjoyed the little shivers it sent through him. Raising the glass, he took another drink. "Do you think she's like Patrick?"

Natalie stilled beside him. He didn't want to ask the question, but it had made a home in the back of his mind since his conversation with Calla the night before. *What if their daughter needed to see someone?* He hadn't pushed fast enough to get Patrick the help he needed and look where that led him. He'd be damned if he was going to let history repeat itself with Calla.

"No, I don't think she is like Patrick in the way *you* mean it."

"What does that mean?" *How did* I *mean it?*

She lifted off him and turned to bend one leg on the couch, facing him. "I mean, if she told you JP is an imaginary friend, I can see why you would be worried about her being like your brother. Your experience with make-believe friends is …"—she lifted her hands palm up—"well … Patrick. But he was going through something *far deeper* than your typical anxieties or not fitting in like Calla is. It's common for kids to have imaginary friends."

"We should get her checked out. Get a referral to a child psychiatrist to make sure."

"It's only an imaginary friend, Jackson. Kids have them. Heck, some adults even have them. Honestly, there's nothing wrong with it. We should let it be for now."

"Let it be?" *She can't be serious.* He set the drink down on the oak coffee table a little harder than he intended and put his head in his hands.

"Unless her behavior changes, yes. You're making something out of nothing here."

He dragged his hands down his face, hoping to wipe away the images of his own visitor from his mind; then her words registered, and he let out a humorless laugh.

"Making something out of nothing? Really, Nat? Patrick *made up an imaginary friend.* We let it be for months thinking he was going to get better. 'No harm if it was helping him be happy' right? Now he's dead because we didn't make him talk to someone, to help him accept things. That's what letting it be and not making something out of nothing got me!" Realizing the last words were shouted, he took a deep breath, absently spinning his wedding band. "Patrick got himself killed doing something stupid because I let his strange behavior be."

Feeling restless, he stood and moved around the coffee table to pace the open area, shaking his arm out and stretching his neck to either side. The ball of guilt that ate at him whenever Patrick came to his mind returned. He felt like throwing up but knew if he did it would just make the feeling that much worse. Ignoring how his failures caused Patrick to pay the ultimate price was the only way he had found to make the churning in his stomach dissipate.

He rubbed his stomach; he needed more alcohol to turn the sick feeling into something warm—something more tolerable. His parents' memories didn't cause these reactions, but with them he didn't carry any guilt. Patrick, on the other hand, he still carried so much guilt that he didn't think he ever really allowed himself to grieve.

His therapist had wanted him to realize he wasn't at fault and that he was only a teenager when Patrick was going through things Jackson wasn't equipped to deal with on his own. Sure, Alex and Marcus were there, and they were going through the proper channels, but it was too late. *He* knew something was wrong, felt it in his gut and held off addressing it—that's what no one ever understood.

"This is why I didn't tell you." Natalie stood and crossed her arms. "I knew this was how you were going to react. Calla isn't like him. There was something wrong with Patrick. He had an undiagnosed condition. He was ill, we all knew it long before he died."

"So you KNEW who JP was and chose not to tell me?" he shouted. "What the h—"

Glass shattered in the hall and he scowled at Natalie before heading to the stairs to see what had broken. At the bottom of the stairs, the one picture of his family he kept on the wall rested face up, their accusing eyes on him from behind jagged pieces of glass. Broken pieces scattered around the frame. Calla stood on the second step from the bottom in her nightgown, hands covering her nose and mouth, eyes wide and teary.

"Seriously, Calla? Why are you out of bed?" Glass shards cut into his foot as he stepped farther into the hallway, the stabs of pain a welcome distraction from the onslaught of memories. "Why did you knock the frame off the wall?"

He may not want the reminders of his deceased family everywhere in the house, but he would rather not have the photos tossed on the floor either.

"I came to get some water, and I didn't do anything. JP did it."

"That's enough with the JP thing," he snapped. "You can't blame someone who isn't real for something you did."

"It was JP though!" Calla pleaded, her eyes brimming with tears.

He pointed up the stairs and snapped his fingers. "Bed. Now."

"I didn't do it!" she yelled and stomped her foot before turning and stomping up the stairs.

"Well done," Natalie deadpanned behind him, obviously angry.

He really didn't need her sarcasm right then and he turned to tell her exactly what he thought of her sarcastic comment but a broom and dustpan were shoved into his chest. Hard.

"Now you get to clean up the glass. I have to go to work."

For the second time in that night, a Connolly woman stomped away from him. She roughly grabbed her keys and yanked open the door. When it slammed shut, the decor vibrated on the walls.

Scratch that. Really angry.

He knew he handled that all wrong and shouldn't have yelled at either of them, but it was like his biggest fear was staring him in the face. Who would willingly accept that?

The broken picture in his hand was the reminder why he lost his temper in the first place and he hated how happy they all were in it. It was the last family photo taken a couple months before his parents' accident—before everything changed.

Natalie was right; he should talk to someone about everything again.

Setting the large pieces of glass and the frame on the first step, he used the broom and dustpan which had been graciously handed him and swept up the smaller shards of glass. The tinkling sound of the glass being pushed into the dustpan almost matched the distant chimes outside. Reaching for the pile on the step, he carried it and the dustpan to the garbage bin under the kitchen sink.

The woman was back and smirking in the window but he paid her no attention, she'd be gone the moment he went out there anyway. He emptied the dustpan and flipped the frame over the garbage allowing the free glass to fall before placing the frame on the counter.

The louder wind chimes had him looking up at the woman illuminated by the light. Her lips were moving but he couldn't make out what she was saying. "I don't have the energy to deal with this," he muttered and turned his back to the woman to put the broom away beside the fridge.

Apologizing to Natalie would have to wait until tomorrow morning, but he could apologize to Calla. He checked the steps for any signs of glass as he ascended the stairs.

"Dad and Mom didn't mean it. They were just upset."

Calla's hushed voice came from her room through the slightly ajar door. He paused to listen, hoping to learn something about this situation to help him not see this as a terrible thing. Natalie didn't seem to think it was as big of a deal as he did.

"Sometimes he does, but he doesn't like talking about you."

Who don't I like talking about?

"Mom says it makes him sad. But you still can't break things because you get mad, and get me in trouble. Hey! I know what will cheer you up! Let's sing your song."

The metal of her door handle chilled his palm as he opened the door a sliver more as she began to hum a melody he recognized. In the mirror's reflection, she was standing at the window with her arms resting on the windowsill. The nightstand lamp cast the room in a muted honey glow.

"Why only lost boys? What happens if a girl is lost? Where does she go? ... There is a whole island for lost girls! Is that where she is from? ... She doesn't like me much. She's always glaring at me … Well, it's rude, and you should tell her that."

A stone fell to the floor at her feet. She bent down to pick it up, and the likeness of Patrick was staring at him from the open window. Jackson pulled back from the door and rubbed his eyelids to rid himself of the image. *What the hell was that?*

He tapped on the door and opened it before walking in—determined to see who was really outside Calla's window.

Her blonde hair lifted as she turned around to look at him with doe eyes. She rested her hands on the windowsill behind her and glared at him. A sharp pain hit his chest at the tears pooling in the angry stare. He felt bad enough for yelling at her before, now he felt ten times worse.

"Can we talk?" he asked as he walked over to her and sat on the side of the bed closest to the window. Raising his arms, he motioned for her to come for a hug he hoped she would accept; whether she took it was up to her.

She rolled her eyes but came over and wrapped her little arms around his neck. He closed his arms around her, kissing her on her head and glanced towards the open window.

Empty.

"I'm sorry for losing my temper, Petal."

At her nod against his shoulder, he squeezed her tighter and gave her a little shake. "How about we get you tucked in. We have a busy day tomorrow and we both could use a good night's sleep."

She stepped back and tilted her head. "You need to stop at the flower shop, don't you?"

"Yeah." He sighed. "I do."

She pulled her sheets back. "Are we picking up cookie dough ice cream at the grocery store tomorrow too?"

Jackson stood, his lips twitching as he pulled the covers over her. "And why would we do that?"

"Because mom slammed the door *really* hard when she left."

"She did, didn't she."

"Yep," she said. "You should probably get the double fudge too."

"Nice try kiddo"—he kissed her forehead—"goodnight."

"Goodnight."

Calla would get her favorite ice cream tomorrow too, no matter what he said tonight and he knew it. He hated losing his temper with her and tried his best to do better each time he was home. Usually, he managed to put his problems aside and enjoy his time at home, but these blow ups were becoming too frequent for his liking.

The night breeze chilled his arm as he walked up to the window. He looked at Calla and pointed to it.

"Leave it open a little," she said.

As he lowered the windowpane slightly, he noticed the small collection of colorful stones on her desk to his right. Memories assailed him in rapid-fire succession as he walked to the doorway. Flashes of Patrick collecting stones when he was younger, and how happy he had seemed. There was so much he would never understand about what happened to his family, so many answers he would never get. He shook his head at the thought and sighed, heading to the door.

"Dad …"

Pausing with his hand on the door, he turned to Calla.

"I'm okay."

He hung his head; the conversation downstairs ran through his mind and shame made itself known as he realized what she might have overheard.

"I know, Petal. I just worry about you and your mom," he said.

She gave him a smile. "I know you do. I love you."

He smiled softly. "I love you too. Don't forget to turn off your lamp. But if you ever need to talk, I'm here for you. I'll always be here for you; even when I'm at work, I'm only a phone call away."

She nodded then reached to turn off the lamp. With an audible click, the room was bathed in darkness. He headed to his own room, making a list in his mind of the phone calls he needed to make the next day before he headed back to work. The things he needed to confront couldn't be put off any longer.

It was time to try to leave the guilt behind. He wanted to be there for his family the best way possible, but he couldn't do that if battling his own demons took up most of the real-estate in his mind when he was home.

He walked past the dresser and headed into the ensuite. Grabbing the toothbrush and toothpaste, he turned on the tap and brushed his teeth. If Natalie felt like she couldn't talk to him about something involving their daughter, he needed to do better. He never wanted her, or Calla, too worried to talk to him about anything. He missed out on so much with working out of town as it was, the idea of missing out on more because he refused to deal with his own issues was unacceptable.

Jackson paused at what sounded like a muffled scream. He spit out the toothpaste and turned off the running water—listening for the sound again.

Tick-tick-tick.

Calla's scream came through the door clearly. The toothbrush fell into the sink and his feet thudded on the wood floor as he ran down the hallway to Calla's room. His hand pushed open the door and he scanned the room for her. All he could see were little fingers with chipped pink nail polish clinging to the windowsill, highlighted by the hallway's light shining from the doorway.

"Calla!" he said as he rushed towards her. "I got you."

He pushed the windowpane fully open and leaned out, grabbing Calla under her arms and around her rib cage. Heart pounding in his throat, he pulled her small frame up and through the opening back into her room. His backside hit the floor hard as he sat with her in his lap, arms around her, one hand cupping the back of her head.

"I got you. I got you," he repeated to reassure himself as much as her, and kissed the side of her head. "I got you." *What was she doing out there?*

Small, slender arms wrapped tighter around his neck as her sobs shook her body. She curled her legs under her, making her seem smaller, and fully surrounded herself with his arms. "Don't turn the lights off. Don't turn the lights off," she whimpered between sobs.

"I won't turn the lights offs"—he rubbed her back—"you're okay."

She nodded against his shoulder, which now felt wet.

"How about we have a sleepover in the living room, like we used to? Grab some pillows and blankets: you on the loveseat, me on the couch?" Her trembling slowed, so he continued. "I'll even let you pick the movie we watch."

She lifted her head and leaned back, giving him a view of her reddened eyes and nose with tear-streaked cheeks. He used his fingertips to wipe away her tears as she sniffled.

"Can we leave the lights on?"

"We can leave every single one on." He would even bring out the flashlights if it made her feel better. "And then tomorrow, when you're calmer, you can tell me what exactly you were doing sneaking out the window."

He pressed a finger to her mouth to silence her when she looked like she was going to argue; he was too rattled from hearing her screams and seeing her hanging out the window to handle the discussion they needed to have the way he wanted. *What was it again? Be responsive, not reactive.*

"I know I hurt you and made you mad tonight. I've climbed out a window or two when I was young when I needed to get away. It isn't hard to understand what happened." Pushing back some hair behind her ear, he smiled at her pinched brows which he smoothed with his thumb. "We'll talk about it tomorrow. Go grab your pillow."

When she was on her feet, she reached up to the window and slammed it shut—locking it with enthusiasm.

She grabbed her rainbow pillow off her bed and hugged it to her chest while she walked towards him.

Glancing at the window, she stuck her tongue out at her reflection, and he shook his head. Something hard hit the window causing her to startle but then she glared.

He followed her gaze and thought he could make out an outline of a person but then it was gone in the next blink. No one could be standing there unless they were on a ladder, and he knew from when he pulled Calla in there was no ladder.

"Come on," he placed his hand on Calla's shoulder as they walked out of her doorway into the hall. "I think there is a bowl of popcorn with our names on it."

The ball in the pit of his stomach didn't feel as heavy while he made his way down the stairs with Calla in tow. Once they were both settled in with pillows, blankets, and popcorn to watch her favorite animated film, he looked over at his little girl, disheveled but smiling, and knew it was time to make the right choice.

CHAPTER 13
NEED A WAY OUT

MERILEE

*H*ow many Lost Boys does it take to ruin a mermaid's oasis? About nineteen.

Merilee had seen plenty of Lost Boys throughout her time there. Wars, plagues, famines and still, most Lost Boys went to the ferryman eager to reunite with their families—not these, however.

The ones this new Pan had guided over not only didn't want to go to the Ferryman to be with their families, precisely the opposite—they were enthusiastically avoiding it. Each one of them had expressed how much Pan was right and how they would have—insert some self-harm activity which caused their deaths— way sooner if they had known Neverland existed.

This bigger problem was forming, which left her faltering. Did encouraging children to become Lost Boys willingly cross a line for Dorathea? She tried to think back as she swam through the pitch-black waters, to a time where such a cruel act had been done previously; there were none.

Vincent was right. There was something wrong with his boy. Whether this was new behavior or not, she didn't know, but she had taken souls down to Hal who had done acts less cruel than that to grown adults; never mind children. The youngest recent addition was only eight years old.

She may not feel much in the way of empathy towards young children, but from witnessing the depths of Vincent's care for his offspring, she assumed the level of pain those Lost Boy's parents were experiencing was intolerable.

Why would Tink encourage such behavior? The fairy was irrational, self-absorbed, and annoying. Encouraging Pan to convince children to do such deeds served no purpose for her directly. Tink wasn't in the position of benefactor, so it didn't make sense. Not much was making sense lately. The tested, tried, and true of Neverland was in a flux and every person around was adjusting to the best of their abilities. Right now, she wanted her oasis back, or her cenote. If she could have both back sans occupants, that would be sublime.

The slightly lighter waters were coming into view, so she needed to get her emotions under control. Vincent didn't need her added energies to thicken the cenote's air, he needed her calm, collected. Near the water's rock bed, the sunlight caught on something shiny, barely visible, but there. *Ah, Vincent had a visitor.*

Vincent told her he asked Pan to get him some trinkets and random items during his visits under the guise of missing home. He produced a way to notify her if he had a visitor so she would know not to surface, which happened to be the mirror attached to a garland floating in the water.

She swam close to the limestone wall on the right as she entered the open area. Two meters in was a hollowed-out portion, its peak the boulder she hid behind to observe Vincent's visitor and learn what she could. Never left disappointed, she heard Tink's voice as she slowly broke the surface, careful not to make unnecessary noise.

"What was my Pan doing down here?"

"MY son was visiting HIS dad."

"He is taking to the Pan role quite well. The idea of the Lost Boys never leaving him was quite appealing."

She barely refrained from snorting at the declaration. A little too well in her opinion. The child was becoming a borderline psychopath paving a straight line to Hal.

"You created that hole in him he believes those children will fill." Vincent closed the book he had been writing in, placed it aside and got to his feet.

"In fact, you did." The translucent woman pointed at him. "You set him up by creating him. Then when you drove off the road and into the lake"—her fingers made a walking motion in front of herself—"killing his mom, and you as well, essentially."

"Because you turned the wheel!" Vincent's shout reverberated off the cenote's walls.

"Still your fault. You were the one driving." She shrugged then smoothed out her hair. "Never should have forgotten me. All this could have been avoided. Now look what you've done to your family. Annelise is dead, Patrick is a Pan, you're at my mercy, and Jackson is without any of you." She wore an expression that appeared both sympathetic and condescending. "You should have remained in Neverland." She shook her head, then sighed, "We both know you make poor decisions though."

"I am not responsible for you destroying my family!" Vincent threw his arms up and tugged on his dark hair, taking deep breaths.

Merilee admired how well he had been keeping himself together, especially with Tink's taunts. She surely would have drowned the fairy, put her body in a sealed jar and buried her in the deepest parts of Hal's domain long ago. Hal would understand her polluting his ocean floor with an annoying fairy; he'd discourage anything from traveling near the spot too. That being had a fondness for inflicting cruelty on those who impose immense pain on others, and since Tink wouldn't stay dead, having her regain consciousness only to suffocate over and over for eternity would amuse him. *How tempting.*

Vincent released his hair and jabbed a finger at the small glowing ball of light. "And I'm *supposed* to forget! That's how it works Tink!" he exploded. "Pans leave for the Real-World. Their coin disappears along with their memories of this place. That's the way it is! How it's always been."

"Yours never disappeared so you shouldn't have forgotten!" the projection shouted back, feet stomping on the ground.

What? From the grimace on the translucent fairy's face, she concluded that was not meant to be shared. *That's interesting.*

"What do you mean it didn't disappear?" Vincent enunciated each word slowly, jaw tight. "They *all* disappear."

She sighed and shook her head, looking annoyed. "Forgot that too?! Ugh, that enchantment was useless."

"What enchantment?"

Yes, what enchantment? She had never heard of an enchantment used on a Coin of Passage before.

"We used old magic and enchanted your Pan coin, so it wouldn't vanish. We thought wrong, your memories of Neverland aren't tied to the coin. Now I must figure out what to do with you since your coin is missing and Patrick knows you're here. You can't simply go missing now, can you? Would cause me too much trouble explaining."

Vincent's eyebrow shot upwards. "You can use your *fairy magic* and take me back to the Real-World. Tell Patrick you took me back. At least then I would be free of this place."

Movement at the top of the cenote caused a shadow

over the two arguing and she looked up to see Pan descend from the opening with loose papers in hand.

"You want to go back to the Real-World? Why?" Pan sounded heartbroken and annoyed. "Don't you want to stay with me?"

"I can't stay here in this never-ending cenote prison alone, Patrick. This is not how I want to spend an eternity."

"I'll come visit so you aren't alone then," stated the smallest of the trio, as though he solved the problem. Smiling, he held out the papers to Vincent, who didn't take them.

"I can't stay here, kiddo. You know I can't."

"You want to go back to Jackson, don't you." Glaring at his father, Pan clenched his fists and crumpled the papers. "You always loved him more," he gritted.

"It's true. You're second born. Never as good as the first," Tink stated matter-of-factly, examining her nails.

"That is NOT true." Vincent glared at Tink, looking much like his son at that moment. He turned to his glaring son and his look softened. "I love you both, Patrick. Not one more than the other."

Tink snorted.

"Shut up, Tink. You know nothing about being a parent or loving someone."

"I know you gave up everything here for Annelise but will give up nothing of your life in the Real-World to stay in Neverland with Patrick. You haven't been here that long and already you want to leave him."

"She's right. You don't want to stay here with me!"

"Patrick, you're not hearing me." Vincent placed his hands on the boy's shoulders and bent down to be eye level with him. "I *can't* stay here. Not won't, *can't*."

"He doesn't need to hear you; your actions say it all."

Sniffling, Pan shrugged off Vincent's hold and sprang toward the opening, letting the loose papers fall to the stone floor.

A Cheshire grin spread across Tink's face. "Rest assured I'll let him know the Lost Boys and I will never let him down like his family. He won't be alone. We will become his *new* family."

"You conniving bitch!" Vincent lunged at the translucent woman, but she dematerialized before he could reach her. Spinning around, he swung his open hand in the direction of the hovering two-inch glow, but she flew out of his reach and followed Pan's ascent. Her laughter and the sound of bells chiming slowly quieted as her proximity dissipated.

Vincent roared, vibrating the air, and reverberating against the limestone surroundings, his eyes shimmering with a light-green glow. "I'm going to kill that fucking fairy."

"I remain hopeful you will one day succeed in that," Merilee said, swimming towards the garland pinned down under a large stone. She dove under the surface to collect the mirror. She began winding the garland around the mirror, following it up above the surface, preparing it for the next use. "She has become most irritating." Finished setting the mirror wrapped in garland behind the stone, she floated on her back towards Vincent.

Head bowed and standing with his hands on his hips, he radiated fury. "This is so frustrating! I can't do anything. I'm stuck here, and it is my fault. I should have written it down; I should have found a way to remember Tink like I promised. None of this would have happened. I need out of here. I *have to* fix this. Fix … Patrick."

"We *will* get you out of here," she reassured, resting her elbow on the ledge, and placing her chin in her hands.

"Where the hell is Simon?!"

"Might want to keep it down with the lion's roar. Don't want anyone peeking down into the hole, do you?"

The English lilt smoothed over her skin like warm honey. *There he is.* His shadow blocked the sun's rays she was attempting to enjoy. She gazed upwards to see Simon's head and shoulders leaning into the opening above.

"Oh, fuck off," Vincent snapped. "Where have you been?"

Simon's smile grew impossibly huge before he plummeted headfirst into the cenote's water. She blinked the water from her eyes and wiped her face, laughing at his theatrics. *Imbecile.*

When he broke the surface, he winked at her and swam to the ledge to her left. He pulled himself up, sitting with one leg dangling into the water, the other bent at the knee, arm resting atop. As he rubbed his coin tethered to his neck, the water droplets began retreating to the water.

"A thrill every time." He ran his hands through his shaggy blonde hair. "Do you know how close I was to getting caught by the glow bug? That's a busier hole there than any I've seen."

She pursed her lips at the seemingly innocent statement.

"Seriously, Mer?" Vincent raised his eyebrows.

"Our boy is growing up. It's adorable."

Simon rolled his eyes and picked up a crumpled piece of paper. "Relax Vinnie, we got this."

"What do we *got*? Seriously Simon, what? My son is Pan and thinks I love my other son more—which is bullshit—thanks to fucking Tink." He began pacing. "Jackson is about to lose his daughter to this damned place. We have no idea where my coin is, so I'm stuck in a freaking cenote, and I miss Annelise." Lifting his arm up, he punched the wall. "Even *that* didn't hurt long enough to make me feel better."

"This is why you should have stuck with the no-kids plan. Half your problems would be resolved right now," Simon supplied.

She pursed her lips. *Was Simon envious of the wall and desired to be punched next?*

"Forgot that, did you? 'Simon, I'm never having kids,'" he mocked.

Yes, he most definitely wished to be punched. Obviously,

Simon didn't hold the same concerns for his physical wellbeing as she did for him.

"Why were we friends again?" Vincent looked to her with bewilderment in his expression. "Do you know?"

"It was my charming wit," Simon answered before she could give her thoughts on the subject. He removed the dagger from his belt and began tossing it in the air by the blade. "Your Neverland life would have been incredibly boring without my presence."

"May I interject a fact you overlooked or forgot to mention in your previous tirade." She held up her hand to stop Vincent from yelling at her, which he seemed about to do. "We know your coin is in the Real-World because it is enchanted to not disappear. Correct? Did you have a coin collection?" She thought of other useless habits she heard humans had. "A necklace? A pin? What is on a Pan coin?"

Vincent rubbed his stubbled chin, a habit she noticed him doing when he was thinking. Hook did that often too when in thought, mayhap it was an older human practice during contemplation.

"An alpine hat with a feather in the middle, vines around the edges and the outline of people flying."

Simon paused his dagger flipping and tilted his head. Eyes going wide, he pointed the dagger towards her. "That makes sense!" He seemed far too excited by his thoughts than the topic warranted. "If a Hook coin has the ship and the Jolly Roger symbol, then the Pan would have that silly hat and people flying."

"Wait, how would you know what a Hook coin looks like?" Vincent eyed both.

Neither she nor Simon answered him. She assumed it was for a similar reason.

"I swear, I will stab you with your own dagger." His pale-green eyes narrowed on Simon. "Repeatedly."

"Promises, promises, Vinnie," Simon replied, unbothered by the threat.

Best explain prior to Simon experiencing blood loss. "Jackson came over when Tink brought Patrick. He was floating on the Neverland Cove bottom when I came across him on my way to see you."

Vincent's back connected hard against the wall. "Jackson was here?"

She nodded, as did Simon. Vincent didn't blink, only stared off at some distant point as he slid down until he was sitting with his knees bent with wrists limply resting atop them.

"After I pulled him out of the water, I watched his coin appear in his hand," she continued. *The quicker he has all the information, the quicker the shock will subside, and Vincent would be useful. No purpose in breakdowns now. What's done is done.*

"And it was a Hook coin. It seems your oldest is going to return and assume the role of your old nemesis," Simon finished for her, his words accompanied by jazz-hand motions.

"Against his own brother." Vincent closed his eyes and

let his head fall back against the stone. "I'm going to fucking kill that fairy."

"Do you think it's appropriate to sound so chipper about the situation?" She snapped her tail at Simon and successfully soaked him.

"You're right," Simon glared at her as he rubbed his coin and the water retreated once more. "A dire tone would be an appropriate improvement to the conversation regarding the most depressing family reunion ever." His dagger handle wobbled in the air as his hand twitched as if he was restraining himself from throwing it at her. "My apologies, Vincent."

"Why didn't you tell me!? You told me about Patrick, why not Jackson?"

Simon sighed and looked apologetic. "Dorathea said he was about a decade too early when she came to order me to return him. So, I figured telling you, or anyone, would be as bad as him being here early." He picked up a pebble and threw it into the water. "Dire consequences and all that."

"I concluded the same. There has also been an influx of Lost Boys and mermaid fledglings the past few weeks. Must be a war or plague in the Real-World because the numbers are higher than usual."

She swam over to where Vincent sat and lifted herself from the water. As she sat beside him in the sunlight, she flipped her hair over her left shoulder and began removing the knots. When she peered at him, she not only saw sadness in his light-green irises, but something akin to defeat. *They needed to fix this.*

"You should have told me regardless," Vincent said, then looked towards Simon. "Both of you should have."

"'Should-have's' have no purpose in this discussion. There is no changing it now," she said gently, and felt relief when Vincent nodded and let his legs fall straight and then crossed at his ankles. He folded his arms and looked down, his eyes moving rapidly back and forth.

"We need to fix this," Vincent said quietly. "Preferably before Patrick catches Hal's interest."

"And we will. From my observations, the more guidance your Patrick receives from Tink, the more irreparable damage will be done. Perhaps *if* someone *knowledgeable* in Pan responsibilities was available to guide him correctly, the consequences may be lessened." She concentrated on a particularly stubborn knot at the end of her blue hair. "Or perhaps, if there was an individual present who could communicate with the new Hook on a more personal level when he arrives; a different, dare I imply, peaceful relationship maybe formed between him and Pan." She dropped the blue strands now free of tangles, and looked at Vincent the way she did a fresh fledgling. "Your full potential in this world is required, and you don't have the means to utilize your *own* purpose."

"How am I supposed to do any of that while I'm stuck down here?"

"Precisely. Let's focus on finding the solution."

"I could bribe one of the Lost Boys to get some fairy dust or get it myself," Simon offered. "Pans keep that stuff close by at all times, but I'd be up for the challenge." The dagger and blade flipped in the air. "Or I could stab the little bugger and take it."

"What the hell, Simon?!" Vincent threw a rock at the blonde's head who smoothly dodged it. "You're not stabbing my son!"

"It wouldn't kill him; I'd make sure of it." Simon laughed. "Only a little blood loss."

"Do you remember where you put your coin?" she interjected and gestured toward the imbecile who obviously wanted to be stabbed by his old friend. "Simon could retrieve it, and that would solve the cenote-prison problem." *Did Simon forget Vincent has his dagger tucked in the back of his shirt?*

"Absolutely. I can do that"—he resumed dagger flipping—"though not as much fun as my suggestion," he mumbled.

"I would have put it somewhere I wouldn't lose it, but I don't remember where that is."

"That's irony." Simon dodged another stone thrown in his direction.

"Next will be his blade, Simon, do take care not to be annoying."

"No promises, love."

The metallic tap tap tap to her right made her turn towards Vincent. She smiled inwardly that she had been correct about him throwing his dagger at Simon next.

The source of the sound was him absently tapping the blade on the limestone next to his thigh.

Tap. Tap. Tap.

Tick. Tick. Tick.

"The watch!" she exclaimed in excitement. *That had to be it!*

Vincent stopped tapping. "What?"

"Jackson had a watch on that had birds flying engraved on it in the corner." She recalled the image, now certain it was the watch.

"Did it have the silly hat?"

"It wasn't silly!" Vincent snapped.

Simon made a face that said, *if you say so.*

"Only the right quarter was visible, the rest was covered by a gold plate. I bet that was it though."

"It would be something I would do."

"Aye, your odd obsession with time"—Simon tucked his dagger into his belt—"Worth looking into though."

"So, we have a plan. Simon gets the watch and then you can get out of here." She hoped it was going to be that simple, although things rarely were.

"On it." Simon looked at the water and shivered. "I really don't like this stuff."

"You dropped headfirst into it to get in here," Vincent pointed out.

"Aye, I did. The fall was the rush, the water landing was necessary. Expelling water from your lungs isn't as cool as I thought it would be." He shivered and peered toward her. "Ready to drown my irritating arse?"

"Always a treat." She grinned, aware Simon knew she took some enjoyment from escorting him out of the underground cave. He drowned three quarters of the way through and had to be revived once they reached Neverland Cove. She would wager part of him expected her to leave him there drowned one of these times; she had threatened to do as much a few times.

She entered the water and at once mourned the warmth of the sunlight.

"Perfect. Good thing I have been tasked with summoning the new Hook now. Makes this a lot simpler." Simon grinned at Vincent and shrugged at the scowling man. "Get ready for the worst family reunion you have *ever* had." With a grimace he reluctantly dove into the water.

CHAPTER 14

TRUTHS REVEALED

JACKSON

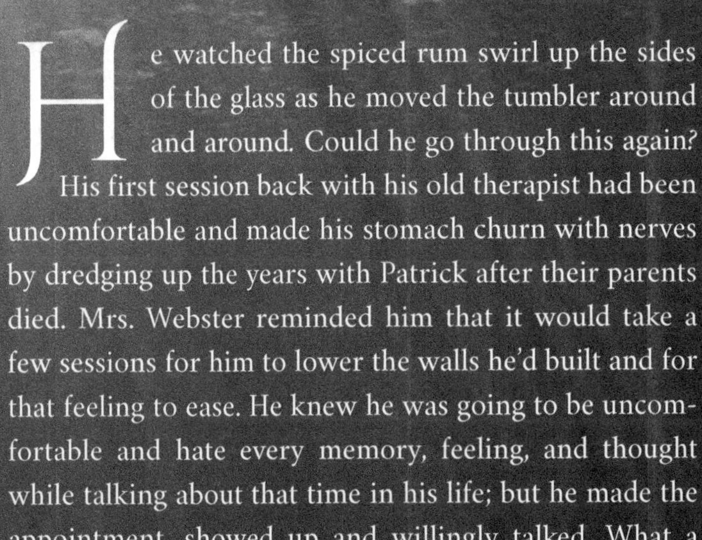

He watched the spiced rum swirl up the sides of the glass as he moved the tumbler around and around. Could he go through this again? His first session back with his old therapist had been uncomfortable and made his stomach churn with nerves by dredging up the years with Patrick after their parents died. Mrs. Webster reminded him that it would take a few sessions for him to lower the walls he'd built and for that feeling to ease. He knew he was going to be uncomfortable and hate every memory, feeling, and thought while talking about that time in his life; but he made the appointment, showed up and willingly talked. What a challenge—and he hadn't even touched on the more recent stuff.

When she asked if there was a history of mental disorders within his family, he hadn't been sure. No official diagnosis was discussed amongst his parents or uncles. Well, other than his brother, but everyone was under the impression his brother's behaviors had been coping mechanisms and not a disorder. At least, he believed that was the case.

But now … what if it was hereditary? Seeing Calla behaving more like Patrick since he began actively watching for it, broke his heart. The looking over her shoulder, avoiding windows, the too-bright smiles when he entered the room, hushed, one-sided conversations he could hear whispered around the corner.

Did he do this to his daughter? Were his genetics the cause? It all felt like his fault. Those questions had been rattling around in his mind over the past week. His relief at being granted leave from work to begin this 'journey of healing' as Mrs. Webster referred to it, had quickly been tainted with regret.

Jackson took a healthy portion of the amber liquid into his mouth and swallowed, comforted by the burn as it made its way down his throat. Had he missed more signs when she was younger? If he had seen them, would he have even recognized them for what they were; or would he have turned a blind eye because why would he want to see those similarities in his daughter? He'd swear he'd seen Patrick too though, the woman and that blonde guy as well. Can two people share a hallucination? He doubted it.

Another healthy gulp of the liquid. Another burn. Hell, he might have to skip the glass and go straight from the bottle with the way his night was heading. Natalie didn't seem as rattled as he would have expected her to be when he had called her at work and relayed what Calla had confided to him. She knew more than she was letting on, he knew it.

"She's asleep and her bedside lamp is on." Natalie sat on the coffee table in front of him, her legs caged by his. Her hands rubbed her scrub-covered thighs before she placed them between her knees. "How many of those have you had, Jackson?"

He leaned back and rested his head on the back cushion, letting out a sigh. "I can't do this again, Nat. Not like Patrick, not with Calla." He rubbed his eyes, trying to erase the images flashing through his mind.

Calla crying for him half out the window layered over Patrick pleading him to never let go. Her whispering to nothing superimposed over Patrick doing the same, both turning and giving him a too-big smile.

"How long has this been going on? Her seeing Patrick?" The words tasted like bile on his tongue, so he washed it down with more alcohol.

The silence stretched between them, until he heard Natalie sigh. "A while."

A while. Calla has been seeing and playing with her dead uncle, for a while ... how long is a while? A month? Three?

"When did it start, Natalie?" He needed answers and Calla refused to give him any after she let Patrick's name slip tonight; when none came and all he got was more unhelpful silence, he lifted his head to see his wife looking at her fidgeting hands.

Leaning forward he cupped his hand over her fidgeting ones to still them. He waited for her eyes to lift to his. "What aren't you telling me?"

She inhaled audibly, then forced out the air in a whoosh. "Here's the thing. Calla and I were looking at your family's old photo album to see which ones to bring out for that remembrance project I wanted us to do. You know, the one where you pretty much told me you wanted no part of because remembering your dead family was pointless."

He nodded. *That was at least four months ago.*

"That's when she pointed to Patrick and said he looked the same. Of course, I was confused, because yeah, he looks the same as the family picture you let me keep up in the hallway. So, then she covered her mouth and said she didn't mean to say it and it just slipped out."

"Okay …" A picture was forming for him from her ramblings, and he was not liking it.

"Right, so then I asked her what she meant about Patrick looking the same. That's when she told me, reluctantly, that JP stood for 'Just Patrick.'"

"You're telling me that Calla told you her make-believe friend was her dead uncle and you what"—he lifted his hand and dropped it back to his leg— "didn't think to mention it, knowing the issues Patrick had?"

"Well yeah, sort of … but it's not like THAT."

"It is like that!" He leaned over and slammed the drink down on the end table next to his seat. *How could she not tell me? She even lied and said she had no idea who JP was, why did she do that?* He wasn't sure if he should be livid or impressed about her ability to lie to him, but he felt betrayed on a level he didn't expect.

"Hey," she said softly as she rubbed his thigh, "she isn't like your brother. I think it's her finding comfort while she's dealing with her struggles socializing at school, on top of the stress that comes with moving to a new house and potentially a new school."

He let out a hollow laugh as he dragged his fingers down his face and clapped them together. "I can't process this right now. I won't." He stood and stepped around Natalie and the coffee table to pace the small open area. "Our daughter is *playing* with and *drawing* Patrick. Do you know how messed up that is? How do you not see that as messed up?" *I can't do this again.* He was calling the pediatrician first thing Monday. "When did she first mention him?"

"In November, and all she said was he was the sad boy who was crying in the side-yard one night, upset that we were selling the house and moving without him."

It was the middle of April now, so that would have been almost six months ago.

"Six months ago? You didn't mention this to me for six months?! What the hell, Nat?"

"I have been trying to tell you for those six months, but I didn't know how to broach the subject without you taking it the wrong way."

His head snapped to where she sat watching him. "The wrong way?! She is seeing her dead uncle and having tea parties with him! How can that not be taken the 'wrong way'? She was out the damned window, Nat. The window! Just like Patrick! I fail to see how any of this could be taken the right way." He scoffed.

"I didn't know that was going to happen," she snapped. "And didn't she do that after *you* yelled at her for breaking a photo frame by *accident*? And it wasn't just like Patrick, Patrick never actually went out the window."

"Seriously?!"

Natalie took a deep breath. "I figured this was her way of discussing how she felt about moving without being vulnerable." Her calm tone was returning but he could see the anger in her eyes.

Un-freaking believable.

"Anything else I should know?"

At her silence, he clenched his molars. "I deserve to know what the hell is going on with our daughter. I may not be around as much as you, but I trust you to tell me the important things."

"She told me Patrick visits her when she leaves the window open."

He stopped pacing and threw his hands into the air. "And that didn't set any alarm bells off for you? Patrick was seeing things before he drowned in the lake. Did it ever occur to you that maybe she has the same condition as Patrick?"

"She doesn't have the same condition as your brother. We don't even know if your brother had a condition."

"I'm making an appointment with the pediatrician on Monday," he said, tolerating no argument.

"I already took her to the doctor. They believe, as I do, that she has an overactive imagination and is trying to communicate things in a way that makes her feel safe."

At that, he stormed into the hallway to the kitchen and pulled the drawing off the fridge, the magnet falling to the floor. Returning to the living room he waved the paper in front of her before crumpling it and throwing it on the couch. "And you didn't feel it important to tell me that you were taking her to the doctor or that any of this is going on?"

"Will you keep your voice down"—Natalie stood—"she's going to hear you."

His nostrils flared as he took slow, deep breaths. He could feel his jaw tick as he clenched his teeth.

"And I didn't tell you any of this while you were out of town because you were working and needed to be able to concentrate."

Is she really using my job as an excuse? He opened his mouth to tell her exactly what he thought of that, but she continued.

"You also don't handle anything regarding your brother, or sleep walking, or imaginary friends well. Like at all."

"Do you blame me?"

"No. Not at all. You asked why I didn't tell you and I'm answering that question. If she had to be monitored or medical intervention was necessary, I would have told you immediately. That wasn't the case though."

She was right, he didn't handle these things well. He felt his eyes sting with frustration. "I can't lose her, Nat. She can't be like Patrick."

Her arms came around his waist and her hands slowly moved along his back. His arms went around her shoulders, using her to feel steady.

"She's not. Remember how I was talking about remembering loved ones and how important it is? That's part of what she is doing. Patrick was around her age when he died. That's a lot to process in and of itself. This may be her way of dealing with her own mortality. Most people think they are going to live to an old age, not die before puberty."

"But to imagine herself playing with him is going a little too far, don't you think?" He rested his cheek on her head, breathing in the fragrance of her conditioner. *Calm.*

"Not really, you see it that way because of what you have been through with Patrick. That is what you are comparing her actions to, and that isn't fair to her or to you. She isn't dealing with the deaths of her parents; she isn't trying to find a connection to a person she was close to and suddenly lost. Patrick *was* doing those things. Your biggest fear is getting close to her and losing her too. Not that you mean to, but you've always kept yourself at a distance."

"It's my job, Natalie. I have to leave town for it." This was not an argument he wanted to have right now.

"You had plenty of job offers in town, but you take the out-of-town assignments. I'm not saying it's a terrible thing. It is what it is. You give her the world, but you are more comfortable observing her world, than being in it. Same goes with me. But I understand the reasons why and you love us wholeheartedly with what you can."

Did I do that? Yeah, I do. "I'm sorry, I try to be a good dad and husband."

"You are a caring father and a wonderful husband; you are the brightest sun in Calla's world, Jackson. She keeps you on this pedestal I don't think you could ever fall from. You changed after the incident with Patrick at the lake; present but somewhat removed. That wall is slowly coming down, and it will be a wonderous day when it does. You'll see."

He never put much thought into why he made the choices he did in the past, but Natalie's words echoed some implications Mrs. Webster had hinted at with her questions. Questions which made him discover some uncomfortable truths. He was terrified of losing Natalie and Calla, and did keep himself at a small distance, constantly waiting for them to be taken away from him.

"You really think she isn't like Patrick?"

Natalie lifted her head from his chest and looked at him, searching his expression for something. He didn't know what.

Then her eyes softened, and she gave him a small smile. "Yes, I am sure."

She put her hand on his cheek and he leaned in for a kiss. "I'm trying to do better."

"I know, and I'm so proud of you. It's not easy, but you made the call to Mrs. Webster, and you showed up. That's a huge accomplishment. You showed up. You got this, and I got you. You need me, I'm here. I'm your girl."

The doorbell rang, breaking the moment.

"I'll get that," Natalie said, giving him a kiss and heading towards the entryway.

Maybe he was overthinking and reaching for similarities between Calla and his brother. It was one of his biggest fears, so that fact was probably making him more sensitive in this situation. He had to do better, starting with not jumping to conclusions.

Natalie walked back into the hallway. "No one was there."

"Kids playing ding-dong ditch this late?" he suggested. He remembered playing that game. Annoyed the Abbotts to no end.

There was a knock at the door and she rolled her eyes. "Coming."

He followed this time in hopes of catching a glimpse of the little buggers. Yet, when he got to the door, he didn't see any kids. Simon was standing on the step, smirking at him.

CHAPTER 15

TAKEN

JACKSON

Coming up behind his wife, Jackson put a possessive arm around her waist and glared at the guy.

Simon nodded and his smirk morphed into a smile. "Hey, Jacks. Figured I'd stopped by and finish that chat we had earlier."

Covering his hand with hers, Natalie leaned into his chest. "Must be kids playing ding-dong ditch. I can't believe we used to think that was a fun game." Natalie chuckled.

Simon smiled even wider and shrugged his shoulders. Then the guy's gaze roved over Natalie with blatant interest and Jackson had the urge to punch him in the face. *What is he, twenty years old and checking out my wife?*

She turned in his arms and gave him a kiss. "I'll be upstairs. Going to take a shower and get ready for bed."

He nodded but his focus was on the cocky blonde.

"Okay, I'll be up shortly. Just want to check something out first." He patted her hand when she ran it across his abdomen, sending chills across his skin.

"Be nice to them if you catch them on the property," she instructed as she moved around him towards the hallway.

Simon's gaze followed his wife's retreating form but when the guy licked his lips, he moved into the doorway blocking his view. "Thin ice, man. Thin ice."

Simon's eyes looked over his shoulder, completely unperturbed by the warning and obviously trying to catch another glimpse of Natalie. "Odd choice of words, given your habit of falling through the crap."

Enough of this. He reached for the cool metal of the door handle and stepped forward, effectively taking up Simon's personal space. The click of the latch was loud in the quiet night. "I don't know who you are but leave me and my family alone."

Simon didn't retreat. He stood with his thumbs hooked in his front pockets. "Even if it means putting your family at risk?" He tsked. "Bad play, Jacks."

"It's Jackson. No one calls me Jacks anymore."

"Lies. I know a particular father and son duo who do."

"I don't have time for this." He suddenly felt like the not-so-crazy one. This guy obviously had a few more screws loose than he did.

"Better make time. We need to find something and then go for a trip."

'Time to go for a trip.' The words echoed in his mind

from the dream he had the week prior. He raised an eyebrow. "I don't think so. I don't make a habit of adventuring off with strangers, especially creepy bastards that stalk me."

Simon snorted. "Stalk? More like babysit. You lead an incredibly boring life, you know."

"I'm going inside, you better leave."

"Or we consider my suggestion." Simon lifted his hands and tapped his left wrist. "Your dad had a watch he always wore, correct?"

"Doesn't everyone?" *What kind of stupid question was that?*

"How should I know? We don't follow time."

We? He looked at Simon's features to find similarities from what he recalled of the blonde woman but nothing that he considered familial stood out.

The guy sighed dramatically and looked up at the night sky. "Really?" He looked back down at Jackson, blue eyes annoyed. "Well, I need to return your dad's watch and you need to come with me. It's that simple."

"You know how stupid you sound? Like I'm going to give you anything, especially something of my father's and blindly follow you."

"Your *father* is the one that sent me to fetch the bloody thing."

"Get off my property." He had enough on his plate to deal with right now, he didn't need some delusion of a delusional person talking like his dad was alive and hanging out somewhere. How would someone even know where to begin to unpack all the baggage that would dredge up. Turning to open the door, he felt a hand grip his shoulder.

"Not going to happen."

Those cocky words came from behind him, and it grated on his last nerve.

Jackson reached over, grabbing the offending wrist and twisted it as he turned back to face Simon. Using his other hand to push Simon back against the wall with a satisfying thud, his hand migrated around the base of his throat. "Back the fuck off and stay away from me and my family."

Simon's eyes dilated and a mischievous grin grew across his face. "You man-handle everyone who strikes a chord? Gotta say, I didn't think you were the aggressive type. Always so calm and collected."

Neon-blue streaks moved through Simon's irises which made him narrow his own eyes. *What is going on with that?*

Pressure was applied to his wrist joint below his thumb, making his hold go lax. A zing of electricity spread through his wrist from where Simon gripped it and traveled up his arm. A sharp jab of pain pricked below his jaw line. Glancing to the three-inch window-pane next to the door, he confirmed Simon had some sort of knife held to him. *Insane and carrying a weapon, lovely.*

"I'm glad you have a temper. You're going to need it."

The stinging beneath his jawline dissipated and

Simon tapped the flat surface of the blade against Jackson's nose with a grin.

"You're insane." He needed to report this guy as soon as he got him away from here. The cameras had to have picked up his image by now. It would be one less thing to worry about in his extensive list.

Simon chuckled. "Not nearly as insane as you wish I was."

Calla's terrified scream seemed to come from all around.

"Leave any windows open with the lights off?" Simon asked, looking up at the sky again but this time seeming to be searching for something.

He didn't bother waiting to hear whatever the lunatic said next, he opened the front door and ran upstairs, taking them two at a time. His open door showed their bedroom curtains billowing in the breeze, and he heard Natalie's, "Jackson?" from the closed bathroom door in the hallway as he rounded the banister. Natalie called to him again as he heard the shower turning off.

"Calla?" he called out as he opened her bedroom door and froze. Her night lamp was on the floor, shining an unnatural lighting on the bedroom. His gaze locked on the window; he noted what he could see in his periphery. The empty bed made his stomach drop, and the sheets pulled from the bed, strewn across the floor and out the window made it feel like he couldn't get enough oxygen. His baby girl wasn't there. His heart stopped then sped in rapid succession as he looked at the likeness of his little brother, crouched on the window's ledge.

"What happened?" Natalie's voice shook as he heard her enter their daughter's room.

Jackson couldn't see her, but knew she looked around like he had; seeing the broken lamp, the bed sheets pulled off the bed and out the window. When she came up beside him, he waited for her to freak out at the sight of Patrick's look-alike.

"Oh my God, where is Calla?"

Brown eyes with glowing ember streaks glared in his direction as a cruel smile crossed its lips. "Come and get her, Jacks." Its gaze went over his shoulder and laughed before it jumped out the window.

Simon whistled a familiar tune as he walked in the doorway, stopping periodically to look at a picture or a drawing. Natalie was seemingly not even aware of his presence.

By her lack of reaction to his brother sitting at the window, he knew it was safe to assume Natalie hadn't seen the doppelganger either.

"I don't know, Nat." He walked to the window and leaned out. Frustrated to see no sign of Calla or the look-alike.

"We have to call the police!" Her panicked tone matched his internal storm.

He walked over and put his hands on her damp shoulders. "Get dressed and call them. I'm going to go try and see if I can find her. She couldn't have gotten far."

"If Pan wants to bring Hook home, then she could very well indeed be *very* far away," Simon said in a sing-song tone.

Who is Pan and what Hook? He shook his head, needing to focus on what was real and finding Calla.

"What are you looking at?" Natalie turned towards Simon, who waved and blew her a kiss, but she looked back at Jackson, frowning.

"I thought I saw a note." He hugged her so he didn't have to look her in the eye when he lied. "I thought maybe she left a note."

Simon leaned a hip against Calla's dresser and tapped his left wrist.

He narrowed his eyes at how comfortable Simon seemed in his home and he didn't like the implications.

"Go get dressed and call the police," he said as he released Natalie. "I'll go for a drive and try to find her."

"Okay, just hurry. I don't like the idea of her out at night alone." She turned and headed to the doorway.

Simon picked up another piece of paper, the outlines of two figures swords fighting bled through. "Lost boy, Lost boy, want to come and play? Never be alone, never age a day," he sang softly and leisurely dropped the paper down onto the dresser. "Never go hungry, never read a book. Battle the pirates, defeat Captain Hook." He saluted to Jackson with his blade and continued to walk towards the window. "Lost boy, lost boy, won't you take my hand—"

"Never be alone, here in Neverland," he finished

quietly. *That was the poem Patrick had been writing and part of Calla's.* His head started to pound.

"What was that?" Natalie asked from the doorway.

"Nothing, talking to myself how things never go as planned."

"Life rarely does," she said and continued out the door and out of sight.

"Still want me to go away there, Jacks? Or you want to grab that watch and go get your daughter?"

There was no doubt about what he was going to do in his mind. He tugged his shirt sleeve up and lifted his right hand, turning it watch-face forward to show Simon the now ticking watch. "Let's get my daughter."

Simon's gaze went to Vincent's watch, then he grinned; looking like he'd won a worthwhile bet.

"Then you can fuck off."

The guy laughed. "Sure, if that's what you want after. I will."

Again, there was no doubt in his mind he wouldn't want to have Simon around after returning his daughter home safely.

"Off to your chariot! We go to Carston Lake, origin of the Connolly family curse."

"You have problems."

"None like you, my friend." Simon patted him on the shoulder, leaving the skin stinging. "And you don't even know half of them yet. Come, time's a wasting."

He followed Simon out the doorway and down the

hallway, tuning into Natalie's worried voice coming from their bedroom.

"We don't know. Our daughter's room was empty when we went in; I thought I heard her scream but I'm not sure, I was in the shower … no. I think my husband was downstairs. He's leaving to see if he can find her …"

He was relieved she was on the phone with law enforcement; Calla would be found more quickly. *She isn't going to end up in the paper like her classmate.* Simon could be leading him on a wild goose chase; or all this could be a delusion in his mind, but he felt truth in Simon's words as insane as it sounded. He would take Simon to Carston Lake like he wanted, but if Calla wasn't there, he was leaving the guy and going to find his daughter on his own.

* * *

"You're afraid of motor vehicles?" he asked as he closed the truck's driver-side door and eyed Simon as he jumped out of the truck bed bedside him. The guy had refused to hop into the passenger side when they left the house and insisted on riding in the box. Normally he would have refused because he didn't need a ticket for that, but no one noticed the guy anyway and they didn't have time to argue.

Simon rubbed his stomach, looking a little paler than usual. "Not afraid. Strongly dislike."

"Well, we're here." He stretched out his arm and indicated their surroundings, "Where's my daughter?"

He had driven farther down Carston Road as Simon's

yelling instructed, around the first bend to the boat launch. The railing continued on either side of the opening with room for multiple vehicles to park on the paved sections. Luckily for him, it was vacant. He wouldn't need to be cautious of locals witnessing him talking to himself—as they would see it anyway. Small blessing in being alone because he didn't think he would be able to navigate another situation right then.

Simon walked past him without answering his question and looked over the railing on the right. "She's there," he said, pointing into the water.

She's in the water? His heart stopped. *Is she okay?* Hurrying to look over where Simon was pointing, he leaned his upper body over the railing.

The eerily smooth surface of the lake reflected the stars and moon, as well as a reflection of himself beside the rocky edge looking back at him—no reflection of Simon. There was no Calla. He should have known and not given into the idea of Simon being able to help with this because it only reinforced that he was losing it. *Why did I hope he was the answer to my problems? Am I that desperate?* The short answer was yes. He was indeed that desperate.

If Simon had been real and knew where Calla was, he could have taken solace in the fact his friendly stalker was a sentient, corporeal being and he was not part of a delusion. The last tendrils of hope for normalcy fizzled out like a lit wick doused by water. Shame cloaked him like a thick fog sprinkled with humiliation. Here he stood at the lake he despised, all because he hoped so badly, he'd finally be able to rid himself of the uncertainty he carried about his sanity.

He bowed his head. Anger rose as he realized he abandoned Natalie to deal with her worry and the police on her own to follow … what? His own conjured stalker? Was this what it was like for Patrick—to have a mind that refused to accept reality and created its own? If he was Calla, he would have run away too—wished he had run away long ago.

Jackson glared at his reflection and his reflection glared back. He despised that surface and wanted nothing more than to have the lake dry up and disappear. This lake caused him more pain than one body of water should for being stationary. A river would make more sense in regard to drownings, but this lake … this lake took three of his family members, completely engulfing two (if he included his dad because it was easier to digest than the alternative) and almost claimed him. It *should have* taken him.

"Guess what, there is no Calla." Not even sure why he talked out loud to the guy.

"Oh, she's there."

Shaking his head, he straightened. "Enough. I have to see if I can find her."

Simon walked up toward him by the railing, looked at him and then back down towards the water directly below. "She's right there," he said, sounding irritated.

"No, she's not."

"Just look! You can see her!" He pointed again.

Jackson leaned over the railing again at Simon's persistence that his daughter was in sight. *One last look?* That's when he caught Simon's movement and felt a hand on his shin pushing his leg off the ground.

Caught off guard, he swung his arms to catch himself, but his bottom half was already going lake-side and heading toward the surface. Legs hitting the chilled water first, he heard Simon's laughter before the rest of his body went under. Bubbles were everywhere in the dark liquid and it was freezing, but he righted himself quickly. He reached for the surface and when he felt cool air on his face, an arm came across his chest and pulled him back under. Pressure surrounded him and he could hear Simon's muffled laughter in the water as he was pulled farther down.

The ticking of his father's watch seemed fitting to be the last sound he'd hear, because as he watched the moon shimmer above him and shrink, he was certain Simon's grip would make sure he wasn't getting out of this alive.

CHAPTER 16
GRUESOME DISCOVERY
MERILEE

"Explain," Merilee enunciated slowly while she contemplated screaming. Why the barrage of unfortunate events continued to surprise her, she was not sure. The atmosphere altered with each passing day, leaving the beauty of Neverland to be desired once more.

Foolishly, she believed an excursion to Glacier Bay with the latest cohort of fledglings would dampen her irritation toward Tink with its macabre scene. She scowled as she pushed yet another frozen corpse away from her person after it assaulted her arm, further irritated with the once ignorant fledgling. The corpse collided into the collection of frozen mermaids bobbing on the surface. An impressive number was beginning to accumulate which raised her concern about the cause of such a substantial number. *This had to be the result of something other than a bet or dare.*

Her companion grimaced as the next corpse was pushed between them by a growling Isla, who was then followed by her counterpart, Odessa. Two of her senior mermaids each agreed to investigate the rumors circulating of mermaids being murdered and bodies dropped in Glacier Bay.

Isla, the unpredictable fire-maned, appeared thrilled by the prospect of retaliation if found necessary. Odessa, who was a gentle soul with a heart as soft as her tangerine corkscrew curls, felt empathy for those caught in such a predicament. Both mermaids volunteered to collect the floaters—as they called them—when the four of them arrived, which left her with Brynn to gather information amongst the frozen.

Brynn tilted her head and bit her lip as she seemingly searched for words. "It is only a rumor, Mer. I overheard some Lost Boys discussing seeing a few pirates place one of ours in a crate and hooking it to the rear of Hook's ship and sailing in the direction of Lava Loch."

"What importance does that hold in this situation?" she asked, not seeing the significance of the statement. While hearing one of her kind being captured by Hook's men was upsetting, it wasn't necessarily uncommon; the tensions between the two groups had been escalating to new heights recently.

She watched Brynn finger-comb her curly silver mane, a habit she exercised when agitated. A growing agitation Merilee herself was intimate with due to the energy shift of the island, as were the rest of her kind.

Brynn's eyes shifted behind her and stayed locked in that direction. "It's possibly significant because I don't see how a charred arm would make it to this place."

Her head whipped around to scan the frozen bodies. Accusations in the sightless white eyes bombarded her sense of responsibility for this disaster. The endless rainbow of varying hues of hair and fins speckled with frost almost concealed her target. About twenty feet from her, a frost-covered blackened arm, bent at the elbow, bobbed along with the other occupants.

"Correct. How does anything charred find itself here, other than being brought?"—she peered over her shoulder at Brynn—"Curious who the owner of the appendage is?"

Brynn blanched, turning a sickly shade of green. Her discomfort could be read plainly in her features, and it pricked at Merilee's skin, or perhaps that was the frozen hair strands surrounding her.

This fledgling heavily disliked any actions with malicious intent. The empathy towards the wounded sometimes became too overwhelming for her, to the point she requested Merilee to isolate her until she had the feelings under control again.

"Venture to Mermaid Lagoon and see if any loose-lipped Lost Boys are meandering about. They divulge more in your presence," she instructed. Brynn's strengths better served them in gathering information, not surrounded by corpses.

Brynn nodded, eyes going back to the burnt appendage. "Share with me later who it's attached to."

"Already planned on it. Now go, nothing to be gained from bearing witness to more." She felt her own relief when the mermaid sighed and submerged herself in the waters. Brynn's discomfort was becoming a tangible force. The fact her own cognitive abilities were affected more severely by those around due to the island's distress was an undesirable consequence of her role of as Mermaid Keeper. Being so intricately connected with a place such as Neverland and its occupants, she was comparable to the likeness of one of those ridiculous mood rings Vincent brought back one trip; only difference being she was an *accurate* reader of the energies. Her emotions were hardwired to be in tandem with Neverland.

Right now, Neverland is irritated and on the verge of screaming.

She pushed the corpses out of her way as she slowly made her way to the anomaly in the group. Mouths gaped open in frozen screams, arms stretched outwards with hands clawed like talons, frozen hair snapped and fell into the water from her jostling. She felt her ire rise as she came abreast of the scorched corpse.

Skin pieces were missing in sections exposing the bone underneath, and a glance towards the tail showed a similar state of scales missing and bones gleaming white under the surface. Pieces of skin shifted under the pressure of her hands as she rolled the body onto its back to expose the facial features—or what remained of them.

Usually, a mermaid was easily identified by the color combinations in their hair, each had a unique set of colors and type. This one's obvious visit to Lava Loch singed all hair from its scalp and face, leaving blackened craters in the skin.

A shiny golden string caught her attention, which rested in the exaggerated hollow of the throat. Only a select few of them received gifts from the Real-World, especially jewelry. Her mind rapidly tallied those she was aware of that wore such things as she picked up the dainty chain. Following along its length under the water until she encountered something small and solid. Taking hold of what felt like a pendant, she wrapped the chain around her fingers and tugged, successfully snapping a link and removing it from the owner's neck—along with several pieces of burned flesh into the water. Her arm took longer to rise than she was accustomed to, as she lifted the inch-tall oval sapphire, encased in swirls of gold.

She knew this piece, experienced some envy towards Leila for receiving it from an earlier Pan. She believed his name was Pierce. The romantic was enamored with Leila from the beginning of his succession into the role.

Merilee clenched her fist around the precious gift and the chain dangled from her palm. She knew why they selected Leila. The lovely soul rarely viewed anyone through a distrustful lens and trusted wholeheartedly in those she encountered—even the pirates.

'Past experiences should not condemn those we have no firsthand knowledge of. If we seek to discover malicious intent in actions, we will find it. Best to live in love and seek understanding.' Leila's voice echoed in her mind.

"Look where love and understanding led you, Leila." She reached out and gently caressed the roughened skin of Leila's head where her once beautiful violet and gold hair flowed.

"Merilee, we gathered all the floaters from the outer waters."

She removed her hand, and turned to see Odessa glaring at Isla, who was using a corpse to rest her arms atop with her chin in her hands and grinning manically. The flush on her pale skin and unhinged glint in her amber eyes was telling. It would be wise for her to remove Isla from the evidence of their lost numbers, the fiery mermaid was positively wired.

"Isla, do not use Juniper as a raft. Be respectful."

Odessa nodded and her glare subsided into plain disapproval when Isla huffed out a breath and pushed off Juniper.

"Thank you." She surveyed the litter of bodies one more time before submerging herself below and swam beneath her former kin towards her companions. "Come, we need to go to warmer waters before we join the rest."

"But Mer, we haven't even evaluated if there was foul

play," Isla whined. "We need to at least look over a few before we leave."

"Once it is wise for us to do so. After tonight's festivities, go find others to bring here to help you search the corpses tomorrow. Have one to keep count of the sundial to keep aware of the time," she explained, noting Odessa's brown skin beginning to develop frost on her shoulders. Turning back to Isla, she felt the manic energy pouring off her in waves.

"Tomorrow?" Isla whined.

"Yes, tomorrow. At morning light. No sooner."

She watched as Isla searched her face for … something. Whatever it was, she must have been left unfulfilled because her eyes rolled in annoyance, and she sighed before crossing her arms slowly.

"We must warn the others to exercise caution," Odessa said calmly and inclined her head to Merilee before going beneath the surface.

Merilee nodded at the entrance and submerged herself into the water—waiting for the irrational mermaid to do the same. She had learned to keep watch over Isla when she was in this heightened state. The instruction to leave it be after Dreilia was pinned to the bow of the ship for all to see was ignored by that one. The vixen tore through five of Hook's men, leaving each one on the side of the Never Bight, gutted and skewered, to be found by their crewmates the next day. She refused to condone such a retaliation but felt deep satisfaction at the macabre scene Isla created. There was no doubt her vengeful warrior would meticulously take note of any injuries found inflicted tomorrow and return each in kind.

She smiled as the glorious image of Isla reigning down justice played out in her mind: fire-red hair billowing out in the waters, amber eyes glowing. *Indeed, that will be something to behold.*

CHAPTER 17

STRANGE WORLD

JACKSON

Jackson broke the surface and inhaled deep gulps of warm air that felt like bliss to his oxygen-starved lungs.

I'm not dead. I wouldn't feel anything if I was dead right?

Blinking the water from his eyes, he turned in a 360, taking in his new surroundings.

I know this place.

He hadn't a clue why he knew it, but he did. Looking to the hills of lush trees, he half expected a collection of brilliantly colored birds to break away from the tree line and fly into the sky.

The nightmare.

His gaze went to the sky but there were no clouds in the shapes of skulls or swords. The sound of water splashing brought his attention behind him to find Simon breaking the surface of the water—laughing.

"Your arms pinwheeled so hard!" Simon mimicked a panicked look on his face. "Aaaaah!" He broke out in guffaws.

"What do you expect, you shit!" he snapped, finding no humor in any of what just happened.

"Not for you to do *that*!" Simon responded and began to swim toward the sandy beach still laughing.

"*Not for you to do that*," he mocked.

He spat out water displaced by Simon's movements and scowled at the back of his head. *Wonder if he'd still help if I punch him, just once.* Deciding to pin the idea for later, he swam to the beach where Simon walked up the shallow waters.

"Did you scream too? I'm pretty sure that was a scream."

"I did not scream," he denied, moving to his feet and walking up beside Simon. "Pinwheel, yes. Scream, no." He pulled his white long-sleeve shirt from his abdomen where it clung and rung it out. Water squished in his sneakers as he continued up the dry sand. "It was a jackass move."

Simon shrugged and lifted his hand to remove his dripping hair from his eyes. "Keeps you on your toes."

He snorted and looked behind him, taking in the scenery and smells with a sense of familiarity. "I know this place." He looked out between the apex of two descending hills covered in vegetation to an ocean that spread as far as he could see, the afternoon sun reflecting off the water. "Why do I get the feeling you know why?"

Returning his gaze to Simon, he noticed the guy glanced in the same direction he had.

Simon's blue eyes shifted to him, and there was an excessively large grin across his face. "Because you've been here before." He extended his hands, fingers splayed, and waggled his digits in a jazz-hands motion. "Surprise!"

"I was? When?"

Simon sobered. "You were. You were sent back. I watched over you. Now your daughter is here, and we have to return her to the Real-World."

"What do you mean by *Real-World*?" He scanned the trees and the water for signs of his daughter. "She's here?"

"Not here, here. At Pan Manor. You know, with Pan and the Lost Boys."

"But where *is* here?" He didn't feel like he was anywhere natural. The air felt too clean, the colors too vibrant, and energy hummed along his skin.

"Neverland, of the Ocean of Souls."

He didn't know how to respond to that. So, he stayed silent as he observed Simon reach up to his shirt and rub the medallion he had seen on him and Patrick's doppelganger and felt his mouth drop. The water began to roll off Simon's hair and collect in a wave, rippling as it made its way down to his feet and into the clear blue water.

"Pretty sweet trick isn't it. Here," Simon said, grinning and reaching for Jackson's right wrist. "Time of truth."

Jackson wasn't sure what that meant but didn't stop

Simon when he clasped his left thumb and rubbed it over his dad's watch. His eyes went wide as the water began leaving his scalp and rolled down his neck. The sensation of being dried on the water's behalf was akin to the feel of a lint roller; only this left his skin dry and clothes light once more. Following the water to his sneakers and then to the body of water—just like Simon's had—he gaped.

"We freaking knew it!" Simon's tone sounded excited and smug. "*That's* what happened last time." Simon tapped the watch several times. "Must have rubbed it when I adjusted my hold on you."

"We? Who's we? What did you do?" *He better not have rubbed anything without my knowledge ... I don't remember him holding me in any capacity. Is any of this even real though?* He felt a pounding in his head begin and felt like he was in a fog. *This is too much. All of this is too much.* He leaned to the side.

Simon slapped his cheek not so lightly and put both hands on his shoulders, giving him a shake. "Hey, none of that. There'll be time for that later."

"Excuse me?"

"Calla," Simon said while he searched his face for who knows what. "We need to get Calla. That's most pressing right now."

He was right, and Jackson would be asking him all the questions later. He shrugged Simon's hands off his shoulders and stretched out the tension from his neck. The smell of the salt water and vegetation surrounding him helped him become grounded.

"Okay. You said my daughter is probably at Pan Manor?"—his voice came out steadier, stronger—"Where is that? And who is this Pan you keep mentioning?"

Simon put an arm around his shoulders and started leading him toward the tree line. "Pan Manor is the home for the Pan and the Lost Boys he guides here."

"So, this Pan guides lost boys to his home and steals little girls?" *What messed up person are we dealing with? If this Pan, or anyone, touched Calla—they're dead.*

He ducked under a branch as they crossed into the vegetation, effectively removing Simon's arm in the process.

"The Pan isn't a pedophile or meant to be a predator like you're taking it. This new one is ... different though."

"Different how?" Not liking the hesitation in Simon's words. *This* Pan had Calla and if he was either a predator or pedophile, then they needed to pick up the pace.

"The Pan has always been the guide for children who die young in the Real-World."

"Wait"—his feet stopped amid the fallen leaves and soil—"die?"

"Yes, die." Simon gave him an encouraging nod, as if to say, come on you can get it.

"So, are we dead? Is Calla dead?"

"Calla is not dead. She wouldn't be allowed in the circumference of Neverland if that was so. She's very much alive," he reassured as he inclined his head. "Best keep moving."

"She's alive but the Lost Boys aren't." *That's only*

slightly comforting. His mind started conjuring all sorts of scenarios involving alive decaying bodies.

"Correct. Think of Neverland as the pitstop for the souls of the young who need time to adjust to the idea of going to the Ferryman; or had a traumatic end of life experience and are needing comfort; or those younglings who want to wait elsewhere than the afterlife for their family members to cross."

"Okay, so those who stay here are the Lost Boys." Remembering the writing below the portraits his mother had drawn, he decided to just ask. "Are you a Lost Boy?"

Did that mean Simon was dead? Do I see dead people?

"To keep it simple, the answer is no. I am not a Lost Boy. I was at one point, but no more," he answered as he took out the dagger from his belt and palmed the handle while scanning the trees.

"You died?"—he needed to clarify this—"You're dead?"

Simon straightened his arm in front of him and stopped walking. Head tilting to the side, the guy sniffed and squinted to the right. He pointed behind them and to the left towards a large fallen tree six feet away. "Get behind that and get down."

Still reeling from the information overload, he blindly obliged. Volleying over the fallen tree, his palm scraped against the bark. Finding the sting of pain oddly comforting, he ducked down, resting against the tree, his legs tucked inward. Simon joined him shortly after with a finger to his lips gesturing to keep quiet.

A loud snarl stopped him from asking what they were doing when they needed to get to Calla. *What animal makes that noise? Sounds huge.* Simon's eyes shifted in front of him at the same time he heard the snapping of twigs. He hesitantly searched for the source of the sound and immediately regretted it.

Twenty feet away, glowing orange eyes were focused on him. *What the hell is that thing?* With the face of a feline covered in white fur, it crouched in the large leaves of the foliage. One hairless limb stepped out, and then the other, slinking towards them; his eyes widened when the body of a mouse, long skinless tail and all, revealed itself.

He shifted, readying himself to run like hell if he needed to, but a blade laid flat against his chest kept him in his place. Another low growl sounded on the opposite side of the tree. Simon's outstretched arm tensed, and Jackson looked up, following the guy's gaze.

An anaconda the color of simmering opal, the width of his couch, perched above him, eyes trained on what he assumed was the mouse-cat creature. He heard another snapping of a twig in the direction of where the mouse-cat had been, and the snake growled that deep growl the same as he previously heard. *That's what was making that noise? A snake that could swallow my truck whole. Fantastic.*

More rustling from the mouse-cat and the opal scales shimmered in a ripple, then the snake lunged over him onto the ground beyond his feet. He followed its trajectory and couldn't blink as he watched the snake slither around the hissing and writhing creature at an unexpected and frightening pace for a reptile of its size. Head rearing back, its jaw opened to reveal rows upon rows of sharp, jagged teeth. The hiss of the creature staring at its own deliverer of death, morphed into a high-pitched squealing as it increased its attempts for freedom.

The blade tapped him on his chest, breaking his gaze from the trainwreck he needed to stop watching, and he eyed Simon. The guy didn't seem half as freaked out by what was transpiring and nudged his chin upwards towards the fallen tree they rested against.

"We're on the wrong side," he mouthed. The terrified squealing suddenly stopped, and Simon looked back toward the creatures.

Jackson didn't want to know what made the guy gulp audibly but forced himself to look. The opal snake faced them, its head cocked to the side—a lump moving erratically in what he guessed was its throat.

The thing is still alive. He felt himself gulp as he realized what a death like that could be like, which he may learn firsthand in the very near future.

"Now Sissil, you just ate …" Simon said, tone wary as he held out his free hand palm up and slowly got to a crouching position, the dagger still keeping Jackson in place.

Oh, he understood he wasn't supposed to move. He didn't hold any reservations about staying exactly where he was and letting Simon handle the situation.

Opal scales shimmered as it slithered slowly towards them inch by inch.

"Sissil …" Simon slowly stood to his full height and moved to stand partially in front of him. "Dorathea will be angry if you eat this one," he warned.

It growled.

"Who's Dorathea?" he whispered, hoping to get an answer and simultaneously not garner the things attention. He didn't want to be another wriggling lump like the still moving one in its throat. A possibility which was quickly becoming more of a reality with each foot the snake—Sissil—gained.

"Dorathea is its keeper," Simon whispered back, then he cleared his throat loudly. "Sissil, stop it."

A high-pitched whistle halted Sissil's progress. It seemed to deflate, then look to the side while it continued to inch towards them. Another whistle caused the snake to slump back and sulkily slither to the right, towards a beautiful woman standing next to a tree.

"You'd be a better keeper if you keep her away from those that need keeping," Simon yelled with sarcasm dripping from his words.

The woman didn't respond but reached up under Sissil's jaw and began patting the beast. A purr began to emanate from the thing and the woman smiled affectionately at the creature. The bond between the two was obvious, and Jackson didn't think he had met a woman who both intrigued and terrified him until then.

"She is that thing's owner?"

"No creature here requires ownership." Her melodic

tone soothed over his nerve endings like woven silk and smoothed the frayed edges.

"I see," he said slowly.

She laughed. "Doubtful."

"Sissil needs a leash. She's a pain in the"—Simon ducked as its tail end whipped where his head had just been—"ass," he finished and glared at the creature.

"Biased perspective." Dorathea extended her arm in the opposite direction of him and Simon. "Bask in the Springs, sweetling."

"Biased because she keeps eating things she shouldn't," Simon grumbled as he offered his hand to Jackson.

Surprisingly, his hand shook as he reached for the offered one.

What a strange place this Neverland is.

He kept an eye on Sissil as he got to his feet, still marveling at the size of the creature. It must be at least twenty-five feet long, seven-feet wide and docile as a kitten in Dorathea's presence.

"Do I want to know what she keeps eating?" He really wasn't sure if he did want to know. What he *did* know, was he felt relief watching the woman and her slithering companion head away from them.

"Anything that intrigues her." Simon shrugged. "Never Creatures, Lost Boys, Pirates, Mermaids." He winced at the last one. "She's been going after me for as long as I've been here."

A memory sprang to Jackson's mind. *'For the love of*

Dorathea, don't lose it ... if she doesn't gut me and use my innards as a bow for this muck up, then she surely will if you lose the darn thing.'

"Would that woman really use your innards as a bow?"

Simon barked out a surprised laugh. "Without hesitation, my friend. She is as lethal as she is beautiful, and don't forget that." Volleying over the fallen tree, Simon turned to him and smirked. "You remember that conversation, do you?"

Did I?

"I remember you saying not to lose something so Dorathea wouldn't gut you." He volleyed over as well and frowned. "What was I not supposed to lose?"

"In due time. We need to get to Pan Manor and back before sunset." The guy gestured at the foliage around them. "The real nightmare begins when the sun goes down." The sound of crunching leaves and dirt filled the air as Simon resumed walking.

"The real nightmare?" he asked, following in step beside his guide.

"Yeah." A humorless laugh left Simon. "The creatures that make Sissil and the Moulines, that thing Sissil ate, look like house pets."

"Lovely ... nothing like adding a doomsday clock to an already stressful situation." He needed to get Calla out of here even more now if there were real life bump-in-the-night creatures that came out at dark. "How far is this place?"

"Not far. It's getting her out that will be most time consuming, I figure."

"Why is that?"

"Depends on the addition to the manor the new Pan made. I haven't been in the new section, so navigating it might take some time if it's extensive," he answered as he tucked his dagger back into his belt as he stepped over a decaying fallen branch. "Whether the Lost Boys or Pan are present will each cause their own set of setbacks too."

While he listened, he scanned the trees when he heard rustling. What looked like a violet-colored monkey swung from one branch and dangled from another by all four limbs, black unicorn horn jutting out from the center of its forehead, and gnashed its teeth repeatedly at him. Glowing yellow eyes tracked him as he continued walking.

"Here's to hoping no one is home, and we hit a streak of luck." As much as the idea of Calla being alone in a strange place concerned him, the idea of her being in a strange place with unknown people made his blood run cold. He had an idea or two regarding what he was going to do to this Pan fellow who kidnapped his daughter, but he needed to make sure she was safe first.

Hang on, Petal. I'm on my way.

CHAPTER 18

PAN MANOR

JACKSON

"*That's* Pan Manor?" Nothing Simon said on their walk to this place had prepared Jackson for the building in front of him. Sure, he had mentioned an addition was added for each new Pan but left out what happened to the old Pan extension.

"The one and only. We'll have to go in through there." Simon pointed to a medieval door; parts of the wooden slats were deteriorated, not sealing the entrance from any elements, but functional enough to keep larger creatures out.

"Why is this place half destroyed?" If it was supposed be welcoming and comforting to children, he felt it fell short of that target, not even in the same direction. Crumbling walls no longer guarded the interior from the elements. The overgrown foliage had begun to reclaim rooms of worn-down furniture due to the crumbling walls no longer guarding the interior. The outer sections were in a worse state, leaving only the stone outline of rooms peeking up through weeds and dirt.

"The Pans are forgotten." Simon pointed to the left, a sole remaining beam jutted out from the building, vines hanging from it like a curtain over a wooden couch, table and chairs. "That was Pierce's addition. He was from 1783RW …"

"RW?"

"Real-World."

He nodded. "Makes sense."

"And that Pan," his tour guide of sorts nodded at the stone outline of the section in front of them beyond the tree line. "That one was the Pan before him. Those still in Neverland who remember him are few and far between, so his rooms are disappearing."

"You mean to tell me that the less people remember of a Pan, the more of the house disappears?" He didn't know the Pan but if he watched over and took care of scared children after death, forgetting him seemed like a disappointment.

"Pretty much. Think of it as the final death a person will experience. When the last person to remember them moves to the afterlife; with them, so does the person's memory. But the new Pans add to it, so it's always there —simply different."

"That's what you meant by you didn't know the new addition, because you don't know this present Pan."

"Yep, so we best get in there. Time's ticking."

"You know the addition that door leads to though?" He sure hoped so.

"Yep, that was Vinnie's." Simon answered, beaming, while looking up towards the sky, then his eyes went wide and he bit his lip.

"What is it?" He scanned the roof but didn't see anything he would find unusual.

"Nothing. Thought I saw something."

He looked at the guy and Simon grinned. "I know that part quite well, and now it's quiet time. Follow me."

Stepping out from the shadows of the trees, he avoided any small twigs or dried leaves as he followed Simon as he led them across the rubble and broken furniture of the older manor. It was rather challenging to keep watch of his surroundings since he wasn't sure what he was keeping an eye out for, but he imagined anything other than a tree would be worth mentioning.

When they came to the door, shadowed by the partial ceiling that remained, the sound of crying met his ears. Simon stilled and put his back to the wall beside the door and motioned for him to do the same. The crying and yelling became louder, as did the sounds of something being dragged or the sound of a struggle. It wasn't Calla but it sounded like a young kid.

"Let me go! I told you I was sorry for picking on her."

He met Simon's gaze and the guy motioned him to stay where he was. Then Simon scooted over to his side opposite the door and got into a crouching position. He figured he would stay standing because if he crouched too, the door wouldn't swing open all the way and depending on how hard it was pushed open, that would be noticed.

"She's in there," he whispered.

Simon put his finger to his lips and nodded, confirming his conclusion was right.

"And she was so ungrateful that I took you out of her class. Not even a thank you. No manners."

A chill skittered down his body as he heard Patrick's voice. He would never get over how similar the Pan was to his brother—it was unnerving.

"I didn't mean to make her cry in class," the other kid wailed. "It was only a joke!"

The door swung open accompanied by a loud creak from the weathered hinges, stopping just as it obstructed his view until the figures moved farther from the entrance. The doppelganger had his hand clenched in the back of the struggling boy's shirt, who he allowed to gain his footing. The kid's face was sporting a black eye, split lip and dried blood under his nose. His shirt had dark blood stains on it as well from what Jackson could see. Recognition hit as he looked at the boy and not his injuries.

That's Dustin, the missing kid in Calla's school. He's in Neverland. His heart hurt as the implications of that settled and he thought of Becky and Calvin, Dustin's parents, whom he and Natalie had talked to during one of the search and rescue gatherings. Their boy was never coming home. No kid should ever be taken from their family and having to endure that kind of treatment was unacceptable. The mere thought of Calla or his little brother being treated like that made his blood boil. He needed to help the kid. His foot must have moved on its own accord, because a hand on his shin that sent a small amount of voltage through his leg had him looking down at an exasperated-looking Simon.

"Did you see her face?" the Pan asked, incredulous. "She looked at me like I was the bad guy. I even think she felt sorry for you."

A yellow glowing ball floated up behind the boys, then over the trees. He could hear chiming bells fading. Pan bent his knees and jumped, lifting a screaming, struggling Dustin into the air and flying over the trees following the chiming light.

"What the bloody hell did you think you were doing?" Simon hissed as he stood. "Do you want to get your daughter out of here or not?"

"Of course, I want to get my daughter"—he snapped and pointed in the direction the boys had gone—"but I have a problem standing by when a kid is being abused."

"This is one of those times where you stay standing by no matter what problem you have with something." Simon got into his personal space and whisper-yelled at him. "If you see something you don't like, but it doesn't have anything to do with getting Calla out of here, you ignore it." He poked him in the chest. "Do you understand?"

He pushed Simon into the crumbling wall with his hand on the guy's sternum and raised a finger into his face. "If I can help save a boy from that sort of treatment I will, because if this Pan can do that to Dustin, he is capable of doing that to my daughter."

"Dustin?" Simon's brows slammed down. "How do you know the boy's name?"

"He's the kid that went missing in Carston. Dustin was in Calla's class."

"Ah. Got it. Well." Simon pushed his hand off his chest and straightened his shirt. "Nothing you can do for him now."

He would sure do something about it next time, Simon's opinions be damned. He flexed his fingers to get the residual tingles out and really wanted to know why that kept happening.

"He won't hurt your daughter."

"What makes you so sure?"

Simon shrugged. "This Pan wants acceptance and approval from her. He won't hurt her."

"How do you figure that?! He kidnapped her."

"He kidnapped the cause of her distress first, then brought her here to show her like some loyal pet showing its owner its catch."

"That's messed up."

"Just like this Pan, but you don't have to worry about

him hurting your daughter. It's Tink you must worry about."

"Who's Tink?" he asked as he stepped back and let Simon walk past him and around the open door. Following Simon into the manor, they stepped into a room that felt like an old Victorian-style home.

"The yellow glow bug you saw fly away that Pan followed when he took off. That's Tink."

Jackson stepped onto the oversized rug and peered around, noting the coat rack and grandfather clock with a pendulum that wasn't moving. His footsteps were quiet against the wooden floor as he followed Simon into the hallway, with throw rugs strewn at the entrances to other rooms. The wallpaper was a truly hideous design that peeked out behind portraits of people in old-fashioned dress. To the left, a door led to what looked like a billiard or smoking room men used to occupy.

To the right was a living room with a small table coupled with a few wing-backed chairs with antimacassars. A fireplace stood empty with the metal gates open and a poker laying across the rug on the floor—abandoned. The next room he passed on his right was a kitchen and dining room with old amenities. At the end of the hallway, was a staircase with an elaborately carved newel and intricately patterned railing which he assumed lead to the upper floor.

"I need to worry about a bug?" Jackson asked, returning to the previous conversation as he ascended the stairs behind Simon. He didn't see why he should be more afraid of a bug than a person who kidnapped children.

"She's a *fairy*. A vindictive little one at that. She has a thing against your family so I wouldn't be shocked if she harmed your daughter in some way," Simon replied, taking the last step to the second floor.

Rooms with beds and linens occupied this one. There was the same wooden flooring as downstairs; small rugs at every doorway dampened the echo of their steps. Different wallpaper but equally as hideous was on the walls. A family portrait hung at the opposite end of the hallway. Six unsmiling faces with pale-green eyes stared back at him. The youngest boys looked familiar.

"My family? What did my family do to this fairy?"

Simon pressed his ear to a door that seemed out of place in this era, raised his hand and stayed like that for a few beats. When he straightened, he bowed his head as he took a deep breath. He looked back at Jackson with a sad smile. "Nothing. Tink is lashing out because she got her feelings hurt."

He felt his eyebrows raise. "You know that makes no sense, right?"

Simon let his head drop back and mumbled something too low for Jackson to hear, the looked at him, almost exasperated. "Tink's a fairy, they don't make sense. Watch out for boys hanging around. Keep quiet. I don't know the layout, so we have to keep an eye out for all doors we *see*."

"All doors? How big do you think this place is?" He

sure hoped it wasn't a large extension because that meant finding Calla would take longer.

"I hope it isn't big like Vi … the last Pan's was," Simon replied as he turned the handle and pulled it open enough for a stream of light to shine on Simon's face through the opening.

"Well?" he whispered as he waited for Simon to move.

After a moment, Simon closed the door to a small crack and looked up at him, lips pinched into a line. The guy tilted his head and then nodded. "I have good news, and bad news."

"Simon, come on. We don't have time for this. Spit it out so we can get in there."

"Okay then. Good news is I know the place. Bad news is, so do you. Keep your head until we are out of here and I will explain everything when we get Calla back to Neverland Cove."

"What do you mean, 'bad news is, so do you'?"

"Keep your head," Simon reiterated.

"Explain and keep yours."

"You're stubborn."

"Explain, Simon."

"That you're stubborn?"

"No."

"You don't think you are?" Simon asked, perplexed. "I think it's obvious."

"I think I'm going to leave you unconscious on the floor if you keep it up."

"Fine. It's your upper level."

Both eyebrows hit his hairline. "Come again?"

"It's your upper level."

"My upper level? As in … my house?"

"Yes …" Simon said slowly. "Are you having trouble with words today?"

It was possible it wasn't even his own personal upper level because the layout was common. *Right?*

"Questions later. Just be thankful we know the layout. It will make it easier."

Simon had a point; it didn't sit well but Jackson nodded anyway. "Alright then, let's go."

"You're taking all this surprisingly well, have I told you that yet?"

He shrugged. "I thought I was schizophrenic for the past decade. If going along with you makes you stop coming around my family and our house, then I'm going to do it."

"Dislike me that much? I've never done a thing to you."

"You make me feel insane because no one else seems to see you."

"Your daughter does."

"Why is that?"

"She believes in the magic of Neverland like all children."

"I'm not a child."

"You are astonishingly observant. Let's go." A wide grin spread across Simon's face, "Oh!" He reached behind himself and when his arm came back around, it had a butterfly knife in it. "Might need this. Everyone's become a little stab happy recently." Simon opened the door and slid through the opening.

He took a deep breath and sent up a silent prayer he would get Calla out of this place and leave with his own sanity intact, but he had a feeling anything Simon would later divulge would be difficult to digest.

CHAPTER 19

PIECES OF PAN

MERILEE

Mermaid Lagoon was oddly vacant when Merilee arrived in search of Brynn. She silently observed the fledgling collecting stones and shells on the waterbed, swimming from spot to spot searching out her treasures. The delight on Brynn's face when she found another prize made the mermaid's gray eyes light up with joy. She cradled her treasures against her chest as if they were delicate and fragile, radiating tenderness.

Merilee found herself calming as she shared this moment of tranquility from afar. *This is what existence here is supposed to feel like.* Peaceful moments during the sunlit hours to balance the havoc under the night sky. Neverland's unbalance created too much chaos for her to truly relax or feel centered anymore. In truth, she noticed all the beings in Neverland were feeling the effects: more temperamental, more aggressive, more manic. Except for Brynn. She reminded Merilee of Leila, the calm eye in a storm. Everything around Leila could be on any extreme end of the spectrum and she would not be affected. In truth, that was probably why the pirates had chosen Leila. She would not have fought them.

Brynn halted in the water and looked over at her with a smile on her face—arms full of shells and stones. She returned the smile and swam towards the silver-haired wonder, feeling gratitude for the gift Brynn had given her without knowing.

Closer, she could see shells and stones in a variety of colors and sizes, with a heavier presence of the green hue. Pointing to the cargo, she tilted her head in question and Brynn smiled, nodding her head upwards.

Following Brynn's cue, she appeared on the surface the same time as her companion.

"I noticed the Lost Boys collecting stones and shells," Brynn said cheerfully. "So, I thought to offer these in a gesture to encourage them to talk."

"They do enjoy their collections lately. Have you talked to any since you came here?"

Brynn shook her head. "I only spoke to two, but they seemed more inclined to speak about their woes over this Pan's behavior. Nothing surrounding Hook and his crew."

"That's to be expected. The Lost Boys from an earlier

Pan will complain of his replacement," she explained as she followed her to Peak Point Rock, watching as the beauty placed her treasures atop the lower sister rock.

"I feel like this was more centered towards a single act they disagreed with." Brynn pinched her brows as she began arranging the collection by color. "They were speaking about how 'the Patrick' they knew would not have done something as cruel as he had."

"They referred to him as Patrick? Were they acquainted with Pan prior to coming to Neverland?"

"Oh yes, they even spoke of their Real-World adventures with him. I felt sympathy for them though."

Interesting, most Lost Boys aren't known to the Pan.

She was intrigued that a mermaid held a tender spot for these recent Lost Boys who were obviously dealing with some moral struggle. Unfortunately, if they continued to be obnoxious and one of their kin did indeed drown one or two, it would obviously upset Brynn.

"You are fond of these two boys," Merilee said.

"Yes. Each is feeling homesick as well, and they mentioned I remind them of home. It is why I believe they will come back for these shells and stones." Finished with her task, Brynn rested her elbow on the rock and placed her head in her palm. "I feel sympathy for those two. They aren't as careless or cruel as the others."

She reached out and touched Brynn's arm when she noticed tears pooling on her bottom lashes. "Your empathy and kindness may be great assets to possess, especially in a time such as this." She removed her hand and caressed the silver tresses on Brynn's head.

Such a tender soul.

She cupped the side of the mermaid's cheek and smoothed a thumb over her cheekbone, soothing some of the sadness from her eyes. "Can you recall their names? We shall protect them until they cross if it will ease your worry for them." A small boon Merilee could give her. Keeping watch over the other mermaids to ensure they didn't act upon their impulses towards some Lost Boys would be exhausting. Already there had been rumors of dragging a few boys to the Ferryman, but she would do her best to ensure those two Lost Boys were protected.

The added bonus of learning about Pan from a peer's point of view could be valuable as well.

"Wren and Oliver. They also mentioned a Hugh, who is even more upset at Pan than they were. Seems he knew Pan from the Real-World too and refuses to leave Pan Manor."

"What did Pan do that upset them so?"

"Brought a boy over who wasn't meant to be here and harmed him. The boy was mean to someone Pan cared about, so he hurt him in retaliation."

Although she could understand the logic, she disagreed with the extremes it would take to bring the boy here. That was not part of the rules. She was not even sure if there was a rule about a Pan taking a life in the Real-World; it never was considered a possibility before. Dorathea would not allow such an action to go unaddressed if it was against the guidelines.

Or would she?

After the incident with Vincent's son in Neverland Cove, she realized how little she knew about Dorathea's knowledge base. At one point, she wondered if Dorathea was omniscient but apathetic towards the tailspin Neverland was in.

"I will let it be known if those three are harmed by the hands of our kin, there will be consequences."

Brynn nodded. Her gray eyes shifted up and beyond Merilee's shoulder and went wide before she covered her face with her hands and turned away.

That's when she heard it. The distant sound of a boy screaming. She searched above where the springs fell from the cliff's side and spotted the source of the scream.

Pan flew overhead with Tink by his side. The short and clipped chimes of Tink's voice gave her the impression she was chastising the young man. It reminded her of how Tink would berate and rant at Vincent. The thought of the irritating fairy being frustrated or struggling with her precious revenge Pan made her lips twitch.

"You really don't like flying, do you?" Pan's laughing tone carried down to her and Brynn. Her skin prickled at the glee in his voice.

"We should fly around the island a few times before I

take you there. If Calla won't enjoy making you scream, I will." His laughter echoed around them, then he tilted his head downwards towards her and Brynn. He raised a hand in salute, his cargo being carried by the back of the shirt with the other hand.

The grin he wore reminded her of Vincent's playful smile but felt macabre in the scene before her.

"Good afternoon to you two. It's a beautiful day, isn't it!" he said cheerfully.

It was similar to watching a predator looking harmless while pawing at its dying prey for enjoyment. She didn't respond, too preoccupied with taking it all in but Brynn's hand came to the side and gave a small wave before returning to cover her face.

What in Neverland is going on now?

She followed his descent towards the low sun in the direction of the gates the Ferryman crossed, the terrified boy crying all the while.

"That must be the boy he brought over which upset the others." Brynn's quiet voice sounded watery. "I thought Neverland was a place of existing to sooth a soul during the transition from life to afterlife, not a place of cruelty."

"It is. This is what happens when one selfish being acts on impulse. Many are affected, and often in negative ways," she answered, mind sorting through the possible ways to deal most effectively with all that had transpired recently.

"He enjoyed the other boy's distress," Brynn said as

she turned and looked to where the Pan had flown. "If Wren and Oliver said he wasn't like this before, what happened to him? Is this what becoming a Pan did to him?"

"Tink happened to him, and I don't think she knew what she was creating when she involved herself in his life." She needed to find Simon and see if he had success with locating Vincent's coin. Pan had yet to threaten Vincent, but emotional and volatile was a dangerous combination. She would protect Vincent and see him reunited with his Annelise, even from his own son if she was forced to. It was one thing she would see through. Still, something nagged at her. "You said the third boy wouldn't leave Pan Manor. Did the boys tell you why?"

"No, only that he refused to leave."

"Why would you refuse to leave if a threat was absent …" she pondered aloud.

"To keep watch over the manor?" Brynn suggested.

"To keep watch over something. I'll bet there is something he is protecting."

"But what? Do you think he brought over another that isn't supposed to be here?"

"Unsure …" She trailed off as a recent conversation pertaining to a granddaughter came to mind. "I'll go to Neverland Cove," she said and narrowed her eyes on the small boat making its way across the waters. "Mayhap I'll find other answers along the way."

"Did you find who was taken to Lava Loch?"

She reached into the cloth wrapping that covered her breasts and pulled out the delicate necklace. Lifting Brynn's hand, she placed the chain and pendant in her palm. "It was Leila."

CHAPTER 20

RESCUING CALLA

JACKSON

Jackson was at a loss for words, which was good for him because he needed to be quiet. When Simon had said that it was his upper level, the guy wasn't saying the layout was the same, it was the exact set up of his upper level when he was growing up.

The same plants on the shelf in the hallway between the bathroom and his room. What would have been the linen closet was the door they came through at the top of the stairs. He could see the entryway and the entrance to the living room and kitchen at the bottom of said stairs.

"I have the bathroom; you check your old room," Simon whispered and jerked his chin towards the second room down the hall.

"How do you know where my old room is?"

"Questions later. Calla now."

"Just how long have you been stalking me?" The idea

of being watched when he was younger made the guy shine in a creepier light to him.

"Not as long as you're thinking." Simon rolled his eyes. "And I wasn't stalking you. I was looking out for you."

"What's the difference?"

"One is obsessive, the other is protective."

"Sounds like you need a hobby either way."

"I had one. Now shut up."

Smirking, he followed Simon into the hallway, noting how he avoided the floorboards that creaked like he used to do when he was younger. That conversation later was more intriguing the longer he was around the guy.

He continued past the stand with his mother's spider plant and globe on it, to his old bedroom door. The indents from him pushing pens into the door to open it after returning from a snack were there. Pushing on the door soft enough to avoid the creak that used to sound, he poked his head inside the sunlit room.

His old desk held old textbooks, his lamp and papers splayed out with highlighters and a pen. The scuff marks on the legs of the desk were even there.

Entering the room, he scanned for signs of any occupants. Checking between the side of the bed and far wall and finding it empty, he lay down and looked under the bed. Vacant other than his worn baseball glove and dust, his gaze moved to his closet door.

Maybe Calla is in there. His little girl always favored closets when she played hide-and-seek.

Heart pounding with anticipation of seeing Calla, he got to his feet and jogged across the room towards the closed doors. As he opened the door, the hinges creaked loudly making him cringe at the sound. *Forgot about that.* He listened for footsteps while moving the hung clothing in both directions, making sure the closet was as empty as it appeared.

A tapping on the doorframe had him turning to see a grim-looking Simon. Jackson raised an eyebrow at the guy's expression and started walking towards him in the doorway. Simon tilted his head to the other room and rolled on his heel to allow him by, then fell in step behind him. Heartbeat thrumming in his ears, he walked into Patrick's old room to see Calla curled into a little ball on the bed.

His feet moved of their own accord, and next he knew, he was kneeling beside the bed with his hand reaching to cup his daughter's cheek. She seemed so peaceful; but her puffy eyes, rosy nose and cheeks told him another story. The dried tear trails on her cheeks broke his heart. Her eyebrows came down and she sniffled.

"Calla," he whispered. "Petal."

Her eyelashes fluttered open and she jolted back. Not wanting her to make any noise to let any of the Manor's occupants know they were there, he covered her mouth. "Shhhh, Calla, it's me. Dad. Shhhh."

Her wide eyes took him in and filled with tears. He gave her a reassuring nod and a smile and she scooted across the bed and threw herself at him; her little arms tightening around his neck, making it hard for him to breathe. He hugged her tightly and held her as she cried silently. Rubbing her back, he felt her trembling eventually slow. "That's it. I got you"—he felt her nod against his cheek—"now take a deep breath for me."

He guided her breathing for a few breaths while keeping an eye on Simon who leaned against the wall, peeking out the slightly ajar door. Simon's eyes met his and Jackson could see discomfort in his features. *What's with him?* Calla hiccupped and he closed his eyes, tightening his hold.

"Alright kiddo," he whispered and kissed the side of her head. "It's time to get out of here." He felt relief when she pulled away from him and gave him a curt nod. Cupping her face, he searched her eyes. "Are you going to help us be super quiet, so we don't attract any attention?"

Calla wiped away her stray tears and nodded. "He'll be back soon, won't he?"

"Possibly. So, let's get going, okay? Want me to carry you?"

"No, I got this." She eyed Simon. "You brought the guy from the store?"

Simon turned to face them, and his expression softened when he looked at Calla. "Looks like you were right. Your dad did need a friend after all."

"Ha ha," he said as he helped Calla off the bed.

She peered up at him and her smile brightened his heart. "I knew he would be a good friend for you, Dad."

A shuffling had them stilling and he waited as Simon turned to check down the hallway again. He lifted his hand with his index finger pointed up, then he turned and pointed to Jackson and mouthed the word 'closet.'

Looks like company's coming. He urged his daughter around as he opened the slatted closet door before joining her; not before he eyed Simon pulling his dagger from his belt.

Once the door was closed, he held Calla in front of him with an arm protectively around her and the other palm over her mouth. Through the slats, he could see Simon pivot behind the closed door which allowed Jackson a view of the figure in the hallway.

As the figure approached, so did the grumblings of a disgruntled kid. He didn't know why he continued to be shocked by the things he saw, but when Patrick's childhood friend Hugh walked into the room, he was stunned. The kid didn't look a day older than he had the last time he had taken Patrick to see him. Except now, the boy had a full head of shaggy auburn hair and a healthy weight on him. The kid no longer looked sickly but like a healthy and hearty young man. His heart panged for the kid in joy if this was indeed Hugh.

"Calla?" the boy whispered. "You okay?" As he turned toward the bed, the kid got a face full of Simon. With a squeak, he was plucked from the floor and pushed up against the wall—feet dangling.

Simon held him in place with a forearm across his

chest with dagger in hand, and covered Hugh's mouth with the other.

"Well, well, well. What do we have here? A Lost Boy who should have minded his own business." Simon's voice made the hairs on Jackson's arms stand on end, but what really bothered him was the fact that Calla seemed to stop breathing.

He felt something wet hit his hand that was over her mouth. Removing it, he put his hand on her shoulders and bent down to check on her. She stared out towards Simon and Hugh and her wide eyes were moving back and forth. The tears pooling on her lower lids spilled over and rolled down her cheeks.

"Stop him," her choked-out syllables barely audible.

"Was he mean to you?" he whispered.

Calla shook her head, then turned to face him. "No, he wasn't mean to me." She frowned. "Would you not help him if he was?"

"I wasn't going to let Simon hurt him. Only scare him a little more if he had." He wiped away her tears and kissed her on the forehead. Straightening, he stepped in front of Calla and pushed the door open. He didn't see a point in remaining hidden if there was only one Lost Boy. Simon had made it seem like a more dangerous situation.

As the slatted door creaked, both heads turned his way.

"Let him go, Simon. If it's just him, you can tie him up or something. We gotta get going." With Calla's hand in his, he led her towards the partially open door. The sooner they got out of there, the better.

The boy's blue eyes went wide, and Simon looked disappointed.

"Jackson?" the boy yelped.

At his name, he stopped and studied the boy more closely.

Simon let go of his hold and took a step back from the boy, letting the kid's feet hit the floor.

"It IS you." The boy's eyes went impossibly wider and shifted between him and Simon. "Why are *you* here?" he squeaked.

"How do you know my name?"

"I'm Hugh."

"As in Patrick's friend, Hugh?" Jackson rubbed his forehead as the dull ache increased. He struggled with the concept of this place, all that Simon had explained so far; but visual confirmation of someone he knew passed away being here was really beginning to make his head hurt.

"You remember me?" Hugh perked up, the same crooked grin Jackson remembered adorning his face.

Of course, Hugh is here. I guessed it was him a minute ago. This is the oddest place.

It was surreal seeing Hugh alive and hearty. His red curls that fell out during his treatments now sprung in complete disarray. He wore a green shirt with a faded picture of a plastic army man on it which was tight around his stomach, and his navy-blue shorts were cut offs like Simon's. Jackson looked for the leather strap he knew Simon and the doppelganger wore but didn't see one on Hugh.

"Looking good kiddo," he said, heart feeling a little lighter seeing the boy doing well. Then he looked to Simon and nodded towards the door. "We're leaving."

"Lead the way, Cap," Simon said, giving him a salute, and smirked at Hugh's grinning face.

He rolled his eyes at the ridiculous nickname and headed to the doorway. Opening the door to search the hallway, he was relieved to find it empty. Calla's hand in his tightened, and he gave her hand three quick squeezes to reassure her he was going to take care of her.

Nothing but the sounds of birds and rustling of leaves outside disturbed the silence of the house. With his eye on the sunlight shining up the stairs he stepped into the hallway, and started leading them to the door at the end of the hallway where they came in from. With each step he heard from the trio behind him, he felt more like he was leading bulls in an antique shop. He knew they weren't being loud, but everything seemed exaggerated with the ache in his head. Glancing back, he saw that Simon was behind Calla with Hugh bringing up the rear.

Hugh grinned as his blue eyes met Jackson's. As suddenly as the grin appeared, it faded, and Hugh's complexion paled. His eyes ping ponged all over the hallway, then over the railing and down the stairs.

Curious what had the boy worried, he stopped walking. "What is it?" Jackson asked.

"Does Patrick know you're here?" he whispered, worry in his expression.

He frowned. "Patrick?"

Simon smacked Hugh on the shoulder, who in turn looked up and glared at the blonde. "Don't hit me," he whisper-yelled.

"Don't talk then," Simon retorted.

"Does he know Jackson is here though?" He inclined his head towards him while directing his question to Simon, who once again smacked him in the shoulder—harder. "Ow." Hugh rubbed his shoulder.

"Stop hitting him." Calla's quiet plea from behind him had Simon leaning and looking in her direction, mouth opening in what would no doubt be a sarcastic comment.

"Please."

The soft word from her had the blonde closing his mouth. His features softened and he nodded. "Only because you asked so nicely."

He turned to see his daughter's cheeks turn pink. When she peeked up at him, he raised an eyebrow and she quickly looked away to step further behind him.

"Hugh, you said Patrick is here?" he asked, returning his attention to the boy.

Looking uncomfortable and eyes on Simon, Hugh nodded.

"For the love," Simon said and blew out a breath. "Yes, Jackson." He huffed out a breath and faced him. "Patrick is in Neverland. Has been for a little while. I told you I would explain once we got your daughter home. So let me keep my word and stop asking questions until we get her out of here." He looked at Hugh. "These Lost Boys are unpredictable."

"I'm not. Not all of us are as erratic as the newcomers," Hugh said testily.

"Either way, most of them would come here and they would sooner stab Jackson and throw his daughter back in that room."

"Stab?" he and Calla said in unison.

Simon sighed. "Stab. S-T-A-B. As in sliced through and bleeding."

Jackson scanned the windows and stairway, slightly more concerned than before. "You're being serious?"

"You're an adult male in Neverland," Hugh answered with a shrug. "Pirate."

"How does that make me a Pirate?"

Simon's long exasperated groan would have been amusing any other time.

"Jackson, you're an adult, and adults are pirates. Hughie here"—Simon gestured towards Hugh with a wave of his arm—"already explained that."

"Dad, we need to get you out of here. I don't want you to get hurt."

"DAD?!" Hugh burst out.

Simon smacked him on the shoulder.

"Stop that!" Calla hissed.

"He talked," Simon defended.

"You said you wouldn't."

"I talked before, and you didn't hit me then," Hugh pointed out.

"Oh, I'm sorry." Simon reached out and cuffed Hugh on the back of the head.

Jackson took a few steps towards Simon and hit him on the shoulder. "Will you cut it out," he hissed. "Stop hitting Hugh."

Rubbing his shoulder, Simon pouted. "But he's the one who keeps talking."

"Only because I was asked a question."

"A question you're not supposed to be answering."

"How was I supposed to know I'm not supposed to answer questions?"

"Because I hit you, Hughie. Not hard to figure out."

"My name is Hugh, not Hughie."

"More like halfwit," Simon muttered under his breath.

Popping Simon on the back of the head for that comment, Jackson took satisfaction in the glare Simon gave him while he rubbed the back of his head. He felt empathy for his Uncle Alex in this moment. Turning to Hugh, he answered. "Yes, I'm Calla's dad."

"That much time has gone by?" Hugh looked perplexed.

"What?"

Voices outside grabbed his attention. It sounded like they were coming from the front of the house, which meant whoever came through the front door would see them if they moved any further ahead. Using his arm to keep Calla behind him, he moved her backwards towards the wall as the door downstairs opened and the voices entered the house.

"Hey, Hugh!" a slightly familiar voice yelled, tickling a memory that he couldn't quite reach. "You will never guess what we saw! Where are ya?!"

Hugh leaned over the railing. "Hey guys, I'll be right down!" he yelled and eyed Simon. "Where you guys heading?" he whispered.

Simon shoved his hands in his pockets and didn't answer.

"I can help." He pointed to Calla and then to Jackson. "You need me, unless you have someone else to help."

"Hurry up, bro! I'm going to make some iced tea for us!"

"I'll get the cookies!" said a second voice from downstairs.

Simon sighed. "Neverland Cove."

Hugh nodded. "Got it. Be there as soon as I can." As he walked past Jackson he smiled. "See you soon."

He smiled back at the kiddo and marveled again at how full of life he was as Hugh headed down the stairs.

"Don't you eat all the cookies like last time! I only got three!" Hugh yelled as his shadow covered the door they needed to reach.

"You better hurry up then. Oliver was talking about how much he missed his mom's homemade chocolate chip cookies."

Jackson followed the shadow's progress as he imagined Hugh and the others going into the kitchen until the shadow disappeared.

"I bet he does, those cookies were amazing." Hugh's voice sounded wistful. "What did you guys see anyway?"

Stepping forward, he looked behind him at his daughter and pointed to his eyes and then to his feet before placing his finger over his lips. She nodded with a look of determination on her face.

"You know the mermaids at Mermaid Lagoon? Well, we saw one who looked like—"

"Let's go," Simon said with a much too cheerful grin.

Keeping Calla close and being mindful of the creaking floorboards, he led them towards the wooden door, hoping Hugh didn't tell the other's they had been there.

CHAPTER 21

OUT OF HAND

MERILEE

"She didn't even care!" Pan whined at Vincent, who stood with a stunned look on his face.

Merilee surfaced from the water in time to catch the whiny statement and almost groaned with annoyance. She had had enough with whiny children for the next season and debated going back to Silent Sanctuary until Pan went back to doing whatever it was this one did.

"I beg your pardon; you did what to a kid?"

Pan rolled his eyes. "He was picking on her and none of the other kids or adults did anything about it. She would cry and cry when Natalie couldn't hear her, and Jackson's never around because he's always working. So, I took care of it like a good uncle should," he said, puffing up his shoulders.

"You killed a kid, Patrick! That's not what a good uncle should do!" Vincent exploded.

"He was neglected at home anyway. His parents won't even notice him missing."

"You are so wrong in this!" Vincent yelled. "You don't get to do that! You don't get to end children's lives because they make someone cry! You don't get to end children's lives. Period!"

"He was the only one," Pan responded, flippantly. "And I did it for Calla. I even beat him up a little for every time he pushed her or threw something at her, and she looked at me like *I* was the terrible person."

"Of course, she did!" Vincent said and threw his hands up in the air. "If you brought him here, and she knows about Neverland because of what you told her, then she knows what happens to kids for them to come here." Vincent paced, hands in his hair. "Take her back."

"He can't take her back yet." Tink's voice preceded her presence and her projection's appearance. "He needs to fix the mess the Lost Boys are creating."

"Do not," Pan retorted, a disgusted look on his face. "That's Dora's job."

Merilee winced. She may not have much compassion towards this Pan but knowing how Dorathea would retaliate to such blatant disrespect made her hope the Keeper didn't know how he viewed her.

"Patrick!" Vincent snapped. "Be respectful. It's not her job to manage Lost Boys. That falls to you and Tink."

"Fine," Pan said cockily and looked at Tink. "You go deal with it."

From the look on Tink's face, she imagined the fairy

wanted to drown the twerp in the water a few feet away. Disturbingly, she found herself agreeing with the fairy. She would do it herself if she could.

"No, you do it. You brought them over. You keep them in line. I've never had such an unruly lot here." Tink pointed to Vincent. "He did a much better job."

"No, he didn't. And you told me I could create my own family with the Lost Boys I brought over, and that's what I did. They all came here and promised they wouldn't leave. So, I will let them do what they want to keep them happy."

"He *did* do a better job as a guide." Tink extended her arm and bent down to eye level with Pan, "He guided them. He kept them from creating chaos and tensions where there shouldn't be any. He sent the ones who no longer served a purpose here to the Ferryman. He did what he needed to do. So. He. Did. Better."

"He left!" Pan yelled. "He left you. He left the Lost Boys. He left Neverland." His voice cracked and a sob escaped. "He left mom. He left Jackson. He left me! He *still* wants to leave me. The only thing he is good at is leaving!"

"Patrick," Vincent said as he started to walk towards Pan but when Pan raised his hand to ward him off— Vincent halted.

"I don't need your comfort, or your 'sorrys.'" His eyes started to shine with hues of amber. "What I need is you to stay here. Not leave me, again. I need Jackson and Calla to stay here. I need my family to stop abandoning me." He glared at Vincent and then at Tink. "I need the Lost Boys to be happy and stay here because *I* need them to."

"At least put a limit on the days they can wreak havoc then," Tink snapped.

"Fine!" Patrick snapped back. "I'll talk to them. I have to check on Calla anyway." With that, he bent his legs and jumped into the air, flying out of the hole at the top of the cenote.

"You happy Tink?! You've broken my son."

"As he said, you left. Seems to be something you're good at. Abandoning those who need you."

"Get out," Vincent growled. "I've got nothing left to say to you, until you fix this and help my son."

"I could simply drown you here and say you left. Would solve your problem of being so insufferable."

Like Hal she would let that happen. If that fairy touched Vincent, Merilee had a special jar with Tink's name engraved in it.

"Or better yet." Tink started circling around Vincent who watched her, hatred seeping from his expression. "I could tell him you couldn't take what he had done to that poor boy and killed yourself." Her laugh echoed off the walls. "Poor boy would never forgive himself—or you."

Merilee tensed; ready to intervene if she needed to— consequences be damned.

"Tell him his dad would rather live out his soul's existence in the abyss than be here with him."

Vincent remained silent and watched her.

"Well?" she spat impatiently. "Nothing to say now?"

She could see Vincent's mind was working in the nuances in his eyes as he continued to stare at Tink. The tension in the air was palpable between the two and the longer Vincent remained quiet, the more agitated Tink became, fidgeting with her hair and crossing, then uncrossing her arms.

A slow grin appeared on Vincent's face, and his eyes got brighter. "You don't know what you're doing, do you?"

Tink huffed. "Of course I know what I'm doing."

Vincent crossed his arms and stepped forward, inches away from the transparent figure, Tink's true form hovering at chest level with him. "No. You don't," he said with more certainty, looking down at the ball of yellow. "You didn't expect how Patrick would react to any of this did you?"

"No idea what you're talking about."

"Oh, I think you do. You took away his family and gave him endless possibilities, but he isn't doing what you want him to do. You can't control him."

Merilee watched as Tink stepped back and Vincent laughed.

"Hurt me if it makes you feel better, but I don't think you will do a thing. He keeps coming back here because he needs his father."

"One day he won't. He won't need you and I won't need you here anymore," she hissed, then disappeared as she flew through the opening.

"We really need to get me out of here, Mer," he said, as he looked over to where she was. "I can't help Patrick stuck in here."

"Simon is working on it," she said and stretched her muscles to ease the tension.

"Where is he?"

"I don't know. He will be back when he is able."

"Patrick is so lost. I need to get him thinking right."

"And you will," she reassured him because she had no doubt that he would do what he needed to make sure his son was helped.

"What do you know of the boy he … brought over?" he asked, not meeting her eyes.

"Only that he hurt Calla, and Pan inflicted injuries on him before taking him to the Ferryman. Which is where he no doubt just returned from."

"I expected many things when Patrick came over, but not that. That surprised me."

"He is caught between worlds and is trying to join the two. Youth rarely think of consequences, only desired results," she said in hopes to soothe his concern.

"But he knows he killed the kid to bring him over, and he still chose to do it."

"Emotions run deep. And from what those who he brought over before this boy have said, your Patrick is acting in a manner they never would have believed him capable of in the Real-World."

"Wait, he brought over friends from the Real-World?"

Now he met her gaze, and worry was swimming in his pale-green depths.

"From conversations at the lagoon, it appears so."

Vincent dropped his head forward and rubbed his eyes. "What a mess."

"Indeed. And Hook is presently kidnapping and murdering mermaids, only to dump their bodies in Glacier Bay. So, Neverland is a mess all around."

"Why is Hook doing it though? It's one thing to mindlessly kill, a whole other to kill with a purpose."

"That has yet to be decided. I have Isla and Odessa taking some others to Glacier Bay tomorrow to inspect the bodies."

"Isla is involved?" he asked and the corners of his lips twitched.

"Yes. I imagine it will be quickly resolved once I allow Isla free reign."

He dropped his hand and he let the smirk spread across his face. "She is a force of nature on her own. So why the visit today?"

"I needed to isolate one of my fledglings in another cenote. She is extraordinarily empathetic and sensitive to those being mistreated, and we had the misfortune of seeing Pan flying over Mermaid Lagoon while carrying the beaten and bloody boy. The boy was crying and screaming."

"Ah. That must have been difficult for her," he said as he took a seat beside his notebook. He picked up his pen and placed the notebook on his lap.

"It was. Since I know the tunnels well, I lead her to her own isolation spot for a time."

"How do you know when she is ready to leave?"

"She enjoys solitude more than company due to her sensitivity. Brynn would love to be left there indefinitely if I let her."

"Brynn? Soft name for a soft heart," he said with a soft smile.

"Quite a fitting name, indeed."

CHAPTER 22

CAUGHT IN THE MIDDLE
JACKSON

Simon passed him in the hallway of the Victorian addition of the manor, reaching the doorway to what remained of Pierce's addition.

The late afternoon sun shone bright behind the lush tree leaves which illuminated the forest in a brighter, richer green. The glowing fireflies fluttering about the furniture only added to the majesty of the view.

Calla had her small hand clasped in his and the other wrapped around his forearm—hugging him close. Glancing down, he saw her eyes were wide and moving in all directions and her mouth was hanging open.

"Everything okay?" He brushed his hand down her hair to her chin and tilted her head up. "You okay?"

She nodded and smiled at him. "I'm alright, Dad. It's just so pretty."

His lips turned up and he turned to take in the scene in front of them. There was a majestic quality to the sight; from the oversized leaves and colorful flowers taking over the rubble of the outer section, to the backdrop of the forest. "You're right. It is a pretty sight."

"Let's admire the scenery from the cove, shall we," Simon said, and inclined his head in the direction of the forest. "I really don't want to be here when Pan returns."

Calla shuddered and he nodded as he ushered her out the door with a hand at her back. Thankfully, they made it to the tree line without incident and he let out a deep breath as he peered back at the manor to search the windows and doors.

"So, this is the Neverland Forest. Let me be your guide."

Calla's giggle in response to Simon's statement warmed his chest. He met Simon's eyes over Calla's head, and mouthed the words, "thank you." The blonde gave him a slight nod and returned his attention to Calla.

"Since you undoubtably have had quite the adventure already, let me show you the calmer parts of Neverland." His gameshow host impression in full swing, he looped his arm for Calla to take. Once she entwined her arm with his, he patted her hand and began walking like a true gentleman. "I'm sure glad you found slippers in the manor. Although pretty, the rocks and twigs will still cut up your little feet."

"Oh, Hugh gave these to me," she responded.

Jackson peered down at the slippers on her feet and smiled at the video game theme. He made a note in his mind to thank Hugh for his thoughtfulness.

"Good old Hughie." Simon grinned at Calla's responding giggle.

"He really didn't like you calling him that."

"No? I thought he quite enjoyed it."

"Do you know Hugh?" she asked.

"I've seen him around but never talked with him much." Simon shrugged. "That might change if he was smart enough to look after you."

"He did look after you, right?" Jackson needed to hear it from her. He wanted to know what had happened in detail since Pan took her but didn't want to push her. None of them needed her to break down right then.

She turned towards him. "Yeah Dad, he watched out for me. When I woke up and JP took me to see what he had done to Dustin, I was so scared. I screamed at him that he couldn't do that and was scared he was going to hurt me too. But Hugh said he wouldn't leave my side or let him hurt me."

"But you were alone when we came in," he stated.

"He probably had to get a drink or something." She lifted a shoulder and dropped it. "He stayed with me telling me stories about mermaids until I stopped crying and fell asleep."

"Did JP—"

"Let's call him Patrick or Pan, shall we?" Simon suggested as he threw a stick into the distance. He winked at Calla and jabbed his thumb in Jackson's direction. "It'll be easier for Daddy-o to come to terms with it that way."

"Let's *not* call me Daddy-o."

"Fine. But no more of this JP stuff. Your brother is Pan and that is that."

"My brother is Pan and that is that." Saying the words felt ridiculous. Then again, what didn't feel ridiculous to him anymore? His life was filled with the odd and the unusual lately. Why would his brother embodying the role of Pan, guiding lost boys' souls to a magical island, and eventually to the Ferryman to cross over to some afterlife realms be any different? It all sounded so fanciful to him. He half expected to be jarred awake at any moment—kind of hoped for it.

When he was younger, he often thought about what happened when a person died. Whether a person had a soul or not; and if so, did they reincarnate to live another life? Does the person rejoin the collection of others in an afterlife? Or was there just simply nothing after a person died? For him, he found comfort in the notion of a soul moving on to live a new life, or rejoining others. The death of his family felt less bleak if he imagined them together in some afterlife that existed.

He'd assumed this little nugget of knowledge of truth about Patrick would have brought him a sense of comfort knowing his little brother lived on. Unfortunately, Patrick's behavior and actions were more than a little disturbing. His brother had kidnapped his daughter after killing her classmate and then proceeded to beat the kid up. Well, he assumed Patrick had been the one who did the beating.

"Did Patrick say why he brought you here?"

"He didn't say exactly. He went on about how he thought I would be happy he protected me." She grimaced. "Like I wanted that to happen to Dustin. I just wanted him to leave me alone, not be brought here." She sniffled. "It's my fault he was taken."

He reached out and stopped Calla, bending down to rest on his heels so he could look into her watery eyes. "It is not your fault he was taken. You had no control over what Patrick did." He waited until she blew out a breath and nodded. "You are only responsible for you. Don't carry that burden on your shoulders."

Her little arms wrapped around his neck, and he hugged her close.

After all that she had been through lately, the absolute last thing he wanted was for her to carry any feelings of responsibility for what Patrick had done. He rubbed her back and at Simon's throat clearing, he noticed the guy was fidgeting and seemed antsy.

"We gotta get going, the sun is getting close to the horizon," was his response to Jackson's raised eyebrow.

He narrowed his eyes at the blatant lie, but let it go. "You good?" he asked Calla as he leaned back and rubbed the tears from under her eyes with his thumb.

She gave him a little smile. "Yeah, let's go home."

"Want me to carry you or give you a piggyback ride?"

"Nah, I'm good. I can walk. Plus, he can't show me the wonders of the forest as he said if you carry me."

Simon grinned and extended his arm. "How absolutely true, M'lady. Come, let's see if we can find fireflies the colors of the rainbows as we walk. They start coming out around this time."

As they made their way to the cove, that is precisely what Simon did. Jackson found himself grateful for Simon's presence and his patience with his daughter. The guy seemed to know when to distract her to keep her mind occupied on the task and not dwell on the dangers they were in, when all the while he could tell he was keeping vigilant of their surroundings. He had made the right choice it seemed in trusting Simon.

When they reached the tree line of the sandy beach, the setting sun was shining a bright amber glow on the trees and water. It reminded him of the embers of a burning log with its brilliant colors.

Calla gasped. "Can I go touch the water? It looks so pretty, Dad." She turned towards him with her hands steepled in a prayer.

Looking in Simon's direction, he received a nod of confirmation. "Yeah, you can go."

She whooped and her little legs hopped over a fallen branch before breaking the tree line. An arm came out from behind a tree and grabbed her around the waist and she screamed.

He lunged forward at the same time Simon yelled her name and rushed onto the sand.

"Samuel," Simon growled.

"Ello, Simon." The man returned the greeting, teeth missing in his wide grin. "Fancy seeing you here, with a little lass to boot." His arm was wrapped around Calla's waist, suspending her off the ground; the other arm rested across her upper chest with a dagger in his hand. That dagger laying on her shoulder keeping them in check. "This be the lass the Pan brought over," Samuel said and sniffed Calla's hair.

He took a step forward at the disgusting display of affection. His daughter whimpered as the man moved back to keep at least ten feet between them. "Don't you fucking do that again."

The man's eyes shifted to him and narrowed as he looked him up and down. "And who might you be?"

"The person who is going to kill you if you hurt her." He didn't think he would ever be in a position to take a life, or whether he could if the possibility ever arose, but he would without a doubt, hurt this man if anything happened to his daughter.

"Kin then. Father?" The man jerked and pointed the blade at Simon, who had moved farther away from Jackson. "Hey now! There will be none of that sneaking around me business." He flicked his knife in Jackson's direction. "What's your business with this one? You are always in the thick of everything."

"Just found him hanging about, thought I would give him a tour of this wonderful place. How about you let her go and I won't have to hurt you, Samuel."

"As if you could. You don't have the balls to kill me. Hook would be pissed at you."

"You may be his favorite, but that little girl has been through enough."

"I'd be thinking Hook would like to meet her. Heard she is important to the Pan. The young boy could be interested in a trade. A coin for a lass. He could buy her back."

He eased closer towards the man and his daughter, who had given up her struggles and now had silent tears running down her face as she pleaded with him with her eyes. *Hang on, Petal.*

"Why aren't you with the Hook and his crew? If you're here, that's where you should be," Samuel asked him while pointing the blade at him and motioning him to back up.

"Not interested in joining his crew. Only came to get her," he responded. Movement in the water behind the man and Calla caught his attention briefly.

"Why would Hook be interested in Pan's coin anyway?" Simon asked, regaining Samuel's attention.

Simon managed to move to the left, far enough to be close to the water's edge, effectively creating a wide triangle with Jackson on the right on the forest side. If he recalled correctly, the section of water directly behind the man and Calla was deeper. He sent a prayer to whoever would listen that the man didn't fall into the water and drag his daughter down with him.

A dome of bright red broke the surface silently preceding a forehead then orange eyes glaring at Samuel's back. He quickly looked away to not draw attention to her and looked at Simon, hoping to catch his attention. *Is this new person a threat?* He didn't know.

"My Captain is needing more treasures. The mermaids haven't been as forthcoming with their treasure trove locations as he had hoped. Seems they would rather die for some odd reason."

The eyes of the red-haired woman narrowed and began to shine a brighter tangerine. When he looked to Simon, the guy met his eyes and rubbed his neck, then balled his fist; thumb extended in a thumbs up as he put it back to his side. He wiggled the thumb back and forth.

"You guys are killing mermaids now for coins? Can't imagine Merilee is pleased with that," Simon said and continued the conversation.

His gaze moved to Samuel and then back to Simon's hand, which was now open with his thumb and index finger touching. Then his middle finger touched his thumb.

Eight. The guy is counting down. He was suddenly glad Natalie bought the baby sign language book when Calla was younger and made him learn a bit of it. His gaze went to Calla who was watching him, and he lifted his hands slightly and inhaled deeply, then lowered his hands and let out the breath. When he repeated the action, she followed his lead and took a deep breath and released it. He needed her calmer for whatever Simon did when he reached zero.

"I reckon she isn't pleased and that's why she let her unhinged-one pin five of our crew to the Never Bight.

Their heads were barely above the waters, so they drowned slowly whenever the waves rippled over their faces. Terrible way to go, that."

Five.

"Why the interest in Pan's coin? He hasn't cared for it until now."

Four.

"That, you'd be havin' to ask him when he gets here. Had me waiting for Merilee to show up but this lass was a better find. He'll be pleased."

Two.

Calla squeaked when the man adjusted his hold on her, and Simon's arm went behind his back and then extended forward letting his dagger fly.

His heart almost stopped as the blade left Simon's hand in the trajectory of his daughter. Determined to get to her, the sand shifted under the soles of his shoes with each step he made until his hand gripped around her slender arm. Simon's dagger sank into the base of the man's neck, a foot away from where Calla's head was.

Pulling her from Samuel's loosened grip, he felt the anger boiling over. He kicked at the man's knee and felt satisfaction as Samuel buckled to the sand while he tried reaching for the handle protruding from his throat.

He cradled Calla close with a hand on the back of her head when she buried her face in his chest.

The gurgling sounds Samuel was making, along with the blood pouring from where the handle was sticking out, turned Jackson's stomach. With eyes wide and wild,

Samuel reached up for the dagger but never got a chance to touch it. A slender arm reached around from behind and came across his chest, pulling him down and back on to the sand.

Red hair clung to the side of the woman's face as she leaned her arm on Samuel's chest while smiling manically down at him. When he made a particularly gross wet rasping sound, Calla tried to pull away and look.

"No Calla, you don't need to see this"—he kissed the top of her head—"hum a song so you don't have to hear anything."

He felt her raise her arms and he saw her cover her ears. The vibration on her humming against his chest reassured him she was okay, and he continued to watch the spectacle in front of him.

Simon came to stand beside him and rubbed Calla's back. She looked up at him and smiled before burrowing back into his chest.

"Do you think we should stop her?" Jackson asked. He really wasn't sure what the etiquette was in this situation. Although he didn't have fond feelings for the man, he wasn't comfortable with watching a man die.

"Nope," Simon said and popped the 'P'. Then shoved a hand in a pocket and rested his arm over Jackson's shoulders. "Isla heard all she needed to. That pirate always loved talking too much and this is her right. I'm not going to take that away from her."

"My dear, dear Samuel. You and I are due for an adventure." Isla's sickly sweet tone carried to Jackson.

She slapped away the hand when it reached for the dagger she was using to pin Samuel to the sand. "No, you don't want to do that. Let me ask you a question. Was it you who took Leila? You and she used to chat often if I remember correctly, you know, back when you had a heart."

Samuel's legs kicked when she twisted the knife and Jackson almost gagged. One look at Simon's grinning face and he was glad the guy was on his side—there was a dark streak in him.

"Oops," Isla said. "Simon dear," her now florescent-orange eyes looked towards them, "will you or the other one be needing Samuel here?"

"We got what we needed from him. He's all yours, Isla."

Her smile was wide and all teeth. "Wonderful," she purred and faced a terrified Samuel. "We get to go for a trip to Lava Loch! You know, where Leila burned to death? Isn't this going to be fun!" she exclaimed, as giddy as a kid told they would get to fill a bag with whatever they want at a candy store.

He held tighter to Calla as she started sobbing and rubbed her back. "Hum, Petal." He wished he could take this away for her.

As a writhing Samuel was dragged by the dagger in his neck into the water, he felt relieved that was over.

"She took my dagger," Simon said irritably.

"That man dropped his when your dagger hit his throat." He pointed to the blade resting on the sand.

"Ooo!" Simon perked up and scampered to the weapon. Picking it up, he examined it. "It's got a good balance. Almost as good as the one Vinnie gave me." He turned and started walking back towards him and Calla.

There was movement in the water and Simon turned, throwing his newly acquired dagger in the direction of the emerging form. A hand grasped it before it met the face of the hand's owner. A blue-haired woman with eyes of aqua.

Did women just swim in the water's here? Or were these the mermaids Simon and Samuel were talking about?

Aqua eyes looked up at Simon, incredibly unimpressed, and she waved the dagger in her grip. He felt his mouth drop open as he recognized her.

She is the mermaid in my dreams—well, nightmares.

With that revelation, he wasn't sure if he should intervene on Simon's behalf; and if he was honest with himself, the way Simon looked as though he was about to be berated by a parent was almost amusing. The guy looked incredibly young at that moment, and the blue-haired woman had her tongue in her cheek, seeming to be choosing her reaction.

CHAPTER 23

SENDING CALLA HOME

MERILEE

"I'm sorry, Merilee. We just had a run-in with Samuel and I'm a little on edge still," Simon said as he toed the sand with his boot.

"I presume Samuel confessed a transgression worthy of his punishment by the two of you?" she responded, still attempting to piece together the events that transpired.

She had come from visiting Vincent, only to see a manically smiling Isla dragging Hook's second in command below the surface. The wired mermaid had ripped out the dagger without any care and handed it to Merilee, pure glee in her eyes as Samuel's scream traveled through the water. She recognized the dagger immediately and almost groaned in agitation. Simon was always involved in the messes; she almost believed if he wasn't in the middle of some sort of chaos he would go to the Ferryman out of boredom.

"Oh, aye. Isla came upon us when Samuel had Calla and was threatening to take her to Hook for Pan to trade his coin. The poor girl was terrified."

"Calla? She is here?" Merilee's eyes searched the beach and halted as her gaze landed on a carbon copy of Vincent sheltering a little blond girl in his arms. Gaze returning to Simon, she raised the dagger he had thrown at her, handle towards him for him to grab. She wasn't about to hurt Simon with it now that her anger had cooled. "I would have preferred more thought and less action regarding Hook's second. That is going to be an action he will not take lightly."

"I know," Simon admitted. "But Calla was scared, he sniffed her and was being creepy." A shudder went through him. "Then talking about selling her to Pan like she wasn't a person. It pissed me off and Isla was already itching to get her hands on him. I figured she could take care of the ass." He walked toward her and took the dagger with the black onyx embedded in the handle. "Now I have another blade since Isla dragged Samuel away with mine."

She rolled her eyes and decided to hold onto Simon's dagger which she had tucked behind her upper back by her chest wraps. A small gasp made her look towards Vincent's lineage, and a girl with many of her father's sharp features was staring at her with red puffy eyes. Poor thing had a reddened nose and tear stains running down her cheeks. She felt the urge to go after Isla and stab Samuel for upsetting the young one in such a fashion.

"Hello youngling," she said with a smile.

The girl's eyes widened, and she looked up at Jackson who hadn't looked away since she joined them.

"Hello again, Jackson."

"She knows you!" The girl's wonder was clear in her voice between the random hiccups and shaky breaths. "And you didn't tell me you knew a mermaid, Dad!"

Jackson broke eye contact with her and looked down at his offspring. "I forgot?" he said, raising a single black eyebrow.

His unsure response was endearing. She could see Vincent's influence in his mannerisms.

"I can help calm her, if you wish."

"Can I go see her?" Calla asked, hopeful.

The fact he looked to Simon for guidance before making his decision wasn't lost on her. She was pleased there was trust building between the two. He was going to need someone he felt was trustworthy in this world.

"Merilee won't hurt her. That's not what she does," Simon said before nodding and returning to his inspection of the new blade.

They walked towards her, Calla slightly behind Jackson, with her hands on his arm in a white-knuckled grip. He remained watchful and guarded as tension emanated from him with each step in the sand.

"I have no intention to harm her," she tried to reassure him but got the feeling that nothing would be reassuring to him at the moment. *Well, nothing other than Simon.*

His hair fell forward over his eyebrows following his curt nod at her words. When they came close to the sandbar edge, they stopped within a few feet of where she was resting her arms.

"Come, dip your toes in the water." She looked at both, hoping it was clear both were welcome to do so.

Letting go of her father's arm, Calla sat on the sand and extended her legs forward, dipping her feet in the warm water. When Jackson stepped closer to her, she wrapped her little arm around his calf and leaned against it. The girl hiccupped and let out a deep breath, smiling as a small orange fish swam next to her toe.

"You've had quite the adventure, haven't you little one?" She picked up a smooth white stone that lay in the sand—similar to the ones Brynn had been collecting. Holding out her hand with her palm up, she offered the smooth flat stone that lay in the center. "I hear worry stones help keep the troubles at bay."

Calla smiled and took her offering. "Thank you. You're nice and very pretty."

"I should hope the first mermaid you formally meet would show kindness. It would look bad on the rest of us if that wasn't the case," she teased. "I'm Merilee."

"I'm Calla." The girl studied her for a moment. "Patrick was nice at first too. But he lied about that. He's a mean boy."

"Yes, that happens sometimes. Especially when a

person is hurting and would do anything for the pain to stop." She felt Jackson's eyes on her, and she continued. "I bet he misses his family and that's why he brought you here."

"Yeah, he said he missed them. Can't you talk to him, Dad?" She looked up at Jackson, who now had both eyebrows raised.

"First, your Dad has to accept that it is his brother who is Pan, and not some look-a-like," Simon interjected. "Makes it kind of hard to have a heart to heart if he doesn't."

"No concerns on that score." Jackson ran his fingers through his hair. "I got to the accepting part during our trip back here through the forest."

"So, you can talk to him and help him feel better like you help me feel better," the little voice offered; hope filled her words.

"I don't think I have much of a choice now. Especially with what Samuel was saying about wanting something from Patrick." He looked at Simon.

Merilee could see the protective streak in Jackson that Vincent once taunted Tink with. She didn't understand how he could still feel that way towards a person who abducted his daughter, but she wasn't known for being protective exactly—well, usually.

A figure emerged from the trees, and she smiled inwardly as a Lost Boy she had thrown in the lagoon bounded towards them. She wondered if Simon was going to throw the dagger he was currently playing with at the poor boy.

"Hey guys!" the boy called out when his feet reached the beach and kicked up sand as he neared. Jackson tensed before turning and stepping to block a paler Calla.

Simon looked over and sighed. "What took you so long, Hughie?"

"Stop calling me Hughie. My name is Hugh," he said, slowing his pace as he approached; then he stopped altogether when his eyes met hers.

She waved at the boy she now knew was Hugh and smirked at his eyes shifting between the three of them, appearing unsure if he should come closer. The fact Hugh was the name of the Lost Boy who refused to leave Pan Manor wasn't lost on her. Her eyes went to Calla. *Hugh was protecting her.*

"I … uh … needed to find my coin. It's been a long time since I buried it when I came here." His voice wavered, then he lifted his index finger to point at her. "Why is she here?"

Simon laughed and looked down at her. "You made a friend with another Lost Boy, or did you threaten to drown this one too?"

"Neither." Her lips twitched.

He looked back towards Hugh. "You scared of a mermaid?"

"No!" Hugh exclaimed, a little too forcefully to pass as believable. "I just don't want to get dunked in the water again by that one. I swear she was going to drown me. All I said was that I needed a break from the Pan."

Simon laughed again. "Yeah, she likes to dunk us into the water whenever we irritate her or need our heads cleared."

A poke to her arm made Merilee switch her focus to Calla who was leaning towards her, eyes glittering with amusement. "Did you really throw them into the water?"

"I did," she responded in a loud whisper, enjoying how her eyes twinkled in merriment.

Calla's laugh floated around her, soothing her nerves and easing her tension. The ripple of its vibrations caressed her skin. If she had to guess, if she went to see the dying reef just outside of the cove's entrance, it would have regained its color and life.

A child's laugh was a powerful force on Neverland, which many were unaware of. That beautifully healing laugh had Jackson turning towards her with a smile and a question in his eyes.

"I'm sorry," Calla said, then looked at Simon and burst into guffaws. "You both seem so angry that a mermaid threw you in the water. A MERMAID! I'd be happy if a mermaid threw me in the water."

"Don't even think about it," Jackson warned Merilee.

"Wasn't even a thought," she said in a placating tone. "She's adorable and not irritating like those two." She inclined her head towards Simon and Hugh.

"I'm adorable," Simon proclaimed.

"According to who?" Hugh challenged.

"Me and Isla," he answered.

"The unhinged one?!" Hugh squeaked. "I'm not sure that's a good thing."

She laughed, feeling the foreign sound come from her throat, a missed sensation. "Hugh may have more survival skills than you Simon."

"Hugh, did you mention us being in the manor to the boys that came to the house?" Jackson asked.

Hugh sobered and shook his head. "To Oliver and Wren? No, I didn't say anything. They were too excited about something else to even give me a chance to talk."

Jackson narrowed his eyes. "Oliver and Wren? Like the boys that hung out with you and Patrick?"

"Umm … yeah. That would be them." The hesitation in his voice was clear.

Her conversation with Brynn came to mind. Brynn had been conversing with a Wren and Oliver who claimed to have known this Pan from his life in the Real-World. Those must be the boys.

"Let me guess, Patrick brought them over?" Jackson's tone suggested he already knew the answer.

Hugh simply nodded, then looked to her before looking down.

"What were they excited about?" Simon asked.

Hugh gave him an odd look, then his gaze ping-ponged between all of them. "Oh nothing. A mermaid was topless, and they had to tell me about it." He rolled his eyes. "You know, boobs are a thing."

What a despicable attempt at lying.

Simon's head tilted to the side, and he opened his mouth in what she predicted would be a statement that would call out the lie—mermaids knew to be covered when around Neverland—but he stopped himself. Perhaps he was noticing the unease in Hugh's mannerisms like she was.

She remembered that Brynn reminded the two Lost Boys—Oliver and Wren—of home. If that was what they were so excited to tell this one, why did he lie now? A possibility formed in her mind, and she would venture she was correct.

Leaning closer to a slack-jawed Calla, she cupped her own mouth with one hand. "Well that certainly would be a sight for boys to see now wouldn't it."

When the girl looked over at her, she made a goofy face which had the desired effect and made Calla laugh.

"But I bet your mother is missing you." Smiling, she reached out slowly—aware of Jackson watching her movements—and cupped Calla's cheek. "We should get you home."

The girl closed her eyes and leaned into her hand, bringing her own small hand up and placing it on the back of Merilee's. The small gesture softened her more towards the child as the offer of her trust was precious. As much peace as she was giving the child, in return, the child was unknowingly gifting her the same.

"Natalie will be terrified and worried to death; it's already been too long," Jackson said.

Simon nodded and placed his new dagger in his belt.

"I want to see my family," Hugh said. "I just want to make sure they are okay and are happy."

"That's not a good idea, Hugh," she warned. "Lost Boy's rarely like what they find when they go back. Very few ever want to, but it has almost universally negatively affected the Lost Boy."

"I don't think it's a bad idea," Jackson interjected. "His family has done many things in his honor and so has the town of Carston." His smile was big as he spoke, as if remembering what he spoke of brought him joy. "He should go, Merilee. It would be good closure."

"All that aside, I need him to help me bring Calla back," Simon said as he stretched his arms over his head. "The weight of the living soul and all that." He dropped his arms and smiled at her. "I can bring her home and play tour guide."

She nodded. "Very well. Don't stay too long over there you two. Jackson will need you here."

"Will I see you again?" Calla asked. "What if Patrick comes back?"

"He's not going to come back for you," Jackson said. "I'm going to make sure that doesn't happen again."

"So here is what you do"—she began—"you never leave a window open, and always leave a light on because he can't come in then."

"Remember Calla, be aware if you hear bells in the air. Pan and Tink are never far away from each other," Simon added.

The water rippled as Jackson lifted his daughter to

her feet and hugged her close. He kissed her on the side of the head and breathed her in. "I'll see you in a little bit, okay. Be good for Simon and hug your mom for me."

"I will. Love you." Calla's voice was quiet and watery.

"Love you too, Petal. Now time to go. The sooner I deal with Patrick the sooner I get to come home."

"Come on little lass. Time to go for a trip. Don't worry, you'll have me and Hughie with you the whole time." Simon walked her into the water with Hugh on her other side.

"Does it work the same as when I came over?" Hugh asked.

"Yes, but you'll feel woozy because part of your energy is going to surround Calla to protect her."

Calla turned around and waved at her and Jackson. Then she looked up at Simon, then Hugh, and nodded.

"Think of Carston Lake and hold the little lady's hand."

She smiled as the trio walked farther into the water before jumping in and becoming fully submerged.

"You put a lot of trust in Simon for letting him take your daughter."

"He hasn't done me wrong yet, and I know I can trust him."

"Why's that?"

"Call it a feeling."

The ticking of a familiar watch brought her attention back to the reason she had been there in the first place. "Did he tell you about needing your watch?"

"He said I needed to bring it but not why."

She held out her hand. "Can I borrow it for a moment?"

"No."

"I will return it very shortly."

He continued to hesitate.

"Simon will know how to find me if I don't return it."

After a few moments of silence, he nodded and undid the strap on the watch. She reached back into her chest wrapping and grabbed Simon's old dagger. She lifted it up to him with the handle first as a trade.

"Don't get into any trouble while I'm gone."

"Not my intention."

With a single nod, she submerged herself into the water, giddiness coursing through her as the watch thrummed with electricity in her palm. *Vincent will finally be free.*

Idly she wondered if she should have prepared Jackson for what was to come but decided it didn't matter.

CHAPTER 24

AWKWARD REUNION

JACKSON

His diaphragm expanded as he deeply inhaled the warm air. Essentially standing in a place of limbo between life and death was awe inspiring. It made sense now why the colors were so vibrant, the sky and waters so clear.

Jackson never would have imagined the past twenty-four hours were real if he hadn't experienced it himself. Calla was abducted by the little brother he thought died years ago; was just escorted back home by a boy he himself had mourned, and a young man he believed was a hallucination for years. Patrick lived on but seemed to be in as much trouble as he was causing which didn't sit well.

The surface of the water rippled where the mermaid submerged herself moments ago. He recognized her the moment she broke the surface and caught the dagger.

The more he watched Simon and her interact, the more he remembered the nightmare and other conversations.

Simon had mentioned the reason this all felt familiar was because he had been here before. Was he remembering then?

He shook his head, trying to clear the fog around the memories he felt were just beyond his grasp. The bantering between the two, and the way Simon looked like he was being berated by a parent, was amusing but also seemed normal; like it was the natural way those two communicated.

"What has the water done to offend you?"

He started at the smoky female voice. To his left was Dorathea a few steps away, her face a mask of indifference. The ends of her dark hair danced in the wind, as did the fabric of her sheet dress; a belt adorned the dress, with a dangling dagger similar to the one in his hand. She continued toward him until she stood next to him and peered into the water herself.

"Where is Sissil?" He scanned the tree line behind them, expecting to see the shiny pink danger rope staring at him from between the trees. Not meeting that creature again wouldn't bother him in the slightest.

"Eating." She stood straight and amber eyes met his. "Where is your daughter?"

"Home."

"Must have been difficult to say goodbye."

"Always is. I'll see her again soon." *The sooner the better.*

"Indeed. Your brother will be upset she has gone." She looked back to the water.

"How do you know he is my brother?" *Does this entire island know who I am?* The idea was unnerving.

"I simply do."

Well, isn't she forthcoming with information.

"It's hard to believe he is my brother, though. He's different. Unrecognizable in some ways," he admitted and huffed out a humorless laugh. "It's almost easier to believe it isn't him."

"He is, and always will be. He is different because he pays the price for another's actions. As do you."

"Me?" He wasn't sure about that unless she was talking about losing Patrick.

She nodded, and that was all the answer he got from the woman. Her head turned in his direction, her sight focused beyond him as she lifted her arm to point behind him. "In time, there will be balance but not before several trials for many have passed."

Following her arm, he saw a ship in the distance. Its sails bowed and inhabitants moved around quickly to avoid objects being thrown at them from the water. He squinted his eyes, trying to see more details to understand. It looked as though people in the water were throwing large rocks or debris at the ship, while the occupants swung swords at the water as they dangled from the lines.

"All have been affected by her actions, and she remains unaware of the repercussions."

"Who?"

"Tink."

"The bug?" He returned to look at her in time to see her lips press in a thin line but turned up at the corners.

"The fairy. The Pan's and Hook's overseer on the island. She caused more havoc than she intended or can control." She inclined her head towards the scene beyond the entrance of the cove. "The effects are spiraling."

"She doesn't seem to be a favorite with people here."

"Once upon a time but no longer. Now others are needed to intervene." She looked at him and it felt like she was seeing into him. "You and your brother, included."

"I'll stay until my brother isn't in danger from that man"—he pointed towards the ship—"then I'm returning to my wife and daughter. You guys can deal with the rest of this. Tink is not my problem."

"You have a more significant role here than you believe. Your family in its entirety does. It's not often a situation including lineage presents itself in Neverland. It amuses."

"Is that a good thing?"

"Necessary. In time, all will be set back on the correct path. While most balk at their paths being forced, at one point they understand the necessity of what has been done, eventually understanding the creation that comes from destruction. Yours is unique and benefits most here, and those yet to come to Neverland."

"When you say my family in its entirety has an important role, do you mean my wife and daughter?"

"In part. Many you know will be needed."

"Hugh and Simon?"

"Among others."

"Such as …?" His frustration was mounting because pulling information from this woman was like trying to get orange juice from an apple.

A streak of blue swam in front of him in the water. It looked like Merilee, and she carried a person, if the dark form was what it looked like. Here, something could be anything though. *Question is—is that person friend or foe?*

"Who does she have with her? Another guy like Samuel?" If she came across another of Hook's men waiting for her, he wouldn't doubt for a second she would drown him for pissing her off.

"One of the others."

* * *

"Who is this?" Jackson asked as he stepped closer to the edge of the sandbar and bent down to grab the man under his arms to pull him onto the drier sand.

The man's head hung low; his long wet black hair collected sand as it dragged along the ground.

"Someone you'll appreciate having here, I suspect," Merilee responded as she pulled herself up onto the sand. "Flip him on his back and grab his left wrist."

"Did you drown this one?" he asked and rolled the man over. "You seem to have a knack for throwing the

Lost Boys in the water from what I ..." Words left him when his father's pale, unmoving face became visible.

"You could say that it's become a necessary action of late."

Her nonchalant tone almost stunned him as much as the fact he had been right with his jest. "Seriously? You drowned him? Where was he?" *Has he been here the whole time? If he is here, is my mother here too? If so, where is she? Did he know Patrick was here? Did Patrick know their father is here?* So many questions running through his head and he wanted answers to them all.

"Pick up his wrist and rub the watch face counter-clockwise and he can answer those questions himself."

He moved to the opposite side of his father from her. The sand moved beneath his knees when he leaned over and reached for the wrist with the ticking watch. Cold skin paired with the dead weight of the arm churned his stomach. It felt wrong to touch any part of him because in his mind, his father had been dead for over twelve years.

"Be sure to move afterwards. He'll need room."

Merilee sat, combing her hair with her fingers— relaxed as can be. As if this sort of thing happened regularly. Maybe it did here, he didn't know. Nodding, he peered down and rubbed the watch with his index and middle fingers which shook. The arm instantly jerked out of his grasp and water expelled from his father's mouth.

Eyes going wide, Jackson scrambled backwards just

in time for his father to flip over to his stomach and go on his hands and knees, back curling as he vomited up more liquid. The water was leaving his hair as well, which left the strands dry.

Gaze going to the watch, he knew then that the watch wasn't simply an accessory. *The water is going back like it had with me and Simon.*

"I remember a time very similar to this." Her smile, along with her tone and kind aqua eyes relieved some of his panic over what was going on. "You behaved the exact same way when you woke up here the first time. Poor Simon looked more panicked than you do right now."

"When I came here before?"

"Yes, when Tink brought your brother over. You somehow came through and were left floating at the bottom of the cove. I came across you and pulled you up and onto the beach in the same spot." She laughed. "Simon came up out of the water behind you, irritate and spitting fire at me for not telling him Vinnie had died."

He suddenly had flashes of being pulled into the frigid water, his grip on Patrick dragging him down, the feel of pressure around him, warm water filling his mouth as he yelled for his brother, a beautiful woman cupping his cheek while her hair floated around him, burning in his lungs, and her voice saying Simon's name.

He met her gaze, and he could see understanding in them.

"Welcome back."

Then what she said prior registered. "Simon came out of the water after I did, mad about not knowing my father died. He knew my father?"

His father coughed and fell on his back with one leg bent at the knee and a hand resting on his chest over his heart. Chest rising and falling in deep breaths, his father sighed and smiled. "I've missed the sunshine." He turned his head towards Merilee. "Thank you, Mer."

"You're welcome. Don't expect me to do that again. It's one thing to do it to Simon, another to do it to you." She shivered. "No thrill in doing that for you."

His father's laugh made Jackson's heart hurt and eyes burn.

"Don't expect me to ask. I don't know how Simon thought it would be a fun party trick, or how he did it every time he visited," his father said as he sat up. Sand that clung to his olive-green T-shirt fell off as he shook the material from the bottom.

He's really here. Alive.

He watched as his father combed his fingers through his shoulder-length hair and seemed to be looking around. "Where is Simon?"

Jackson caught Merilee's eye movement in his direction, and he braced himself for his father to turn around. *Will he be happy to see me? Will he even recognize me?* The sudden urge to jump in the water to avoid this situation overcame him, but his butt was frozen in the sand—legs useless.

"Hey Simon, thanks for getting my watch back …"

His father's voice died as he caught sight of him. He looked exactly the same as Jackson remembered him, only a few years older than he was. The same pale-green eyes widened slightly.

"Jackson?"

All he could do was nod.

"Why are you here?" His father's head whipped around to Merilee. "Why is he here?! He isn't supposed to be here."

No, I'm not, but the least you could do is say Hi.

"You two look eerily similar. It's like you are twins," she said instead of answering his father's questions.

"Are you kidding me? Why is he here, Mer? You two were supposed to bring me my watch and leave my son in the Real-World, where he is safe! I'm going to kick Simon's ass for this. That guy is so careless and doesn't think before he does anything."

Merilee rolled her eyes.

Jackson snapped out of his daze and got to his feet. "You're not going to do anything to Simon." His tone came out with more authority than he intended but he was not about to let the guy be hurt—especially by his father.

"Excuse me?"

"You can stop yelling at her too. She didn't bring me over. And you're not going to do anything to Simon. He helped me get my daughter back after she was kidnapped and brought here. I agreed to help him."

His father's harsh laugh sounded bitter. "Simon is

nothing if not resourceful. He could have brought Calla back without bringing you to Neverland."

"I'm so glad the first time I see you, you are pissed to see me."

"It's not like that and you know it."

"How would I know it? Simon helped me, he helped all this"—he waved his hand in the air—"make sense. That I wasn't fucking crazy, and did you miss the part where he helped me get my daughter. Do you have any idea how terrified she has been through all this? And if you were here the entire time, why didn't you do something? Where the hell were you?"

"I was trapped in a god-damned cenote for the past who-knows-how-long!" his father shouted back; getting to his feet.

"You don't seem stuck now."

"If Simon hadn't done what he had, you would still be stuck where you were." Merilee sighed. "And from the presence of the Biped with your son here earlier, I assume all is as it should be."

His father shoved his hands in his pockets and growled. "What did Dorathea say to you?"

"That you are an ass."

Merilee snorted and grinned. "Looks like you angered him, Vincent. May I suggest not touching Simon when he returns? Your son appears to be protective of our grown Lost Boy."

"Noted." His father ran his hand through his hair and

tugged on the strands as he looked skywards. "Where is Simon?"

"He and Hugh Brodwick took Calla home."

"Little Hugh is here?"

"Yeah, he died of Leukemia almost three years after you and mom—well, died. He also watched over Calla I guess while she was in Pan Manor. She felt safe around him."

His father nodded. "Lucky for her he was there then." He ran his hand through his hair, agitated. "I'll just have a talk with Simon. He still shouldn't have brought you here. You know that don't you?"

"You should be grateful he did. I wasn't giving anything of mine to him when he actually talked to me and told me he needed me"—he gestured to his father's wrist—"to give that to him. It seems you needed that to get out of wherever you were."

"Better to have fought you for it than bring you here," his father snapped.

"You are angry at the wrong person, Vincent," Merilee reprimanded, but her tone was gentle. "Simon is not the reason you're hurting. He did what he had to, to achieve the results needed. You cannot fight the inevitable."

"I know," his father gritted, then breathed deeply through his nose and sighed. "I know."

A silence fell between the three of them. So many emotions were running through Jackson as he looked at his father. Happiness, anger, confusion, regret and all the emotions in between which his mind restlessly ping ponged around.

The sounds of distant shouting and that of a cannon being shot came from across the water. He turned to see smoke rising from part of the ship and a man being pulled overboard by two figures he assumed were mermaids. In his periphery, his father and Merilee turned in the same direction.

"Nightfall is coming," his father said. "We best get to cover Jacks before the Larnack comes out to play." He came to stand in front of him.

It was unusual to be able to look at the man at eye level and still feel like the little boy who needed a hug. "What's a Larnack?" His voice cracked a bit, so he cleared his throat.

"Remember your pet gecko?"

"Yeah."

"Like that, but the size of our house and with quills like a porcupine."

"Perfect. Are any creatures small here?"

"Other than the Lost Boys and the Mermaids? No."

"Lovely." He could not wait to go home.

"It is good to see you," his father said and wrapped his arms around his shoulders and squeezed. Then he released him from the hold but kept one hand on his shoulder. "You have your coin, right?"

Jackson frowned. "My coin?"

His father turned to Merilee, who was lowering

herself into the water. "Seems Simon left out some crucial details. You sure I can't beat him?"

Delicate shoulders shrugged. "According to my knowledge, those two had a daughter to save from a psychotic Pan and volatile fairy. Covering Neverland basics and its occupants without having your son's mind go into a tailspin would have been challenging enough in the fleeting time they had. *Some* details would trump others."

"Fair enough." He turned back to Jackson. "Did Hugh or Simon mention stopping anywhere or doing anything else before returning here?"

"Hugh wanted to see his family. He seemed upset when he saw me and realized how much time had gone by."

"Mer, do you mind staying here until they return to tell them we've gone to the den at Peak Falls. They should be back shortly and before nightfall."

"I will be remaining in the area to retrieve Brynn for the evening-time festivities. I can pass along the message."

His father clapped him on the shoulder and gave him a little shake, a smile spreading across his face. "Looks like I have a lot to catch up on with you."

CHAPTER 25

FAMILY SECRETS

JACKSON

Jackson followed his father up the steep hill at the back of the cove. The waterfall that fell to his right blocked the entrance to the underwater tunnels that led to Merilee's hideaway, where his father had been conveniently stowed away by Tink.

He shivered as he recalled his father explaining that the only way out was to have Merilee swim him out, but he would run out of oxygen and drown three-quarters of the way through. Hence, their hesitation to try without the guarantee of the watch's protection. The fact Simon had willingly done so to visit his father multiple times showed Jackson how loyal and dedicated the guy could be, and he didn't even know the whole history between Simon and his father.

The loose rocks shifted under him as he stepped on the worn path, made in a zig zag pattern up the side of the hill. It had been well hidden in the back, but he was told his father and the Lost Boys used it often when they used to jump from the top into Neverland Cove's water when they sought a rush.

After cresting the top, his father walked a few feet onto the flat grassy surface and put his hands on his hips. "I forgot how beautiful it was here."

The orange rays of sunshine bathed him as he stepped up beside his father. The surface of the pond a few feet in front of them was so still, it looked like a mirror. It was twenty feet wide, but widened slightly inland, with various boulders and leaves placed around the widest edge in the form of makeshift chairs or benches.

He smelled the grass as he walked over to the edge of the water where it transformed into a waterfall, curious how the surface could be so still and yet be flowing off the cliff to the water below.

"Physics doesn't have the same principles here, Jacks."

"I'm noticing that."

His father's sight was still off towards the half-set sun. The ship's ripples from the breaks in the water widened and caught the orange glows of the sun.

"Looks like that Hook guy and the mermaids came to a truce?"

"No, not a truce." His father shook his head, then turned to him. "An impasse. Both parties acknowledged stalemate."

"Why is there so much hostility between the two?"

"Many reasons I'm told. It all seems to stem from Tink's actions."

They headed towards the end of the pond where three large trees stood, each ten-feet wide and embedded in a mound of earth that was as tall as Jackson. His father went to the middle tree and the vines that trailed down the side of the trunk. He brushed the vines away with his arm and the leaves lit up to bright green as he came in contact with it.

"After you." His free arm disappeared as he swung it into the tree.

Jackson's eyebrows drew down and he came to stand in front of his father, peeking around to the side of the trunk. Small glowing leaves on vines ran across the top of the passage, illuminating the wooden walls and a path into the earth mound behind the trees. The smell of oak, moss and soil invaded his nose as he stepped into the tunnel; crouching slightly as this was obviously meant for smaller individuals.

Smaller like Pan and the Lost Boys.

'I was a Lost Boy, but not anymore.' Simon's words came to mind then.

'... he was angry I didn't tell him Vinnie had died.' Merilee's voice drowned out the sound of his steps.

He rubbed his forehead as he rounded the bend and came to an open furnished room.

'That part is Vinnie's.' Simon had said back in the Pan Manor.

He sucked in a breath as things started to click into place. *'Mer, do you mind remaining here until they return to tell them we've gone to the den by Peak Falls.'*

At the sound of footsteps nearing him, his father stopped to stand beside him.

"You were a Pan, weren't you?"

Putting his hands in his pockets, his father looked around the room lit up by the trailing vines and their leaves weaved throughout the ceiling. "I was. For a long time. Until I met your mother." He patted Jackson on the back and walked into the open room with a grin on his face.

He moved past a seating area on the left with rickety looking chairs with wool blankets thrown haphazardly over the backs, a card game left in play on the small tabletop under a coating of dust, and stopped at an antique-looking chest. The snick of the metal clamps seemed loud in the quiet, as did the metal hinges creaking from the weight of the lid as it opened. Reaching inside, he was moving the contents around before he straightened, holding a cloth pouch with a leather drawstring.

"How did you meet mom if you were a guide for lost boys' souls?" Jackson never knew how they met and when he asked his uncles, they both got the same confused look and couldn't remember.

"I met her and her brothers on the hill near Carston Lake. She was catching fireflies in the tall grass and accidentally caught Tink in a mason jar instead," his father said as he walked past an easel in the back that was placed on one side of a large fur rug, the other half had a worn spot and pillow propped against the wall. He reached into a wicker basket beside the fur which had pieces of branches and other materials sticking out.

A cubby carved into the dirt wall above the table caught Jackson's attention. It had other cards and older-style games, along with a few candles, cups, small plates, and a small pouch. He stepped down the slight incline towards the table and reached into the hollowed-out cubby. Picking the pouch up, he could hear marbles clinking with the movement.

"She captured Tink? The evil fairy everyone keeps mentioning?"

That couldn't have been good.

"The one and only," he confirmed while focusing on whatever it was he was looking for. "Tink wasn't how she is now back then. She and I were playing hide-and-seek before we were going to stop at an orphanage in Drisdale."

"The town an hour away from Carston?"

"Same one. There was a terrible flu sweeping through it and many children weren't surviving." He paused as he sat on the worn-out spot on the fur, legs stretched out and crossed at the ankles, a small piece of wood and knife in hand.

The movement seemed so natural, as if he had done it a couple dozen times, which he very well could have.

"It would be hard to see that. I have a hard enough time when Calla has the flu, let alone watching children sick enough to pass away from it." His stomach turned at the thought of what it must have been like for his father to witness children that sick, over and over. The idea of being a Pan with those responsibilities was not for the faint of heart.

"It was difficult. Sometimes knowing what comes after for them loses its comfort. Those are the times Tink and I would play before we went. That dusk though, while I was counting in the grass while Tink hid, I heard this amazing laugh." His father closed his eyes and smiled. "It was full of so much joy it made the heaviness of the tasks ahead disappear, and I couldn't stop myself from smiling. That's when I saw your mom, beautiful brown eyes full of excitement and a smile that lit up her face more than Tink's glow did."

"Mom had a contagious laugh."

His father opened his eyes and looked at him—still smiling. "She did. Distracted me enough I forgot Tink was in the jar your mother handed me. Which didn't endear her to Tink. I think that's the first time Tink was ever jealous of your mother."

"The first time?"

"Come, take a seat," his father said, pointing to one of the stuffed sleeping bags propped up against the right wall as he put down the large satchel he had been looking through. "Patrick told me you had married your high school sweetheart. He spoke fondly of her."

He carried the pouch he was certain was full of marbles, to where the four stuffed sleeping bags sat and adjusted his position until whatever it was stuffed with shifted to a more comfortable position. A sharp stab of pain on the top of his left butt-cheek made him wince and he leaned forward as he reached behind and grabbed Simon's dagger he forgot was there.

"Yeah, they were close. Nat became like the big sister that kept me from being overbearing. She also never hesitated to give him heck if he did something stupid." He chuckled as he placed the dagger next to his hip. "Sometimes she even beat me to berating him for doing something stupid."

"Sounds like you two made a good team in looking after your brother."

"Not good enough," Jackson mumbled as he untied the leather strap around the pouch in his lap.

"Why would you think that?"

"Because of where he ended up." His fingers pulled apart the fabric, revealing a collection of multi-colored marbles.

"He ended up here because of Tink, not anything you didn't do."

"I could have mentioned something sooner to Alex and Marcus about his strange behavior," he said as he dumped the pouch on the floor beside him. Whoever owned these had a clear preference of the color green.

"Tink was already interfering by then I assume. She mentioned how you were a pain in her ass because you kept saving Patrick from her plans."

At this, he looked up at his father. "You talked to her?"

"She would come down and brag all about how much fun she was having playing with Patrick to rub it in that I was helpless to stop her. Then she would rant about how you were always getting in the way," his father explained, whittling away at the wooden branch, his own pouch open beside him. "I would laugh and say you would never let anything happen to him, and I was right."

"But something did happen to him."

"And you followed him over from the Real-World. You would die to protect him. That says a lot about how far Tink had to go to get him here. You did well."

"Why does Tink hate our family? And is mom here somewhere? Are you here because you were a Pan?" He had so many questions.

"I forgot Tink, like we do when we leave Neverland to grow up. It hurt her feelings and she blamed your mom. So, the night your mother died, Tink brought me here expecting me to be happy to be back."

"Seriously?"

His father nodded. "From what I understand, she thought if she removed the person I left Neverland to be with, then I would happily return. And when that didn't happen, she went after Patrick."

"So … are you dead, or not?"

"I'm not dead, and neither is your brother. Pans are alive but their aging is paused while they are fulfilling the role. Either they go to the Real-World when they find *their Darling* and live out their lives, or they choose to cross with the Ferryman because more of their family has usually passed on and crossed by then."

He looked up at the glowing leaves trying to process

what his father had said. To be fair, this whole situation had been a lot to process. His brain was about to start misfiring or short-circuit soon. *How could a simple thing like 'forgetting,' make a being so angry she would destroy my family?*

"If you're here, is mom?" He hadn't seen any women except for Dorathea, and he got the impression she was an anomaly. She held a different aura around her.

His father's sad eyes met his. "No, she would have crossed with the Ferryman. Tink brought me here, and since she enchanted my coin to not disappear when I left Neverland, I was stuck here without it."

"That's why I needed your watch Jackie-boy. His coin is inside." Simon's voice came from the direction of the entrance just as he and another guy came into view.

"Calla safe?"

"Snug as a bug in her own bed. Your wife is over the moon she is home," Simon said with a bow. "You're welcome."

"Thanks for getting her home. I owe you."

"Don't forget to thank Houston." Simon waved in the other guy's direction. "He might take offense."

The new guy was only slightly shorter than Simon by half a foot. His auburn hair was an unruly mess, and his clothes were way too small, coming up his calves and forearms.

Jackson's eyes widened as recognition hit. The blue eyes and freckles were the same as a young Lost Boy he once knew.

"Hugh?"

"In the flesh!" His voice was noticeably lower, with a squeak on the 'e'. "You don't have to thank me. I know you'd do the same for me if the roles were reversed. I didn't know this place was here though! This is *such* a cool hide out," he stated as his eyes wandered over the room.

Simon laughed as he walked over to a stuffed sleeping bag beside him. The guy bunched a lump of filler to prop himself up as he leaned on his side, one leg bent. "Someone gets to fast-track through puberty, Neverland style."

"Mr. Connelly?" Hugh's eyes went wide. "What are you doing here? Wait, did *they* send you to come get Patrick?"

"Hush, Hughie. Jackson's got the marbles out." Simon said and lunged for a handful.

"Hello, Hugh. You seem to have grown out of your clothes." His father chuckled.

Jackson swatted the guy's hand away from the pile, only to have him use the other one to grab a handful, a cheeky grin on his face as he leaned back, tossing a marble in the air and catching it.

"You're annoying sometimes, you know that?" he informed him.

The blonde saluted him with two fingers and winked.

"Simon and Marcus used to play marbles often when they came here," his father said.

"Uncle Marcus knew him?" He pointed to Simon.

That's a shocker. He really couldn't imagine Marcus playing marbles though, or any activity with Simon without it turning into a competition. Those two seemed to share a similar disposition.

"Yeah, he did. So did your uncle Alex. Except Alex would refuse to play marbles with those two because it inevitably turned into them pelting each other with the glass balls."

"Marcus was a cheating crook. He always had the best Tolley and there was no way anyone could make the shots he did."

"You hid that Tolley on him and he still beat you with Annelise's," his father said, pointing the piece of wood with the bark shaved off at him.

"He played for bloody keeps too," Simon grumbled, and Hugh laughed.

"I can imagine Alex pinching the bridge of his nose after the marbles started flying," Jackson said.

The scene he imagined of Alex doing just that while counting to ten as Simon and Marcus whipped marbles at each other, made him grin.

"Oh yeah, the nose pinch was standard practice. Your mother would sit right here," his father said and pointed to the seat beside him next to the easel. "And use her sketchpad as a shield from marbles gone astray, all the while laughing."

"Poor Ann was always in tears by the end of it," Simon added.

"So, you were here before? With Patrick's mom?" Hugh's brows came down. "How?"

Simon chucked a marble at Hugh as the guy walked over. "He was a Pan, Hughbert."

"No way!" His eyes went wide as he turned to Jackson's father.

"Way," his father said.

"That's so cool."

"Any who." Simon rolled his eyes. "It's nice to see you out of your cenote. Merilee is no doubt disappointed she doesn't get to drown me now."

"She didn't seem too keen on drowning me to get me out." His father smirked.

Simon snorted. "You're everyone's favorite."

Hugh grabbed a stuffed sleeping bag and dropped it at the end of the one Jackson sat on, "The blue-haired one drowned you? On purpose? With your permission?"

"No other way to get out of the cenote Vinnie was in except through the underwater tunnels."

Hugh shivered.

"Why are you older?" Jackson asked, perplexed.

"It's cool right! Guess since I went over after being here for so long my appearance aged."

"You look older too," he told Simon. "But not as much." Jackson pointed to his own 5 o'clock shadow on his chin, "You have more facial hair."

Simon scratched his jawline. "Yeah, happens every time."

"Patrick doesn't seem to look older, and he was

visiting Calla weekly. Multiple times a week some weeks from the way Natalie and Calla talked about it."

"That's because he is alive, and his form is in stasis until he relinquishes his role as Pan," his father explained. "Then the Pan coin—"

"Disappears and they forget about Neverland," Simon finished. "It's the thank-you card from the deities," Simon said theatrically. "You give up your life to guide the lost souls and to give comfort to them. So when you are done, you can cross to the Ferryman to essentially die and be with your deceased family, or you can live out a life in the RW."

"Speaking of coins, where is Jackson's?" his father asked.

"I have a coin?"

Simon glared at his father. "I was getting to that."

His father waved the knife in his direction. "Sooner than later would be ideal. Best he knows so he's prepared. He's going to have multiple targets on his back now that *you* brought him here."

"I had to," Jackson interjected, not liking the accusation being flung in that statement. "Don't think for minute you can pin me being here on him. It was my decision."

"You followed the dictate," his father gritted.

"Wouldn't you?" Simon challenged.

"A dictate from who?" Hugh asked, head swiveling between his father and Simon. "And yeah, *why* does Jackson have a coin?"

Simon reached into his shorts pocket and flipped a coin in the air towards him. Catching the cold metal in his palm, he examined the silver piece. It was the same size as the ones he'd seen the others wear around their necks. The skull in the center and crossed swords underneath laid atop a ship on water and was bordered by vines with thorns. A sense of ownership of the coin was instant and unexpected. About as unexpected as the sort of calm that blanketed him the longer he held it.

"I remember this," he said quietly. "This is the pirate coin I dropped by Carston Lake that night Patrick fell through. Why did you take it?"

Simon—who had been arguing with his father—stopped arguing and looked down at the marbles in his hand.

Patrick's screams came back to his mind and brought the memory of icy water splashing into his face and the feel of being submerged completely. Chills formed tiny bumps over his skin as the memories continued. Him yelling in the warm water and fluid filling his lungs. Merilee in the water. A void of nothingness. Merilee out of the water and Simon talking to him but more confusion. More icy water and icicles hitting his neck as he swam out of the dark lake before collapsing; Simon talking again.

"Did I drown?"

"Yeah, you did," Simon said cautiously. "You were only dead for maybe three minutes Neverland time. Like no time at all."

"Jacks?" A hand landed on his shoulder, and his father was sitting on his heels beside him. "You're looking kind of pale there. Talk to me."

"I died. I never knew what happened that day. It's kind of a mindfuck to learn all that I have in the past day, and to top it off with *that* ..." He shook his head, then threw a marble at Simon who was still looking at the dirt floor. "I kept dreaming about it because it was real. I tried to save Patrick and I ended up drowning myself."

Simon nodded. "Yeah, that sums it up."

"No way!" Hugh said in disbelief. "Patrick really knows how to put people through the ringer to get here, hey."

Simon sat up and smacked Hugh on the arm. "Shut up."

"Simon," his father's tone was full of warning.

The blonde huffed and rested his arm on his drawn-up knee and threw a marble into the open pouch. "When you drowned, your coin appeared. Happens to everyone. But you were brought back because you weren't meant to be here yet. So, Dorathea made me take you back."

"That's why I could see you and no one else could?"

"That's a bit more complicated. You have a connection to Neverland because you died here but you could see me because I had your coin on me."

"Why didn't it disappear?" he asked his father.

"Because of the kind of coin it is, that particular one doesn't disappear until you cash it in, so to speak, with the Ferryman."

"What kind of coin is it?" Hugh asked hesitantly.

"You're part of the Hook legacy, and you have the Hook coin," Simon said in a rush.

Hugh's gasp was loud in the silence. "Dude!"

Simon threw another marble at him, successfully hitting him in the forehead.

"Ow."

"So that's my endgame when I die? To be this … Hook?"

"Yeah, that's about right," Simon said and his father glared at him.

"I'm not doing it."

"You don't really have a choice," Simon informed him.

"My father had a choice." The tension in his father's grip on his shoulder increased when he spoke. "I want a choice. I am not going to go around killing mermaids and attacking young boys. That's not me. I won't do it."

"That's not what the Hook's purpose is," his father said, squeezing a little tighter and giving him a little shake.

"I need some air." He shrugged off the hand on his shoulder and got to his feet. Hugh leaned to the side and he stepped around him, mindful not to hurt the boy. He could hear his father and Simon's harsh whispers behind him. The smooth marble in his hand helped to calm his racing heart as he headed to the entrance of the den.

CHAPTER 26

THE HOOK'S ROLE

JACKSON

Fresh air would let him clear his head and help him be able to think. He thought of himself as a level-headed and open-minded person and he knew it would take time for him to find acceptance in some things, but this, this was pushing his boundaries of belief. Not having a choice in what he did when his life ended was not a reality he ever entertained. He imagined reuniting with deceased family members or some sort of reincarnation happening. Becoming some medieval treasure-hunting pirate with a penchant for violence against beautiful creatures and young boys? Not his idea of being rewarded for leading a good life.

The green glow of the leaves curtaining over the entrance was brighter in contrast to the darkness beyond them. The vines brushed over his palms as he moved them aside, revealing an eerily dark version of a once magical-looking plateau.

The water of the pond was so still, he could see the bright white of the moon and its craters clearly on the surface; two stars twinkled next to the glowing orb but nothing else. He approached the pond; side stepping the larger sitting stones and taking a seat on the larger stone bench. He rolled the marble around in his palm in a vain attempt to relax.

The sun had fully set and the sky was void of stars, except the two high in the sky in close proximity to the moon. The reflections on the ocean surface were shifting with the waters in irregular patterns. Squinting his eyes, he tried to make out the cause of the peculiar waves. Periodically, something would break the surface before returning to the water and soft sounds that weren't quite loud or clear enough to be distinguishable made it to his ears.

"You can hear them, can't you?"

His father sat beside him and kicked a stone into the still pond with his shoe before crossing that foot over his other ankle.

"I can hear *something*," Jackson admitted as he kicked a rock into the too-still water. He didn't know what he was hearing but the sound was soothing, like the ripples traveling across the pond's surface and cutting through the moon's reflection.

"That sound you're hearing is the mermaid's singing and luring the grey souls. Their song makes the souls less combative while they are being taken to Hal for repair. That's why it's so soothing."

"How did you know I found it soothing?"

His father raised an eyebrow.

"Right ... this was your home before Carston." He pocketed the marble and ran his hand through his hair.

The soft undercurrent hum in the air was doing an excellent job of easing some of his tension. Now that he knew it was the mermaids singing, he could distinguish different tones in the sound when the grey souls broke the surface. To go down into the water to be closer to the source of the sounds was appealing from this distance; he could only imagine what it would be like in close proximity. "Do I want to know what a grey soul is? Or who Hal is?"

"Grey souls are the ones who walked the line bordering moral and immoral." His father gestured towards the ocean in front of them where Jackson had been looking. "They end up in the Ocean of Souls because they weren't moral enough to line up for the Ferryman but weren't immoral enough to go straight to Hal for mending. And Hal, he is responsible for the broken or damaged souls in need of mending."

"Like purgatory?"

"That is one term for what some consider the darker side of the afterlife; the place where the damaged souls get tortured and such. Other belief systems have their own versions of Hal and his domain."

"By your tone I'm guessing that isn't what it is?"

"I am sure it is a form of torture for them. Hal must mend what is broken and that must be painful for the soul, but without that repair, they never get to cross or return for another lifetime like many chose to do. It's his purpose. We all have a purpose."

"The Hook has an actual purpose? Doesn't seem like a useful one."

"Yes, and it isn't what you thought. The Hook, in this Neverland dynamic, is the captain of the crew responsible for saving the grey souls from the Ocean of Souls and delivering them to the Ferryman. This Hook has been here since I was a Pan, and from my understanding was fine until Tink brought me back here. He also needs to be removed and taken to Hal from what the mermaids have been saying he is doing. The man is broken now since things shifted."

"Where is he now?" There was no sign of the ship, or anyone for that matter.

"Daytime is the Hook's time; nighttime belongs to the mermaids. Anyone caught in the waters rarely makes it out alive. Both parties get more"—his father paused and scratched his neck—"aggressive and focused on their task."

"I'll stay until Patrick is safe because I feel responsible for him being here. But after that, I'm leaving."

"Jacks ..."

"No, I'm not staying. I'm going to live my life with Natalie and I'm going to watch Calla grow up. Neverland is going to have to find a new Hook or wait until I die in my old age."

"I don't think you get to decide when you stay here."

"No? Then who does? A Deity? Fate? A psychopathic fairy?"

"The result is inevitable, the journey there is up to you. I know you've been through a lot. I didn't get the life I wanted to live out, so I understand why you're angry—but trust the process. I have seen so much while being Pan that I cannot do anything *but* trust the process."

"That's you. I can't accept that." He refused to believe he wasn't going to be with Natalie or Calla. The coin clinked against the stone bench as he put it down beside him.

"Keep it on you. If anything happens to you while you're here and you don't have it on you, you might not make it to the Ferryman. You'll enter the Void until you become part of it." His father placed the metal coin in Jackson's hand and curled his fingers over it. "You may not like it Jackson but be smart and safe while you're here. Your rejection of the rules doesn't negate the rules the others here play by."

Jackson nodded, more for his father's sake. "I need to be alone."

When his father continued to sit beside him, irritation prickled his skin. "I need to be alone. I'll be in shortly. Just need to clear my head."

"Okay." His father nodded and patted him on the back as he stood. "I'll talk to Simon and start making a plan on how to deal with Hook and your brother, so he doesn't end up with Hal too."

A clinking beside him had him looking down on the

bench to see his father placing Simon's dagger next to his thigh.

"Stay close and don't take too long. The Larnack isn't the only creature in the night that would love to play with you."

"You would know," he responded. Then a thought popped into his head as he watched his father walk back to the vine-covered entrance—curiosity riding him. "What year were you actually born if you were here before?"

His father's white teeth gleamed in the moonlight. "December 8th, 1896."

Jackson felt his face go blank at the date, and his father chuckled before heading behind the curtain of glowing vines.

1896? If it's 2010, that makes him—he quickly did the math—*114?*

He scrubbed his face with the palms of his hands, then blew out a breath.

His father's words ran through his mind as he picked up the coin which sealed his fate and rolled it over his knuckles. The prospect of his little brother going to a place like Hal's realm made him sick to his stomach. He didn't know exactly what his brother had been up to that warranted a trip there, but from Wren and Oliver going missing to being here … he was sure he wouldn't like the answers when he found out.

Simon said he would explain things once Calla was

safe, so he'd start asking when he was ready to deal with more.

A rough hand covered his mouth and nose, cutting off his air. His own came up and clawed at the hand, trying to break the seal it created but the pressure only increased against his struggle. Jamming his elbow back, it collided with a solid body and a satisfying *'oomph'* came from whoever it belonged to. The grip didn't give. He went to straighten up, hoping to push the person off balance when something hard cracked against the side of his head, causing his vision to dim and him to slump back against what he assumed was the assailant's body.

The feel of something warm trickling down the side of his face registered as his vision swam. A blurred figure came in front of him.

There's two of them. Shit.

His lungs began to burn with the need for oxygen—adding insult to injury.

Then a warm breath was at his ear. "You yell, I'll cut your throat no matter what the Captain wants," warned the deep male voice.

The feel of something hard and sharp along his throat made any thoughts of calling the man's bluff evaporate. Not like he could yell if he couldn't take a breath anyway. Another sharp hit to his skull sealed any decision he might have made about going against these men's wishes.

"Just for good measure. Can't have that Simon boy running out here. Might get a bit messy then."

The grip left his mouth and his chest expanded as his lungs filled with what they craved. Unfortunately for him, it increased his dizziness. When he felt hands grip his ankle, and arms snaked around his chest, he opened his eyes and became nauseous as the world tilted. His head lolled to the side as he was lifted off the stone bench by the two men.

He had a voice and limbs, but all were useless because he couldn't use either no matter how much he tried. Never had he felt so helpless. Well, never had he gotten clocked in the side of the head that hard. Frustrated, he tried again to focus to get a sense of where they were going: to the cove or into the forest? *Maybe the Larnack will come and scare the men off—or eat them.*

A breeze blew up the back of his shirt and caused a shiver to go over him. That's when he remembered the drop off on the opposite side of where he and his father had climbed.

The men stopped and another breeze blew over him.

"On the count of three," the man behind him whispered.

"One."

Are they seriously going to throw me off the side?

He was swung to the right: their grips painful on his skin.

"Two."

Shit, I'm about to get tossed. I could try to take them with me. As much as he tried, he couldn't get his arms to cooperate and move to grab the arms around his chest.

Another swing to the right with more momentum. He

had no idea what was on that other side but he could hear water to his left—he sure hoped it was water. If his limbs decided to work in the water, it wouldn't be so terrible.

"Three."

A final enthusiastic swing to the left and he felt the grips around his chest and ankles let go. Then he was weightless, before he felt nothing but gravity taking him down.

CHAPTER 27
MEET CAPT. HOOK
JACKSON

The two figures leaning over the cliff's edge were shrinking as he attempted to focus. *I wonder what the void is like?* Because he knew he didn't have that damned coin on him. His hair covered part of his vision from the wind of falling, but he didn't care, only wished he would wake up and be next to Natalie.

Natalie. Her brown hair and deep-brown eyes always captured him, as did the spattering of freckles he would run his fingers over as she slept. She fit into his arms perfectly.

He smiled at the image. Then he abruptly hit a net of sorts and began rolling. Round and round, until he landed on a firm surface and got a face full of sand.

Groaning at the pounding in his head, he coughed and opened his eyes.

He was lying on a small beach; a dingy floated nearby

with an occupant he couldn't quite make out. Another man a few feet away was walking towards him, wearing a beige button-up shirt, black slacks, and a sword dangling from his side.

"Looks like they roughed you up a bit," the man said. A boot flipped him over onto his back, successfully getting sand in his eyes and making the world tilt. He blinked, trying to rid them of the sand as arms snaked underneath his and his upper body was lifted.

"I hope you are what the captain needs you to be 'cause I sure am tired of this," the man mumbled, more to himself it seemed, as he dragged Jackson across the beach.

His vision focused enough for him to follow the divots in the sand from where his heels dug in, to where the cliff met the ground. A large fishing net was pegged into the sand and the other side was secured halfway up the cliffside.

One of the men who threw him off the side was falling and hitting the net as his eyes closed. He silently wished the net would disappear and the man would fall flat on the sand, especially if he was the one who clocked him in the head.

"Hurry up! The songs got quiet," another man behind him whisper-yelled. "The mermaids will be back soon and I sure as shit don't wanna be in this dinghy when that happens."

With the sound of water lapping nearby, coupled with the increasing smell of sea, he knew they were close to the large dinghy. The air left his lungs in a grunt when his back collided with the ground and a boot on his sternum pushed him further into the sand—making inhaling difficult.

He opened his eyes, glad the world no longer spun as harshly, and pushed at Beige-shirt's leather boot that was restricting his air. A calloused hand grabbed his left wrist and wrapped a thick rope around it. He slammed—well more like nudged—his hand against the man's wrist but had his right wrist caught in a grip and the rope wrapped around that wrist tightly to his other.

Seriously? The first time I'm alone in this place and I get hit in the head twice, thrown over a cliff and now tied up. Simon is never going to let me live this down. For some reason, he knew Simon would get his dumb ass out of this situation. His father would no doubt come with Simon, but he didn't know how the man would react. Berate him? Be annoyed? He didn't really know what to expect from his father anymore. There was a lot he didn't know about his father.

Clinking got louder and a man with khaki pants and a black polo bent and grabbed him by the legs again. This time Jackson tried to wriggle his legs out of the hold. He opened his mouth to tell the bastard just where he and his buddies could go, when a cool sharp object rested against the side of his neck, and he froze.

"Be a good little captive and I won't slit your throat," Beige-Button-Up said from the other end of the shiny blade.

Jackson narrowed his eyes but remained quiet; he'd left any desire to die back in the Real-World.

The man who dragged him here and tied his wrists, smiled at his lack of response. "That's a good fella. Might survive this after all." The boot lifted from his sternum at the same time the blade left his throat.

Purple-Button-Up climbed into the dinghy in his periphery.

Once again, he was thrown like a sack of grain and landed unceremoniously on the hard wooden planks in the dinghy.

Shit, that hurt.

The wood felt damp and abrasive against his palms as he pushed himself up onto his knees and sat on his heels —finding himself face to face with Samuel.

"You?" Anger rose, as did his confusion at the sight of the man who grabbed Calla before he was dragged by a dagger in his throat into the water by a pissed-off mermaid. His pristine white shirt was free of any blood splatter, but it was the neck which was sans wound that had confusion winning the silent battle over anger.

"How are you still alive?" He didn't know what the rules were here regarding injuries and what a person could survive. Bleeding out and drowning were high up there on the things-he-doubted-anyone-could-survive list; even here, in this place. He lifted his bound hands and touched the tender spot by his temple, hissing in a breath when he made contact. Blood glistened on his fingertips when he brought them away.

Samuel's grin was all teeth. "Thanks for confirming what I suspected."

"Anytime," Jackson said with a shrug. The statement made no sense, but he didn't have the mental capacity to try to understand it right now.

His hands gripped the edge by his side to catch himself from falling as the boat shifted. The two others were pushing the boat farther out into the water before they hopped inside, Black-Button-Up taking a seat beside Samuel and Beige on the beam behind him.

So, it's four against one.

Not the greatest odds for him if he tried to get out of this situation. Oddly enough, he felt more like he was about to be reprimanded for missing a board meeting than being captured by soul collectors. Being surrounded by four men who were in their forties, in button-up shirts and polos, and slacks or khakis, didn't exactly exude physical danger; the swords, and axes on them however, did.

He assessed the restraints while glaring at Samuel and the one who bound him.

"Is this necessary?" he asked, shaking his bound hands in front of him.

"Tying your arms up?" Samuel asked.

"Clearly," Jackson drawled. "Is there a point? Not like I'm going to jump out into that." He gestured with his head to the water.

"Don't know you mate," Beige-Button-Up replied,

then shot a look toward Samuel. "Gotta make sure you make it to Hook."

Water splashed and a shrill screech split the air. A grey arm flung itself over the side of the boat with fingers clawing at the panels where Jackson sat. Wet hair plastered to the person's grey face, covering most of the features as it became visible over the side.

He scuffled across the sole of the small boat trying to get away from the grotesque sight and the horrible gurgling sound it made.

Black Polo stood and extracted his sword from its holder around his waist and sliced the arm off the soul, eliciting a scream from the being. The extremity fell to Jackson's feet with twitching fingers. He gagged when dark sludge oozed out the severed end. Black Polo picked up the arm and flung it over the side with a splash.

Water splashed and something gurgled behind Jackson, then a rancid-smelling appendage came over his shoulder and nails clawed into his chest. "Shit!"

His back hit the side with the force of being pulled back by the soul attempting to crawl into the dinghy using him as leverage. The burn of the fingernails imbedded into his skin was almost distracting enough for him to ignore the smell wafting from the appendage. Putrid and sour, so pungent he could practically taste it. Bile rose into his throat but the watery gasp in his ear had him lurching away from the soul while he pushed at the cold, slippery arm.

Black Polo sat and wiped his hand on his khaki pants,

making no move to come at this one. To Jackson's surprise, Samuel removed his own sword and leaned over, swinging the blade.

He winced from the deafening shriek near his ear. The pressure of the arm disappeared the same time he heard another splash behind him, and the dinghy rocked slightly. The dismembered arm fell into his lap. Black sludge smeared on his jeans' leg from the appendage and bile rose in his throat.

"Do you need a minute alone with the arm?" Samuel sneered.

"You're sick."

The connection of Samuel's fist to his jawbone was solid and knocked his head to the side and back.

Shit, that hurt. He spit blood onto the floor beam. The appendage twitched in his lap and he gripped onto the flesh and threw the arm behind him and into the water. Little drops of that-which-he-was-not-about-to-identify sprinkled on his hair and he was quite sure a droplet landed on his forehead.

"No shame if that's what you're into, but I pegged you for liking the younger, more alive ones," he taunted Samuel.

The cartilage in his nose cracked with the force of the next blow. Warmth trickled from his nose onto his upper lip then down his chin. His eyes watered from the pain radiating from the break, but he forced out a humorless chuckle. "Guess not."

He rubbed his forehead, ridding it of the questionable liquid and wiped his hands off on his pants.

"Why are ye hitting the man?" a distant voice yelled from the ship coming into view around the bend.

"The bloke keeps speaking when he shouldn't," Purple-Button-Up yelled.

"Bring him up. I want a word with him."

"Aye, Captain," Samuel yelled. "Maksim, release his bindings but keep a hold of him until he's on board."

Purple-Button-Up leaned forward and started tugging on the ropes around Jackson's wrists.

So, Maksim is Purple-Button-Up.

"Sasha, you handle the dinghy," Samuel instructed.

Black Polo nodded.

Sasha it is.

He rubbed his wrists as soon as he felt the ropes leave his skin. When he wiped the back of his hand against his upper lip, it came away bloody. The flow of blood was slowing but not as fast as he had hoped. Guess he didn't have super healing here like Samuel.

The ship he had seen in the distance many times was massive as he looked up the side to where a man stood at the top and kicked a rope ladder down the side. The three-mast ship was an older-style vessel. He had always admired the craftsmanship of this era. Traveling back in the 1700s and earlier would have been a feat not for the faint of heart. Cannon barrels protruded from the lower deck, sails drawn up, but the ends could be heard flapping in the breeze along with the metal reels and connectors.

A hand on his left arm pulled him to his feet and shoved him towards Samuel and Beige-Button-Up, who were already climbing the Jacob's ladder.

"Get a move on and don't fall. No one here will save your sorry ass," Maksim sneered.

He raised an eyebrow at the animosity coming from the men. Samuel—he could understand the hatred; he smashed the guy's knee the last time they interacted. But the other two, he had no idea why. Well … other than he hurt their pal.

There was the one he didn't know the name of though; that one sounded more resigned while he dragged Jackson across the sand. Even when he was threatening to slit his throat there wasn't the malice behind it: more performance, maybe? *Is he more friend than foe?*

The wooden beam knocked against the side of the ship, accompanied by the jangling of the chains which made up the rest of the ladder. Following the others' lead, he ascended the unsteady ladder, praying he wouldn't fall. Movement in the water caught his attention, and the silhouettes of numerous souls moved beneath the surface, eliciting a shiver from him. Yeah, diving into the water with the grey souls wasn't on his bucket list.

With each step on the wooden beams, the feeling of rightness became stronger. The closer to the deck, the more at home he felt; it was a feeling he was not keen on because he needed to be alert and not comfortable in these men's presence.

"There be the mystery man of the hour," a robust voice said as Jackson's foot hit the deck.

"I've been waiting to meet ya since I heard Simon was walking around with a man and little girl in tow. What's yer name?"

"Jackson." He didn't see a point in withholding that information. "I presume you're the Hook?" The man had a damned red tricorne hat with a long feather sticking out of it. The justaucorps style coat hung to his knees and was left open, revealing a gold and black waistcoat and white shirt. The man only needed a lacy cravat to match his black breeches and knee-high socks to complete the stereotypical pirate captain look.

"Aye," he said with a flourishing bow. "Now, explain how ye came to be here."

"I'd rather just leave," he said.

Hook began stepping around him with arms behind his back, and his silly hard-soled shoes clicked against the deck.

"One doesn't just leave this place. Unless ye're like that Simon fellow, which I know ye're not. Ye, are different."

"Don't know what you mean."

"Ye be lost but not a grown Lost Boy like him." Hook stopped in front of him and narrowed his eyes. "Ye do look familiar though."

Jackson kept quiet; he could see the madness in Hook's eyes as the swirls of amber moved through his irises—much like Patrick's had whenever he had seen him lately.

Are the glowing eyes a Neverland madness thing?

Hook sighed. "Very well, on to more important matters. What did ye do to my Smee?"

"Your *smee*? What's a smee?"

"My right hand. Samuel is his name. I sent him to the Cove to capture the blue-haired viper." His breath was rank as he leaned in close. "But when some of my men arrived to collect them … no Smee or viper."

"Ask him," Jackson spat. "He's standing right there." He gestured to Samuel, who was leaning against the beam, arms folded. "He can tell you what happened. He started the whole thing."

"That's where we have a bit of a problem. Ye see, he isn't Samuel. He's Theo. Samuel's twin."

"Oh shit," Jackson said out loud.

"Aye, oh shit, indeed," Theo said. "So tell me, what did you do to my brother that you were so shocked he survived? Because, I don't believe he did survive since we haven't seen or heard from him since earlier this afternoon."

"Maybe he went for a walk, or a swim." Jackson's mind raced to see a way out of this.

Theo tsked. "He would have returned by nightfall if he was able."

"Bad form, Jackson. Lying is not the way around

here," Hook chided. "A little fairy told me you would have the answers I need about Smee."

Freaking fairy. He was only ever told about one fairy and if she was in Hook's ear, who knows what kind of trouble he was about to find himself in.

"Do what you will with him but don't kill him. She said he was the key to getting that coin," Hook instructed.

"What coin?" he asked. *Patrick's? Simon's? Mine?*

"Where's Smee?" Hook's tone was hard.

"I don't know." He didn't lie, he had no idea where the fire-haired mermaid took the guy.

"Mayhap Theo can help you remember." His tone turned light as can be, as if saying he brought cookies to the party.

"My pleasure," Theo said as he straightened from the beam and walked towards Jackson.

"Stepan, come," Hook said, turning and heading towards the small set of stairs to the upper deck.

Theo's gaze followed Beige-Button-Up as he walked between them, shoulders stiff and looking like a puppy about to get beat by his owner. Theo dropped the mask he had put on and scowled at the duo.

Stepan's footsteps echoed as he followed Hook up the steps and gradually faded.

"Wow, he replaced your brother quick."

Theo's fist connected below Jackson's diagram, forcing him to fold over, and knees hitting the wooden deck. He coughed as his stomach heaved.

"Take it you're not a fan?" he wheezed. A hard grip on his upper arm had him staggering to a standing position, a pissed off Theo in his face.

"Tell me what you did to my brother?"

"Busted his kneecap," he replied with a grin. "You'll have to talk to a mermaid to find out the rest. A red headed one."

"Good to know," Theo sneered.

"Think he's talking about the one who taunted us the other night with how the others died on the Bight?" Maksim inquired from behind.

Theo lifted his boot, which connected with the side of Jackson's knee eliciting a sickening crunch. Pain shot from his knee up his thigh and down to his toes. He would have gone down again if it wasn't for Maksim holding him up by his arm, but he couldn't hide the groan as the pissed off brother got in his face again. When the man's boot hit his other knee, he swore and fell to the deck, Maksim's hold no longer keeping him up.

"Get the ropes."

The wood felt rough on his cheek as his face rested on the deck. His arms were pulled behind his back and he assumed it was Maksim who was starting to tie his wrists once more. Rough hands grabbed him by his jaw and turned his face up painfully.

"That was payment in kind. Once Hook's got what he needs from you, you'll wish you never came to Neverland." He released his face.

Jackson snorted but instantly regretted it as pain shot through his face from the broken nose. "Already there."

Anger flashed in the man's face a moment before he reared back and hit him in the same spot at the side of his skull as before. This time as his head spun and vision went blurry, he didn't fight it. He hurt—everywhere.

"Where should we put him?" Maksim's voice was distant.

"Attach another rope to his hand and tie him to the mainmast. He can stay there until Hook gets his coin. I'll cut the damn thing off Pan's neck along with his head for making Samuel go after the mermaid keeper."

Jackson felt himself falling into the darkness of unconsciousness, appalled at the words he was hearing but unable to do anything but fall deeper. Maksim's laughter was his macabre lullaby into the dark.

CHAPTER 28

SAVED BY A FAMILIAR FACE

JACKSON

The sun's rays lacked the usual comforts for Merilee as she sat on the sister rock at Mermaid Lagoon. She felt nostalgic, and craved her conversations with Vincent and Simon, when their teasing and laughter were commonplace in a more pleasant time. She found herself swimming to the spot she used to frequently occupy in calmer days.

The lagoon was quieter than earlier visits. No Lost Boys yelling and destroying the vegetation or polluting the waters with the debris. Sounds of the springs made a soothing backdrop to the birds chattering above. She ran her fingers through her hair as she went over the facts Isla and Odessa's party relayed from their trip to Glacier Bay.

It seemed most of the bodies showed puncture wounds of assorted sizes, and a few others came from Lava Loch. With more fledglings missing, her concern rested with finding and retrieving those who were unaccounted for. She had to stop more from going missing before Hal felt it necessary to intervene. He was the most patient being she ever interacted with, but that storm all mermaids could sense below his surface was something she never desired to experience; especially if her responsibilities were those not being taken care of.

The silver-haired beauty appeared in front of her, her grey eyes sad. Merilee had hoped last night's festivities would have helped Brynn adapt or desensitize her to the plight of others. That was not the case.

Isla—who had accompanied Merilee to Mermaid Lagoon—appeared next to Brynn and grinned widely at her.

"What were your findings?" Merilee asked.

"There is a man on the deck, secured to the mainmast," Brynn replied.

"Out in the open?" Isla asked, her head tilted to one side.

"Yes, and beaten quite badly." Concern laced the light-haired beauty's reply.

"Broken for all to see? I bet he's bait." Isla bit her lip and nodded rapidly, making her red strands bounce in the air.

"Bait for who?" Brynn asked, frowning.

"The Pan. Hook probably wants him to come there so he can capture the boy and take his coin. It's what the Smee was saying before Simon's dagger went through his throat," Isla answered.

"Brynn, stay near the ship. If he gets thrown over-board, you will be there to rescue him from the water or souls," she instructed as the mermaid grimaced at Isla's words. Having Brynn stay close in case something happened to Jackson had a dual purpose; it lent Vincent's son aid if he required it, and it also kept Brynn excluded from the fighting that was inevitable.

"As you wish." Brynn gave her a small, thankful smile before disappearing into the water.

"More likely he is bait for Simon then, not Pan," she said while she counted the crew members visible on the deck from a distance. "Hook would know about his Smee by now. Can't imagine it being a coincidence that he has a person involved with your adventure on the beach beaten and tied to the beam."

"Possible, but that"—Isla raised a hand from the water to point up towards the springs above—"makes me believe I am correct."

She followed the direction Isla pointed. Pan was sitting on the top of a tree looking out towards the ship. There was no sign of Tink, but the tiny fairy was never far from that one.

"Indeed. I wonder how the man found himself with Hook in the first place."

Did something happen to Vincent or Simon?

"This idiot let him get taken from Peak Falls," Simon announced angrily as he walked out of the tree line, pointing at a pissed-off Vincent walking beside him. He hopped onto Peak Point Rock and sat heavily on the stone, resting an arm on his bent knee. Simon's hair was a mess, likely from rubbing his hand over as he was apt to do when frustrated.

"I didn't *let* him get taken," Vincent snapped. "He needed space, and I gave it to him. How would *you* have liked me to handle *my son*, Simon? You've been berating me since we discovered he was missing. It's not like you weren't there as well."

That one didn't appear to be in any better shape as he took a seat on the grass beside the large rock and placed his feet on the sister stone where Merilee sat.

"Don't you blame any of this on me. I was in the den explaining this mess to Hugo. I did my part and kept *your son* safe. I managed to take him to Pan Manor from the cove, get his daughter and then back to the cove without incident or harm." Taking out Samuel's dagger, he turned to glare at Vincent. "He was alone with you for ten minutes and he gets taken. Excellent job, *Dad*," Simon sneered.

"He wouldn't have been taken if you hadn't brought him over in the first place!"

"This again?!" Simon threw the dagger, blade-over-handle, and caught it. "You need to get past that."

"No, I don't." Vincent leaned his elbows on his thighs and put his head in his hands; his fingers peeking through his hair.

"Fine, take it up with Dorathea. Better yet, trade your other son for Jackson since he's on the Jolly Roger. Problem solved."

"Ooo, yes please!" Isla agreed, obviously thrilled with the idea.

Vincent's head shot up at that remark, his eyes radiating green. "Are you serious?"

"Yes," Isla answered bluntly.

Simon pointed to her. "She gets it. What about you Mer?"

"The Hydra of solutions, Simon. That would only solve the most immediate problem, and cause more for us to deal with," she said as she noticed the spot where Pan had been earlier was now vacant. "Are either of you aware of the purpose for taking him?"

"Could be a number of reasons but it all depends on how much Hook knows." Simon sighed.

"Either way, we need to get to him before something happens to my son."

"Your son's already been beaten," Isla said with enthusiasm.

"What?" Simon and Vincent said in unison, turning to her.

"Bloody, bruised and tied to the mainmast on the deck." Her amber eyes lit with excitement. "You seem familiar."

Merilee sighed at the topic change. That one could never stay on topic. "This is Vincent all grown up."

Isla's smile beamed as her eyes took in Vincent with appreciation. "Welcome back, Vinnie. So that dark-haired fellow from yesterday was your son?"

"Yes. He is."

"And the psychopath Pan," Simon grumbled.

Vincent punched Simon forcefully in the arm.

Simon winced as he rubbed the spot. "What? He is, isn't he?"

"The mental state of Pan isn't a concern to be focused on at present." Merilee picked up a smooth stone Brynn had left on Peak Point Rock and held it up to examine. "There is movement on the ship and Pan is on the bird's nest."

"Jackson can't be in the middle of that," Simon said as he reached into his pocket and held up the Hook coin.

"He's a *Hook*," Isla squeaked.

"Why do you have that still?" Merilee demanded.

"Found it on the bench next to Peak Falls Pond along with my dagger."

"He's without his coin and defenseless?" She was shocked at the recklessness.

"That's what I said." Simon lifted his arms and dropped them.

"Yes," Vincent gritted and stood. He turned and stepped onto the grass; his hands balled into fists. "I'm going to the beach for a boat and then going to get him."

"We'll gather a few distractions and meet you there," Merilee told Simon, then nodded at Isla who submerged herself. "I have Brynn near the ship keeping watch if Jackson needs aid in the water."

"Thanks, Mer," Simon said and stood up, pocketing the coin, and flipped the dagger one final time. "Think Hook knows his successor is on board?"

"Let's hope that is not the case since you hold his coin."

* * *

"Why don't ye come down here boy." Hook's voice sounded close. Jackson opened his eyes a sliver to see the backs of some truly hideous black boots a couple feet from his face.

"Now why would I do that?"

At the sound of Patrick's voice, he tried to tell where his brother was, but the sunlight intensified the throbbing in his head. That's when it registered how sore his body was. Everything on him hurt, and his stomach roiled. Wasn't limbo supposed to be free of pain and suffering? Because he was feeling all the pain and he was suffering.

"Ye're here for a reason and I be thinking it has to do with this fella."

There was the snick of metal that rang through the air and he froze when Hook extended his arm and tapped the blade tip against his abdomen.

His brother floated down to the deck from wherever he had been and glared at Hook. "Leave him alone. He doesn't belong with you."

"A trade then?" Hook removed the blade and poked it carelessly into the deck at his side to rest his hand on. "Your coin for the fella's release."

"His release, and I won't tell Merilee where you are keeping the fledglings."

Hook picked up the sword and pointed it at Patrick,

who held a smaller version of the sword in the same manner.

"I will have that coin. Whether ye give it to me or I take it off ye."

The grin his brother gave the captain was malicious and his eyes were streaked with amber. "You can try."

Their swords clashed together as they started swinging at each other.

He needed to stop this. This is what he stayed in Neverland to stop. Agony shot through his side as his arm was lifted at an awkward angle and he was lifted and forced to his feet.

Theo sneered at him and looked back at his Captain and Patrick dueling. A circle of the crew formed and were cheering on their Captain, booing as Patrick slashed the man's arm.

He was impressed with the swordsmanship his brother displayed and then he remembered the many times he had seen Patrick when he was younger, sword fighting an imaginary foe.

"You've served your purpose," Theo said in his ear as he lifted a knife to Jackson's throat and led him backwards.

"How you figure that?" He felt the blade cut into his skin as he spoke. A loud cheer went up and Jackson frantically searched the circle for Patrick who was holding his arm but grinning. He needed to figure out how to get to his brother and help him. Sure, he had no skill with a sword, and they would be grossly outnumbered, but he needed to do something.

"Hook was told you were the key to obtaining what he searched for, and it's within his reach." Theo leaned in close to Jackson's ear, "this is for Samuel."

The deck beneath his feet vanished as Theo let go of his arms and pushed him back by the blade at his throat, slicing into more tender skin. An enthusiastic cheer rang through the air, and as he fell towards the water, he prayed that cheer didn't mean Patrick had lost.

Hitting the water on his back felt as bad as the belly flop off the diving board he had done at the swimming pool in sixth grade. He kicked his legs as he went under, trying to reach to the surface when he felt small hands grasp onto his arm. Strands of silver floated from behind him and caressed his cheek. The sensation of being lifted carried a sense of déjà vu which eased his panic slightly. *Yet again, another time a mermaid has saved my life here.*

He broke the surface near the back of the ship and took big gulps of delicious air.

"Easy there. I got you."

The familiar soft voice felt like a gut punch. He could hear men shouting and more metal clashing on the ship along with women's voices shouting indistinguishable words. It felt like he was in a daze because the chaos faded into the background as the mermaid who saved him, turned to him and smiled.

"You're Jackson?" a silver-haired mermaid asked.

He nodded, his eyes taking in every detail of her face.

"Vincent's son?"

He nodded again, unable to form words.

Her eyes went wide when they focused on his neck. "Oh dear."

Feeling her palm press against his throat caused the stinging to increase, but he couldn't react.

"I'm going to take you somewhere safe," she said with teary eyes.

"Kay," he whispered. That was the one syllable he managed to get past the lump in his throat.

"Don't worry, Merilee sent me. I'm Brynn" She gave him a reassuring smile, obviously misinterpreting his response for discomfort. "Take a deep breath. Here we go."

He took a deep breath and closed his eyes as the water engulfed him. Then Jackson felt them maneuvering through the water at a fast pace.

Right then, he didn't care why Patrick was on the ship, where his father was, or how his body felt like it had been through a meat grinder. In that moment, he was the child who lost his mother too young and finally got to see her again—even if he knew it wasn't her.

CHAPTER 29

WHO IS BRYNN

The seaweed stung as the mermaid named Brynn wrapped his wrists where the ropes had rubbed them raw. Jackson stared at her from the ledge he sat on, unable to look away. Her face was a carbon copy of how he remembered his mother. The only difference, well other than her white and silver scales and tail fin, was her matching silver hair. His mother had been blonde like Patrick and her eyes a warm mahogany brown, not the slate grey of this creature.

"You'll be safe here. We came here when the Lagoon was full of Lost Boys and were never bothered," she spoke as she grabbed more seaweed from his side and gently took his other wrist. "Once you're rested, you can leave through that tunnel behind you. It leads to the north side of the Neverland Forest. Pan Manor is just a few minutes' walk west of here."

Even her voice is the same.

"How long have you been here? In Neverland, I mean," he asked, curious to know more about her.

"A short time compared to many."

"Any memories of being a tadpole? Are mermaids tadpoles at one point?"

Her laugh is even the same.

Entering this hideaway from the small entrance, the blue hair of a certain mermaid he recognized appeared under the water behind Brynn.

Merilee broke the surface; her aqua eyes roved over him, pausing with a slight flare at the seaweed around his neck before going to his wrists which Brynn finished wrapping. The shimmer of concern came and went so quickly, he would have missed it if he hadn't been looking directly at her.

"No. No memories of being a tadpole I'm afraid." Brynn smiled softly, then looked to Merilee. "Only waking surrounded by water and Merilee greeting me with kindness."

"Seems she has a knack for finding lost things in the water," Jackson said as she swam to the opposite side of him.

"That's how I found Jackson. Floating at the bottom of Neverland Cove," she explained in response to Brynn's knitted brows.

His mother used to look at his father that way when he defended his and Patrick's shenanigans. His arms itched to wrap around this mermaid and pretend—if only for a moment—that he was holding his mother again.

"Seems you have a knack for *being* a lost thing in the water," Brynn pointed out.

"Only since I met Tink," he grumbled. How such a small creature could cause such havoc in his life was baffling.

"The most lost creature of all." Sad grey eyes erased her teasing smile.

He wanted that smile back. Yet, how anyone could have sympathy for that fairy was beyond him. As far as he was concerned, he wouldn't mind if she was thrown into oblivion; or if Hal decided to pick apart her deranged soul piece by piece. He would deliver her himself to this Hal if it meant his brother wouldn't suffer that fate.

"Would you like me to go check on the others now?" Brynn asked Merilee.

When the mermaid nodded, Brynn reached into the side of her chest wrapping and grabbed something he couldn't see. Her fingers that were still around his wrist, gently moved his hand palm up and placed something small in the center. When her hands left his, it revealed a shiny white stone the size of a large marble. She smiled at him before she submerged herself below the surface and he followed the white form as it glided out of view.

"She has developed this habit of collecting small stones and gifting them to the Lost Boys."

"Why does she look like my mother?" He knew if

anyone would be able to answer that question, it would be her.

"I suspect because she was." Merilee plucked the small white stone out of his hand and lifted it up into the streak of sunlight.

"Was?"

"We don't retain the knowledge of our Real-World life like other souls," she explained and returned the stone to him.

"But my father said she was in the afterlife." *Wouldn't my father know if my mother was here?* He turned the stone around in his palm, the golden specks shimmering in the sunlight.

"I would assume he mistakenly believes so," she said. Leaning her elbows back on the ledge next to his hip, she began moving the water rhythmically along her fin. "Your mother's life was ended by Tink, which makes her a mermaid fledgling. Vincent knows this, but if he told you otherwise, then perhaps all his memories of Neverland have not returned."

"Tink killed all of you in the Real-World?" *If that is the case, why hasn't anyone or the deities dealt with her?* It didn't make much sense to him, unless it was purposeful; a way to use her and replenish the mermaid's numbers.

"Gosh no. Various supernatural beings left unsupervised by one deity, or another, was the cause though. This existence is the deity's apology to us for their negligence."

"Doesn't seem like much of an apology."

"It is."

Getting to go back would be a better one, although he guessed explaining how a person survived some gruesome deaths would be rather difficult.

"Has my father seen her?" *Because that would not go over well.* He rubbed the seaweed wraps, trying to alleviate the itching that had started.

"No, he hasn't, and it should remain that way for now. We have more pressing matters that need our attention."

He didn't miss her pointed look and message behind those words. "Which pressing matter are you talking about, exactly? The homicidal fairy? The maniac pirates? Or the vengeful brother of the man Simon and the redhead killed?" From where he sat, there was a lot that could be considered under that category.

"You failed to mention the Pan problem," she pointed out.

Lifting the edge of the smelly seaweed, he was fascinated with the improvements of the abrasions on his skin. The deeper cuts were less red and angry, clean cut, instead of ragged. "I just need to talk to my brother and that will sort itself out," he replied, distracted.

"Don't be so confident in that. Verbal communication didn't have an effect when it came from Vincent."

He didn't like her tone. It was condescending; a little like a pat on the head. "I know Patrick, maybe better than our father. Siblings tend to bond when their parents 'die.' He'll listen to me."

"Doubtful."

Doubt was written all over her features, and the stabs of irritation pricked him. "You don't know him like I do."

"Neither do you since he came here. He's become broken in his attempts to find peace," she snapped.

"He is not going to Hal, and you aren't going to take him there." His temper flared hot and his hand itched for Simon's dagger.

A cool feeling in his palm caught his attention and the shiny sapphire in the handle of the dagger glinted in the sunlight. *I could make my point real clear. All it would take is a small lean sideways to sink the blade into the delicate skin at her neck.*

"If Hook gets his coin, then that won't be a concern," she replied gentler.

He shook his head to clear the images and thoughts of stabbing the lovely creature beside him. Jackson clenched his now empty palm. Breathing deep through his nose, he mentally counted the number of partially washed-out bloody spots on his jeans "So … uh … Hook didn't hurt him or get Patrick's coin like he wanted then?"

She nodded, aqua eyes piercing. "Pan flew off shortly after I arrived at the Jolly Roger."

"Good. Hook's not going to touch my brother or his coin." Jackson huffed out a breath, feeling more like himself. "Okay, help me understand. Why does Hook want this coin? Do you guys get one of these coins you all seem to be so concerned with here?" He hoped if he asked the questions, this strange feeling would go away.

"No, but we collect and keep the coins of the grey souls we take down to Hal," she said slowly.

"I bet the pirates are always looking for your treasure trove."

He could feel the weight of the dagger in his hand again. Could imagine the blade piercing the skin.

"They have never been aggressively seeking it until now. They do not keep the coins of the grey souls they deliver to the Ferryman either."

"That seems backwards." He took deep, controlled breaths and focused on her melodic voice hoping to rid himself of the intrusive thoughts.

"Balanced. Not backwards. We do not crave the coins; therefore, we are keepers over them. Pirates crave the find, revel in the search. They receive fulfillment or reprieve when they collect the grey soul and deliver them to the Ferryman. Then they crave the reward again, so they search anew."

"I thought Hook was the bad guy," he said, thankful his heart rate was returning to normal. A shot of whiskey would be useful right about now.

"There are no good or bad here. Only a purpose. Tink is what threw it off. She interfered with your family and disrupted it all by bringing Vincent back."

"What was thrown off?" *He* felt thrown off. The weight in his palm had disappeared once more, leaving him more confused by the relief and disappointment that warred inside of him at its loss.

"The balance, Jackson." She frowned at him. "Are you feeling unwell?"

"Looks like I have to get a move on then." He got to his feet, glad to note the pains in his knees from when Theo kicked each one was mild. Looked like the wraps on his knees were magic too.

"Where are you going?"

"To talk to my brother. If things are as off as you say they are, I won't have you or any other mermaid taking him down to Hal to be—*fixed*. I'll talk some sense into the kid."

"Perhaps it's best to wait for Simon or Vincent," she suggested, her opinion on the matter clear.

"I can manage my brother."

"Here." Her arm went to her back and reappeared, only to offer him Simon's dagger. "In case you have need for it."

The sapphire glinted and the smooth blade shone in the sunlight. He took her offering, praying she didn't see how unsteady his hand was, and tucked it into his belt and away from her neck. "Thanks. I'll fix this."

"You are a loyal brother. I hope Pan is wise enough to realize it."

"It's my fault Patrick is here in the first place; so, it's my responsibility to make it right."

"Tink is responsible for him being here, not you." Her eyebrows knitted.

"If I would have helped him more, he wouldn't have turned to her for comfort. I failed him."

"We all have choices, Jackson."

"And I am going to fix the mistake I made ten years ago." He stepped onto the soft green grass behind the ledge. "Oh, Patrick mentioned Hook holding fledglings somewhere. Maybe one of his crew would know more about that."

"Interesting. It appears Isla, or the redhead as you call her, will get another adventure."

"I met a lovely gentleman named Theo, who would probably have a wealth of knowledge," he suggested and grinned at Merilee's knowing smirk.

Giving a dramatic bow, he pivoted and began to make his way up the tunnel Brynn mentioned earlier. His mind whirled with what to say to his brother and just how he was going to fix this.

CHAPTER 30

CONVERSATION GONE WRONG

JACKSON

The front of the manor held only slight differences to the way Jackson remembered it from his childhood. What was once a white front door was now canary yellow, matching the sunflowers that grew in the flowerbeds in front of the house. A small cluster of stones placed in the bottom corners of the soil reminded him of the clusters Patrick would make for their mother. He looked to the right and left of the manor, but no one was walking about.

Wonder where everyone is?

Hugh had mentioned Oliver and Wren, but he had yet to see them. The forest was even empty of most creatures which he was thankful for because he really did not want to run into a Mouline or Sissil again.

Footsteps were the only warning he got before a hand came down on his shoulder and spun him around. Auburn hair pulled back into a bun was the first thing to catch his attention. The wide blue eyes and freckles along with the hair was a combination he recognized. The shiny blade he held to the boy's throat, however, was not. He had no intentions to hurt anyone, so he quickly dropped his hand and stepped back, putting the dagger back in his belt with a shaky hand.

"Sorry, Hugh. I don't know why I did that," he apologized and ran his hand through his hair.

"Yeah, no worries, Jackson," Hugh said wearily. "You've had a rough go with the pirates from what I hear. Shouldn't have come at you from behind."

"Yeah, I sure have." From the look on Hugh's face, he rattled he kid; well—young man.

Footsteps and snapping twigs announced the approach of two young adults. Both around Jackson's height of five-eleven, one with a short brown military haircut and a scowl aimed at him; the other, curly black hair going in whichever which way and biting his lip in the way a person did when trying to hold back a laugh.

"Thought Jackson was a friend, Hugh," the scowling one said as he stood beside Hugh and sized Jackson up.

"Stop being so prickly, Wren," the curly haired one said through a laugh. "Jackson isn't like Patrick."

"Wren?" he said, seeing the similarities in the young man. He studied the features of his companion who was in good humor. "Oliver?"

"You bet!" Oliver replied, blue eyes beaming.

Hugh looked almost guilty as his cheeks were turning

a telling shade of pink and he found his feet remarkably interesting all of a sudden.

"You took them home?" Jackson could not help the disapproval seeping through. Hugh knew better.

"We have every right to know what happened to our families. Patrick lied to us," Wren defended, fists clenching. "He said to come for a swim, then brought us here."

"That's what he did?" His heart sank at his brother's actions. "He drowned you?"

"Dared us to swim to the bottom of the lake and we couldn't swim up," Oliver said and clapped Wren on the back, who shoved the hand off. "Wren here is grumpy because Molly Kleese is married to Kyle Patterson. His dreams of wedded bliss have crashed and burned."

"Shut up, Ollie. I'm mad because Patrick said we were here for a visit. Not that we could never go back."

"That's what he said? A visit?" Jackson shook his head in disgust, anger rising towards his brother. When the two nodded in confirmation, he growled. "I'm going to kick his ass."

"Not before I do." Wren went to move past him but he grabbed the young man's upper arm tightly.

"No one touches him. You got that?" He pulled Wren back and got into his face. "I will deal with Patrick. No one will lay a hand on him. It's my fault he is here, so if you want to be pissed at someone be pissed at me. Hell, you can even take a swing at me if you want; but that's after I make sure Patrick is set right and doesn't have a noose around his neck over his damn coin."

"Fine," Wren growled and shook his grip loose. "Go talk to him before I do."

"Stay here"—he pointed his index finger at all three and then to the spot in front of them—"because I don't know how he is going to take you three like this and I really don't want to deal with more than I have to right now."

He pivoted once they nodded, albeit reluctantly, and his boots crunched over the debris on the forest floor as he made his way to the front door. The smell of the tulips and daisies became more noticeable as he approached the front porch. Going up the three steps, he hesitated with his hand on the door handle. He wasn't even sure what he wanted to say to Patrick, if he was being honest with himself.

So many emotions warred with each other inside him. Relief that Patrick was safe from Hook; anger that his daughter had been kidnapped; disbelief that his brother would kill Dustin and bring him here; all the while an undercurrent of happiness that he got to see the kid again, as messed up as this situation was.

"You turn it and push to open it," he heard Oliver loudly whisper from the trees. A smack sound followed by an *'oomph'* had him closing his eyes and taking a deep breath.

Did I really expect the equivalent of three twelve-year-olds to be quiet when I needed them to be?

Turning the handle, the door opened soundlessly, and he walked through. He caught his reflection in the hanging mirror above the entry table on the left, not nearly as bruised as he should have been from his adventures with Theo. The smell of baking made his stomach clench with the need to go home.

"Where are all the Lost Boys? I haven't seen any around for half the day!" Patrick's whiny tone floated from the living room.

"Some I sent to get supplies for this evening's campfire and the more unruly ones I sent to the Ferryman."

"You what?!" Patrick shrieked.

"You said you would talk to them. You did not. Therefore, I took care of it," the woman snapped.

"You had no right to do that! I was going to talk to them eventually, and you were the one who told me I could make my own family. Then you took them away!?"

"Something she is far too comfortable with doing," Jackson mumbled under his breath, assuming the woman was the infamous Tink.

"And I got a little distracted when I noticed Hook's ship. Why was my brother on Hook's ship, Tink? I didn't know he was still here or else I would have stopped those stupid pirates from hurting him, even if I am still kind of mad at him for taking Calla without saying hi." He sounded so forlorn, like the caring brother he once knew.

"I have no idea."

Jackson growled at the blatant lie and rounded the corner.

"Because she"—he pointed to the glowing ball on the fireplace mantel—"told him to look for me."

"Jacks!" Patrick stood up, eyes wide and mouth forming into a grin which slowly faded. "What do you mean, 'Tink told him'?"

The translucent blonde woman materialized and leaned against the fireplace, wearing a green dress that hugged her curves and seemed to be made out of giant leaves. She crossed her arms and huffed, looking for all the part annoyed; but her tapping foot told him something entirely different.

"Why would I tell Hook that?" Tink said as she examined her nails. "Do you really think I would do that to your brother, Patrick?"

"Yes," he replied before his little brother could.

Tink rolled her eyes again. "You simply hate me because I've helped Patrick be happy where you could not."

Patrick's brows knitted. "Tink wouldn't do that to you, Jacks."

"Seriously?" He held his arms out wide. "Why *wouldn't* she. Look what she's done already."

"She's helped me," Patrick defended.

"She's the reason you were unhappy in the first place," he shot back, raising his arm to point at the vindictive pain in his ass. "She killed mom."

Patrick gasped. "No she didn't! She saved dad when their car went under. Tink did her best to save mom."

"She probably held him in place and made him watch

her drown," he shouted. The slight smirk he caught on the transparent woman's face gave him a sick feeling in his gut, telling him it was a real possibility his guess was right. "She is the reason all this is happening."

"No, she wouldn't do that." Patrick shook his head. "Why would you say that?"

"Because it's true," he said, almost dumbfounded by the cruelty of that being.

"No, it's not!" Patrick shouted. "Tink wouldn't hurt anyone."

"No? She will just convince you to do it instead." He needed his brother to believe him.

"I don't hurt anyone."

"What about Dustin? You brought him here, didn't you?" he argued. Anger at his brother's ignorance coursed through him. "How did you get him to Neverland?"

"That's different, he was bullying Calla." Patrick's eyes narrowed. "Something you should have stopped since you are her dad. But did you stop him? No. I did."

"By killing him?!" he said in disbelief and pointed at his brother. "Don't tell me you haven't hurt anyone because I saw you coming out of the back of this place with Dustin. He was *not* happy to be here. In fact, he was bleeding, and bruised, and pleading with you and crying."

"He was hurting Calla! I stopped it! I did that because I cared. You know what you didn't do when I was being bullied? Stopped it or care! Tink did though, she helped me. She even brought over Hugh and stopped his pain."

Patrick's shouts turned broken as his eyes started to shimmer. "She helped him, like I helped Calla."

The thought never occurred to him that his brother would care for the fairy that took him away and destroyed their family. The betrayal and hurt in his brother's features cracked something inside him. His brother's pain was palpable in the air.

"Hugh and Dustin are different, and you know it," he said in a softer tone. "Hugh was sick. As thankful as I am to her if she did bring him here, for ending his suffering, Dustin was a healthy ten-year-old boy. They are not the same, Patrick."

"Neither were we," Wren added as he came into the room, followed by Oliver and Hugh.

"Who are you?" Patrick asked, tilting his head to the side.

Tink's expression darkened, and her nostrils flared.

"We went to go see our families," Oliver said. "You lied to us."

"Oliver?" Patrick's gaze moved between the three. "Wren?"

"I took them after I'd seen how old Jackson was," Hugh said and shrugged.

"Hugh?" Patrick's face fell. "What have you guys done?"

"Looks like your brother took them away from you too," Tink said, tone sad but malice in her eyes.

"Why?" Patrick yelled, eyes streaking with amber. "Why does every one leave me! Why am I not good enough to stay for!" His hand went into his blonde hair and tugged hard.

"I never left you," Tink whispered.

"You *need* to leave him alone. He was getting better before you came into his life," Jackson growled.

"You're just mad I brought Calla here," Patrick spat.

"Of course, I am mad about that! What father would not be pissed his daughter was kidnapped?! In what world would that be okay?"

"Did I get a hug from my big brother when you saw me again? No."

Patrick paced, mumbling under his breath, the translucent woman following his movements with her eyes.

"You know, Dad wasn't even excited to see me."

"He wasn't too thrilled to see me either," he admitted begrudgingly. "Dad doesn't want to see us here," he pointed to the ground as he slowly stepped towards a now still Patrick. "Not us personally, but here—in this place."

"Tink was right," his brother whispered. "No one cares about me."

"We care about you, and we care about what you are doing."

"You don't care!" He shook his head. "Ever since you met Natalie, that's all you cared about. All that made you smile was when she called, or she came over. You only let me tag along because you felt sorry for me."

"That's *not* true, kiddo."

He couldn't believe his brother would think that. A quick look up to a smirking Tink helped him understand why he did though.

Patrick covered his ears and closed his eyes. "Shut up, shut up, shut up!"

His fingers went around his brother's smaller wrists and pulled them away from Patrick's ears. Leaning down to be eye level with him, he hated the confusion he could see in those dark eyes.

"*We* care about you. *I* care about you, Patrick. Always have. But you're *hurting* people." He took the well of tears pooling on Patrick's lower lids as a good sign. "You can't hurt people and think everyone is going to be okay with it."

Patrick's eyes shifted over his shoulder to where he knew Hugh, Oliver, and Wren were standing. The tears spilled over when he blinked, but a coldness entered his eyes. "Tink thinks I'm worth staying for. Dad wanted to go back to stay with you. Calla wanted to go back with you, and now you took away my friends! I hate you!" Patrick screamed. Twisting his wrists free of Jackson's grasp, he moved back and away from him.

Why didn't they listen and stay where I told them to?

He'd felt Patrick coming around to a common ground he could work from, but that was all blown to hell now.

He followed Patrick as he went towards the window and grabbed his upper arm. The conversation was not ending like this, and he was not letting his brother fly off. Patrick tried to shake off his grip, but he was set on finishing this conversation; too much was on the line to have any other outcome.

A sharp pain ripped through his abdomen. Intakes of breath echoed around the room, and Patrick's angry features went lax before morphing into a face of shock. His brown-amber eyes bounced down and up to Jackson's face; horror replacing the shock.

"I … I … I'm sorry." Patrick's hushed words barely registered. "I'm so sorry Jacks, I … I … didn't mean to. I don't know what happened. I … I …"

Blinking, he tried to make sense of what he was seeing. What looked like a kitchen knife protruded from his abdomen, his brother's small hand wrapped around the handle. He followed the arm attached to the hand, to confirm that yes, it was indeed his brother's hand on the knife in his stomach. "You stabbed me?"

More pain shot through his torso when his brother pulled his hand back, knife included. He cried out as it left his flesh. He'd never been stabbed before, so he was shocked by how much it hurt. His hand flew to his gut and blood seeped through his fingers as he applied pressure and bent over.

"You'll pay for this," Tink hissed in his ear before she disappeared, and the glowing fairy went out the open window. He did a quick scan of where Patrick was but there was no sign of him.

"Jackson!" Oliver was at his side and put his hand over his to add more pressure.

"I'll be fine." He breathed, in harmony to Wren calling Patrick's name outside.

"Maybe you should go home," Hugh suggested as he ducked under Jackson's arm relieving some of the strain of staying upright.

"I can't believe I'm agreeing with Hughbert, but I think he's right on this one." Simon's blonde head appeared under his other arm and replaced Oliver's hand to slow the bleeding.

"Where did you come from?" The sense of relief he felt having Simon near was immense.

"Figured I'd check here for you once we seen you get dumped off the Jolly Roger. I knew Merilee had Brynn there in case something happened to you. We weren't sure where she would take you though." The guy removed his hand and swore as the blood continued to seep out. "But you should go home. Let us deal with Patrick and Hook."

"Have you met Brynn?" he asked, wanting to change the subject as they made their way out of the manor.

"No, I haven't."

That eased some of the hurt he had harbored when he suspected Simon knew his mother was here and didn't tell him. "Ask Merilee to introduce you sometime after we deal with my brother and Hook." He grunted, then grimaced as the stairs down the front porch jostled his stomach. "Better yet, bring my father when you do."

"Why?" The mischievous uptick to Simon's mouth

told him the guy wanted to know the reason why but would do it either way.

"You would want to be there when he meets her. Trust me," he said, his own mischievous smirk making an appearance. His vision started blurring and his body was beginning to feel weighed down with every step they walked towards the forest. "I can't leave it like this, Simon."

"I know, Jacks," Simon sighed. "I know."

Part of him felt like he lied because the longer he stayed here the more he simply wanted to go home. He would regret it if he did, so he knew that wasn't a feasible option. His little brother was hurting and needed to get away from Tink. If Patrick refused to leave her, he would deal with her and Hook himself to keep his brother safe from them—and Hal.

CHAPTER 31

I'M NOT OKAY

JACKSON

The sounds of angry whispers invaded his blissful sleep.

Jackson listened for the voices, and relaxed when he recognized Simon's and Hugh's. Simon probably did something to piss off Hugh or called him another ridiculous version of Hugh. His hand moved to where the knife went into his abdomen and was thankful that only a raised line remained.

When they had been traveling through the Neverland Forest, Dorathea made an appearance. It was amusing to watch the boys get tongued-tied around her as well as be wary when she placed her attention on them. Almost as amusing as Simon arguing with Sissil after the giant snake took a swipe at him. Dorathea had actually smiled at the odd fighting between those two, before lecturing Simon on letting Jackson get so poorly mistreated and even refusing to let him pass off any blame to his father.

It would seem Simon had been tasked with keeping him unharmed over the past decade and that extended to his time here in Neverland. He had laughed at the satisfied look Simon gave Dorathea when she swung her arm outward and hit Hugh in the gut after he teased Simon for being in trouble.

Shortly after, the jar of salve the woman carried in her satchel was brought out. When the neon lime sludge made contact with his skin, he passed out from the searing pain that went through him.

Guess the pain was worth it because I'm pretty much healed. Not that he would ever volunteer for that treatment again. Shuddering at the thought, he cracked his eyes open and was greeted with glowing leaves attached to trailing vines on the ceiling. *The Den.*

Rubbing his face with his hands, he sighed and sat up from his makeshift bed on the lumpy stuffed sleeping bag on the floor. Oliver and Wren were playing some sort of card game on the little table, but their eyes kept shifting to Simon and Hugh in the entranceway. Getting to his feet, he extended his arms above his head and leaned to one side. His stomach pulled a little but nothing that concerned him. He would have to thank Dorathea before he left if he didn't run into her before that.

"What did you do now, Simon?" he asked, partially joking but curious what had Hugh so riled up.

"Why would you assume I did something?" Simon responded, turning away from a scowling Hugh. "How are you feeling?"

"Tell him," Hugh said to Simon's back.

"Tell me what?" he said slowly.

Simon turned and hit Hugh in the stomach with the back of his hand, and Hugh punched Simon's shoulder in return. "I'm getting to it," Simon gritted.

"What's going on? Is it Patrick? Did something happen to him?" His mind was a whirl of possibilities, no outcomes he would want. He never would forgive himself if he failed his brother again.

"What? No," Simon said, waving his hand dismissively. "Pan is alive and crazy as always. Look let's go outside. Fresh air will do you good."

He looked to Hugh who glared at Simon but briefly met his eyes before dropping his gaze to the floor. Oliver and Wren were watching from the table, looking uneasy when they noticed him looking at them. Sighing, his sneakers kicked up dust as he walked towards the entrance. He could feel the eyes of the boys on him, feeling like he was walking on death row or some other spectacle of doom.

Outside, little glowing pixies the size of dimes flew about the still pond in various hues of the rainbow. Simon stood by the makeshift bench with his head bowed and hands on his hips. The hum of the mermaids' songs lent an eerie element to the already ominous feeling in atmosphere.

He had yet to meet the Larnack but knew better than to be out at night in this place, especially without a weapon and the sun was almost down on the horizon. He needn't have worried though, noting Simon had two daggers: one on his side, the other at his back in his belt.

"Where's my father?" he asked as he came up beside the solemn-looking blonde.

"He went to see if he could track down Merilee. Wasn't too pleased with his youngest when he saw you two days ago. None of us are."

"Two days?" He thought it was only a few hours.

Simon nodded. "Dorathea's salve is also a sedative. It knocked you out for a while."

"But Patrick is okay?"

Simon looked down and nodded.

Relief flooded him. "I was getting through to him, but then he saw those three and lost it," he recounted, frustrated with how the conversation went. "I'll get to him next time, I have to."

"Jacks, something happened to Natalie," Simon said and looked up at him.

He'd never seen him look so uncomfortable; no, remorseful? Then his words sank in.

"Excuse me? What do you mean something happened to Natalie?" His heart picked up speed in his chest.

"There was an accident and Natalie didn't make it."

"No"—he shook his head—"no, you have to be mistaken. Is this some ploy to get me to stay here and replace that damn Hook asshole because that is a really shitty thing to do, Simon."

"You don't know how much I *wish* it was a ploy. I had a bad feeling when we left Pan Manor, so I stopped in and checked on Calla and Natalie when we got you to the den."

His throat closed up before he could say the word. Whether it was a sob or scream, he didn't know, because he felt like doing both. The whoosh of blood in his ears sounded in rhythm with the pounding in his chest.

"She drowned, Jacks." Simon's eyes shifted around before he crossed his arms and blew out a long breath.

Natalie's dead? My Natalie? A particularly sharp pain shot through his chest and he rubbed at the spot. He leaned over and rested his hands on his knees, trying to keep his breathing steady. She drowned. *My Natalie ... Gone. Drowned.*

"Was she at the pool?" he breathed, not wanting the details but needing them no matter how much it was going to hurt. She was an excellent swimmer, so it didn't make sense to him.

"A vehicle accident." Simon met his gaze.

You're going to regret this. Tink's words rang in his mind.

No ... she didn't ...

"Wait, I thought you said she drowned?" he said slowly, watching Simon as he kicked a stone into the quiet pond, causing ripples to dance across the surface like an arrow to the waterfall.

Simon gave him a sympathetic look.

"You have got to be fucking kidding me!" he exploded. He straightened and ran his hands through his hair and tugged, pulling his head back and yelled out his frustration.

In every scenario he had run through in his mind, Natalie had always been a guarantee when he got back. Not having her, he wouldn't know how to breathe. She was the best part of him—of their daughter.

Calla.

If it was true, his daughter was all alone and he wasn't there for her. He had to see for himself that Natalie was dead, and Calla was alright.

Decision made, he searched for the path he and his father used to climb the steep hillside. Spotting the worn-out path, he headed towards it with long, purposeful strides.

"Where are you going?" Simon asked.

"I have to see for myself and check on Calla. If Natalie is dead, so is that bitch of a fairy," he yelled back.

He heard Simon curse and then footsteps heading away from him.

"Hugh, keep an eye out for Vinnie and tell him we went to the RW," Simon shouted.

The loose dirt fell as his sneakers displaced it as he made his way down the path. He needed to see his daughter, his heart hurt with the knowledge that she could be hurting, and he wasn't there.

What a clusterfuck this is turning out to be.

All he had needed to do was leave when Calla did. That was it. He didn't have to stay and talk to Patrick; but the kid was hurting and honestly, he wanted to protect him because he failed to do that before.

If he lost Natalie because of this though, the blame would rest on his shoulders too.

His feet landed as he jumped down the last few feet to the sandy beach.

"You want to reel it back a bit there, Jacks," Simon said as he landed behind him.

"What are you doing?"

"Coming with you."

He turned and poked Simon in the chest. "I don't need a babysitter."

"No"—Simon knocked off his hand—"but you need this to go anywhere."

His metal coin with the skull and crossed swords shone in the fading sunlight when he held it up.

He grabbed the coin from Simon's grip and closed his eyes as a current went through him. It was a pleasant feeling—energizing. Opening his eyes, he nodded in thanks and continued into the water until he was knee deep.

His reflection stared back at him, looking determined and eyes shimmering with pale green. *Huh, must be a Neverland thing.*

Simon's reflection came beside his and grinned a mischievous grin. "Ready to go for a trip?" Simon asked.

Raising an eyebrow at the statement he would now forever associate with Simon, he nodded. "Think of where I want to go?"

"And rub the coin face clockwise. See you at Carston." Reaching up to his own coin hanging on his chest, he winked and turned as he fell; back hitting the water first.

"See you at Carson," he repeated, silently grateful he wasn't going there alone.

Taking a deep breath, he moved his fingers along the raised ropes that bordered the coin and thought of Calla. Closing his eyes, he pictured the lake that took away so much and turned as he fell, dreading what waited for him at home.

* * *

The leaves crunched under the soles of his sneakers, echoing in the still night. It had been the start of spring when he was thrown into Neverland, and now it was late fall. Simon had simply shrugged and said time moved differently in Neverland but a gnawing sensation in his gut kept nagging at him. He remembered Hugh looking confused at the manor about Calla being his daughter and asking how much time had gone by. At the time, he thought the boy had lost track of how long he was in Neverland, but looking around it was clear time moved much faster here.

"Just how much does time move differently between the two?" he asked Simon, who had refused to look at him since they left the lake.

"It all depends. On what, I don't know. Sometimes hours in Neverland equals a week, a month."

"You're telling me a day there could be a month here?" Anger rose at Simon's pursed lips and quick nod.

He turned onto Sterling Street, the familiar elm trees lending shadow from the streetlights. As he walked under the first streetlight, he noticed Simon slowing. Confused, he raised his eyebrow and gave the blonde a look.

"Almost two-and-a-half-years." Simon sighed.

"What?"

Growling, Simon walked up to him and faced him. "It has been almost two-and-a-half years. The general time difference is a week for every hour in Neverland. Sometimes it's more, but it's been a little over two-and-a-half years."

He quickly did the math for his time in there.

"You're telling me that my five days in Neverland cost me two-and-a-half years here?"

"Yeah." Simon sighed. "That's what I'm saying."

"And you didn't think I would want to know that!" He balled his fists, feeling his nails dig into his palms.

"Of course, I thought you would want to know. I wasn't *SUPPOSED* to tell you but I'm telling you now."

"Probably because I would figure it out when I noticed how different things were when I got home." *Unbelievable.*

"I tried to get you to come back here earlier, but you wanted to '*save your brother*,'" Simon mimicked him, then grabbed his dagger and started flipping it. "I did what I had to do but Natalie was never part of the equation. Had I known *THAT,* I wouldn't have brought you to Neverland in the first place."

A new wave of anger prickled over his skin like little pins of ice. "But she was *always* part of the equation that is my life. Hell, I went to Neverland with you to get Calla with the bonus that you would disappear so I could live a normal life with her and my daughter. You should have told me."

"Hey. I'm telling you now."

"Yeah, you did," he said, placing his hands to the back of his neck and looking up through the barren tree branches, enjoying the pull in his muscles and attempting to release some tension. Needing to move, he continued to his house with his strides eating up the path. His house came into view and Uncle Marcus walked out the front door and jogged to the older black Chevelle parked in the driveway.

Was he visiting or did he live there with Calla now? He hadn't thought about who her legal guardian would be if something happened to them. Natalie had been on his case about drawing up a legal will with their lawyer, but he never got around to setting up an appointment.

Simon grabbed him by the arm and moved him behind one of the large elm trees. "Unless you want to explain where you have been for the past two-and-a-half years, I would stay out of sight," Simon explained at his scowl.

The purr of the engine filled the empty street and he leaned his back against the tree, feeling the bark scratch him through his shirt. He heard the gears shift as Marcus put the car in gear. As his nerves began to hit, he focused on Simon as the guy obviously watched Marcus drive away.

Sure, he was pissed at the guy for not telling him about the whole time difference thing, but he did tell him. Simon had always had his back since the grocery store. Actually, he'd had his back since his first trip to Neverland according to Dorathea. He could admit he was grateful for him tagging along now because yes, he did need a friend or someone to rely on here.

"Alright, you can go," Simon said with a nod of his head in the direction of the house.

Taking a breath and blowing it out, he pushed off the tree and headed to the familiar, white two-story house with blue trim, and a now bright-purple door. If he took a guess, it was Calla who picked out that color. The windows downstairs were dark, but Calla's bedroom window was illuminated by a soft light. The flowerbeds were empty of the flowers Natalie kept there, with weeds growing throughout.

His heart rate increased as the soles of his shoes hit the wooden stairs to the landing. The metal door handle was cold against his damp palm when he gripped it but it only turned partially—locked.

He banged on the door and listened for footsteps. Cupping his hands to block the porch light, he tried to look through the slim etched windowpane. No movement but he remained hopeful because of the light on upstairs.

"Maybe she's not home?" Simon suggested, picking his nail with the blade tip.

"She's here. Her bedroom light is on." He banged on the door again and returned to the window. Someone walked by the railing on the upper floor towards the stairs.

Running his hands through his hair, he stepped back and waited impatiently for Calla to open the door. He could hear footsteps at the landing, and then the door handle jiggled before the door cracked open a few inches, revealing his daughter's wide-eyed gaze.

"Calla," he breathed and pushed the door open enough for him to wrap her in his arms. Jackson squeezed her tight and rested his head on her blonde hair. She was at least a foot taller since he seen her at Neverland Cove.

"Dad?" she whispered against his chest.

He felt her arms raise and wrap around him hesitantly.

"Yeah, Petal, it's me," he said, emotion thick in his throat. "I'm home."

"Home?" she parroted, jerking back slightly and dropping her arms. Her brown eyes that were the same as her mother's searched his face. "Where have you been?"

He frowned at the accusation in her voice—the anger. Placing his hands on her shoulders, he leaned down and searched her face. "I've been at Neverland, Calla."

"Neverland?" She shrugged his hands off her shoulders and stepped back farther into the entryway. "Where is that? You didn't think to at least call mom? Or me?"

He turned to Simon, who was leaning against the doorframe, hoping he had some insight into the situation. "She doesn't remember?"

Simon's lips pressed into a thin line and he simply shook his head.

"Who are you talking to?"

His daughter was leaning to the right and looking in Simon's direction. Wariness entered her eyes as she took another step back. "I think you should leave."

"What?"—he must have heard her wrong—"You want me to leave?"

"Yes, I want you to leave," she said again. "You didn't care enough about mom or me to come home or call, I don't care that you're here now."

"Calla?" He frowned. "I'm here to see you. To see if you're okay. I'm sorry it took so long to come home, but I'm here now."

She was already shaking her head. "I don't want you here."

He rubbed the ache starting in his chest. A *tick-tick-tick* filled the air surrounding the entrance.

What the hell is going on?

"Calla, you don't mean that. Look, I can understand you being angry with me but believe me when I say I would have come home sooner if I could have."

"Why couldn't you? If you loved us sooo much, why didn't you?" She scoffed. "Sooner. How much sooner?"

"Petal, let's sit"—he motioned to the living room—"I'll explain."

"Explain what?" she snapped. "Where you were when mom refused to sell the house until one of us came home? Or when mom was dealing with the investigation? Because I showed up in my room one night after being missing for over a month talking about my dead uncle and the missing kid at school being beaten up? Do you know what it's like having kids scared of you because they think you and your dad had something to do with a missing classmate? Do you know how everyone looked at me when I was saying my dead uncle was alive? Or how much mom had to defend me?" She tapped the side of her head and made a self-deprecating look.

"They thought we had something to do with Dustin?" That possibility hadn't even crossed his mind.

"They did, now everyone thinks I made it all up. Funny part, I don't even know why I would say something like that." She threw her arms out to the side. "I don't remember anything from when they say we went missing until I was home."

"I—"

"Or"—she pointed her finger at him—"how about when she would be crying at night, missing you, wishing you would come home."

He ran his hand down his face, imagining how that would have been for her to be there so young. Leaning his head back, he took a slow breath through his nose trying to collect his thoughts.

Oh Natalie, I am so sorry.

Calla was right, he wasn't there when he should have been. He never should have stayed to help his brother; Patrick made his choices years ago. Natalie and Calla needed him here, and he failed them in that.

"Exactly. But if you loved her as much as she said you did, where were you when she died *almost a year ago?*" her voice broke then, tears flowing over her lower lashes. "Do you know what it's like to bury a parent while your other one is missing? And thank whatever God there is that Marcus quit his job and relocated here. Who knows where I would have ended up."

He felt a hand at his back and found Simon standing beside him. His lips turned up on one side in a sad smile and Jackson swore he could see pain in his blue eyes as he looked at Calla.

"Yeah … I know what that feels like, and I am so unbelievably sorry I wasn't here for you. And for your mom. If I could have called, I would have. Please believe that, Calla. You two are my world." He took a step toward her, and she took a step back. "If I could have come home, I would have. In a heartbeat."

Her lip quivered as she looked back at him, so much hurt emanating from her it broke his heart.

"But … You … Never … Did … " she whispered brokenly. Sniffling, she pulled the long sleeve of her pajama top over her hand and wiped away her tears roughly.

"No"—he bowed his head—"I didn't." And he knew that decision would haunt him for the rest of his life.

"I need you to go." Her broken words barely a whisper. "I can't be around you."

The hurt in her words had him nodding in agreement. The last thing he wanted to do was hurt her, and if she needed him to go—he would.

Tick. Tick. Tick.

With each staccato beat, his irritation at the sound grew. The shiny gold clock mounted on the wall behind Calla caught his attention and he had the urge to rip it off the wall. It didn't belong there.

"I'll meet you outside, Jacks," Simon said quietly, squeezing his shoulder gently before his footsteps took him outside.

"Can I give you a hug before I go?" It was selfish of him, he knew, but he needed to hug his little girl. "Please." He wasn't above begging.

"As long as you go after," Calla said through a watery smile.

He returned her watery smile with his own and opened his arms as she walked up to him and wrapped her arms around his waist. He closed his arms around her and tried to blink away the stinging in his eyes. This was goodbye for now for him, and the realization broke his heart. The pressure around his waist increased and her little form sobbed, so he increased his hold, pouring as much love into her as he could.

"I love you, Petal," he said, running his hand over her blonde hair and pressing his lips to the top of her head.

"I love you too, Dad." She squeezed him and then released her hold, taking a step back.

He cupped her cheek and wiped away a tear that slipped down. "Your mom was an amazing woman and I see so much of her in you."

She nodded at his words but created more space between them; so, he let his hand fall.

"Be safe, Dad."

He took one last look at his baby girl, from her messy blonde hair to her bare feet sticking out of her pajama pants. Then he met her eyes and tilted his head in goodbye and headed towards the front door, turning the lock on the handle before he closed the door behind him, and breathed the cool fall air.

When did everything go so wrong?

"You okay, Jacks?"

Am I?

No, he didn't think he was. He looked to Simon who had his back leaning against the wall, arms folded and looking at him like he was a bomb about to go off.

The whole reason he went to Neverland, other than getting his daughter back, was to live a normal life without this guy lurking about. Now, he was a widower, his daughter turned him away in his own home and from the sounds of it, Carston thinks he kidnapped a ten-year-old boy and his own daughter before disappearing.

There was the metallic snick of a deadbolt behind him; the finality in that one sound cut deep.

"Am I okay?" he said slowly. No words came. He went down the stairs, allowing his heavy steps to bleed out some of the anger roiling inside him. His quick stride ate up the distance as he hit the sidewalk heading back towards the lake.

Am I okay? No, I'm not. Not one bit.

He picked up his pace and sprinted down the sidewalk, hearing the staccato of Simon's steps in pace behind him.

Am I okay?

No, and he didn't think he would be again. Didn't want to be. The sidewalk disappeared and the paved road towards the outskirts of town was all he could see in the streetlights, and his sprint turned into a run.

Why did he keep trying to be more than he was?

'I'll be okay, Jacks. Don't worry.' Patrick's voice from their conversation about him considering college. He believed him and failed to see what was happening right under his nose.

Jacks! Patrick's scream overlapping with the splash of water and chimes. He failed to save him from falling into the lake; literally pulled out of his arms and dragged to another world.

Calla's screams joined the torment in his head, and he picked up the pace.

I failed to keep my daughter safe in so many ways.

Patrick took her right out of her bed. Simon had to save her from Samuel because he didn't evaluate the beach situation correctly. He never came back with her and instead let Simon and Hugh take her; leaving her to vet all the questions by herself. How terrible would that have been for her? He could imagine the questions and looks she would have received. Hell, he had been on the receiving end of those a few times in his life.

He turned the bend, and the lake came into view reflecting the moon and stars like another night sky.

'I got you. You need me, I'm there. I'm your girl.' A sob caught in his throat as he heard Natalie's words that helped him realize she was his home. She brought him peace in his chaos when his family started falling apart, and how did he thank her? By having their family be torn apart the same way, and by his choices because he failed to fix what he broke with Patrick.

I'm not okay, Nat.

"Jackson!"

Hell, he even failed to keep *himself* safe for five minutes the first time he was alone in that damned place. How did he think he could protect anyone if he couldn't even protect himself?

A grip on his forearm shook him from his thoughts and he slowed, then stopped running. Bending over, he rested his hand on his knees as he gasped in big gulps of air. Simon was in a similar position, doing the same.

"I haven't run … that far since Marcus … bet me

a tolly ... he could run farther than me." Simon bowed his head, then squinted at him. "Working it out?"

"Yeah ... working it out."

"I am sorry," Simon said and straightened, resting his hands on his hips.

"I know. It's not you I'm pissed at."

"Oh?" he questioned, a dubious look on his face. "That's a relief. You were kind of growing on me."

"Yeah, you're still annoying though."

Simon huffed out a laugh and then held out his hand. "We good?"

He clasped the hand and gave it a squeeze, letting it go as he straightened. "Let's go take Patrick to Hal."

"Wait, what?" Simon blinked and narrowed his eyes. "Vincent isn't going to like that plan."

"My father's preference is not my problem." He vaulted over the guardrail and grabbed the coin out of his pocket.

"It will be when you're not pissed off or hurting." Simon landed behind him and turned him around. "You know what taking him to Hal will mean, right? Will you be okay with being responsible for that?"

He spread his arms wide. "What do I have left to lose?"

"More than you're thinking right now. Vincent may not get over that."

"Tell me"—he dropped his arms—"how does one kill a fairy?"

Simon's face morphed from concerned to wicked. "Fairies don't stay dead."

"She's going to wish she could. I'm going to take care of those two and have a little fun while I'm at it."

"Lead the way, Cap."

Jackson smirked and lifted the coin, admiring the way the skull and crossed swords shined in the moonlight.

That nickname is starting to have a nice ring to it.

CHAPTER 32

BROKEN BONDS

JACKSON

"What's the plan then? Go into Pan Manor and grab your brother by the shirt and drag him to Merilee?"

"Something like that," Jackson answered, rubbing his thumb over the coins face. The water rolled off his hair and down his shoulders allowing the night air to touch his skin. His white shirt released its hold on his abdomen.

He would never feel Nat draw circles on his stomach or back while they talked. It was another punch to his gut, another tally against Patrick and this whole place.

"I'm pretty sure Tink will have a problem with that." Simon stood in front of him, blue eyes searching.

"Good, let her come at me." He didn't care. She had a special type of hell coming to her, and he would see that fulfilled. He reached out his hand to Simon. "Dagger."

"What are you going to do if the Lost Boys are there?"

"Did you get older?" He leaned into Simon's personal space. "Yeah, you might actually have a wrinkle now. Careful, you might look my age if you keep going back." He had meant it to tease, but it was surreal seeing Simon look like he was in his mid-twenties.

"Of course, I did." Simon glared at him and pressed against his shoulders, moving him back. "I'll look like you by the end of the week with how much I have to chase after you and Hughston's lot."

Jackson raised an eyebrow and wiggled his fingers on his still outstretched hand. "Dagger."

"Fine." Simon huffed, reaching behind him before slapping the sapphire adorned dagger into his palm. "I still think you should talk to Vinnie before going after your brother."

An exhilarated-sounding 'whoop' from above him had him turning to watch someone fall into the water at the bottom of the waterfall. Raising a hand to shield his eyes from rogue droplets, he noticed Simon doing the same but with a huge grin on his face.

Hugh's head popped out of the water, auburn hair matted to his head.

"Nicely done, Hughbert!" Simon whooped. "I didn't think you had it in you."

"Neither did I," Hugh admitted. "What a rush!"

"Impressive," Jackson agreed.

He looked towards the forest line illuminated by the rustic orange of the setting sun. If he ran, he could make it to Pan Manor in time before whatever nocturnal creatures came out to play. If they even existed.

His shoes dug into the sand, and he began to make his trek across the beach. To the left, he could still see the confrontation with Samuel in his mind. How scared Calla had been and how useless he was. *Kicked the guy's knee?* Simon had saved Calla; not him. Isla had dealt with the man who held his daughter; not him.

"You don't want to go that way." Hugh's voice came from behind him.

"Why not?" he snapped.

"Because I think you need to see what's on the other side of Peak Falls."

"Not interested in Neverland drama. I need to deal with my brother."

"Even if Hook has your dad and a mermaid that looks like your mom?"

His feet stopped short, and he pivoted. "What?"

"Tink told us."

"I wouldn't believe a damn thing that fairy says." Shaking his head, he started back towards the trees.

"I saw them on the boat myself though," Hugh shouted. "Wren and Oliver have too."

"How? Is the Jolly Roger next to the beach?" Simon countered, not sounding too convinced either.

And why would she even tell them that? What did she get out of it? But why would Hugh lie?

"With the looking glass we found in the Den. Come

up and see for yourself," Hugh urged. "Wren and Oliver are up there keeping an eye on them."

He stopped again and placed his hands on his hips and took a deep breath through his nose. If what Hugh was saying was true, he couldn't leave his father and mother with a psychopathic man on a ship no matter how much he wanted to deal with his brother.

Sighing, he pivoted and headed towards the path leading to Peak Falls.

"Let's go see what we're dealing with then, shall we," he said while walking past them, the excitement in his tone a mockery of how he was feeling inside. "Maybe Merilee will offer to take Patrick down to Hal herself afterwards. Two birds with one stone."

"You're taking Patrick to Hal!?" Hugh squeaked. The boy was beside him, brows pinched. "You can't take Patrick to Hal. Try talking to him again."

"Tried that. Got a knife in the gut for it. Not doing *that* again." The rocks on the path shifted under his weight.

"Will you do something," Hugh whisper-yelled as he fell behind him as the path narrowed.

"Like what?" Simon whispered back. "He has a point."

"What happened to talking to him like Mr. Connelly wanted."

Like my father wanted. He scoffed at the thought. *What a joke. If he wanted to talk to Patrick, all the power to him; but he better do it before I get to him.*

He was going to get his father off that damned ship,

make sure his mother didn't get killed again for nothing other than existing, and then he would deal with his brother. His father wasn't going to convince him otherwise.

"Jackson?"

"This isn't up for debate," he snapped. "You don't want Patrick to go to Hal? You go talk to him. Try not getting stabbed while you're at it." He looked over his shoulder and noticed Hugh's hesitation. "Precisely."

"Maybe he would listen to me," Hugh suggested, lifting his chin in challenge.

"Considering seeing you three at the Manor—after I told you guys to stay put, I might add—was the reason he lost it in the first place, I highly doubt that will be the case."

Renewed anger towards those three pushed him to move faster up the incline. If they had just listened and stayed put, who knows what could have happened. Natalie might even still be alive, and Calla wouldn't have pushed him away for abandoning them. But no, they had to come barging in, mucking up his progress with Patrick.

"I'm sorry, Jackson. I didn't know that would happen."

Cresting the incline, he could see the two other boys standing on the other side. One careless; one hot headed.

"Great, I'm sure that means a lot to Natalie." He picked up a handful of stones and threw them into the still water on the pond. The water splashed and droplets created ripples in the too-tranquil surface, sending chaos along its calm—much like this place and everyone there had done to him.

Nothing here deserves to be that peaceful.

"Hey!" Simon snapped. "What happened to Natalie is NOT Hugh's fault."

No, but he played a part. They all did. If Patrick hadn't freaked out, that homicidal fairy probably wouldn't have lashed out. She seemed oddly protective of his little brother, which annoyed the hell out of him. *Where did she have the right to retaliate on his behalf?*

A hand pressed against his shoulder causing him to spin and his fist swung. Simon swiftly ducked and avoided it. Something pressed behind his ankle the same time Simon stood with his arm coming across Jackson's chest. In one fluid move, the pressure against his ankle and chest increased effectively kicking his foot out from under him causing him to fall backwards, landing hard on his back. Blood pounded in his ears. He glared up at Simon who was kneeling beside him and scowling from above, his hand pressing flat on his chest keeping him on the ground.

"You need to calm the hell down," Simon growled, pushing on his chest to emphasize his point. His hair glowed orange by the rays of the setting sun behind him. "I know you're hurting; you're pissed off and if I could take it away I would. If I could bring back Natalie, I would. But blaming Hugh and swinging at me isn't going to bring her back."

"Get off me." He pushed Simon's hands off his chest,

only to have a blade pressed to his throat. The look in Simon's eyes was not one he had seen before, so he raised his hands palm up and froze.

"You don't get to lash out at those who want to help you. I won't let anything more happen to your family. I've been there since before you were born, Jacks. I watched you and your brother grow up. Watched over you, Natalie and then Calla when she came to be. I *know* how much you're hurting. But I'm sure not going to have anything happen to my best friend on that ship because you don't have your head on straight."

He searched Simon's expression and could see the anger but there was worry in his eyes too. He had forgotten that Simon could be affected by what had happened. Simon had been there for his family long enough to see three generations. Of course, Simon cared about his father and his family, even if he never verbalized it.

Movement in his periphery let him know the other boys were standing nearby, silhouetted by the last setting sunrays. He couldn't blame them for Natalie, they were only easy targets; shame flooded him.

Lowering his left hand, he patted Simon's leg. The blade left his throat and he nodded, relieved when Simon's hands went to his back to put the dagger back in its usual holding place. Simon pushed to his feet, then reached down and offered his hand which he clasped to be pulled up.

"You guys okay?" Oliver asked hesitantly, eyes bouncing from Jackson to Simon and back again.

"Perhaps Patrick killing Natalie was a touch too far?"

He whirled around at Tink's words, throwing his own dagger at the transparent woman standing fifteen feet away near the den's entrance. The blade went through the woman's stomach, a few inches below the glowing blob that was the hellish being.

Hatred for her was like nothing he had ever felt before. This one creature destroyed his family because her feelings got hurt unintentionally. He would make her pay for every minute of pain his family had felt. If only his aim had been truer, he would have started his repayment right then.

"What nonsense are you blathering about now?" Simon drawled at Tink, coming to stand on his left. "Nice throw by the way," he complimented, tone sounding delighted and in complete contrast to the emotions bleeding off him a moment ago.

The woman looked sympathetically at them, which made his blood boil. What right did she have looking at any of them with sympathy when she caused all this?

"I tried to stop Patrick, but he was so angry that you took his friends from him. He was determined to take something away from you."

"Bullshit. Patrick loved Natalie like an older sister," he spat.

"Did he though?" She walked towards them slowly

with her hands out to the side. "You heard him in the Manor."

He had, and it had blindsided him. Patrick had never mentioned anything about feeling abandoned or replaced. They had been close, or at least he had thought they were. Maybe he didn't know Patrick as well as he had thought. If he could plunge a knife into his abdomen, was he capable of hurting Natalie if he was angry enough?

An ominous growl sounded, and Tink froze, eyes going wide. The woman disappeared, the yellow glow shooting over his head to be replaced with the sharp, jagged teeth of a familiar opal-scaled snake.

Simon crouched down like he had, his dagger reappearing in his hand. Hugh, Oliver, and Wren scrambled to the opposite side of Peak Falls, where he remembered being thrown off.

Sissil's forked tongue shot out and flicked in the trio's direction. A quieter rumble came out of the creature as it slithered towards the three Lost Boys.

"Jump, Hugh!" Simon shouted.

The trio didn't hesitate, obviously seeing the jump to the net a safer bet than Sissil, and their forms disappeared off the edge.

"She reacts too quickly for you," Dorathea cooed as she walked out to the clearing and was greeted by a purring Sissil. She rubbed the snake's scales and smiled.

"Sissil can eat Tink?" Jackson asked with raised eyebrows.

"A little indigestion for the snake might be worth it to have the fairy digested; that has to be painful." Simon said with a wicked grin.

"Your blade almost found purchase in this beauty." Dorathea said and continued towards him, holding his dagger in her hand, "Take care where you aim this next time."

"Yes ma'am." He had a feeling that if his dagger had hit this woman's companion, his dagger would have been returned in a far more painful way.

Something shiny caught his attention on the ground near where the boys had been standing earlier. Not caring whether the giant snake took a bite at him or not, he left Simon to talk to Dorathea. She probably didn't want to speak to him anyway.

Sissil's eyes followed him, but the snake didn't make a move towards him, so he relaxed slightly and jogged the short distance to his destination.

Bending down, the wood felt cool against his skin. He straightened and examined the makeshift looking glass. Spotting the Jolly Roger on the horizon, he lifted the end to his eye and peered through. The magnification was surprisingly strong, and the Jolly Roger came into view at once.

Men moved about the deck; Hook was at the helm but seemed to be focused on the prow. Following the deck, past about a dozen crew milling about, he paused at the sight of his father bound and sitting next to a rusted cage under the mainmast. His father looked positively livid and kept looking in the cage he sat beside, because in that cage was Brynn. She was leaning into Merilee who had her arms wrapped around her protectively while glaring at any man who approached them.

Guess that secret's out of the bag.

"What you see?"

"Exactly what Hugh said, except he left out Merilee being captured as well." He took the looking glass away from his eye and handed it to Simon.

Scanning the clearing now void of their company, he turned back. "Where is Dorathea and your favorite snake?"

Simon snorted. "Away from here."

"What did she want?"

"Is that Annelise?!" Simon looked at him with shock on his face.

"That would be Brynn."

"That's why you wanted me to bring Vinnie to meet her," he said before peering through the looking glass again. "Oh, Vinnie is pissed."

Yeah, he could only imagine what his father was feeling at the moment.

"Did you see the dinghy headed this way?" Simon handed him the looking glass and pointed towards the ocean.

Spotting the dingy in the water, he was taken aback by the sight of Stepan rowing while a squirming Theo was tied up on the sole of the boat. Three chests were on the stern of the dingy. "What do you make of it?"

"Not too sure but there is only one way to find out."

"And what way is that?" He put the looking glass in his back pocket, having seen all he wanted to see.

"Talking to him of course," Simon said with a shrug.

"Looks like those three have the same idea." He pointed to the three figures standing sentry by the burning lanterns on the beach.

"I don't think she was telling the truth about Patrick."

His eyebrows pinched at the random statement.

"I don't think Patrick killed Natalie," Simon reiterated. "I know he cared about her."

"Let's get those three off the Jolly Roger." He patted Simon on the back. Peering over the edge, he found the net he remembered directly below where they were standing. Lifting his foot, he stepped off the edge and felt the breeze whip his face as he became weightless.

Whether or not Tink lied made no difference to him. Her comments had planted a seed of doubt in the shaky ground he had left with Patrick; and that seed had already taken root. As far as he was concerned, Patrick was broken and was capable of anything now.

CHAPTER 33

TO THE JOLLY ROGER

JACKSON

"Remember to stay on course," Stepan repeated for the third time. "Keep to the plan."

"No need to be concerned about me," Jackson responded as he followed the movements of the grey souls under the water. The way they swam in an organized chaos around and over each other, never colliding, was mesmerizing. There was a grace to the vision, a masterpiece to the harmonious tones of the mermaids he could now hear.

"Why do they have a faint glow?" he asked no one on the dingy in particular. The Lost Boys were currently in the three chests, and Simon sat in front of him beside their unexpected ally grumbling about the plan. He wasn't even sure if the guy was paying attention.

"Their life essence is what glows," Stepan answered, lifting the oar to put back in the water as Simon did the same for the opposite side. "Damaged as they may be, they are still a part of something grander. That can't be snuffed out as easily."

"Do we really think this is going to work?" Simon griped. "How are they going to believe you managed to catch both of us when Samuel couldn't even catch one."

"Pain is distracting. Muddles judgement. That fairy came about after the crew brought the man onboard speaking of the Pan disposing of that one's wife." Stepan dropped his gaze, "almost bragged about it. Upset the man and sweet mermaid fiercely. I believe that was her goal. Hook is consumed with his quarry and is distracted by his greed."

"Deranged is what she is if she thinks that anyone is going to believe her," Simon quipped.

Is she deranged though? Anything is possible.

He never thought Patrick was capable of half the acts he had heard he'd done but some he witnessed himself. Patrick lashing out at Natalie, taking her away from him because that's how Patrick felt about what he had done with Hugh, Wren and Oliver wasn't as unbelievable as he would have thought a week ago.

A hard connection to his shin jolted him from his thoughts and he glared at Simon who was readjusting his position.

He tried to rub the sting out of his shin with his opposite leg. "I'll give you a split in your lip to match the one on your temple if you do that again."

"As if you could, tied up as you are," Simon scoffed,

but his look turned serious. "He wouldn't do that to Natalie."

He wished he held half as much conviction as Simon. The guy was looking at him so intently, almost like he was willing him to believe but he looked away. He wasn't willing to embrace the same possibilities with open arms; disappointment a drink he no longer could swallow.

"I don't know if the boy did do it or not," Stepan said quietly. "But for what it's worth, I'm sorry for what happened to your wife. A man should never have to feel the pain of being widowed."

"Sounds like you know something about it," he said, while trying to calculate how much longer until they were at the ship. His wrists were starting to itch from the rope binding them behind his back.

"I buried my wife after raiders went through our village," Stepan admitted. "My sons as well."

"Where were you when it happened?" Simon asked.

"Out hunting boar with some of the other men. Never forgave myself."

"That wasn't your fault though," Simon said.

"I am responsible for providing for and protecting my family, especially during the time when I was alive."

"Is that why you want to cross over? To be with them?" he asked, trying to piece together the puzzle that was Stepan, the new rogue Smee who was about to betray his Hook.

"Aye. I've saved enough souls here to repent for my

failings. I'm ready to let go of the guilt and hold my family again."

"It'll be a relief for you," Simon commented but held Jackson's gaze. "Letting go of your sense of responsibility for what happened to them."

He knew what Simon was getting at, but the guy didn't understand just how much his shortcomings had failed his family. He was as responsible for Natalie's death as Patrick was. Hell, he might as well have held her down in the water himself. Maybe he should ask Merilee to take him to Hal too.

If he couldn't find a way to make it up to Calla, or if she refused to have him in her life, he would remain here but watch over her for as long as he could. Then he would ask Merilee to take him to Hal because there was a glaringly bright flaw shining through the crack in his heart: he wanted to see them all bleed for their part in his family's pain.

"We're almost there," Stepan's words broke into his thoughts. "Those boys ready?"

He stomped twice and three separate double thuds sounded, as instructed. He nodded and rubbed his thumb over the rough rope.

The Jolly Roger loomed in the distance, its occupants moving across the deck illuminated sections of light throughout. Near the bow, there remained a cluster of men who stood next to their bounty as he'd seen from Peak Falls. Anger burned through him as he thought of Brynn, probably scared in that cage.

He held no reservations about doing what was in his power to set her free, even if that meant throwing each man in his way overboard. Each one of them could swim with the grey souls for all he cared—she did not belong there.

"Do you really have to hit me in the head again though?" Simon lifted his bound hand off the oar to touch the droplet of blood trailing down the side of his face, effectively smearing it.

"Won't be as hard as the first time," Stepan smirked. "Only has to look the part, not break the skin. Don't forget what we discussed. I talk, you fellas wait for the signal."

The ship's stern had become close enough for him to see the definition on the windowpanes of the captain's cabin. The details in the wood he never paid attention to last time he was this close were something to be admired.

Shouting could be heard up above, and he met Simon's uncertain gaze. He got the impression Simon was looking to him for reassurance this once, so he inclined his head.

Stepan stood and he hoped he wasn't making another mistake by trusting in Stepan. The four young men that were with him put their trust in him and he was determined not to let anyone else down—even if it killed him.

"Let's do this."

* * *

Merilee felt rage emanating from Vincent and welcomed the emotions barrage on her senses. The trembling fledgling in her arms abhorred the onslaught compounding with the malicious comments from the men around them. Some members of Hook's crew had been taking delight in recounting in great detail the deaths of multiple of their kind. She planned to return the favor to each one of them.

"The others don't seem to be coming for you," taunted the one she'd heard referenced as Maksim. "Think they're tired of you?"

Responding to the nonsensical question would only agitate Brynn more, and she had no desire to cause her additional distress.

"Cowardly for you to take her while the mermaids have obligations to Hal," Vincent ribbed. "Knew you wouldn't be able to during daylight hours?"

Maksim's fist connected with Vincent's jaw with a sickening smack causing Brynn to flinch. Spitting blood into Maksim's face, Vincent smiled, eyes streaking light green. "Untie me and we'll see how many more of those you land."

"Just why do your eyes glow like the captain's?" Maksim leaned closer and his hand shot out to grasp Vincent's face, his fingers turning white from the pressure. "Could you be the captain's replacement?"

"Stepan is back," someone yelled from the crow's nest.

She could see the man's mind working to figure out Vincent, who simply raised both eyebrows at the blood-speckled man.

"He has that boy Simon, and the fellow Theo threw off the ship."

No. No. No. She refused to believe that statement. Simon knew better than to come aboard the Jolly Roger with Jackson. As far as her awareness went, Simon was on strict instruction to keep Vincent's son alive; which would be incredibly difficult in the present situation.

Maksim huffed and shoved Vincent's face to the side before hollering for hands to help load the supplies.

"I hope they are okay," Brynn's voice came out small.

She caressed the fledgling's hair to lend her comfort. Pain crossed Vincent's features as he followed the motion of her hand with his gaze. She understood the turmoil that Vincent's features had been expressing since Brynn was brought onto the ship in a fishing net. From what Jackson had relayed, his father believed his wife was in the afterlife waiting for them, forgetting that his wife was killed by a supernatural force—hence, becoming a mermaid fledgling. The reality was painful for him, although he successfully tempered his expressions quickly to avoid inquiries from Hook's crew.

Men came up from the lower deck, she assumed from loading the supplies. There were seventeen crew members left on the ship by her calculation, eighteen including the new Smee. The men's voices became louder as an unmoving Simon was carried slung over a man's shoulder towards the cage where she sat. His body was unceremoniously dumped in front of the cage and rolled into the metal bars. Blood trickled from a gash to the side of his temple; his cheekbone was swollen and adorned with another gash that was slowly bleeding.

"Oh no," Brynn whimpered, leaning towards Simon and out of her embrace. "You poor boy," she whispered. Her arm fit easily through the spaces between the bars as she reached to gently move Simon's blonde locks away from his face.

"Ah, the Captain will be thrilled to have you back," Maksim sneered. "I preferred thinking you drowned when Theo threw you overboard."

"Where is my pal, Theo?" Jackson asked, looking amongst the men.

"Had to be dealt with for doing just that and breaking Captain's orders," Smee growled, roughly shoving Jackson farther back towards the cage she occupied and caused him to almost lose his balance.

"Pity, I was looking forward to seeing him again," Jackson said, sarcasm dripping from his words. He met her gaze before his eyes went to his father and then stayed on Brynn; inspecting her until some of the tension left his shoulders.

He came for his parents. Although, she suspected Brynn's presence influenced the decision more heavily than Vincent's.

"I send you for supplies and to deal with a traitor, and you return with just the man I wanted to see." Hook's voice traveled from beyond her sight and the glee in his tone made her skin crawl.

The men quieted and parted to allow Hook to stroll

closer with his hands clasped behind his back. At one point in time, she had many conversations with this man. Enjoyed discussions of strategy and tales of his time in the Real-World.

Now, the sight of his crooked smile beneath the thin black mustache held no appeal—only a desire for the contraption to cease its prattle. For once that pompous red coat of his wasn't to be seen. The obnoxiously crisp white of his silk shirt was contrasted by his long curly black hair which fell past his shoulders, and the black of the long waistcoat with gold accents.

She noted he still possessed his favorite sword with a golden pommel, which hung from its scabbard along his waist. As he neared to stand in front of Jackson he turned slightly, allowing her to confirm his Hook coin was still embedded in the golden quillon.

Maksim stood next to Hook, adjacent to a stoic Smee—that his lip curled at the man's presence didn't go unnoticed by her.

"I've decided ye will make a nice addition to the crew."

WELCOME ABOARD

"Excuse me?" He could not have heard the man correctly.

Join his crew? Not gonna happen. He focused on controlling his facial expression to not let the building anger at the sight of his parents ruin the plan—a feat he found more challenging than he'd predicted.

"Ye heard me," the pompous man said adjusting his golden cufflinks. "I want ye on my crew."

Well, this is unexpected. Utterly insane and ridiculous—but mostly unexpected.

The speed with which Maksim's head whipped towards Hook with a look of utter disbelief made it obvious to him the man felt the same way he did. It might be worth it to agree simply to see how upset the man would become.

"Not interested."

"Wasn't a choice. Ye see, ye intrigue me," Hook said. "Ye have gained the loyalty of that one." He waved a hand in the direction of a motionless Simon. "This new Pan seems to be fond of ye, enough to risk his life and coin to come here. Even that insufferable fairy is fixated on you."

"Passing amusement for them." He shrugged. His eye twitched at the mention of the 'insufferable fairy' who started all of this mess.

"Not so. Ye have value here and I be thinking it would benefit me to have ye aboard."

"I don't want anything to do with someone who takes pleasure in caging and killing mermaids." He inclined his head towards said mermaids.

If Hook wanted him on his crew now, then maybe he could use this to his advantage. Part of the plan was to free the mermaids and his father; if he could accomplish part of it without any fighting—it was worth a shot.

Stepan stiffened slightly beside him, and he felt the man tug sharply on his ropes. *Yeah, yeah. Stick to the plan.*

"With ye here, I wouldn't need them. I want the Pan coin and as the fairy said, bring ye onboard and the Pan will come."

Could it be that easy?

If he agreed to stay part of the crew, would that garner Brynn and Merilee's freedom? He could consent to staying on the Jolly Roger in exchange for their release and then slip off tomorrow morning. His heart began to beat harder at the prospect. If he agreed, then Patrick would surely come, eliminating any struggle to find him —which made it easier for him to be taken to Hal.

"Of course, if ye agree, a boon will have to be paid so I know ye aren't going to cross me and my men." He leaned forward, his breath carrying tones of mint. "Can't have ye slitting our throats and taking the ship now can we."

"You do like to hear yourself talk, don't you," his father said, sounding utterly bored.

"I have yet to decide what to do with ye, wanderer."

"I have," Maksim growled. "Get your new buccaneer to dispose of your replacement."

He eyed the man in the purple shirt. What did he know about the Hook's replacement? Did he know it was him?

"My replacement?" Hook tilted his head. "Explain."

"That one with the mermaids. He's your replacement," Maksim said.

His stomach dropped. *Why does he think my father is a Hook?*

"His eyes glow like yours Captain, and he has been seen with the mermaid keeper. Think about it, why would a mermaid try to protect a man from pirates in Neverland unless he was going to replace the one killing her kind."

"You like to talk nonsense too, don't you Maksim," his father said, saying the man's name, over-enunciating the 'M'.

"Smee, bring the man here," Hook instructed, eyes narrowed.

Stepan tugged on his rope as he passed behind him, and he felt the rope's tension give way.

Almost show time.

His father's eyes were pinned on Hook, anger radiating from him and his eyes did in fact have a slight glow to them.

Stepan stumbled when his father shoulder checked him as he gained his footing, landing him against the cage. Brynn's inhale could be heard over the shouts of disapproval from the other men who were milling about pretending to be busy.

Stepan cuffed his father on the back of the head like a disapproving father and Jackson almost laughed at the incredulous look his father gave the man. He roughly grabbed his father's arm and escorted him towards their little group.

Looking annoyed, his father was positioned to stand to his right and Hook's left and Stepan stood behind and in between him and his father. The anger in his light-green eyes wasn't directed towards him, he knew, and those irises moved from the top of his head to his feet. It would appear to their companions he was being sized up by the newcomer, when instead he was being looked over for injuries. Some of the glow left his father's eyes.

"So, ye are my replacement. Smart not to mention it when my men brought you aboard."

"That's the rumor."

A cold blade moved up his arm while a familiar handle was pressed into his palm. In his periphery, Stepan was leaning over pretending to tighten his rope like they had discussed—so he winced for effect.

"And I'd say I'm long overdue." His father made a show of looking about the ship and at the crew. "These men and this ship need an upgrade."

Maksim reached over and grabbed his father's shirt in a fist causing Hook to take a step back and scowl at Maksim as he moved into the spot his crewmate had previously occupied.

"You respect the captain and his ship," he growled, getting into his father's face.

"No," his father said coolly. The glow increased again, and his eyes widened fractionally.

Something breezed past his ear with a notable *'swoosh'* sound. He watched with a strange sense of satisfaction mixed with a sprinkle of horror as a slender, three-foot pole impaled itself into and out of Maksim's neck, pausing three quarters of the length through.

Showtime.

Pandemonium struck as Hook's crew hollered and scrambled around each other, calling for weapons and avoiding other sharp spears projecting through the air.

Hook jolted and squawked in surprise.

The mermaids have arrived.

Maksim released his father, stumbling back and reached up to grab the end of the weapon protruding from the front of his neck. Eyes wide, his hand slipped off the spear slick with his blood and he fell to his knees. He met his eyes before falling forward, face connecting with the wooden panels of the deck with a sickening thud, unmoving.

He let a grin creep onto his lips. He caught movement to his left and Hook hustled theatrically towards the stern, arms flailing as he called for Smee.

Allowing the rope to drop to the deck, he rotated his wrist and readjusted the familiar dagger handle in his hand and met his father's stunned look; he who also brought forward his freed hand with his own dagger in his palm.

Stepan's assistance was as shocking to him earlier, so he understood the feeling.

His father leaned back in time to narrowly miss the knife aimed for his throat. Grabbing the hand attached to the knife, his father tugged it down the same time he rammed his elbow into the offender's nose. The man howled and the knife clinked as it hit the floor.

Jackson's eyes widened as his father flipped his dagger into the air, caught it blade extended backwards, and stabbed into the man's neck in one fluid motion.

"Good form," he said, strangely admiring the skill.

His father laughed as he pulled the blade out and let the body fall to the floor, blood spattering as he did. "Like riding a bike."

"Whoop! Let's do this!" Simon's enthusiastic holler came from behind them as he threw an abandoned spear, impaling a black-shirted Sasha in the stomach. The guy teetered near the railing holding his stomach as Stepan—with Brynn over his shoulder—pushed him by the shoulder over the railing.

Brynn was using her hands to cover her face and his anger surged at the sight of her discomfort. Stepan said something to her, and she nodded her head. The man's arm came up and patted her comfortingly on the back, then he leaned her over the railing, and she left his sight.

"Get Merilee off of here," his father instructed as he bent down and grabbed a short sword from Maksim's belt.

Simon grinned wildly and nodded. "Me and Vinnie got this." He laughed and flipped his dagger.

His feet carried him towards Merilee now out of the cage, her nails deep in a squirming man's throat.

Viciously personal but justified. He ducked as an errant spear flew near his head and knelt beside her, the man no longer squirming with his throat in her crimson-covered hands. Her free arm came out, aimed for his throat but he clasped it before it made contact. Her glowing aqua eyes fixated on him, and she hissed.

"Easy," he coaxed. "Let's get you off here shall we. I'll throw some men overboard for you to play with."

Her eyes focused and she smiled. "I knew I would be fond of you." The mermaid's voice at night had a musical lilt to it that soothed some of his anger.

"I don't need calm right now, so how about you don't speak," he suggested.

She pressed her lips together as she grinned and inclined her head.

He reached out and wrapped one hand around her back and the other under her smooth blue fish tail. The scales felt soft as silk against his forearms which surprised him. He got the sense not too many were allowed to touch a mermaid's tail. *Forbidden.*

Standing with her slight weight, he moved easily towards the railing with her deadly arms wrapped around his shoulders. Simon and his father moved fluidly together, as if they had done this many times before and he guessed they had. Hugh and Wren were clashing swords with others of Hook's crew, while Oliver swung a metal hook at the end of a rope at a man and laughed when the man fell overboard with flailing arms.

Merilee touched his face and he turned to look at her as he came to the edge.

"Thank you," she mouthed the words instead of putting lyrical words to them, which he appreciated.

"You're welcome. I'll call in a favor when this is done."

She tilted her head and furrowed her brows but nodded slowly as he leaned over the railing.

He straightened his arms and she leaned away from him, twisting as she fell towards the water and entering it seamlessly like a professional diver. The rainbow of colors intermingling with the grey souls and the few men struggling to stay afloat while acrid arms of grey flesh clawed at them was a sight to see. He hoped the mermaids' vengeance would ease some of the pain he could imagine they felt losing their kin. Once he called in his favor, he would feel his own ease.

He pushed away from the railing and walked towards his father and Simon who had three men on their knees, hands up in surrender. Prone bodies that lay in his path had to be stepped over and he held a new respect for his father. There was also a wave of relief his father didn't remember his time in Neverland while he was being raised by the man. He surely would have had his ass kicked more than once.

"Jackson, what do you want us to do with these ones?" Simon asked and toed his boot at one of the men.

"Why are you asking me? This isn't my ship."

"It's not yer ship and never will be." Hook's shout of outrage came from by the helm. Wren and Stepan had the man by his arms and were dragging him squirming down the few steps to the deck. Wren's face was hard and smeared with blood while Stepan only had on a few specks from what he could see.

"Got right into it, did you?" he asked Wren with a lift of his eyebrow.

Wren shrugged but the corner of his mouth turned up and there was a gleam in his dark eyes.

"We already said we would serve the new Hook," one of the ones on his knees said. "We only want to help the souls cross, not go after the coins. Torturing and killing creatures like the mermaids is not what we want to do."

"Just why are you so willing to kill the mermaids?" he asked Hook as he walked over to where Wren and Stepan had stopped near one side and out of the way. The man's eyes were glowing blue and looked half wild.

"To find their treasure trove at first. Then it became great entertainment for me and my men when my interest waned," he answered.

"And then you moved to the Pan coin?" he took a guess.

"Precisely. The ultimate treasure to have." The man's look turned wistful. "Just to hold it would be worth the boy's life."

"You were after the Pan to simply hold the damned coin?" That sounded like an incredibly simple reason. Too simple, there had to be more. "You'd kill the boy for that?"

"It's only one boy. Another would come." Hook's gaze went to his father. "Another always comes. I've killed my replacement before, well Smee had. But I was planning on making this Pan suffer."

"Why?" *What made Patrick so special?*

"I was told to and in return I would get his coin."

He felt his anger boil over and he leaned into the smug man's face. "Told by who?"

"A fairy friend."

Freaking fairy. The control on his anger snapped and his right arm went back and then connected with the man's face. His hand wrapped around the man's throat and energy flowed between them, energizing him and Hook's eyes went wide in realization. Blood from the man's broken nose trickled down onto his hand and he lifted his other fist and slammed it into the man's face again. Thoughts of his mother in a cage, scared; his brother being tortured by this man because of that damned fairy flooded his mind. His fist came down again and connected with a sickening crack.

"Jackson." His father's voice sounded far away.

He tightened his hold on Hook's throat, enjoying how his face began to turn red. The splash of the mermaids and grey souls called to him. He leaned over and bowed Hook's back over the railing. "I should throw you overboard and let the mermaids have their piece of you. You don't deserve to be captain of this ship or hold that title. No vile creature who enjoys torturing others should be in a position of power."

"Jackson!" His father's voice was louder now, but the call of the mermaids was louder.

"Bad form, mate," he said in Hook's ear.

He slipped his foot behind the man's boot and kicked his leg out from under him as he increased the pressure on his throat, until Hook's body went over the railing. Releasing his grip, he watched in satisfaction as the man fell towards the kaleidoscope of rainbow and grey.

"Jackson!" Patrick's excited shout had his head shooting up to the crow's nest and followed him as he floated to the deck. "You did it! Thank you! Now I don't have to worry about that Hook."

His hand shot out and grabbed his brother's beige T-shirt and dragged him close. He ignored Patrick's surprised squeak, satisfied when that mocking smile left his face though. How dare the kid be happy and have the gall to thank him.

"Why did you do it?" he growled, pain lashing through him at the thought of his brother having a hand in Natalie being torn from him and Calla. The guilt that flashed across Patrick's face cracked the remaining hope he had that Tink was lying on Peak Falls. Small hands lifted to cover his and tried to pry his fingers open. He only increased his grip, and his hand began to shake.

"Jackson, let go of your brother." His father's words were soft but stern.

He could see his father slowly approaching from his right. "Why did you do it?" he repeated, his voice shaking. He wasn't even sure which emotion caused it. Anger? Hurt? Betrayal? Sadness? Hopelessness? Because he was feeling them all.

"I didn't mean for it to happen," Patrick wailed and increased his efforts to pry his fingers open. His feet scrambled and failed to push himself backwards before lifting off the ground and into the air. "I was so upset and then she was there and then I don't know what happened."

"Dead!" he shouted, his voice cracking. "She's dead, Patrick!"

Patrick's face crinkled up in pain and his eyes brimmed with tears. "I don't know what happened," he cried.

"You killed her! You took the one person who helped make this world makes sense to me." He clenched his jaw, trying to regain his composure. "Calla thinks I abandoned them and refuses to be near me because of you."

Patrick's feet landed on the wooden deck with a heavy thud, no longer fighting to release his shirt from the hold.

He refused to be swayed by the tears spilling down Patrick's face as he shook his head repeatedly.

"I don't know what happened," Patrick whimpered.

"Let your brother go, Jackson." His father's hand covered his trembling one. "We will figure this out."

What is there to figure out? The word brother was being whispered throughout the bystanders and his teeth clenched at the reminder of their audience.

"There is nothing to figure out. He's damaged"—he turned to his father and avoided Patrick's widening eyes —"Let go of my hand."

His father shook his head. "Not going to happen. He isn't going where you're thinking. I won't let that happen. Give yourself some time to cool off, you're not thinking straight."

"I'm thinking straight; you're not. He's killed kids, beat up my daughter's classmate, kidnapped my daughter, stabbed me in the stomach, and killed my wife." He shouted the last part to emphasize his point. "Something you can relate to, and you want me to *let him go*? I'll drag him down there myself if I have to."

He turned towards the side, dragging Patrick by the shirt with him.

"Dad!" Patrick's high-pitched plea had him grinding his molars.

There was a tearing noise and the resistance left his grip. His father held a dagger, he held a piece of cloth, and Patrick was flying off into the distance.

"What did you do?!" he roared.

"Stopping you from doing something you will regret," his father shouted back.

"Get off my ship!" he yelled.

His father's eyebrows shot up into his hairline. "I beg your pardon."

"Get. Off. My. Ship." He enunciated each word slowly, unable to find any forgiveness in what his father had done. He had every right to send Patrick to Hal, and because this man couldn't face the fact his little boy needed to go there, he set him free to kill or kidnap whoever he wanted.

The tick-tick-tick of his father's watch had him narrowing his eyes on the damned contraption. That sound was always present in the worst moments of his life, and he wanted it gone. "The blood of the next kid he kills is on your hands now. Get off my ship."

Raising his hands palm up, dagger hanging loosely by the handle off his thumb, his father slowly backed away. "I'll give you time to calm down. You need to think about what you're doing here, son."

He didn't need to do anything or think about anything involving Patrick anymore. Jackson knew where he stood on the issue and if he ever got his hands on Patrick, he would be sending him to Hal regardless of his father's pleas.

"There is a dinghy port side you can take to Neverland. I'll send someone to collect it at sunrise." There was nothing left to say to his father.

He walked over to the starboard railing and rested his forearms on the wooden piece. The melodic hum of the mermaids' song seemed to invade his body on a cellular level, and he let himself be taken under by the harmonious tones.

Betrayal from his family cut deep. His father of all people should understand what he was going through and yet he saved Patrick from the necessary consequences of his actions.

He huffed out a breath. *What a family bond they had.*

Opening his eyes, he watched the clouds move gracefully through the sky, illuminated a deep purple and pink by the rising sun. He could almost see the shape of a skull forming through the valleys and hills in the clouds and he smiled.

For now, he was home.

A sharp pain shot through his chest at the word home. The home he wanted so desperately to be present, no longer existed. A week ago, he would have given anything to live a normal, undaunted life with Natalie and Calla. A life free of people only he and his daughter could see. Yet, he had given up everything—including his family—in the end. He had willingly come to Neverland in hopes of ridding himself of the person who now felt more like family than his actual blood kin.

He would miss Simon.

He sighed. Self-pity would get him nowhere fast, and in the end, it had been his failing that caused his current predicament. Below in the water, Brynn stared up at him, concern in her pinched features. His losses had saved his mother from another undeserved death and to have her free and living—even if she had no memory of him—was a victory in his mind. He'd sleep better knowing he hadn't failed her in the end.

He raised two fingers to his forehead, saluting her and giving her a small smile. She didn't seem satisfied and opened her mouth to speak but shut it without voicing whatever it was she was going to. Then her small 'thank you' floated up to him, and he nodded.

"You going to stare at the water for hours or are you going to tell us what to do with these bodies." Simon's words sounded annoyed behind him.

Pushing off the railing, he was perplexed to see Simon leaning against the main, flipping his dagger and looking impatient. The three pirates that had been on their knees were now standing in a straight line: along with Stepan, Hugh, Wren, and Oliver. A quick scan of the deck showed barrels turned over with the contents strewn about the still bodies.

What a mess.

"Why are you here, Simon?" he asked as he leaned

against the railing and crossed his arms. "You four don't need to stay here. You can leave. I don't need a crew."

The fewer people on the ship to harass him, the better. He could use the distraction of being overwhelmed with his new duties for a while.

"Sorry to disappoint you," Simon said as he sheathed his dagger and strolled forward, kicking random objects out of his path. Bending down, he grabbed a black baseball cap. "But that decision doesn't seem to be up to you." He brushed the dust off the cap while he continued to approach him. "You may not think you need me, but you do."

Jackson raised an eyebrow "And what makes you think that?"

Simon shrugged. "Because a little girl once told me you needed a friend, and I have nowhere else I'd rather be at the moment."

"Nor I," Hugh said.

"Me neither," Oliver agreed.

"Exactly," Wren said.

He sighed. "You're not going away, are you?"

Simon smirked and held out the cap. "Nope," he said and popped the 'P'.

Jackson snorted. He could see why that annoyed Alex; it was irritating to be on the receiving end of that 'nope.'

"Well then, so be it," he said, as he reached for the ball cap and placed it backwards on his head. "Would that mean you're my second in command since we're delivering Stepan to the Ferryman shortly?"

A rather pleasing idea.

"Consider me your Smee." Simon saluted him with a huge grin.

"Welcome aboard," Jackson said, turning toward the seven men lined in a row who were patiently watching him. "I'm now the captain of this ship, and you can call me Captain Hook."

The End

EPILOGUE

HAL

HAL'S REALM

The arguing voices echoed down the hall as he made his way to the chamber meant for the souls needing to remain concealed. Neither man noticed him when he leaned against the stone doorway and crossed his arms—too busy arguing a point of little significance.

They always did this. Each soul that required his assistance followed the same pattern: denial, anger, bargaining, depression and lastly—acceptance.

Unfortunately for these twins, one was now stuck in this room until the cycle was complete.

Anger being the current stage.

"Don't you see? I had to do it! Why can't you see that?" Theo pleaded.

Samuel was shaking his head before his brother even

finished his plea. "When you see you were wrong, then I will get to see you again."

"You were killed!"

Samuel grimaced. "It wasn't pleasant but it was Isla taking me up to Lava Loch that did it; which ya have to admit was deserved. We did some nasty things to those creatures."

The familiar aroma of sea water and damp earth enveloped him and the corner of his mouth turned up. "Perhaps I should join you in Neverland. Seems delightfully chaotic."

"It has had its moments, Hal," Dorathea said as she came to stand beside him.

"Our guides fell into their roles seamlessly. I believe it would be best for Odessa to take Samuel back to the Ferryman; he is ready, and I would prefer his presence not upset Merilee and her new brood." His mermaids were already currently displeased with Hook's men and wanted to torture the ones in the west wing chambers for information about the ones still missing. Fortunately, the task belonged to him, which was where he was heading before he stopped here.

"I will instruct her on the importance of confidentiality in this."

"Indeed," he said, and pushed off the stone wall. A guide which he personally looked forward to fixing was waiting—not that he would admit as much.

"The one guide will need to be watched though. His

essence is darkening and he is not meant for this realm. Have your apprentice ensure that does not continue."

Dorathea's gaze was still locked on the arguing twins in the room and he could see her fingers twitch as her eyes narrowed slightly.

He placed his hand on her delicate shoulder. "I will deal with Theo as I did Samuel. You have done your part; this is mine."

Her hazel eyes met his and he knew her patience was waning by the swirls of white streaking through her irises. "As you wish, brother."

ACKNOWLEDGMENTS

Thank you to my Peterri Clan - Peter, CJ, Dasher and Klo. Thanks for being such amazing humans and being there for support and encouragement while I created this world. I love you guys!

Thank you to Maizie M, Karrie R, and Miranda R for providing me with feedback as I brainstormed. I appreciate you immensely, as well as your patience while being my sounding boards!

Thank you to my Beta Readers: Angela F, Brandon M, Serina M, Jessie R, Karen A. and Hailee M. Your feedback was so encouraging and enlightening. I will be forever grateful for your time and willingness to take a chance on my writing!

ABOUT THE AUTHOR

As the daughter of a poet, Terri was introduced to writing at a young age. Poetry was where her passion for writing started. She is an avid reader of many genres and feels there is value in all stories told, particularly stories pertaining to human nature. She resides in a small city in Alberta, Canada.